Claire

Initia
D

D1296215

Coming closer, Lane took off his robe and sat on the edge of the bed. Julia made no resistance as he began to remove her nightgown. As she usually did, Julia remained passive as Lane began to caress her; but then, as always seemed to be happening to her of late, that unbearable tension began to make itself known, threatening her composure. Gritting her teeth, Julia told herself it would soon be over.

Tonight, however, Lane seemed to be in no hurry. He continued to stroke her for minutes on end. Her breath quickened to the point where she had to part her lips in order to get enough air into her lungs.

Her eyes were closed, and when his mouth found her breast, she shuddered. His mouth moved lower, trailing hot darts of flame wherever it came in contact with her quivering flesh, and now her body began to tremble like a leaf in a storm.

"Julia..." he whispered, "don't fight me. Make love with me..."

Also by Helene Sinclair

Stranger in My Heart
The Bayou Fox

Published by
WARNER BOOKS

Twilight of Innocence

Helene Sinclair

WARNER BOOKS EDITION

Copyright © 1985 by Helene Lehr
All rights reserved.

Cover illustration by Robert Sabin

Warner Books, Inc.

WARNER BOOKS

A Warner Communications Company

WARNER BOOKS EDITION

Cover illustration by Sharon Spiak

Warner Books, Inc.
666 Fifth Avenue
New York, N.Y. 10103

 A Warner Communications Company

Printed in the United States of America

First Printing: May, 1988

10 9 8 7 6 5 4 3 2 1

This book is affectionately
dedicated to

Gary Lehr

chapter
<u>one</u>

"They say he's enormously wealthy. . . ."

Clair Eastwood raised her lace fan to cover her lips as she addressed her friend, and soon-to-be sister-in-law, Julia Trent. Both young women had just descended the curving stairs and now stood in the arched entry of the ballroom in the Eastwood house, one of the largest on Beacon Hill.

Even though the party wasn't scheduled to begin for another quarter of an hour, guests were beginning to arrive in fancy equipages driven by smartly groomed drivers. No one wanted to miss a minute of the festivities to be held here on this June evening of 1875; it was considered by most to be the social event of the season.

"His name is Lane Manning," Clair went on, giving Julia a brief glance. "Daddy met him two days ago at the Men's Club."

Julia's dark blue eyes swept over the elegantly attired guests to the man in question. He was tall, head and shoulders over every other man in the room. His face was partially

1

averted, but she could see that his hair was black and slightly wavy. Almost every young and unmarried female present stood close enough to the man to dart a coy smile in his direction at every opportunity. He, in turn, was regarding them all with a polite indifference that bordered on open boredom.

"I've never seen him before," Julia said to Clair. "Why is he here?"

Clair shrugged in a delicate way, absently touching the pearl collar that encircled her throat. "As you know, Daddy is on the board to raise money for an addition to the library. I understand that Mr. Manning made a sizable contribution. I suspect Daddy was hard-pressed to ignore the amount of the donation and probably reciprocated with an invitation."

The girl paused to view the gathering in the lavishly decorated ballroom. Liveried waiters, hired just for the occasion, moved discreetly through the crowd, some of them offering champagne in fine fluted glasses and others holding trays of colorful canapés that ranged from Russian caviar to simple wedges of cheese. In an alcove surrounded by latticework and potted plants, a twelve-piece orchestra was, for the moment, playing a lively polonaise, though no one was as yet on the dance floor. French chairs richly upholstered in crimson brocade had been placed along one wall as a convenience for those ladies who wished to rest between dances. At the far end of the large room an archway of intricate plasterwork led to huge lace-covered tables filled with silver platters of food.

Almost every member of Boston's society was present, Clair thought to herself with no little satisfaction, pleased that she and her family were associated with such an elite group. It must be dreadful to be outside the pale. Her attention again returned to Lane Manning.

"Of course, he doesn't live here in Boston," she confided to Julia from behind her fan. "He lives in Philadelphia in a big mansion, I've heard tell. He's twenty-eight, and he's single!" Her hand moved up to pat her brown curls, and she gave Julia an impish grin that suggested she might try to change that situation.

This display of enthusiasm drew a smile from Julia. Petite and vivacious, Clair was seventeen, two years younger than Julia. With a small sigh of wistful longing, Julia's gaze dropped to view Clair's very fashionable gown of mauve velvet, the full skirt of which was embellished with russet-colored silk thread artfully embroidered into a pattern of trailing leaves. The square neck was cut low enough to reveal the soft swell of her pert bosom. Julia's own gown, while made of the finest watered silk, was buttoned to her throat, for her father forbid her to wear anything less conservative.

"He is very handsome, don't you think?" Clair whispered, nudging Julia with her elbow.

Without much interest, Julia again looked at the man. At that moment he unexpectedly turned in her direction and stared at her in a bold manner. His eyes were gray—a cold gray that reminded her of the ocean during a winter storm. Julia hastily turned away.

"I suppose that some women would find him handsome," she murmured to Clair, uncomfortably aware that the man was still staring at her. "But he's too . . ." She hesitated, searching for a word that wouldn't sound offensive. "Well, he doesn't appear to be too refined to me," she concluded lamely. "Certainly I don't find him as attractive as Mark."

Clair giggled at the observation. "Of course you would say that tonight, of all nights." She slipped her arm through Julia's. "Come on, I'll introduce you."

Julia hung back, her natural modesty affronted at the thought of becoming a part of the simpering group of young women who were so blatantly flirting with the tall stranger. "I don't think . . ."

"Don't be silly!" Clair tugged on her arm. "After all, you are the guest of honor. Besides"—she emitted another trilling laugh as Julia reluctantly moved forward—"I'm sure Mr. Manning will be relieved to meet the one unmarried woman in the room who isn't plotting to trap him into marrying her." Clair quite brazenly pushed through the ring of young women until she was right in front of Lane. "Mr. Manning, may I present Julia Trent? The party tonight is in celebration of her engagement to my brother Mark."

Lane Manning gave a slight bow. "Miss Trent." His voice had a deep, rich timbre. He smiled as he straightened, but his eyes still had that bold look as he regarded Julia. "I must say that Mark Eastwood is a most fortunate man."

Julia found herself looking up into those gray eyes set beneath dark brows. They were heavily lashed, of a length that would cause any woman envy. She suddenly fastened on the word that had eluded her minutes ago. Masculine. That was it. Lane Manning was too masculine. Although he was dressed formally and in good taste, his black broadcloth jacket did little to conceal those broad shoulders. Even his muscular thighs seemed to resent the confinement of his well-cut trousers. Julia's cheeks flamed with her unconventional thoughts.

"Thank you," she managed faintly, remembering her manners. "I understand you live in Philadelphia, Mr. Manning. Do you plan on being in Boston long?"

"Only long enough to conclude the business that brought me here. Several weeks, I should guess."

Without appearing to do so, Lane Manning studied the two young women standing before him. Clair, at seventeen, was as ripe as a luscious peach. It would take no more than five years for her beauty to dim, for her delicious roundness to expand to an unattractive plumpness. In contrast, Julia possessed a cool beauty of the type that would become more arresting with the passing years. Her hair was the color of the champagne in the glass he was holding and was infused with just as many sparkling glimmers of light. It was worn simply, drawn back from her face and fashioned into a smooth chignon. The effect emphasized her oval face and delicate features.

"Mr. Manning purchased the warehouse on Commonwealth Avenue," Clair was saying to Julia. "He's going to have it refurbished."

Julia smiled. "Do you own many warehouses?" she asked, more for something to say than because she really wanted to know.

His laugh revealed excellent teeth. "A few. I'm involved in importing and exporting goods. And I dabble a bit in timber."

"How very interesting," was all Julia could think of to say, grateful to see Mark coming toward her. Julia couldn't help but compare the two men. Tall and thin, Mark Eastwood wore his clothes with a natural flair denied a man of a more muscular build. He had light brown hair and a full mustache. Julia didn't approve of Lane's clean-shaven face; it exposed too much. She was right, she thought to herself, a trifle smugly. *Mark is far more attractive than Lane Manning.*

"Darling." Mark touched her arm as he came to stand beside her. "My father's ready to make the announcement, then we'll have to lead off the dancing." Turning from Julia, he regarded Lane with an arched brow. "Good evening, Mr. Manning. I'm so glad you could join us." Though Mark's voice was congenial if cool, his attitude was noticeably condescending.

"The pleasure is mine," Lane responded cordially, his

expression giving no indication of his dislike for Mark Eastwood. He had made a snap judgment, perhaps; but his first impressions were usually on target. Yesterday he had spent the better part of an hour in Devlin's law office while the papers were being drawn up for the sale of the warehouse he had purchased. Mark had been in and out of the room several times, long enough for Lane to perceive his major characteristics. Completely without humor, Mark was a man to whom propriety and appearance were all-important. In short, he was a rigid, unbending snob.

"Are you enjoying yourself?" Mark asked, almost as an afterthought.

"Very much," came the low murmur, and Julia wondered if she imagined the dry tone of his voice.

Julia slipped her hand beneath Mark's arm and watched as Devlin Eastwood held up his hands for silence. When he had the crowd's attention, he announced the engagement of his son to Julia Trent.

Seeing her father coming toward her, Julia's smile brightened. She thought him very handsome. Though his dark brown hair was receding from his forehead, his sideburns were full and thick, as was his short beard.

With the polite applause of the crowd as a background, James Trent shook Mark's hand, then turned toward Julia. She tilted her head to receive the light kiss on her cheek; but he gripped her hand a bit tighter than necessary as he whispered: "I'm so glad. You'll be safe with Mark."

The music began just then, and Mark led her onto the dance floor before Julia could question her father's strange remark. Safe? Safe from what? She glanced back at him, seeing him take another glass of champagne from a passing waiter. Was it her imagination, or was her father looking tired of late?

Then Julia forgot her father as she let herself flow into the beauty of the waltz. Mark was an excellent dancer, as were most of the young gentlemen she knew, for lessons in this important social grace were a part of everyone's education, including her own.

Placing his glass on a nearby table, Lane sighed. He guessed he was supposed to circulate, to dance with one of the young women who were watching him with expectant eyes. The prospect didn't appeal to him at all. Without much enthusiasm he requested a dance from the girl nearest him.

As he danced by Julia and Mark, Lane gave Julia a nod and smiled at her.

Julia's answering smile was stiff. In motion, Lane reminded her of a black panther.

"Strange fellow, that Manning," Mark commented tersely, leading her to the far side of the room so as to distance himself from the object of his conversation. "I can't imagine what my father was thinking of, inviting him here tonight."

"Clair says he's very rich," Julia ventured and was rewarded with an annoyed look.

"Money isn't everything," declared Mark, to whom it meant everything. "The man is an upstart, a nobody," he went on in a tone that matched his expression. "It takes more than wealth to create a gentleman of the old school. He looks like a dockworker, and his manners aren't much better."

Wisely, Julia said no more on the subject. Mark's occasional spurts of temper always took her by surprise. She stole a glance over his shoulder at Lane Manning. Whether he looked like a dockworker or not was open to question, but she could honestly say she found no fault with his manners.

Lane, always uncomfortable in formal settings, did his best to be courteous and attentive to the girl he was dancing with, but was much relieved when the music ended. She had the fanciful name of Bunny—short for Beatrice, she was quick to explain as Lane began to escort her back to her mother.

"Oh, Julia!" Bunny called out before they had covered half the distance. "It's a marvelous party." She paused before Julia, who was standing with a group of friends, and took care to keep her hand linked through Lane's elbow in a possessive manner, anchoring him in place.

"Thank you," Julia responded with a smile, giving Lane only the briefest of looks and directing it toward the center of his forehead. The way he stared at her was most unsettling. She wished that Mark was by her side, but he was dancing with his mother. "I'm so glad you and your family could make it." She turned to face Bunny again.

"Wouldn't have missed it," Bunny assured her with a toss of her red curls. "We'll be leaving for Newport in a few weeks. Will you be there?"

Julia nodded, somewhat surprised by the question. Everyone went to Newport for the summer.

Bunny then arched a brow at Lane and flashed her most dazzling smile. "Do you summer at Newport, Mr. Manning?"

Gravely, Lane shook his head. "Business does not permit me such pleasures, Miss Ramsey." He flinched as the girl's shrill giggle assaulted his ears. Placing a hand on her elbow, he firmly continued the brief journey that would place her back in the care of her mother.

That accomplished, Lane moved toward the wall and stood next to a malachite vase that was almost as tall as he was. He glanced around the room, observing Julia as she mingled with the guests. There was an inbred graciousness about her that was totally unaffected, casual, as if she had been born with it, never having had to learn it. To Lane's way of thinking, very few women had this indefinable quality that set one woman apart from all the others.

Lane hesitated a moment, then approached her to request a dance. With no trace of coyness, Julia accepted.

"Have you known Mark a long time?" he asked conversationally. A faint floral scent emanated from her hair to tease his senses.

"Yes," Julia replied. "Mark's family and mine have been friends ever since I can remember. Of course, since my mother died we don't see as much of them as we did before. . . ."

"Surely you see Mark regularly?"

"Oh, yes," Julia nodded. "Mark calls every Sunday afternoon."

Lane raised a brow and looked amused. "I take it he then proposed to you on a Sunday afternoon?"

She appeared momentarily flustered. "Oh, Mark never proposed to me. That would have been most improper."

A smile played lightly in the corners of his mouth. "Who did he propose to?"

"He spoke to my father, naturally," came the swift retort. "And Mr. Eastwood was there as well. They decided we should get married."

Lane considered that a moment but refrained from showing the surprise he felt. "Did no one consult you?" he asked at last. His gray eyes held hers in a compelling way.

"Of couse they did," she replied with a small laugh, sounding disconcerted by the question. "My father would never force me to marry anyone."

"But it was already a fait accompli when they told you?" he murmured.

Thick golden lashes lowered to fan her cheeks. "Well, yes, I suppose it was."

Lane hesitated, then asked: "Do you love him?"

After a moment's astonishment, she stiffened. "Mr. Manning! I do believe you are out of line. . . ."

"Improper?" Lane suggested, a shade mischievously.

"Definitely," she stated tersely, not at all charmed by the twinkle in his eye.

The dance ended, and Julia was relieved when Lane released his hold on her. She had thought it far too tight. Trying not to appear ill-mannered in her haste, she moved away from him.

For the next hour, Julia danced, mingled with the guests, and tried to ignore the fact that her new shoes were pinching her toes. It was well after eleven o'clock when she heard her name being called and turned to see Agnes Eastwood hurrying in her direction. Mark's mother advanced in a swirl of garnet-red taffeta and grasped Julia's hand.

"Come with me, my dear. There's someone I'd like you to meet. You've heard of Mrs. Southworth, haven't you?"

Julia regarded the older woman in surprise. "The outrageous Mrs. Southworth? The one who writes those novels?"

Agnes laughed softly. "Yes. But she's all the rage now, you know." She paused, looking confused, then brightened as she spied her quarry. "Oh, there she is, standing with Mr. Manning."

Julia checked a frown. There were over two hundred guests milling about, and she seemed to be bumping into this man at every turn. She smiled shyly at the author as Agnes introduced her. The woman was tall, thin, and flat-chested, with yellow hair of such a flamboyant color that it was to be doubted whether nature had provided it.

"Oh! The lucky bride-to-be," Mrs. Southworth exclaimed, squeezing Julia's hand. "My sincere congratulations."

"Thank you," Julia said, then added: "I've read *The Deserted Wife*, and I enjoyed it very much."

"Did you? How delightful of you to say so!" ending forward slightly, she tapped Julia's arm with her fan. "Mark is such a splendid young man." She again viewed Agnes, who was beaming with the compliment. "You must be very proud."

"Oh, I am," Agnes agreed hastily. "And so looking forward to having Julia as a daughter-in-law. Her mother and I were very dear friends. . . ."

Julia tried to pay attention to the conversation that now ensued, but she was very much aware of a pair of gray eyes that never seemed to leave her.

Finally there was a lull, as both Agnes and Mrs. Southworth ran out of steam at the same time. And into that lull came Lane's voice as he requested another dance.

"Oh, yes, Julia dear," Agnes said with an emphatic nod of her head. "Go along. We've monopolized enough of your time."

With no recourse, Julia allowed Lane to lead her onto the dance floor, now crowded with couples who whirled and glided to the strains of Strauss. Again she was conscious of his overly tight hold on her. Suddenly Lane's hand moved against the small of her back as he firmly avoided a collision with a man who was more than a bit inebriated and in high spirits. Feeling the increased pressure, Julia stumbled, causing him to pull her even closer.

"Are you all right?" he asked quietly, inclining his head to study her face.

"I'm fine," she said quickly, too brightly. "It's my shoes . . . They're new. . . ."

"Ah. . . ."

efore she could protest, Lane had propelled her out onto the terrace. The June evening was mild, the air scented with early summer flowers. A full moon softened night shadows, tipping leaves of trees and bushes with pale ivory.

"Tell me," Lane said, as they walked across the flagstone walkway. "Did you really read *The Deserted Wife*?"

Julia was glad the shadows hid her flush. Her father never allowed her to read such books.

When she made no immediate response, he laughed. "You didn't, did you?" He seemed amused. "What would you have done if the outrageous Mrs. Southworth had questioned you in depth?" Lane thought her answering laugh enchanting and wondered if he could provoke another such response. He couldn't count the times a woman's laugh grated on his nerves. He had long decided he couldn't live with a woman whose laugh set his teeth on edge.

"Appear foolish, I guess," Julia speculated at last, toying with the silk sash around her waist. "Actually, I did sort of skim through it. Clair has a copy."

"I understand that Miss Eastwood is leaving for Vassar in the fall," Lane said as they paused by a trellis that supported a profusion of rambling roses. "I suppose you attended that school as well?"

She shook her head. "No, I was tutored at home. Father did consider Vassar but decided my education would be better served at home, under his personal supervision. He himself chose the subjects I was to be taught." She related that with a pride that was not lost on Lane.

"And what were they?" Lane asked, liking the sound of her voice. Inside, the dance had ended and another begun, but Lane was reluctant to excuse himself from Julia's company. He found her refreshingly straightforward and without guile or artifice.

"Oh...." She gestured. "It changed over the years. When I was very young, music, penmanship, and reading took preference. As I became older that changed to French, Latin, history, mathematics. . . .''

Turning slightly, Julia placed a white hand on the black wrought-iron railing that delineated the terraced area. She had lovely skin, the color of tea roses, Lane thought. That is, what he could see of it. More than half the women present were displaying bare shoulders and a seductive curve of bosom. He thought it odd that Julia's dress was long-sleeved and high-necked, revealing no more than an inch of her throat under her chin.

"I'm surprised that your father didn't at least consider a finishing school for you," he said after a moment.

A smile curved her lips. "Father always maintained that finishing schools were a waste of time and decided that my mother was quite capable of teaching me all the social graces."

"From what I can see," Lane murmured, "she's done an admirable job."

Julia raised her head to look up at him. "And you, Mr. Manning? What school did you attend?"

He looked sheepish and, to her, suddenly younger than his twenty-eight years. "If you are referring to college, I did not attend any."

"It doesn't seem to have placed any impediments in your path," she noted archly.

"None whatsoever," he agreed cheerfully; then his manner turned somber. "I . . . want to apologize for offending you earlier this evening."

"That isn't necessary," she demurred softly, lowering her eyes.

"I still think Mark's a most fortunate man. I . . . suspect you had many suitors to choose from," he speculated after a moment, unable to contain his curiosity. For the life of him,

Lane couldn't understand why a woman like Julia would accept a man like Mark Eastwood. She was beautiful, well-bred, intelligent. He felt certain she could have had her pick of any eligible bachelor in Boston.

She looked up at him, her blue eyes widening. "Oh, I don't think so."

He drew back in surprise. "Don't you know?"

"Not really," she replied, amusement dimpling her cheeks. "I have no way of knowing if any gentleman approached my father and was refused permission to court me." She tilted her head to one side. "Are things done so differently in Philadelphia?"

Slowly, he shook his head. "Well, perhaps not," he conceded. "I would say that, in your case, it would be a matter of degree, rather than difference."

They fell silent a moment. The music wafting through the open doors was as soft as the night air, and just as sweet. Beneath the moonlight, Julia's pale hair glowed with a silvery sheen that caught Lane's admiration. He opened his mouth to speak, but a harsh voice preempted his words.

"Julia!"

She started and turned to face the man who had just come onto the terrace. "Yes, Father?" Anxiety caused a little line to mar her smooth brow. Her father rarely raised his voice to her.

James came closer, giving Lane a hard look as he did so. "It's most unseemly for you to be out here alone with Mr. Manning. I suggest you come inside immediately!" He held out his arm for her to take.

"Yes, Father." Obediently, Julia placed a hand on the outstretched arm and, without a backward glance, followed her father back into the ballroom, leaving behind the faint, lingering sweetness of her perfume.

Leaning on the wrought-iron railing, Lane watched them go, a puzzled look on his face. Other couples were strolling the terrace, catching a breath of cool air after the closeness of the ballroom. He and Julia had hardly been out here alone. Then he shrugged. Doubtless James Trent was one of those overly protective fathers, standing a constant guard over his daughter's virtue.

Lane felt a moment's compassion for the lovely Julia Trent. From all indications she would be passed from the hand of her father to the equally strict embrace of Mark Eastwood.

Glancing around, Lane noticed that the crowd was beginning to thin. Removing his watch from a vest pocket, he decided that the hour was late enough for him to take his leave.

Inside, Lane located Agnes Eastwood and thanked her for the invitation. As she escorted him to the front door, his eyes scanned the ballroom. Julia was dancing with Mark. If she noticed his departure, she gave no sign of it.

When the party ended some two hours later, Julia couldn't contain a sigh of relief. She was tired, her feet were beginning to throb, and when she finally settled herself beside her father in the carriage, she resisted the impulse to take off her shoes. She sat quietly, listening to the monotonous clip-clop of the horse's hooves, sounding loud in the stillness of the early morning hours. She felt vaguely troubled, but didn't know why. This should have been one of happiest nights of her life; instead, she felt a dissatisfaction that she couldn't explain. Turning her head, she observed her father. He was staring out the window as if he were alone. He was not a talkative man at the best of times, but tonight Julia found his silence disturbing. Finally, she spoke hesitantly.

"Father, what did you mean when you said I would be safe with Mark?"

For a moment, James made no response. Then he turned toward her. "Nothing, really." He patted her hand, but his voice was distant, as if his mind was not on what he was saying. "Just an expression, my dear. I'm sure you know that the only safety and happiness for a woman is in a good marriage." He fell silent again, apparently lost in his own thoughts.

The carriage rolled up to the front entrance of their house on Beacon Street. Three-storied with a gabled roof, it greatly resembled its neighbors, constructed of brownstone and fronted by a red-brick sidewalk. The dark mahogany door swung open before they reached it, and the housekeeper, Mrs. Beale, smiled a welcome.

"You needn't have waited up, Mrs. Beale," James said kindly as he handed her his hat.

"No trouble, Mr. Trent. I'm not at all sleepy. Can I get you anything before you retire?"

"Thank you, no," he replied, heading for the stairs, and Julia was again struck by the weary slump of his shoulders.

Mrs. Beale regarded Julia. "And you, Miss Julia?"

"What? Oh, nothing for me, thank you."

"Peggy is asleep," Mrs. Beale called out as Julia started to go upstairs. "But I can wake her...."

"No, don't do that. I can manage."

In her room, Julia closed the door. Her bed had been turned down, the ruffled counterpane folded neatly over a chair, and a single lamp burned softly.

Absently, Julia undressed, then donned her nightgown, nudged by a growing concern for her father. He just wasn't himself of late, though she couldn't quite put her finger on the problem. He wasn't ill; at least, she didn't think so. It was just that he was . . . distracted. Yes, that was it.

She sighed as she sat down at her dressing table and removed the pins from her hair. Probably it had something to do with business, she mused. If so, she could never question him. Her father felt strongly about women discussing business matters. In his opinion, that was not a suitable topic for a lady.

Picking up the brush, Julia applied it vigorously to her pale hair before plaiting it into its usual night braid. Peggy, her personal maid, usually did this for her, but Julia saw no need to disturb the girl's rest just for this simple chore.

In bed, she rested against her pillow, wide awake, her thoughts turning to Lane Manning. "Strange fellow," Mark had said, and Julia thought that was true, though not in the sense Mark had meant it. Lane Manning was unlike any man she had ever met. Even now, in the darkness of her bedroom, Julia imagined she could still feel those gray eyes watching her. Worse, she all too clearly remembered the burning pressure of his hand on the small of her back. She hadn't liked that at all! A gentleman always held a lady lightly. Why, when Mark danced with her, she wasn't even conscious of his touch!

Well, no matter, she thought, pulling the covers closer and resolutely banishing Lane Manning from her mind. The chances were excellent that she would never see him again. Best just to forget the interlude.

chapter
two

Standing by the bow window in the front parlor of her home, Julia stared outside. A gentle rain fell steadily, forming silvery drops that quivered delicately on leaves and glistened palely on blades of grass.

The house seemed oddly silent. Julia clasped her hands tightly at her waist, finding the stillness unnerving. Not two weeks had passed since her engagement party. How could her life have gone from such serenity to such chaos in so short a time?

"Miss Julia?"

Turning with a rustle of black silk, Julia offered a wan smile to the housekeeper. Mrs. Beale's eyes were red and puffy, and she kept dabbing at them with a crumpled handkerchief.

"Frank has the carriage ready," she said in an unsteady voice, not moving from the threshold.

"Thank you, Mrs. Beale," Julia murmured softly, pausing at the sound of the muffled sob. Her own eyes were dry, and she hoped that Mrs. Beale didn't think this was due to a lack of feeling, because the truth was that she had no more tears to shed. "Will you tell Peggy to fetch my cape and my black silk bonnet—the one without any adornment?"

Nodding her graying head, the woman moved away, her handkerchief pressed against her lips.

For a moment, Julia stood where she was in the center of the room, feeling a curious disorientation. She glanced around, trying to shake the sudden sense of unfamiliarity that gripped her.

He used to sit in that chair reading the newspaper, the lamp warming one side of his face, brows drawn down as they always were when he was concentrating.

Walking toward the chair, Julia's hand brushed against the antimacassar pinned to the back. She had made it quite some years ago. How many? Five; yes, all of five. It wasn't the best of its kind because she hadn't then been proficient, but he had insisted that it remain on his favorite chair, even though years of washing had yellowed the lace.

She turned, hearing Peggy enter the room. The girl's eyes were downcast beneath the starched white hat that covered her black hair. Wordlessly, she offered Julia the bonnet. Without bothering to look in the mirror, Julia put it on, then stood motionless while Peggy draped the cape over her shoulders.

"That's all. Thank you, Peggy," Julia murmured, not watching as the girl left the room.

A few minutes later, Julia stepped out onto the front porch, waiting until the coachman came up the steps, umbrella in hand.

Inside the carriage, she leaned back against the cushioned seat in an attitude of weary acceptance. The wheels moved along the brick-paved street lined with handsome, well-constructed houses. Almost all of them were fitted with wooden window boxes, but even the flowers appeared flat and gray on this gloomy afternoon.

A fitting frame for her own mood.

She didn't want to think about the last four days, but her mind refused her wish, playing the events over and over like a nightmare that had no end.

Her father was dead.

Julia's initial shock upon hearing that announcement had barely enough time to dissolve into grief when a second, even more difficult shock to bear, was thrust upon her, tinging grief with horror: he had taken his own life. It had happened away from home, at her father's place of business, a small consolation for Julia. A clerk had heard the shot and, upon investigation, found James Trent dead by his own hand.

And Julia didn't know why. No one did. There hadn't been a note or a clue. The loss was a cold, hard knot in her breast, all the more terrible for not being understood.

And now, this morning, two days after the funeral, she had received a letter from Devlin Eastwood requesting that she meet him in his office.

Well, perhaps ''request'' was not the right word, she thought, chewing her lower lip. ''Command'' would have been a more apt description of the curt message.

She sighed, seeing they were nearing their destination. Most probably, Mr. Eastwood would have legal papers for her to review and sign. She hoped the process wouldn't be too complicated.

The carriage halted. Julia glanced outside at the four-story brick building but made no immediate move, waiting until Frank opened the door to assist her out, again using the umbrella to protect her from the unrelenting drizzle.

''I shouldn't be too long,'' Julia said to him as they walked to the front entrance. A sudden gust of wind flattened her cape against her body and set a few raindrops to defying gravity as they pelted one side of her cheek.

"You take all the time you need, Miss Julia." He opened the door for her. "I'll wait right here for you."

Julia nodded, gathered her skirt, then quickly ascended the stairs to the second floor.

It was the first time Julia had been in Devlin's law office, or any office for that matter. She was surprised at the size of it. It was much larger than she had thought it would be. The windows were closed in deference to the rain but did not mask the clattering sound of traffic in the street below. One wall was fitted with glass-fronted bookcases. The law books they contained were imposing, of great size and handsomely bound in leather.

Receiving no greeting from the occupants of the room, Julia hesitantly advanced toward the large walnut desk, the top of which was now cluttered with papers. Devlin's pipe rested in an ashtray but was unlit.

Devlin himself sat behind the desk in a large leather chair. He was an attractive man, but grave in his bearing, with a razor-thin smile that could chill the most enthusiastic adversary in a courtroom. He was not smiling now.

"Sit down, Julia."

She did so, obeying without question, casting a tentative glance at Mark, who was standing to the side of the desk, clad in dark brown trousers and a maroon jacket that she had never seen before. He gave her a brief nod but did not speak. Still, his presence was reassuring to her, and she relaxed. Mark would explain anything she didn't understand.

Devlin shuffled the papers in front of him for several long minutes, leaving Julia with the distinct impression that he was stalling for time, trying to collect his thoughts.

"I've been going through your father's papers, which he

left with me for safekeeping,'' he said finally, without looking up. "Naturally, I've never looked at them before . . . before he died. I've spent the last two days trying to sort them out. . . ."

Julia shifted in her chair and again looked at Mark. The expected reassurance was nowhere to be found. He was now standing by the window, his back to her, hands clasped behind him. A definite feeling of unease came over her.

Devlin gave a great sigh and frowned until his brows met over the bridge of his nose. "Julia, I know this will be a shock to you, but the plain fact is that James Trent was not your father."

The rain against the window seemed very loud in the silence that greeted his words.

Whatever she had expected to hear, that declaration was the remotest possiblity. Julia didn't know whether to laugh or to become angry at such an absurd statement. Giving Mark another glance, she saw only his back.

Before she could say anthing, Devlin continued in a curious monotone. "I don't know who your real father was, but I do know the identity of your mother. . . ."

"What are you saying!" Julia cried. She got to her feet, but felt so weak she had to sit down again.

Obviously there was some ghastly mistake, she reasoned, trying to control her whirling thoughts. James and Amelia Trent had been her father and mother. She remembered no other, could recall no time in her life when those two people hadn't been around her, caring for her.

"It's true, Julia," Devlin said, sounding impatient with her outburst. He observed the clock on his desk as though he had allotted this distasteful task a certain amount of his time and was annoyed that his schedule was being upset by unnecessary questions. He viewed Julia again and spoke sternly. "Please listen to me. I realize this is difficult for you, especially coming so soon after..."

Closing her eyes, Julia took a deep breath. She didn't believe this for one minute.

"As I've said, we don't know the identity of your real father, but your mother was James Trent's sister. James was, in fact, your uncle."

There was another long silence while Julia tried to absorb his words. She pulled her cape closer, staring at the rain that coursed down the panes of glass, shimmering like ribbons of silver satin. "How do you know this?" she managed at last, feeling chilled to the bone.

Devlin picked up the sheaf of papers in front of him. "These letters tell the story." Extending his arm, he placed them in front of her, but she made no move to touch them. "I'm certain you will want to read them when you're calmer. In any event, they are now your property."

"Where is she now?" Her tremulous lips could barely form the question.

"Carolyn Trent died eighteen months ago in San Francisco where she...ah...lived for many years. You were actually born in that city. Your mother was not married at the time. As I've been able to put it together, James and Amelia were childless and had no hope of being otherwise. They agreed to take you into their home when you were no more than an infant." He leaned back in his chair and thoughtfully rubbed his chin. "There were conditions, however," he went on, staring off into space. "Your mother was never to contact you in any way, and James and Amelia were to be given a free hand in raising you as their own daughter."

Julia looked down at her hands in her lap. They were trembling, and she pressed them together. No need to lose control. "Well, then," she said in a barely audible voice that was nevertheless steady, "there's no disgrace in being adopted—" She broke off as Devlin loudly cleared his throat.

Sitting up again, he once more regarded her. "I'm afraid, Julia, that you were never legally adopted." He paused a moment so that she could fully understand the implications of what he had just said; then he continued. "I really can't say why James would overlook such an important step, but I gather from the letters your mother wrote that she refused to give you up in any legal sense." Julia paled, and Devlin gave her a sharp look, his aloofness momentarily dissolving in the face of the more immediate concern of having to deal with a fainting woman. Turning in his chair, he motioned to his son. "Mark! Get her a glass of water!"

Roused from his unremitting contemplation of the scenery, Mark hurried to do his father's bidding. Pouring water from a decanter on a side table into a glass with an efficiency that would do credit to a waiter, he held it to Julia's white lips.

Julia took a few sips, then waved him away. With great effort, she channeled her thoughts, trying to concentrate on the shattering revelations that were being presented to her. "Is this why my . . . my father killed himself?" she asked Devlin.

"I sincerely wish I could say that was the sum of it," Devlin murmured. The anxiety, the grief, the bleak despair of the girl seated before him touched Devlin not at all. He had long since schooled himself to disassociate himself from the emotional problems of his clients. "James killed himself because he was bankrupt. I won't go into the details of what happened." His hand moved through the air in a disparaging gesture that, despite her fogged state of mind, Julia recognized. "I'm certain you wouldn't understand."

"But I want to understand!" she implored, leaning forward in her chair.

Frowning, his fingers drummed the polished surface of the desk, an impatient staccato that Julia ignored. "Well, it began during the Panic two years ago, in 1873. James lost the bulk of his resources at that time. Apparently when Carolyn Trent died, whatever monies she possessed were forwarded to her brother, supposedly to be held in trust for you. In trying to recoup his losses, James . . . well, he invested that money, too."

Julia sat motionless, hardly able to listen to Devlin's droning monologue of disaster. She felt as if she had been stripped of her identity.

"Last Friday," Devlin continued in the face of her insistent stare, "the stock market, as well as the Gold Exchange, suffered a severe setback. While it caused great inconvenience for us all, James had no cushion on which to fall back. All of his money is gone—a blow from which James could not recover." He paused a moment, sighed, then added, "And, although it distresses me to tell you this, the house you are living in is mortgaged to the hilt."

Julia regarded him wide-eyed, unable to believe all these shocking facts.

"The bank is calling in the mortgage. You will have to vacate the premises within thirty days." Devlin's voice betrayed no compassion; nor, in fact, did he feel any. He had always prided himself on being able to judge a man's true character and now felt deceived by James Trent and his sordid little secrets from the past.

Julia didn't take the time to wonder at the coldness in his voice; there were too many other matters to concern her right now.

"Vacate?" she echoed faintly, as if she'd never heard the word before.

"You will have to move out, Julia! Any furnishings and

personal possessions you have are, of course, yours to do with as you see fit." He got up, appearing anxious to leave. Bending forward, he placed the packet of letters in her numb grasp. After exchanging a meaningful glance with his son, Devlin hastily left for the outer office, closing the door behind him.

Julia sat very still, only dimly aware that Mark came to stand behind his father's desk.

Finally she gazed up at him, startled to see the bright flush that stained his cheeks. She waited for him to come to her, to take her in his arms and tell her that everything would be all right. But he didn't move, keeping the desk between them as if it had become a welcome barrier.

"Julia . . ." The crimson in his face deepened, and he stretched his neck as if his collar had suddenly become too tight. "I'm damned sorry that all this had to happen. But you can understand . . . I mean, under the circumstances, it would be impossible for us to . . ."

She regarded him for a moment, sternly ignoring the sinking feeling in the pit of her stomach. "What are you trying to say, Mark? She was distantly surprised at her calm voice as she asked the question. But perhaps that was because somewhere deep inside her she already knew the answer.

He wet his lips, and his eyes roamed the room in an effort to avoid looking at her. Stammering, his face still flushed, he let his words tumble out. "Dammit, Julia, this is not something that can be kept secret. The news will be all over town in a few days. Just about everyone at the bank knows what happened. I can't possibly marry a woman who doesn't even have a last name, a woman whose mother was a . . ." He stopped abruptly and began to move the papers on the desk in an aimless fashion.

Julia stood up, grateful for her returning composure. This

was Devlin's doing, she decided. She had seen, though not immediately recognized, the look Devlin gave his son just before he left the room. I've done my part, it said. Now you do yours. But as she observed Mark's anxious face, she had a nagging doubt. Disdain crept into her eyes as she studied the man to whom she was supposedly engaged. He was a proper Bostonian; genealogy was of paramount concern to Mark. Only hours ago she would not have questioned this. But why should she feel ashamed? she wondered bitterly. She had done nothing wrong.

"I suspect that my mother was not the first woman to have given birth to an illegitimate child. . . ."

Mark ran an agitated hand through his hair and for the first time seemed to grope for words. A sudden flaring of his nostrils indicated that he had found them. "Your mother was a prostitute, Julia!" The words flew at her on a wind of accusation that suggested she should have known this. "She ran a brothel in San Francisco. You were born in one of those . . . those houses!" He glared at her as if she had become distasteful to him. "She probably didn't even know who your father was. . . ." He sniffed and gestured. "I'm sorry. There can be no marriage between us."

Prostitute? Julia confessed to herself that she had only a vague idea of what that entailed. Such a subject had never been discussed in her home, certainly not in her presence. Her head moved up. Actress! Of course. Everyone knew about those women. Even she had heard the whispers, the innuendos that branded those fiery rebels as something other than symbols of ideal womanhood. Of course, she had never actually seen one. The only time she had been permitted to attend the theater—properly chaperoned—was when a concert was being offered. Even the opera had been viewed with suspicion by her father, who considered it to be a decadent form of entertainment.

Inclining her head, Julia glanced down at the letters in her hand, then headed for the door, where she paused. Turning, she viewed Mark as she would a stranger, which was exactly what he had become to her in these last minutes. If someone had asked her yesterday, Julia would have said she knew Mark very well. Had she actually been going to marry this pompous weakling? she wondered with a jolt of surprise. She had come in here expecting her fiancé's strength to see her through a difficult time. What she had found was a man with clay feet.

"Tell me something," she said softly, regarding him with curiosity. "What would you have done if all this came to light after we were married?" As she waited for his answer, she was grimly amused to see his flushed color recede to paleness.

He shifted his weight from one foot to the other before he spoke. "I . . . don't know," he admitted, refusing to meet her eye. "I really don't know. I'm just glad it didn't happen that way. It would have made everything hellishly awkward."

She cocked her head to one side and spoke reflectively. "You know . . . I'm glad, too. It would distress me greatly to have placed you or your family in a position of . . . awkwardness."

"Um . . ." Mark toyed with the papers on the desk, still not meeting her eye. "If you need any money, I think I could persuade Father to . . ."

"That won't be necessary," she cut him off. "I will do just fine, thank you." Raising her chin, Julia turned from him, refusing to give him the satisfaction of seeing her despair.

But as she left the office, Julia's shoulders slumped, and she wondered morosely if anything would ever be fine again.

Somehow she made her way back to the waiting carriage and settled herself within its dim confines.

As it moved away from the curb, she looked outside. Though the afternoon had not yet wended its way into evening, a lamplighter had already begun his rounds. Julia watched as, one by one, the streetlights began to glow, creating soft islands of brightness in the gray mist.

She kept her mind carefully blank until at last the carriage stopped in front of her home. Although from all accounts, Julia thought wryly, it would not be her home much longer.

Stepping from the carriage, she raised her head. The rain had stopped, but the grayness of the sky remained unabated. For some reason it reminded her of Lane Manning's eyes. She had caught a brief glimpse of him at the funeral, but he had neither approached her nor spoken to her. Probably he was on his way back to Philadelphia by now.

Inside, she handed her hat and cape to Mrs. Beale, then went into the study at the rear of the house. It was not a large room, but two tall windows made it light and cheery in sunny weather. In the center of the room were two desks, positioned front to front. This had been the room where her tutors had conducted their classes, with herself as their solitary pupil.

Crossing the carpeted floor, Julia placed the letters on one of the desks and stared at them for a long time, wondering why she felt so little curiosity as to what they contained. Perhaps, she thought, the constant barrage of blow upon blow in these past days had inured her to feeling anything. And she didn't know which was more stunning: the news of her birth, or Mark's rejection. Her engagement to Mark, her life with Mark, was over. Why wasn't she more upset about that?

Julia allowed her thoughts to turn inward, searching her

heart for sorrow; it was there, all right. But not because of Mark Eastwood.

In a weary gesture, Julia rubbed her temples, for the first time feeling a resentment against her father.

Uncle! she silently corrected herself as she sat down. But it was no use. James Trent had been the only father, surrogate or otherwise, she had ever known. And so he would remain in her mind for the rest of her life.

Her resentment was short-lived, dissipating almost as it surfaced. He must have been more than desperate to do what he had done. Certainly he could not have known that Mark would have acted in such a reprehensible manner. "Safe," her father had said on the night of her engagement. The thought produced a humorless laugh.

The door opened, and she saw Mrs. Beale poke her head into the room.

The woman's eyes filled with concern as she viewed the slim girl behind the desk. Something had happened, of that she was certain. It was not her place to ask questions, however. Instead, she said, "It's almost time for supper. . . ."

Julia shook her head. "I'm not hungry."

Mrs. Beale's face folded itself into a disapproving look. "You've eaten nothing since breakfast! At least let me bring a sandwich and a pot of tea," she coaxed.

"Yes, that would be fine." As the door closed, Julia reached out and plucked a letter from the top of the pile.

For the next two hours she read one letter after another, taking an occasional bite of the sandwich Mrs. Beale had placed in front of her, and just as absently sipping the hot tea.

It was all true. There were, of course, no letters written by her father, but for some reason he had saved every one written by his sister. From Carolyn's replies Julia could tell that James Trent had alternately pleaded and threatened his sister in an effort to turn her away from the life-style she had chosen, all to no avail.

There was, however, one thing that Devlin had either overlooked or not recognized. Carolyn Trent not only knew the name of the man who was Julia's real father, but also she had been very much in love with him. He had promised to marry her, then deserted her, leaving her pregnant and alone in a strange city. And from the accusatory tone of the letter Julia now held in her hand, even James Trent had at that time turned his back on his sister's scandalous behavior. A woman then befriended Carolyn, giving her food and shelter until her child was born. The woman ran a brothel on San Francisco's notorious Barbary Coast. Once there, Carolyn had never left, and, in time, when the woman died, she had taken over the management of the establishment.

From that point on, everything Devlin told her was true. Julia couldn't help but wonder if James and Amelia Trent would have taken her in if they had had children of their own.

It was a question she would never be able to answer.

When she was through reading, Julia sat there for a long time, staring into space. At some point, Mrs. Beale had come in and lit the lamp, taking the dirty dishes with her when she left.

Julia didn't notice. She now understood the reasons for her strict upbringing, her father's insistence on her maintaining a conservative wardrobe, the constant chaperoning, even when she had been a small child. They must have thought she would go the way of her mother.

Finally she got to her feet, feeling stiff. No wonder; it was past ten o'clock! She picked up the letters, hesitated, then placed them in a desk drawer.

The staff would have to be let go, she realized as she locked the drawer and pocketed the key. There was no money with which to pay them. She debated as to whether she should tell them what had happened, then decided she would say nothing; they would learn of it soon enough. Reference letters would have to be written for them all. She'd begin that task in the morning.

And as for herself . . . Julia sighed deeply, not wanting to think about that just yet.

Picking up the lamp, she left the study and slowly ascended the stairs.

On the landing, she paused. Raising the lamp, she studied the portrait of Amelia Trent, painted some five years before her death. Julia wondered why she had never before realized that there was no resemblance at all between herself and the woman she had called Mother. The woman's hair was black, her eyes brown, her face round.

I saw what I wanted to see, she thought sadly, and knew in her heart that this woman would always be known to her as Mother.

Lowering the lamp, she headed down the hall to her room.

Opening the door, she saw that the bed had been turned down. Peggy was waiting to assist her, but Julia dismissed the girl, feeling the need to be alone.

Besides, she thought ruefully as she put the lamp on a table, she'd better get used to doing things for herself.

Although she was certain she would be unable to find any rest this night, Julia fell asleep almost immediately, a sleep of mental exhaustion, uninterrupted by dreams.

chapter
three

Morning presented a clear blue sky. The storm had passed, taking with it the chill of the previous day but not its memories.

Opening her eyes, Julia's heart seemed to still for a moment as remembrance flooded her mind.

It had not been a dream.

Turning her head, she glanced about her room, seeing the bright yellow curtains at the window, the cheerful green of the flocked wallpaper, the warm mahogany of the furniture. Nothing had changed; everything had changed. She had never felt so alone in her life.

With great effort, Julia dragged herself out of bed, wanting desperately to return to sleep, to the blessed oblivion it provided.

Setting her mouth in a firm line, she resisted the temptation. There was a household to run, and the habit of years could not be ignored.

After she had washed and arranged her hair into its usual

chignon, she dressed, again in black. Then she went downstairs to what would most certainly be a solitary breakfast. The dining room seemed huge with herself as the only occupant.

As she ate, Julia pondered what she must do. The household staff, including Frank, who doubled as coachman and gardener, totaled six. All would have to be paid their wages and given letters of reference before they were sent on their way.

And where would she get the money to do that? She couldn't recall a time in her life when money had been a consideration in anything she did; money was to be spent, not thought about.

The sound of her fork scraping the last of the eggs from her plate gave her pause. She stared at the border, then touched it with a fingertip. Gold. Certainly it must be worth something. Holding up her fork, she studied it, though she needn't have. She knew very well that it was solid silver.

When she finished her coffee, Julia summoned Mrs. Beale. As briefly as possible, she explained her financial situation to the woman, then instructed her to inform the staff that this would be their last week. All, she stressed, would be given favorable letters of reference and an extra week's pay.

Mrs. Beale was silent for such a length of time that Julia was about to speak sharply to her.

"I don't know how to tell you this, Miss Julia," she said at last. "But, well, it isn't enough." Her voice was only a whisper as she said that, and she wrung her hands in a nervous gesture that was quite unlike her. The carpet caught her attention, then the window, and finally Julia. "I know you're not aware of this, but the fact is, none of the servants have been paid in over three months. . . ."

"What!" Julia's mouth gaped.

"It's true," the woman said sadly, appearing to be about to cry. "During the first week of March, your father—God rest his soul—called me into this very room and told me there was no money to pay the staff's wages. A temporary financial setback, he called it. He asked me to tell everyone, and to tell them there'd be a bonus if they stayed on. Well, except for Phoebe—you remember, she left at that time—we all stayed. It's not always easy to find as good an employer as your father was. Mr. Trent always treated us fairly. He demanded we work hard, and that was only right. But he was never mean or stingy. Never said a word about the food we ate or the candles we took to our room at night."

Julia's sigh came from the deepest part of her. Even though she had no doubts as to the veracity of Mrs. Beale's story, she found it incredible that she could have been so unaware of what was going on around her. Ever since her foster mother died, Julia had had a say in everything involving the household, except money. Money was business; therefore it was a man's prerogative.

And why did no one ever take the time to consider the fact that women might be left to deal with it! she fumed silently. An urge to throw something was sternly repressed.

Bleakness enfolded her in a cold embrace, and for a minute Julia considered going to her room to hide, to disassociate herself from this treadmill of misfortune that seemed to have no end.

Foolish notion. There was no place to hide. She shrugged off the moment's weakness and forced herself to concentrate on this new problem.

Julia's dark blue eyes, when they finally raised to view Mrs. Beale, gave no indication of her thoughts, and she covered her distressed surprise with an ease that she could only thank Amelia Trent for supplying through many years of guidance: one did not display emotion before servants. Julia stood up and spoke briskly.

"Inform everyone that they will receive their back wages by the end of this week. And the bonus my father promised," she added firmly.

It was later that same day when the cook, Mavis Stoddard, approached Julia, who was in the study compiling a list of the possessions she was planning to sell.

Mavis, a widow, was in her late fifties. Heavyset and large-boned, she nevertheless retained a certain earthy prettiness. Fine crinkles around deep-set hazel eyes indicated an easygoing, good-natured personality.

"Mrs. Beale told me we were all being let go by the end of the week," she said, coming to stand before the desk. The white apron she was wearing was floor-length, and only the long sleeves of her dress showed the black she had donned in recognition of Julia's state of mourning.

Julia nodded in answer to the observation. "But through no fault of your own," she hastened to say.

"Oh, I know the reasons, all right," Mavis said in a tone that suggested they might not be all that important. "She also said that you were going to stay on here for a few weeks until you decide where you want to go." She looked at Julia for confirmation.

"Yes," Julia responded, wondering what the woman was leading up to. She didn't think she could handle any more surprises right now. "I'm sure you'll have no trouble at all in finding another position." She smiled reassuringly. "Cooks with your talent aren't easy to find."

Mavis blushed with pleasure. She was very proud of her achievements, and it was nice to be appreciated. "Oh, I'm sure I'll find a place easy enough," she conceded, trying to sound modest and not quite succeeding. "But who's going to do for you in the meantime?" she demanded, folding her arms across her ample bosom and giving Julia an indignant stare. "You can't stay here all by yourself!"

"I'll manage." Julia gathered her notes into a neat little pile.

Ignoring the unspoken dismissal, Mavis stood her ground. "Well, if it's all the same to you, I'd like to stay on until you actually leave the house." She raised a hand as Julia started to speak. "Don't you be worrying about the money. I've some set aside. And you've got to eat, don't you?" Her grin was at once coaxing and affectionate. "Besides, it'll be a vacation of sorts, cooking for just the two of us."

Julia hesitated, then gave her a grateful smile. Until this moment, she hadn't given thought to the fact that, when everyone left, she would be alone in the house; the prospect wasn't appealing. "Thank you, Mavis. I'd be happy to have you stay."

When the woman left, Julia went upstairs. She spent the next few hours going through her father's desk, which was in the sitting room that adjoined his bedroom. Here she found several more proofs of debt: a small bill due a bootmaker, a somewhat larger one due a tailor, and one that was over five hundred dollars owed to the dressmaker who made Julia's own clothes.

Putting the bills aside, Julia resolved to pay them all.

That night as she brushed her hair, Julia regarded the pile of debts on her dressing table. Such an innocuous stack of paper; such a legacy to be left behind after a lifetime of diligence and hard work.

Even though she had thought there were no more tears, her eyes filled, droplets spilling over, blurring her vision until she abandoned the braiding of her hair. Crawling into bed, she pulled the covers up and sobbed softly into her pillow.

The next morning, once again composed, Julia left the house early. By noon she had arranged for most of the furnishings, including the gold-bordered china, to be sold. The servants received their back wages, plus the bonus promised by her father. Before the week was over, they had all left the house, with the exception of Mavis.

On Monday, as she had done for the past seven years, Mavis hooked her shopping bag on her arm and went to the market.

Feeling restless, Julia wandered around the nearly empty house in an aimless manner.

For the past two years she had seen to the running of her father's household, planning menus, making certain the guest rooms were always in a state of readiness. Her father had left her completely in charge when a dinner party or social function was in the offing. And, until six months ago, her lessons had consumed a good four hours of each day. Now, with only herself and Mavis, there was little, if anything, for her to do.

She would have to find some sort of employment, she decided, pausing to straighten a picture frame that was already perfectly situated. Working for a seamstress, perhaps? She had to squelch that idea; sewing was not something she did well.

In the hall, Julia paused again, biting her lip as she stared at the pattern created by the fanlight over the front door.

Being a governess was one post for which she might qualify, if the matter of references could be overlooked. Trouble was, there wasn't one family in town that wouldn't immediately recognize her. Discounting the fact that they might close the door in her face, Julia couldn't bring herself to confront her former friends and peers in such reduced straits.

Finally, coming into the front parlor, Julia seated herself at the piano and began to play a soft and melodic piece by Bach.

Halfway through the rendition, Julia lifted her hands from the keyboard, hearing the back door slam in a most definite way. A moment later an irate Mavis stomped into the room, waving the empty shopping bag as if it were a red flag.

"For years I've been doing business with that man, and now he has the nerve to sass me!" Her voice was loud, her face crimson with outrage.

Julia frowned and shifted her weight on the piano bench until she was facing the woman. "What are you talking about, Mavis?"

"Mr. Bateman!" she exclaimed heatedly. "Seems like our credit's no good anymore!" That was proffered as if she had received a personal insult. " 'Cash on the line!' he says. He'll not allow us to buy so much as a loaf of bread till the bill is settled." Tirade spent, she grew somber and her voice lowered, taking on an apologetic note. "It's pretty high, Miss Julia. I've been charging the groceries for a couple of months now."

Julia sighed, feeling incredibly weary. Mark had been right, she thought dispiritedly. The news is all over town. "I'll see what I can do in the morning," she said quietly, and waited in silence as Mavis left the room.

Inclining her head then, Julia let her fingertips rest lightly on the ivory keys of the piano, feeling a friendly smoothness that beckoned her further touch. She would miss the instrument greatly, for it had afforded her many hours of enjoyment.

The following morning, Julia came quickly down the

stairs, her bonnet held loosely in her hand, its ribbons billowing in her haste.

Best to get it over with, she thought to herself. The piano would have to go, and probably everything else as well. Even with all debts paid, she would need money once she left here.

At the foot of the stairs, she detoured to place her reticule and bonnet on the hall table, then went into the kitchen to inform Mavis that she would be going out for a few hours.

"Will you be home in time for dinner?" Mavis asked, pausing in her task of kneading dough. She brushed her hands free of flour, then wiped them on her apron.

"I'm sure I will be," Julia replied with a nod. "What I have to do shouldn't take too long."

"Well," Mavis sighed, knowing full well what Julia was about to do, "I don't see that it will be a problem if you're not on time. The roast will wait. . . ."

Going back into the hall, Julia grabbed her bonnet, then paused, viewing the silver platter that seemed to mock her in its barren state. It was empty, as it had been for day after day now. No calling card rested on its gleaming surface, no message beckoned her attention.

Her mouth compressed with her bitter thoughts. She had been hoping that one of her many friends would come forward with an offer of at least a temporary shelter; but not one of them had even called on her. They had, of course, all attended the funeral. But that was before the circumstances of her birth had been revealed.

Again her eyes sought the empty tray, and Julia began to realize that, in the full sense of the word, she had no real friends. All her acquaintances had been chosen by her parents with an eye toward respectability and acceptance.

She supposed the reverse was also true: she was no longer considered to be either respectable or acceptable.

With a sigh, Julia raised her eyes to the oval mirror and was just about to put on her bonnet when the front doorbell rang. She put it back on the table next to her reticule.

"I'll answer it, Mavis!" she called out.

Crossing the foyer, Julia opened the door and blinked in surprise. "Mr. Manning!" She looked up at him—she had forgotten he was so tall. Though the day was warm, he was neatly dressed in tan trousers with a matching frock coat over a white shirt, ruffled down the front.

Lane smiled as he removed his hat. "I'm pleased you remember me."

She stared blankly, making no move to admit him. "Are you . . . are you here to see me?"

"Indeed I am," he responded with a nod, still smiling.

Julia stood there feeling foolish. It went against everything she had been taught to invite a man into the house when she was alone and unchaperoned. Of course, Mavis was in the house, but that was hardly the same thing. Glancing up and down the street, she wondered how many curious eyes were watching from behind curtained windows. The street itself was quiet, the sun blazing through trees, dappling grass and walkways with irregular shadows. Next door, a cat yawned and stretched, moving himself to a more sunny spot on the lawn, casting an accusing eye at Lane's carriage for disturbing his nap.

Seeing her hesitation, Lane said, "I realize it is a bit early to receive callers. If the time is inopportune, I can return later in the day. Or tomorrow."

Julia swung the door wider. "Come in," she murmured, curiosity getting the better of her. She couldn't think of one reason why this man would be calling on her.

Closing the door, Julia led Lane into the front parlor, taking care to leave the pocket doors open. Though the thought crossed her mind to send for refreshments, she quickly discarded the idea. That would only prolong his visit, and she had no wish to do that.

If Lane was surprised by the barren state of the room, he gave no indication of it. One side was completely devoid of furniture, the rug showing a more vivid color where the horsehair sofa had protected it over the years from the effects of light and sun. At the other end there remained two chairs with a table between them. Not so much as a knickknack graced the mantel over the stone fireplace. The only amenity to be seen was the large piano, a fringed shawl covering the top and artfully draped down the side to conceal its wooden legs.

Lane watched as Julia crossed the room and sat down in a chair. Only in the depths of those dark blue eyes was he able to detect a hint of the sorrow she had to be feeling. Her head was high, her bearing proud, despite what he knew she had gone through in these past two weeks. No hysteria, no look of long-suffering martyrdom, no paleness of face. Whatever she was feeling would never be revealed in public. It was evident to him that she had spirit and courage. He approved.

"Devlin told me that you and Mark are no longer engaged," he said quietly. Although he thought Mark Eastwood a fool, the young man's decision to break his engagement didn't surprise Lane in the least. Bostonians were, if nothing else, predictable.

Her nod was curt. "That is correct, Mr. Manning." Her cheeks pinked and grew warm. Obviously everyone knew she had been jilted, and why.

Coming forward, Lane placed his hat on the table but

remained standing. "He also told me that you have to be out of this house in a few weeks."

"That is also true."

Julia shifted her weight and smoothed the skirt of her black bombazine dress. The color, so unflattering to most women, actually looked good on her, Lane thought to himself. He decided it would be inappropriate, however, to tell her she looked attractive in mourning.

"Have you decided where you will go?" he asked her.

"Not yet." Julia viewed her clasped hands and thought of the empty silver tray. What would she do if no one came forward to offer her assistance?

Thoughtfully, Lane inclined his head. "You have no family? Cousins, perhaps?"

"None that I know of." Was he going to offer her a job of some sort? she wondered, viewing him with growing interest. And if not, did she dare to ask for one?

Lane walked to the fireplace and stood there a moment, looking into the empty grate, then he motioned toward the piano. "Do you play?" he inquired casually.

"Yes," she replied simply, not mentioning that she was quite proficient at it.

He nodded but made no further comment on the subject. "It would seem that you are in a difficult position," he murmured, placing a hand on the mantel.

Julia made no answer.

Turning, he faced her again. "I . . . ah . . . might have a solution."

She gave a short laugh. "If you have, I'd like to hear it."

Tilting her head, Julia turned her face toward him in such a way that the bloom of her cheek was suddenly caught by a ray of sunshine that crept through the lace curtains, reminding Lane of an early summer rose. For the first time, he noticed that a thick fringe of silkiness framed those fabulous deep blue eyes. Again he was struck by her delicate beauty, aware that this was the first time in more than nine years that a woman had caught his eye for longer than a passing glance.

He hesitated only briefly, but his eyes were level as he regarded her. "You can marry me."

For a second she could only gape at him. What kind of a man would joke at a time like this? She frowned at him and moved restlessly in the chair. "I do not appreciate your sense of humor," she exclaimed indignantly.

"I was not being facetious," Lane protested quickly. "I am asking you to marry me, to be my wife."

Julia seemed incapable of speech for the moment. Lane stood quietly, watching the play of emotion that crossed her lovely face.

Uncomfortable beneath that unrelenting stare, Julia put a hand to her throat and finally found her voice. "You can't be serious!" she said at last.

"But I am. Very much so."

He was standing before her, feet planted wide, hands clasped behind him. He did look serious.

"We've met only once, Mr. Manning," she pointed out with a small laugh, turning away from those gray eyes. There was a directness to them that she had never encountered before. "I can't imagine that you have feelings of love for me."

He shook his head, his demeanor still serious. "Love has nothing to do with my proposal, Miss Trent," he said with an honesty that took her by surprise. "Quite frankly, it is time for me to settle down, to raise a family. When I make a decision, I do so very carefully. I wouldn't even purchase a

horse unless I was convinced of its health and speed...."
He smiled disarmingly.

Julia viewed him doubtfully. She sincerely hoped he
wasn't about to ask her to open her mouth so he could
inspect her teeth.

"And as I've said," Lane continued, not noticing her
expression, "it's time for me to begin my family. I would
like to have at least five children, preferably three boys and
two girls."

Three boys, two girls? Julia kept a straight face. "That
sounds reasonable," she murmured innocently.

Lane missed the sarcasm; in fact, he seemed pleased with
her assessment. Coming toward her, he settled himself in
the remaining chair and gave her an intent look. "You
yourself said that your engagement to Mark was effected by
others."

"Mark—" She broke off, realizing she had been about
to say that Mark loved her; but of course he didn't. If he
had, he never would have allowed his father to talk him into
breaking their engagement. Or had it been Mark himself
who wanted to discontinue it?

"This time," Lane noted quietly, "the choice would be
entirely up to you."

Getting up, Julia went to the window, needing time to
think. She wasn't considering his proposal; it was too
absurd. Yet this was the first time a man had proposed to
her. Surely a woman deserved a few minutes to relish such
an important event. Mark had never said: "Will you marry
me?" Never. It had been her father who had approached
her, telling her that Mark had requested her hand in marriage. What had Mark said to her? Julia concentrated. He
had said: "I would like permission to speak to your father."
Julia remembered that she had blushed and nodded. In an

indirect way, she supposed that could be termed a proposal. Yet, in the final analysis, she had left the decision to someone else. What if her father had said no? Julia confessed to herself now that she would not have made any objection, certainly not a forceful one; it never would have occurred to her to disobey her father.

Intrigued in spite of herself, Julia turned to look at Lane. What would her father's reaction have been to this proposal? Instinctively, she knew.

"Do you know that if you had approached my father with this request, he would have refused you?" She watched him with interest, and Lane saw the hint of sorrow return to her blue eyes. It did not strike him as odd that she referred to Trent as her father; a habit of a lifetime is not easily broken.

"I have no doubt that he would have refused," Lane admitted with a nod of his head, well aware of the social reception he had received from most Bostonians. Business, of course, was another matter. Then he returned her look, adding a small smile. "But I am not asking your father; I'm asking you."

It crossed her mind to ask him if he felt sorry for her; but as soon as the thought presented itself, Julia dismissed it. Lane Manning was not a man to feel sorry for anyone, not even himself. Again she looked out the window. The cat was nowhere in sight. The street was still quiet, empty of traffic, but she had no doubt that neighbors, hidden from her view, were avidly counting the minutes that Lane Manning remained inside her house. She could even guess what they were thinking: the apple doesn't fall far from the tree.

"Why do you want to marry me?" she asked finally in bewilderment, still not quite believing him. No man proposed marriage after only one meeting; it was simply not done.

"You are well educated, for one thing," he answered candidly. "In good health. More important to me is the fact that you conduct yourself like a lady. Your social graces are impeccable."

She raised a brow at that. "But my origins are not," she noted softly. "Perhaps you are unaware that James Trent was not my father, and that my mother—"

"I know all about that," Lane interrupted with an impatient wave of his hand, taking her by surprise. "I never judge a man on the basis of his parentage. I see no reason to do otherwise with a woman." Julia shot him a look that was frankly disbelieving. Seeing it, Lane murmured, "I confess to not having been gifted with the prejudices of the well-bred people of your acquaintance. I did not say I was without my faults," he added wryly.

"Are you telling me that you want to marry me simply because my social graces are ... impeccable, as you put it?" She resisted the urge to laugh. Coming back to the chair, she sat down again.

"Not entirely," he admitted, then continued in a brisker tone. "You are beautiful." That was delivered in such an impersonal tone, Julia thought he could be describing the weather.

"And is that important to you?" she questioned, trying not to look as dubious as she felt. Despite his declaration, Julia knew very well that she was no beauty. Even Mark at his most gallant had never paid her such a compliment.

"I would say so. To be honest, I can't imagine anything more tedious than viewing a plain woman across my dining table night after night." Lane smiled when she still hesitated. "Most women would welcome the opportunity to marry a rich man," he pointed out.

"But I am not most women," she retorted swiftly, her

tone cool. "If I were, I doubt you would be asking me to marry you." The rather cavalier manner in which he was treating the subject of marriage was beginning to irritate her.

"Still, if a person has a choice," he said reasonably, "I should think that being wealthy would be preferable to being poor."

"That would depend, Mr. Manning," she retorted in some annoyance, thinking him gauche for harping on his finances. One either had money or not; one did not, however, discuss it!

Lane began to sense her discomfort and realized that his wealth or lack of it was of no concern to her. He found that most refreshing. Lane did not deceive himself into thinking that his attraction for women was based on his charm. He paused, took a breath, then asked bluntly and with great seriousness: "You are a virgin, I presume?"

For a moment Julia didn't react. Her upbringing had been such that she had never heard that word spoken aloud. And since she had only a vague idea of what took place between a man and woman in the privacy of their bedroom, the meaning wasn't entirely clear to her. But she did know that unmarried girls were virgins and married ones were not. Having put that together, Julia's face flushed with what she took to be an insult.

She sprang to her feet, her flushed color deeping the blue of her eyes. "Mr. Manning! How dare you! You would never presume to take such liberties if my... if I were properly chaperoned."

The outburst seemed to take him by surprise. "I beg your pardon? Oh, I see. Please believe me, I did not mean my question to be offensive. If I have worded it indelicately, I apologize. But it's vital information."

"I don't care how you word it!" Julia's shock gave way to anger. "I will not dignify such a question with a reply."

He regarded her appraisingly, half amused and half annoyed by her outrage. "My apologies," he murmured quietly, but didn't appear contrite. "I'm a man who speaks his mind."

"Obviously." She didn't sound mollified. Pausing, she gave him the coldest look she could summon.

Lane pursed his lips. "You were, after all, engaged to Mark Eastwood for almost one year. . . ."

Julia had no idea what he was talking about, and told him so.

"Well, it's not unheard of for a man to take advantage of his betrothed," Lane said carefully, "to seduce her into his bed. . . ."

"You make a grave mistake if you judge other men against the ruler of your own behavior!" she exclaimed hotly. "You've made an issue of the fact that you consider me to be a lady," she added scathingly. "Might I inquire as to whether it is your custom to question a lady as if she were . . . an actress!" Lane raised a hand and rubbed the bridge of his nose to cover his smile. Julia caught it anyway but saw nothing amusing. "Certainly no gentleman would speak as you are doing here today."

There was a moment of silence while they stared at each other.

Then a stern look came into Lane's eyes, banishing any trace of amusement. "Do you think I would not question your father on something as important as this issue?" he inquired in a stiff tone that prompted her to think she might have been out of line.

"I . . . don't know," responded Julia in a shaky voice.

"Of course you don't," he said easily. "You were never present when these things were discussed. When a man's child is born, he would like to know that it is his own. I see nothing out of the ordinary in that.''

Julia couldn't either, and for the moment she didn't know what to say. All she did know was that she didn't like this conversation at all.

Lane viewed her a long moment, then said softly, ''You haven't answered my question.''

''Mr. Manning!'' Her chin jutted out, and she trembled in her outrage. ''This has gone far enough. I must ask you to leave!'' She paused abruptly, appalled at how high her voice had risen. No one had ever elicited such a reaction from her before.

''Please, Miss Trent . . .'' Lane raised a hand in a placating gesture. ''I assure you that I have no intention of taking advantage of you. In fact, my intentions are honorable ones,'' he stressed earnestly. ''And my proposal is sincere.''

Julia listened, not at all swayed by the persuasive tone he was using.

Reaching out, Lane picked up his hat from the table, then got to his feet. Hands clasped at her waist, Julia was regarding him in stony silence.

''I'm sure this has been a trying time for you,'' he said in a low voice. ''And no doubt my offer of marriage came as a complete surprise. It would be unfair of me to expect an immediate answer. I'll return next week for your decision.''

Julia was of a mind to decline his offer on the spot, but she had an idea that he would further pursue the subject, and right now all she wanted was for him to leave. In silence, her back rigid, she escorted him to the front door, where he paused, regarding her for a long moment before he spoke.

''Do think about this very carefully before you make up your mind,'' he urged. ''I assure you that you will live in the style to which you are accustomed, and I promise that you will never want for anything.''

Julia raised her chin and wished he would go. ''I will think about it, Mr. Manning,'' she replied, not having the slightest inclination to do so. Her circumstances would have to be dire indeed before she would even consider marrying such a crude, boorish man as Lane Manning. He bowed slightly, and she frowned at the sight of those broad shoulders that threatened to undo the seams in his jacket each time he moved.

''I would deem it an honor if you would accept,'' he said softly, straightening.

Again, the force of his masculinity made itself known, causing Julia to recoil mentally from its impact. ''I . . . cannot possibly give you an answer now.'' She took a step back in an effort to distance herself from him.

''I understand. I'll call again next Wednesday at three o'clock.'' Lane went to put his hat on, then hesitated. ''A few weeks ago, I said to you that I thought Mark Eastwood was a most fortunate man. I would like to say now that I consider him a fool.'' Placing his hat on his head, he stepped out into the sunshine.

Julia didn't watch his departure. Closing the door firmly, she decided she would be unavailable to callers next Wednesday.

chapter
four

Sunlight slanted through the window, flowing like melted butter across the well-scrubbed kitchen floor. It didn't matter to Mavis that the house would soon be vacated, eventually to be occupied by others. The kitchen was her domain, and she would have it no other way than spotless. No one could have said that it was her job to scrub and polish, but she performed those tasks in her kitchen. The rest of the house could collect dust with no bother on her part, but here it was different.

Nor did she grow slack becuase there were only two people to eat what she cooked. It was a matter of pride that she did her best. Lifting the cover from a pot on the stove, she sniffed appreciatively, casting only a casual glance at the door as Julia entered the room.

Without any greeting, Julia sat down at the trestle table, her manner displaying utter dejection. She and Mavis had been sharing their meals this past week, for the dining room furniture had been sold.

She had traveled from one end of the city to the other,

and there was no employment for her, absolutely none. She had expected her lack of experience to be a problem but not a gigantic obstacle that appeared impossible to surmount; nor did it help matters any to learn that everyone in town was whispering about her.

Mavis was still bustling efficiently at the stove, the clatter of pots causing a strident noise. Julia put a hand across her eyes, closing them briefly. She had not been sleeping well this past week, tossing and turning on her bed, frustration growing with the swift passage of days that brought her closer and closer to the poorhouse.

Lowering her hand, Julia looked up as Mavis placed a bowl of soup in front of her, then sat herself down at the other end of the table.

For a few moments, Mavis regarded Julia with troubled eyes. Poor girl, she was thinking, suddenly sorry that she had no daughters. Two sons she had, but they were long since gone. One was in the Oregon territory, the other a sailor on a cargo ship. Julia had always been kind to her, Mavis reflected, never uppity or condescending. Mavis knew she was going to miss that bright smile of Julia's, though, in truth, she hadn't seen much of it these past days.

"Have you decided what you're going to do?" she asked at last, buttering herself a slice of bread.

Slowly, Julia shook her head, her mind on an incident that had occurred the day before. She had just emerged from a milliner's shop, having unsuccessfully sought employment there, and had seen Clair and Mrs. Eastwood heading in her direction.

In dismay and anger, she had watched as Agnes, catching sight of her, quickly ushered her daughter to the other side of the street. To her credit, Clair had turned around and offered a tentative smile before again being prodded by her mother. Not so Bunny Ramsey, whom Julia had encountered earlier in the week. That girl had walked by with her nose in the air, eyes focused on some distant point, leaving Julia with the impression that she had become invisible.

It was as though she had suddenly contracted a deadly disease, Julia thought, dipping her spoon into the broth without appetite.

"Well, if you ask me," Mavis continued, undeterred by Julia's silence and unmindful of the fact that she hadn't been asked, "I think you ought to accept Mr. Manning's proposal. It doesn't appear to me that you have much choice."

"I don't even know the man," Julia retorted with a sigh of irritation, sorry now that she had told Mavis the purpose of Lane Manning's visit.

Mavis shrugged at that and took a bite of the bread. "You thought you knew young Mr. Eastwood," she pointed out, "and look what happened there." Despite the fact that Julia had mentioned only that her engagement to Mark had been terminated, Mavis knew very well what had happened. Gossip was rampant among servants, and the marketplace was an excellent source of information. Mavis herself never indulged in such gossip, of course. Few servants were blessed with employers of the type that she was privileged to serve.

And, still viewing the slim girl on the other side of the table, Mavis made a vow that she would never carry tales about this one.

Julia swallowed a spoonful of soup. Though it was tasty, alive with herbs and seasonings, rich with vegetables and pale slivers of chicken, she pushed the bowl away.

"I suspect Mark's father had a great deal to do with that," she murmured. The words sounded hollow even to her own ears.

Mavis gave a snort and brushed the bread crumbs into a

neat little pile. "I'll bet no one tells Mr. Manning what to do!" she said succinctly, giving a curt nod of her head for emphasis. "He's his own man. Anyone can see that." Mavis had caught a brief glimpse of Lane as he was leaving and thought she had never seen such a handsome man in her life. She couldn't understand Julia's hesitation. If someone like that had proposed to her, she would have accepted in an instant.

An annoyed look lowered Julia's brows and darkened her eyes, but Mavis didn't seem to notice. Then Julia silently chided herself. Mavis was a good sort. Her advice, wanted or not, was put forth in good faith. Under the circumstances, the woman could hardly be reprimanded for her forwardness.

Finishing the last of the bread, Mavis got to her feet, heaving a great sigh as she did so. "Well, you'll have to make up your mind soon," she murmured. "He's coming to call this afternoon." She gave Julia a level look. "Why don't you change your dress, spruce up a bit? I'll make some tea."

The bell rang just then, and both women regarded each other in surprise. Lane wasn't expected until three o'clock; it was now only one-thirty. Quickly, Mavis went to answer the door.

"It's about time," she grumbled to herself, knowing full well how Julia had been waiting for her friends to call on her. Mavis thought it an outright shame how the good people of Boston had turned on an innocent girl.

But when Mavis opened the door, she saw Mark Eastwood standing on the front porch, looking dapper in a high silk hat and carrying a walking stick. For a second, Mavis just stared at him. Mark eyed her up and down, clearly annoyed with the hesitation. Leaning lightly on his walking stick, his tone impatient, he informed her that he wanted to see Julia.

Though she would have much preferred to slam the door in his face, Mavis reluctantly directed him to the front parlor, which, aside from the bedrooms and kitchen, was the only room that still had some furniture in it. She eyed Mark with a certain contempt only servants can express. Imagine him turning down the likes of Julia, she thought with a curl of her lip. He'd never do better, no matter how long he searched.

Leaving Mark standing in the middle of the room, she went to fetch Julia.

"Mark! I didn't expect to see you. . . ." Julia exclaimed as she entered the room a short while later, concealing her surprise at the unexpected visit.

He didn't immediately respond and stood there absently rolling the ivory head of his walking stick between his fingers. Julia noticed that he did not bother to remove his hat. The discourtesy stung all the more because she didn't think it was deliberate. Mark never forgot to remove his hat in the presence of a lady. Julia could draw only one conclusion from the omission.

She gestured toward a chair and summoned a welcoming smile. "Would you like to sit down?"

"No, no. I can't stay long. My father is expecting me back at work as soon as possible."

"I understand," she murmured, then injected a bright note into her voice. "How is Clair? I . . . haven't heard from her in a while."

"Fine, fine," he said quickly, sounding uneasy with her question. "She and Mother have gone ahead to Newport. They left last Friday. My father and I plan to join them this weekend. . . ." With the back of his hand, Mark brushed his mustache, a gesture Julia knew him to make when he was nervous.

She looked away and said nothing. It would serve no

purpose to mention the fact that she had seen both Agnes and Clair less than twenty-four hours ago.

"Will you . . . be leaving town?" Though he made an effort to look concerned, Mark's true feelings were all too evident to Julia.

"I have not yet decided," she answered shortly, refusing to let herself be annoyed or hurt by the hopeful expression she was seeing on his face.

He nodded, then said, "I . . . ah . . . understand that you have been selling your furniture."

Pausing, Mark looked around the near empty room with distaste, as if it were dirty instead of sparsely furnished. His lips twisted into something resembling a sneer; it made his narrow face most unattractive, a trifle weasel looking, Julia thought. Why had she never noticed that before?

"It has been necessary for me to sell a few things," she admitted, wondering why he was here. Obviously he hadn't changed his mind about their relationship.

Hunching his shoulders, Mark cleared his throat. "I've persuaded Father to write you a bank draft." He fumbled in the pocket of his jacket. "Here. I hope it will . . . will get you settled."

She looked at the paper he held out to her, but made no move to take it. "I don't want your father's money," she stated flatly, raising her eyes to meet his. Did he think she was a charity case? she wondered angrily. She'd get down on her hands and knees and scrub floors before accepting money from Devlin Eastwood or his son.

His face flushed darkly. "Dammit, Julia!" he all but shouted at her. "You make it sound like this whole thing is my fault!"

"And you've made it sound as if it were mine!" she

snapped back, and knew a moment of intense satisfaction at the astonished look on his face.

Glancing away for a moment, Mark drew himself up to his full height. "I see no need for this discussion to degenerate into a shouting match," he declared pontifically, now viewing her as though she were a naughty child. Mouth hard and tight with disapproval, he jammed the paper back in his pocket. "I'm here only to offer what assistance I can." He waited for an expression of appreciation, and when none was forthcoming, he frowned in a way that reminded Julia of his father. There was a small silence that Julia did nothing to alleviate, then Mark wet his lips, his tone softening in the face of her stony look. "I . . . didn't mean to imply that any of this is your fault."

He didn't sound entirely convincing. Seeing his hand come toward her, Julia took a step back. She had no doubt that he was about to pat her shoulder in a patronizing gesture, something he did rather often, now that she thought about it.

With a sigh, Mark's hand dropped to his side. "I meant what I said. I really don't think it's your fault. I know you're not to blame." Inclining his head, he regarded the head of his walking stick with an interest that suggested he was viewing it for the first time. "It's just that . . ."

". . . you judge a person by their parentage?" she suggested softly, thinking of what Lane had said to her.

His head jerked up, and he gave her a sharp glance. "Why . . . yes, of course!" His nostrils flared as he caught her look of contempt. "What a foolish thing to say, Julia! Really, I did think you were brighter. . . ."

She raised a brow. "I learn quickly, Mark," she said in that same soft voice. A light of mischief came into her eyes; she had nothing to lose. "Tell me, Mark," she said in the same tone, "did you ever ask my father if I was a virgin?"

Shock bleached his face of color. "My God, Julia! How can such words come to your lips?"

Prepared for his reaction, Julia persisted. "I ask you again, Mark. Did you?"

"I . . . of course not!" Color crept up his throat and stained his cheeks. "It wasn't necessary! I knew very well . . ." He halted suddenly and gave her that same look she had seen in his father's office. This time it didn't faze her at all. In an abrupt movement, mouth compressed so tightly that it disappeared beneath his mustache, he began to leave the room. "Don't say I didn't try to help you," he muttered over his shoulder.

Julia didn't bother to escort him to the door, listening to the staccato sound of his boots as he crossed the tiled foyer. She stood in the parlor until the door slammed shut with a force that resounded throughout the house. Walking to the window then, she watched Mark enter his carriage. She could see his profile, grim, unyielding, as he stared straight ahead, and the only feeling Julia could recognize within herself was relief.

With a firm step, she turned from the window, at once knowing what she must do. She had been offered the solution to her dilemma. It would be foolish of her to cast it aside and hope that something better might come along.

Thus resolved, Julia hastened to her room to change from her morning gown into something more suitable for receiving guests. She was just about finished when she heard the doorbell ring for the second time on this Wednesday afternoon.

Giving her hair a final pat, she went downstairs, her manner determined.

A few minutes later Julia again entered the front parlor, this time to greet Lane Manning. He was wearing a bottle-green frock coat and dove-gray breeches. She saw that Mavis had placed a tray on the table with a pot of tea and two cups.

"Good afternoon," he said pleasantly as she came into the room.

As he politely removed his hat, Julia smiled and bit her lower lip to prevent the threatening tears. She hadn't realized until this moment how much she resented being treated as a nonentity. "Please sit down, Mr. Manning. Would you like a cup of tea?" At his nod, she sat down and picked up the silver pot.

She was again wearing black, he saw, the material this time silk instead of bombazine. The skirt was domed like a bell, and had a trim of black lace just above the hem. Dropped sleeves narrowed to her elbow, then flared at the wrist. A black satin ribbon was fastened around the high neckline, and she wore no jewelry. Lane couldn't help but admire her cool poise.

"Have you given my proposal some thought?" Lane asked, getting right to the point. He seated himself and placed his hat on the table.

She nodded once as she filled the cups with tea. "I have, although I confess that the lack of feeling between us troubles me."

Lane gave a short laugh at the observation, then scowled at the dainty little cup before picking it up. "You are referring to that foolishness called love, I presume. When a man marries for love, he marries for all the wrong reasons."

"I see . . ." She didn't really, but wasn't about to argue the point. "You have never been in love?" she ventured after a moment.

"No."

The word was short, but Lane had hesitated a moment too long for Julia to believe him.

So, she mused, picking up her cup, at some time in the past, love had dealt a harsh blow to Lane Manning. Well, that emotion hadn't been too kind to her, either. Bleakly, Julia wondered if it had even existed. Had Mark ever loved her? She thought of the expressions reflected on his face when he had viewed her earlier in the day. Distaste and disapproval were the least of them. She had also detected an impatience, a need to distance himself from her. His visit, she suspected, had been prompted only by a nagging need to fulfill an obligation, at least partially.

Lane took a sip of the tea and grimaced; it was not his favorite beverage. He studied her a long moment before speaking. "Do you . . . dislike me?" He watched her closely.

Julia blinked. "Why, no . . . no, I don't dislike you." She gave a small, embarrassed laugh. "But that is hardly a basis for marriage."

He raised a dark brow. "I'm glad you don't dislike me," he commented, ignoring the latter part of her statement. "Now I ask you: do you love me?"

Taken by surprise, Julia drew a sharp breath. "Of course not! I don't even know you!"

He smiled, rather condescendingly, Julia thought. "And I don't know you, except superficially. But you have all the outward qualities that I would choose to have in a wife." He gave a short laugh. "It would seem that we are both taking a chance."

There was a small silence while they both directed their attention to the tea. Lane did not feel it necessary to tell Julia that he had been searching for a wife for the better part of a year now; he knew very well the type of woman he wanted. Given more time, he would have courted Julia in the accepted fashion, perhaps even become fond of her. But he had long since given up hope of becoming emotionally

involved with a woman. That had happened to him only
once, with disastrous consequences; he neither hoped nor
wanted to repeat the experience. Still, a man must have a
wife and a family or everything he worked for would be of
no use in the end. He had amassed great wealth, built
Manning House, and now he needed a wife to grace its
rooms and halls, a wife who would give him children. Lane
was convinced that a fortune and a house, however large,
were empty accomplishments without a family as a foundation.

Carefully, Lane now placed the fragile cup back on its
saucer, then cleared his throat. "May I speak plainly?"

"I wish you would."

"I realize there is no love between us, and I'm sure you
would think little of me if I professed something I didn't
feel." Frowning, Lane gazed speculatively across the room,
for the first time noticing the absence of the piano. In a lazy
movement, he leaned back in the chair. "You are not so
naive as to believe that every marriage is founded on love?"

"No. . . ." She swallowed. But she had been in love with
Mark. Hadn't she? Julia suddenly wondered if she knew
what real love was. Perhaps what she had experienced with
Mark was habit, familiarity? She sighed. She'd never know,
so there was no use in speculating.

"Then why do you keep pressing the issue?" Lane asked
shortly, sounding infuriatingly logical.

Clenching her teeth, Julia resolved to mention love no
more. "A few minutes ago you asked me if you could speak
plainly." She gave him a guileless look, wondering if she
could shatter his annoying calm. "May I?" At his nod, she
asked, "Would you still want to marry me if my . . . virginity
was in question?" Carefully, she studied his expression; it
did not alter.

"No," he responded quickly in his blunt fashion, then smiled. "Would you like to tell me differently?"

Slowly, she shook her head, sorry now that she had brought it up. "You can rest easy on that score," she said stiffly.

Julia sipped her tea, trying to regain her composure. She was unsettled. Most of the time she had known how Mark would react to any given situation. Occasionally his sudden show of temper had taken her by surprise, but she could not honestly say that his attitude changes had ever surprised her. This man Manning, however, refused to act in an acceptable manner. Julia was uncertain as to how to deal with it; these decisions had always been made for her. There had always been an older woman present when she was in the company of a man. All Julia had had to do was follow the woman's lead and act accordingly.

She continued to regard Lane in silence, her mind working furiously. She didn't know if she even liked this man. But she did know one thing: she respected him.

Putting her cup down, Julia sat up straighter and gave him a level look. "I don't seem to have much choice, Mr Manning. You have been honest with me, and I appreciate that. I will accept your proposal."

"Good!" He slapped his hands on his knees, looking pleased with himself. It was, Julia thought glumly, as if they had just concluded a business deal. Getting to his feet, he held a hand out to her, his demeanor businesslike now. "I will send a man around tomorrow to see to the disposition of your remaining furniture. If there is anything you wish to keep, just tell him. He'll pack it and set it aside." He paused, then added, "If you have any outstanding debts, I will see to it that they are satisfied."

"There aren't any," she replied softly, with dignity.

He nodded. "Then if it's convenient for you, we will be

married the day after tomorrow. I'll make all the arrangements. I had thought a quiet wedding, if you agree to that.''

''Yes,'' Julia murmured with a slow nod of her head. It was clear to her that Lane Manning was used to being in a position of authority. He spoke as if he were issuing orders he expected would be carried out instantly, with no objection.

''Pack such clothes as you will need for a six-week trip,'' he instructed in the same brisk manner. ''It will be warm where we're going. I'll have the rest of your clothing and personal possessions sent to my home in Philadelphia. We'll return there directly after the honeymoon.''

In a slow movement, Julia raised her head to look at him. Honeymoon? The very word sparked a flame of terror in her breast. Strange, the word in connection with Mark had produced nothing but anticipation of seeing London, for that was where they had planned to go.

Picking up his hat, Lane headed for the hall. Julia trailed along, feeling numb.

''I'll come for you on Friday at two in the afternoon.'' Pausing, he gave her a questioning look. ''Is there anything I haven't covered?''

''I think you've covered everything, Mr. Manning.''

A broad smile softened the angles of his face. ''In view of the fact that we are to be married, I think we can dispense with the formalities.'' Bending forward, he kissed her lightly on the cheek and was gone.

When the door closed, Julia put a hand to her cheek. On those rare occasions when Mark had kissed her, she had felt only the tickle of his mustache. It was a bit disconcerting to feel a man's lips on her flesh. She wasn't entirely certain she liked it.

chapter
five

Fastening the last of the buttons on her dress, Julia pinned a small watch to her bodice. The gold glinting against the black silk appeared frivolous. She was debating whether to remove it or not when the door opened.

Mavis took one look, blanched, and hastily crossed herself.

"Oh, Miss Julia! You're not going to wear that to your wedding, are you?"

The woman's face held an expression of shock as she came into the bedroom. She was viewing Julia's black dress with as much horror as she was capable of expressing.

Uncertainty flooded through Julia as she glanced down at the dress she was wearing. She, too, had had doubts as to what to wear on this day. "But I'm in mourning," she cried, "and I will be for some months to come!"

"No woman wears black to her own wedding!" Mavis exclaimed with convincing authority, appalled at what she was seeing. "It simply won't do!" She raised a hand as Julia opened her mouth to speak. "Do you want to cast a pall over your marriage before it even begins?'' Without waiting for an answer, she hurried to the wardrobe and flung open the doors. ''How about this?'' She pulled out a bright yellow dress and thrust it at Julia.

''No!'' Julia exclaimed with just as much shock as Mavis had displayed. ''I cannot possibly wear bright colors. . . .''

With a sigh, Mavis laid the dress aside. ''All right, how about this one? It's dark blue. . . .'' She waited hopefully.

''No, no! That's too formal!''

Undaunted, Mavis reached back into the wardrobe. Dresses came and went, held up for inspection and discarded. Finally, after more than an hour, they both decided on a pale gray lawn dress. Although the style was rather plain, the dress did have a white collar and cuffs.

The issue having been resolved, Mavis went to do her own packing. Julia changed her clothes, then cast a critical eye at her reflection in the pier mirror.

Well, it will have to do, she thought, giving it up. Mavis was undoubtedly right; she had never yet seen a bride dressed in black. Quickly, Julia gathered the dresses on the bed and put them in a box.

With a small frown of contemplation, Julia then turned and surveyed her room, wondering if there was anything she had forgotten. Her trunks were downstairs in the front hall, packed with the clothes she was taking with her. The rest of her clothing and personal possessions had been placed in boxes and crates that rested in a corner, waiting to be shipped to Philadelphia.

Lacing her fingers together, Julia took a deep breath, trying to ward off an ever-increasing feeling of nervousness.

Today was her wedding day; she could face that. What filled her with apprehension was the coming night. What would be expected of her? What was she supposed to do? Julia hadn't the faintest idea.

Going to the window, she pushed the curtains aside, her eyes scanning the street below. It was not quite one-thirty; Lane wasn't scheduled to arrive until two o'clock. Julia couldn't figure out whether she was anticipating his arrival or dreading it. Yesterday he had stopped by briefly to inform her of their itinerary: they would be married here in Boston, after which they would take the train to New York, where they would spend the night at the Fifth Avenue Hotel. The following day they were scheduled to leave for Athens by boat. Once there, they would board a packet for the island of Santorini.

Too restless to stand still, Julia backed away from the window and began to pace her room, her nerves taut and becoming more so with each passing minute.

At various times she had spoken to newly married women, but the only subjects discussed were how they were going to furnish their new houses, and how difficult it was to find good servants to keep them functioning properly. Occasionally, sights seen on their wedding trip were revealed, but never, ever, was anything of a personal nature mentioned.

Something happened; Julia knew that. But what it was she didn't know!

Educated, Lane had called her. Now Julia was disgusted by her ignorance.

With a deep sigh, she sat down at her dressing table. So lost in thought was she that when the door opened a moment later, she didn't look up.

"It's almost time!" Mavis exclaimed, coming into the room. She spoke cheerfully, happy with the thought that Julia's future was apparently secure. Her own future, too, looked bright. She had secured another post as a cook and planned to begin her new duties at the beginning of the week. Mavis then pursed her lips as she closed the door, viewing the pale gray dress. "What a shame you won't be able to wear a wedding gown," she murmured. "No matter how often a woman marries, she is a bride only once."

"There'll be no one there but Lane and myself, so what difference does it make?" Julia sat there toying with the brush, her tone absent, eyes fixed on a distant point in space.

Mavis lowered her chin and regarded Julia with a thoughtful expression. Something obviously was troubling the young woman, and she had an idea what it might be. She shook her head and sighed. She'd been in this house for more than seven years and knew firsthand of the conventlike atmosphere in which Julia had been raised.

"Is it tonight that's bothering you?" Mavis asked quietly.

The quick start, wide eyes, and flushed cheeks told Mavis her question was right on target. Without asking for permission, she pulled up a chair and sat down on it.

"Believe me, there's nothing to be afraid of!" She paused a moment, as if considering her own statement, then went on to say, "Well, there is a bit of pain involved. That's usually only the first time, though. After that, a woman gets used to it."

Julia moistened her lips. It? And just what was it? "I . . . it's just that I don't know what to expect."

" 'Course you don't," Mavis said quickly. "That's nothing to be ashamed of. Why, on my wedding night, I was as innocent as a lamb, let me tell you. I thought I was being split apart." She gave a short, loud laugh, nodding as if she found the recollection amusing. "Guess they heard my screams in the next town."

Julia paled, and she put her fingertips to her throat.

"Screams?" Her voice cracked on the word. And what was that business about being split apart?

A look of surprise widened Mavis's eyes. "Why, bless my soul," she breathed in wondering fashion, leaning back in her chair. "You really don't know anything at all, do you?"

Miserable, Julia shook her head. Mavis glanced at the clock. Lane was scheduled to arrive in fifteen minutes.

Mavis shrugged and took a deep breath. "Well, it's this way. I'm sure you've noticed, from time to time, a certain bulge in the crotch of a gentleman's trousers." She made a face and waved a hand in a vague gesture. "They refer to it as their manhood."

Then, warming to the subject, Mavis bent forward and lowered her voice as she continued to explain the mysteries of the initiation that turned a girl into a woman. The blood drained from Julia's already pale face.

When Mavis concluded her recitation, Julia was silent for a long moment. She clasped her shaking hands tightly in her lap, her body trembling with fear at the impending assault it would have to endure. Then another thought struck, and she viewed the older woman with imploring eyes. "I . . . I won't have to disrobe, will I? I mean, take off my nightclothes?"

"Of course not!" Mavis exclaimed, sounding indignant at just the thought. "No gentleman would demand anything like that. At least not of his wife," she qualified. "Some men do get peculiar notions at times, but there are places— and certain types of women—to cater to those baser needs."

Julia shuddered in distaste, wondering what could possibly be baser than what had just been described to her.

"Certain types of women?" Julia murmured the question.

Mavis gave a short nod. "Prostitutes, my dear. They sell

their favors." At Julia's blank look, she added: "They sleep with men and get paid for doing so."

Julia averted her gaze. Now, armed with this new and frightening information, Julia was amazed that any woman would follow such a course; yet her own mother had done so!

"Do men actually enjoy this thing?" she asked after a moment, finding it difficult to believe.

"Well, they seem to," Mavis answered with a smile. "I guess it's just nature's way; there wouldn't be any babies if one of us didn't like it, would there?"

Julia shook her head. That, at least, made sense. "How often . . . I mean, this is not going to be an every-night occurrence, is it?"

Mavis's shoulders rose, then dropped. "That depends on the man," she replied, then added, "But I must warn you, when they're young, their blood runs hot."

"Surely I will be allowed, on occasion, to . . . decline his . . . advances?"

Drawing in her chin, Mavis looked doubtful. "Well, of course, if you are ill. . . ."

Julia turned away a moment, mouth tight. "Safety there may be in marriage," she muttered. "But apparently only at the cost of freedom. . . ."

Mavis made a face and sighed deeply, features blending into irony. "What freedom?" she asked dryly, then waved a hand. "Freedom to work for others? To be at the beck and call of many instead of one?"

"But I don't love him!" Julia lamented with a catch in her voice, blinking her eyes against the sting of tears that threatened what composure she still had.

"That is not always given to us," Mavis said softly, moving uncomfortably in her chair, remembering her own happy marriage, and wishing Julia could have the same. "Sometimes," she said carefully, "there is love at the beginning, and it doesn't last. . . ." She hesitated, wanting to mention Mark; but she didn't. No woman could live with that one, she thought ruefully, and not have everything turn sour in a week! "And sometimes," she went on, trying to brighten her voice, "it's the other way around."

Julia brushed away a wayward tear that had managed to slip through her defenses. There was no chance of that happening to her, she thought. "I don't think I'm going to like this," she murmured with another shudder of distaste.

"Nor are you expected to," Mavis responded quickly. "In fact, I can tell you that a man would be shocked to discover that his wife was enjoying her marital duty." She wagged a finger at Julia. "That's what it's called, you know: a wife's duty. You must remember that. A woman has many crosses to bear in life, and this is only one of them. Pray to God that you become pregnant quickly. Then you will be relieved of this burden for a while; maybe even a year, if you're lucky."

"How will I know when I'm pregnant?"

"Your monthly flow will stop; that will be your first sign. Then you will get nauseous every morning for several months; but by then, of course, you'll know for certain because you'll begin to show."

Julia swallowed, feeling nauseous right now; the alternative seemed just as dreadful to her as her wifely duty!

Downstairs the bell rang with a clamor that caused Julia to jump from her chair.

"I don't think I want to go through with this!" she cried. She couldn't possibly marry Lane Manning, she thought frantically. She couldn't possibly marry any man!

"Now don't let yourself get upset," Mavis said soothingly.

"It'll be over before you know it." A broad smile creased her face. It always pleased her to know that she had done a good turn for someone.

The bell rang again, sounding more insistent.

"Oh, I don't think I can. . . ." Julia felt cornered, on the verge of hysteria. Taking a step back, she viewed the closed door in rising panic, half expecting it to burst open from the impact of a broad shoulder.

"Nonsense!" Mavis chided in a brisk voice as she got to her feet. Coming closer, she patted Julia's arm in a maternal way. "It's only the first time that hurts so much. After that, it's only a minor discomfort." Giving Julia a smile of encouragement, she hurried downstairs to admit Lane.

When Julia descended the stairs a few minutes later, she hoped Lane couldn't detect her nervousness. Even covered by gloves, her hands felt icy. She stared at Lane, suddenly aware that she knew absolutely nothing about him. She listened as he gave Mavis a few final instructions, then he offered her his arm.

Julia said a hasty good-bye to Mavis, who wished her well, and a short time later found herself seated beside Lane in a handsome victoria.

The minister was waiting, the papers were filled out, and before she knew what happened, Julia was married to Lane Manning.

Right on schedule—Lane seemed to have everything scheduled down to the minute—they arrived at the train station.

Julia sat in the parlor car beside the man who was now her husband and felt only apathy. Beneath her glove, she could feel the weight of the heavy gold band that encircled her finger with frightening finality.

It was done, she thought in amazement. I am actually married, now and forever.

Lane had purchased a few magazines for her to read on the trip. Mechanically, she opened one and stared down at it. Then, unable to help herself, she glanced at Lane's lap from the corner of her eye. The bulge was there, all right. Why had she never noticed it before? Mavis told her it would get bigger, but Julia didn't quite believe that. No part of a person's body changed shape. The idea was too ridiculous to credit.

Facing forward again, Julia compressed her lips. She had agreed to change the course of her life and must now make the best of it. There would be no turning back. The landscape, as well as the next hours, passed in a blur for Julia.

It was after nine o'clock by the time they arrived at the Fifth Avenue Hotel. Standing in the plush lobby with an outward patience belied by her quivering stomach, Julia watched Lane sign the register. The clerk snapped his fingers with a show of bureaucratic importance, and a uniformed bellboy immediately came forward to collect their trunks. A moment later they entered the caged elevator and were summarily transported to the fourth floor with a speed that left her dizzy.

The two-room suite Lane had rented was the best the hotel had to offer, sumptuously furnished with Duncan Phyfe pieces and lead crystal vases filled with fresh flowers, courtesy of the management. The chairs were upholstered in peach and green damask, and in the sitting room a table had been set for two, the fine silver reflecting the amber glow of the gaslights.

Julia saw none of it. Nothing, that is, except the bed visible through the doorway of the sitting room. It loomed before her eyes like some gigantic beast, overshadowing everything around it.

At a discreet tap on the door, Lane went to open it. A waiter entered, pushing a cart that held covered bowls of food. He carefully arranged them on the table, after which he deftly lit the candles in the candelabrum that served as a centerpiece. The tasks were accomplished in efficient silence.

Julia was hardly aware of his departure. Clutching her reticule in her hands with a fierceness that left her knuckles white, she stood in the middle of the carpeted floor as if she had been planted there. Lane had removed her cape from her shoulders and was standing in front of her, a quizzical look on his face.

What did he want now? Julia wondered nervously.

"Would you like to take off your hat and gloves?" he suggested with a small smile.

Hat? Gloves? Reaching up, Julia removed the pin that held her hat in place and hastily removed her gloves, handing everything to him in an almost placating gesture.

Clearly Lane hadn't expected it. For a second, he just stood there viewing the articles of clothing that had suddenly materialized in his hands before depositing them on the nearest chair.

Taking hold of her arm, he led her to the table. "In view of the hour, I thought we would be more comfortable if we ate here instead of in the dining room. I've ordered pheasant, but if you prefer anything else, I'll send for it immediately."

"No, no. This is very nice." Nothing would ever be nice again, she thought miserably. He was holding the chair for her, and Julia sat down, her back ramrod straight.

Lane picked up a bottle of wine, and Julia quickly put her

hand over her glass. "Thank you, no. I'm . . . I don't drink spirits."

Solemnly, Lane nodded, then proceeded to fill his own glass.

Although he tried to keep the talk flowing smoothly, Lane soon realized it was hopeless. Julia offered nothing but one conversation stopper after another, replying with an unembellished yes or no every time he spoke. She toyed with her food, taking minuscule bites and chewing interminably before taking another. She was delaying the meal in such an obvious way, he had to check a smile.

More than an hour went by in this manner. Lane began to fidget, and Julia continued to nibble at her food until he felt certain their supper would run into breakfast.

At last Lane put down his coffee cup and got to his feet. Fork in midair, Julia looked surprised, as if he had done something totally unexpected.

"It's almost midnight, Julia," he noted quietly. Placing a hand on her still-raised one, he gently lowered it to the table, prying the fork from her grip. "I think it's about time we retired."

Julia sat in her chair as if carved from stone. Everything Mavis had told her came rushing foward, cresting into a wave of fear that was paralyzing.

Seeing she had no intention of moving, Lane bent forward, put his hands on her elbows, and raised her to her feet. Closing her eyes, Julia sagged against him.

"What the . . .? Julia? Julia!" Lane patted her cheek, but there was no response. She was as limp as a rag doll in his arms. Picking her up, he carried her into the next room and deposited her on the bed.

Disconcerted, Lane stood at the side of the bed, feeling helpless. Now what was he supposed to do? he wondered.

Call a doctor? But no, it was just a fainting spell. Women had them all the time. He should know; he lived with three of them.

He frowned, glancing at her slim waist. Of course! She was too tightly corseted, and the endless meal she had just sat through had probably exacerbated the condition.

Leaning over, Lane began to undo buttons and ribbons. This was the first time he'd ever undressed a female, and he found the profusion of clothes an absolute maze to get through.

He finally managed to get the dress off and was about to fling it on the nearest chair. Feeling something made of metal, he turned it inside out and stared curiously at the framework of coiled wire, wondering what the hell it was. Then he concluded that the contraption probably supplied extra support for her skirt.

Shaking his head, Lane threw it on a chair. He didn't give a second glance to the cotton padding that formed the bustle; he knew what that was. Then came the petticoats— she was wearing two, one long and one short. They both landed on the chair next to the dress. Wide supporters hung from her shoulders. Baffled, his eye followed it down, and he realized it was holding up her stockings.

"Incredible!" he murmured to himself. No wonder women fainted with the least exertion.

Julia's trunk was on a stand at the foot of the bed. Opening it, Lane located what he assumed was her nightgown. And, my God . . . long sleeves and high neck, just like everything else she wore!

Julia was still unconscious, her face looking young and vulnerable. Pausing, Lane allowed his gaze to travel the length of her. He hadn't realized just how lovely she was.

Her body was flawless, exquisite in its perfection. Unable to resist, he reached out to caress a softly curved shoulder.

Aware that she would be recovering her senses shortly, Lane awkwardly pulled her nightgown over her head. She was a dead weight, and it was no easy task.

There. At least she was clothed again. Lane rested a moment to catch his breath. Finally he walked toward his own trunk, located a nightshirt, and struggled into it.

Then he sat on the edge of the bed and waited.

Julia opened her eyes with as little warning as she had closed them. She stared at him a moment, trying to get her bearings, then sat up. Feeling dazed, she looked down at her nightdress, then up at him, unable to smother a startled cry. She knew she hadn't undressed herself, and there was only one other person in the room.

"What . . . what happened?" she asked, sounding as if she was trying to catch her breath.

"Nothing yet," he remarked wryly.

She looked mortified. "I'm sorry. I'm not in the habit . . . I mean, I guess . . ." She trailed off and tried not to cry. Her fingers plucked nervously at the sheet, and she gave some thought to pulling it up over her head. As Lane started to reach for her, Julia jerked away from him. "You had no right to undress me! What sort of man are you!"

His hand fell away, and he lowered his head, his gray eyes dark as they viewed her from beneath black brows. "Right?" he echoed softly. "As your husband I have every right to do what I did."

"You do not!" she countered defensively, wondering if that was true.

He ignored her outburst. "As for what sort of man I am, I suspect that in time you will discover the answer to that on your own." He crawled into bed, giving her a sharp look as he did so. "I do hope you're not going to swoon each time I touch you," he growled. As he turned toward her, his nightshirt became entangled in his legs. Angrily, he tried to pull it loose. "I do not normally wear one of these," he muttered, trying to free himself from the clutch of flannel, "but under the circumstances . . ."

"What . . . do you normally wear?" was all she could think to say.

His head jerked up, and he looked surprised. "Nothing." His hand came toward her.

"The light . . ." Julia whispered tentatively, still clutching the sheet with both hands.

Pausing, Lane frowned at her. "What about it?" She made no answer. Then, with a grunt, Lane reached over and extinguished the lamp. It was so dark he couldn't even see his hand in front of his eyes. His movements had again caused his nightshirt to become tangled. "I can't wear this damn thing," he grumbled. "It gets in the way."

Julia was aware that he was removing his nightshirt. A soft plop told her it landed on the floor. That meant he was naked! Panic tightened into a hard lump in her throat. As he again reached for her, Julia shrank away from him, pressing her slender body into the mattress as if she might be able to hide herself in its softness.

With a sigh of exasperation, Lane said, "Julia, you're really making too much of this. I promise I will be as gentle as possible. . . ." No response. He sighed again. "This will be difficult enough without you acting as though I were some sort of ogre," he muttered, more to himself than to her. Narrowing his eyes, he peered through the inky darkness. Her face was only a pale blur, but he didn't have to see it to know she was frightened. He had expected her to be nervous, but not terrified!

Damn, he thought. Drawing away, he sat up and turned on the light again. Unmindful of his nakedness, he crossed the room to where his jacket was hung on a chair.

With a gasp, Julia closed her eyes and averted her face, but that quick glance was more than sufficient to imprint the image of him on her mind forever. It seemed to her that he was covered with hair! It was thick and wavy on his chest, narrowed to a point on his flat abdomen, and flowed into a dark triangle that only partially covered his—Julia searched for the word Mavis had used—manhood; Hair was also on his legs and even the lower part of his arms! Did all men look like that? she wondered in amazement.

Removing a cigar from the pocket of his jacket, Lane lit it and came back to sit on the edge of the bed. Perhaps she needed a few minutes to compose herself. He was a reasonable man. Let her take all the time she needed. Taking a few puffs on the cigar, Lane gave some thought to delaying this business until tomorrow night; but by then they would be on the boat, where the beds were narrower. He glanced at Julia from the corner of his eye. She was as rigid as a block of wood! Would she be more compliant tomorrow? Somehow, he thought not. Anticipation of a happy event was one thing; waiting for the sword of Damocles to fall was quite another. He would be doing them both a favor if he got it over with tonight.

Suddenly becoming aware of how quiet she was, he quickly turned toward her. "You're not sleeping, are you?" he demanded, peering down at her to assure himself that her eyes were open.

"Hardly," she murmured so softly he could barely hear her. As if she would ever rest peacefully again, she thought to herself, pulling the covers up under her chin.

"Well, try to relax. . . ."

Lane took a few more puffs, unaware that Julia's blue eyes were boring into his back with something like astonishment. The insensitive clod! she fumed silently. Did he really expect her to relax while he was perched on the edge of the bed, clothed only in his hair?

Minutes ticked away in silence. A gray stream of cigar smoke drifted by, and Julia concentrated on it, trying to will her heart to cease its pounding. At the sound of the cigar being stamped out in the ashtray, she gave a start that shook the bed.

The light went out again, and Julia clenched her teeth to prevent their chattering

Feeling his hands on her body, Julia stiffened. He was not ungentle, that much she discerned through her fear. When his hand touched her breast, she resisted the impulse to draw away, but when it dropped to her thighs, she clamped her knees together in a reflex action. Mavis had said nothing about this! Stubbornly, she kept her knees together until the hand moved away.

Lane easily felt the tension beneath his questing touch and began to realize there was only one way to consummate his marriage: do it as quickly as possible. He didn't like the idea, for he had never in his life taken a woman against her will.

Muttering a soft curse, he positioned himself on top of her, pushing her nightgown up and out of the way. He bent his head, intending to kiss her, only to discover she had covered her face with her hands.

"Good Lord," he moaned, almost defeated. He was still for a moment, then put his hands on her buttocks, pulling her toward him and slightly raising her body. He entered the moist warmth, moving as gently as possible until he encountered the resistance of her maidenhood. One forceful thrust was all that was necessary. He heard her slight whimper, but she made no other sound. His own release followed quickly.

Moving away from her, Lane lit the lamp.

Christ! he thought to himself, feeling annoyed. Over the years he'd had sex many times, with many types of women, but this was the first time he'd ever found it to be a frustrating chore!

"I'm sorry," he said awkwardly. "I didn't mean to hurt you, but it is unavoidable, you know." He spoke defensively, without fully realizing he did so. He frowned at her, his square jaw set at a belligerent angle.

Julia shivered, feeling chilled, and moved to the far edge of the bed. Was she expected to put up with this every night? The prospect wasn't a thrilling one. Gradually, she became aware of a warm, uncomfortable stickiness between her legs. Blood? Mavis had told her there would be some; but she had said it would be only a few drops. . . . Julia waited a few seconds; the feeling persisted.

Wiping her damp palms on the sheet, Julia's heart began to thump as she contemplated what was most likely the remains of her torn insides. Clamping her teeth against a cry of fright, she threw the covers aside, then ran for the bathroom in such haste that her feet barely touched the floor.

Brows raised, Lane watched her progress, momentarily surprised at the swiftness she displayed. Getting up then, he located his robe, put it on, and went back into the sitting room, where he poured himself a stiff brandy. He wondered if all wedding nights were like this one. Easy to understand why a man usually got married only once.

Tilting his head back, Lane drained the glass, then returned to the bedroom. From the continuous sound of running water, he assumed that Julia was taking a bath. No doubt her baths were as time-consuming as her meals, he thought grumpily. Shucking his robe, Lane got into bed and fell asleep almost immediately.

Some minutes later, Julia peeked around the door, relieved to hear the sound of his deep, even breathing. In a grip of suffocating apprehension she had examined her body with great care; there were a few crimson spots on the back of her nightgown, but she didn't seem to be bleeding anymore.

An incredible weariness now engulfed her. A while ago Julia would have said she'd probably never sleep again; now, sleep was all she craved.

With only a towel draped around her, Julia tiptoed to her still-open trunk, fished out a clean nightgown, and hurriedly donned it.

Cautiously, she eased herself into bed, casting a wary glance at the man beside her, ready to run back into the bathroom if he so much as moved. The light was still lit, but it was on his side of the bed. Fearing to wake him, Julia decided not to extinguish it.

Expelling a deep breath, Julia let herself relax. In retrospect, it hadn't been all that bad, she decided; probably she could live with it. It was, after all, her wifely duty. And no one had ever accused her of shirking her responsibilities, she thought virtuously, closing her eyes.

chapter
six

Though she fell asleep quickly, Julia didn't sleep for long. Every time she turned over, she came in contact with Lane's nude body. He was so big, he took up most of the bed, and no matter how much distance she tried to put between them, their bodies seemed to touch each time either one of them moved. Even when she managed to put a few inches between them, the heat of his body reached out to her, enveloping her in an uncomfortable warmth that prompted her to kick off the covers.

Toward dawn, Julia awoke with a start, smothering a gasp of fright. In that first, dreamlike moment of awareness, she was certain that someone was trying to strangle her. Reaching up, her shaking hands encountered Lane's arm flung across her throat. When she tried to move, she discovered that he also had a leg across the bottom part of her, a position that allowed his manhood to snuggle against her upper thighs. She grimaced at the intimacy, but didn't dare touch it.

Placing her thumb and forefinger around his wrist, Julia

gingerly raised his arm from her throat and carefully moved it to his side. A ragged sigh of relief escaped her lips, and for just an instant, she thought longingly of those blissful nights alone in her own bed. Sitting up, she then squirmed out from beneath his leg. Lane gave no indication of having his rest disturbed.

With as little movement as possible, Julia got out of bed. The lamp was still lit but seemed dimmer beneath the encroaching light of morning.

Hands on her hips, Julia regarded the sprawled-out form that was taking up most of the bed. Against the purity of the white sheets, his body appeared even more hirsute than she had first supposed.

Disgruntled, she glanced around the room. Chairs. She wasn't about to sleep on one of those! Her gaze returned to the man on the bed. She cocked an ear. He was snoring! A surge of annoyance swept through her. How could he sleep while she was wide awake!

Going to the window, she stared down into the street below. It was empty, gaslights glowing forlornly across the empty expanse that was Fifth Avenue at five-thirty in the morning. Overhead, the night sky was giving way to a brightening in the east, subdued and colorless due to the clouds that hovered low on the horizon. It was promising to be a dreary day.

Turning, Julia walked back to the bed. Lane hadn't moved; apparently nothing disturbed his rest. Reaching out, Julia poked at him, tentatively at first, then harder, until he at last turned over.

"Big, hairy brute!" she muttered to herself. About to get back into bed, she paused, staring thoughtfully at her pillow. Picking it up, she carefully positioned it between them.

There! she thought in grim satisfaction. Let him hang on to that!

The next time Julia awoke, it was after eleven o'clock. Heavy, brooding clouds obscured the sun, and only a dismal gray light gave any indication that the day was well under way. Lane had already gotten out of bed. Throwing the covers aside, Julia was prepared to do the same when the bathroom door opened and Lane emerged—once again clothed only in his hair. Quickly, Julia pulled the covers back in place.

"Good morning," he said pleasantly, heading for his trunk.

Julia glared at him. "Do you . . . do you always walk around like that?" she asked stiffly, careful to keep her eyes on his face.

Lane continued to rummage through his trunk for a moment longer until he located the shirt he wanted. Shrugging his arms into it, he viewed Julia with an innocent look. "Only in front of my wife," he replied, raising his chin to get at the top button.

"You must have a robe in there!" she sputtered, pointing to his trunk.

"I suppose I have," he replied easily, reaching for his trousers. "But I would have to take it off to get dressed," he added reasonably.

Mouth compressed, Julia averted her gaze and viewed the wall as he proceeded to button the front of his pants.

"Would you like me to leave the room while you dress?" he inquired casually, with a lift of his brows.

"I would indeed!" she replied curtly, still staring at the wall, seeing a wallpaper that depicted overblown roses in a most unnatural hue of green.

"Well, if you'll give me a minute or two, I'll be glad to oblige."

The cravat went on; then he sat on the bed to pull on his boots. Turning her head, Julia gave him an annoyed look, but he ignored it. Picking up his jacket, he grinned down at her.

"I'll put this on in the other room."

When the door closed, Julia finally got out of bed. The manners of a dockworker, Mark had said. And, by God, he had been right! Julia thought to herself.

She had unbuttoned her nightgown and was just stepping out of it when the door opened and Lane peered in at her. Clutching the garment, she held it in front of her. Had her eyes been daggers, they would have pierced him with deadly impact.

"Would you prefer to eat in the dining room?" he asked, displaying that infuriatingly innocent grin. "Or would you rather I had something sent up here?"

"I would prefer to eat in the dining room!" Julia's voice was terse, her words measured.

He went to leave, and she dropped her gown; he turned, and she hastily raised it again.

"Do hurry," he urged. "I'm getting hungry. It's almost noon!"

Julia gritted her teeth as the door closed. "If you hadn't kept me up half the night, I would have awakened at a reasonable hour," she grumbled to the empty room, flinging her gown in the general direction of her trunk. It missed and fell on the floor, but she didn't bother to pick it up.

After she had washed, Julia stood before her trunk and chewed her inner lip. What did one wear on a boat? she wondered. She had never been on one. Most of the young people she knew had taken the Grand Tour; she had not.

She glanced out the window. It wasn't raining, but the clouds were dark and ominous. Finally she selected a dark blue linen dress, wide-brimmed straw hat, and a paisley shawl.

Almost an hour had passed. Julia didn't care. If she had to lose sleep, Lane could suffer a few hunger pangs, she thought as she left the room.

The caged elevator transported them to the first floor with the same swiftness it had ascended to the fourth, and Julia was much relieved when she vacated the contraption.

In the dining room a short while later, Julia felt more relaxed. At least Lane had his clothes on. All this prancing about in the nude was totally uncalled for, she thought primly.

They were no sooner seated when, it seemed to Julia, they wre surrounded by a swarm of waiters, each of whom addressed Lane by name. Water glasses were filled, china and silverware appeared, and Julia and Lane were each handed a bill of fare with a flourish and a bow.

Lane seemed unaware of the fawning attention of those around him. *But perhaps,* Julia thought, *he is so used to it that he no longer notices it.*

Power. That's what Lane Manning had, she realized with a start. And not all of it was due to his wealth. Some mèn, by the very nature of their self-assurance, commanded respect.

Julia opened the bill of fare. Lord, she was hungry! She couldn't remember a thing she had eaten at supper last night.

After they had ordered, Julia toyed with the stem of her water glass, feeling suddenly uneasy. What was he going to say about last night? she wondered. Fainting like that! She had never fainted in her life. She darted a quick glance at

Lane. He smiled at her but she was beginning to distrust those innocent smiles of his; they usually preceded something she didn't like.

He didn't say anything. That made her even more nervous.

When the crowd of waiters had thinned somewhat, Julia found herself regarding her husband in amusement. "I take it you've been here before," she remarked as she unfolded her napkin.

Absently, Lane nodded. "I usually stay here when I'm in New York."

Their meal arrived. The constant hovering of the attentive waiters precluded any conversation other than of a general nature, a situation for which Julia was grateful.

When they had finished eating, Lane removed his watch from a vest pocket.

"It's getting on to three," he remarked conversationally, returning the watch to his pocket. "We'd best be getting down to the pier."

While Lane settled their bill, Julia returned to their room to repack the few clothes they had used.

Downstairs again, Lane saw to it that their luggage was placed in the hired carriage, after which they were conveyed to the pier.

With some interest, Julia viewed the boat anchored nearest to where the carriage had halted.

"Is that the boat we'll be taking?" she asked as Lane assisted her from the carriage. A strong wind gusted off the water, and she put a hand on her wide-brimmed hat to secure it in place.

"Yes, it is," he replied.

The captain was on deck, and though Julia could not hear his words, sailors suddenly hurried forward to gather their trunks, careful not to step in Lane's way while they were doing so.

Amusement returned. "I suppose this is the boat you usually take whenever you leave New York?"

"As a matter of fact, it is," he agreed. Taking her arm, he led her to the gangway. "I own it."

Pausing, she gave him a look of astonishment. "You own this boat?"

"Among others," he responded with a smile. "Come along. We're scheduled to sail in about thirty minutes."

As they boarded, Lane viewed the vessel with no small degree of satisfaction.

The *Sovereign* was a refitted clipper. Constructed of Malabar teak, the boat was capable of moving either under sail or steam. It was 244 feet long and 44 feet wide in the beam. A line of gold leaf encircling the hull just below the main deck gave the vessel a trim and graceful appearance.

Except for the captain and crew, Julia and Lane were the only passengers aboard.

The day was overcast, the sea high, and they were not an hour into the voyage when Julia began to feel queasy. She sat on deck, a blanket covering her from the waist down, and tried to concentrate on Lane's voice instead of her stomach, which was beginning to rebel against the constant movement of the boat.

Resigned, Julia shifted her weight and regarded Lane with what she hoped was attentiveness, nodding her head as he spoke. He was standing in front of her, one hand resting casually on the wooden railing.

Briefly, Julia gave some thought to going down to her cabin, ostensibly to rest, but she didn't know where it was located. They had boarded at four-thirty in the afternoon and had been on deck ever since, watching land and civilization recede from view. There was nothing to see now except an expanse of gray water that seemed to reach to the end of the earth.

"Julia?"

"Yes?" she answered quickly, aware that her attention had wandered. Resolutely, Julia swallowed and said nothing of her increasing distress, refusing to allow Lane to see yet another sign of weakness in her.

He gave her a quizzical look, obviously puzzled at not receiving an answer to his question. "I asked you if you've ever been to the Mediterranean. . . ."

"No. No, I've never been there."

"I know you'll enjoy it. It's a beautiful place."

"I'm sure it is," Julia murmured. The breeze strengthened and set the bottom part of Lane's jacket to flapping. He wasn't wearing a hat, and his hair was becoming tousled and wind-tossed.

"And, in my opinion," he went on, "Santorini is the most beautiful of the Greek isles."

Julia nodded, longing to be there right now, this minute. If it didn't move, she was all for it.

Leaving the railing, Lane came to stand beside her chair. Julia wondered how he could keep his balance. The rolling motion of the boat was becoming more noticeable. "Is this your first voyage?" he asked.

"Yes, as a matter of fact, it is." And please, God, let it be my last, she prayed silently.

Lane gave a small chuckle and rubbed his chin. "I guess there's a lot we have to learn about each other. We know so little; but all that will change during the coming weeks. . . ." He paused as he saw the captain walking in their direction.

Amos Huckabee was a giant of a man, so tall that even Lane had to look up at him. He had a ruddy complexion and thick, ginger-colored hair that curled around his collar and crept down his cheeks in neat sideburns.

"Good afternoon, Mrs. Manning," he said, touching the brim of his hat, then he grinned at Lane. "Looks like we're in for a bit of weather!"

Julia gave a small sigh, wondering why the man seemed so jovial at the prospect. "Does that mean we might run into a storm?" she ventured, sounding anything but jovial.

"Nothing to cause concern, Mrs. Manning," he replied hastily, giving her a reassuring nod. "We'll only be on the fringe of it. The main body of the storm is to the west of us. Of course," he qualified somberly, "if the wind shifts, we might have to batten down."

In some trepidation, Julia glanced beyond the captain to the grayness; even the water was gray, waves chasing one another, each one appearing more menacing than its predecessor as they all headed for a distant shore no longer visible. Julia returned her attention to the men as she heard the captain speaking to Lane.

"They're about ready with the evening meal," Captain Huckabee was saying.

"Fine!" said Lane enthusiastically, then held his hand out to Julia. "Shall we go in to supper?"

Supper? The word sent a shiver down her spine. "Yes, of course," she said brightly, trying to clamp her teeth together and smile at the same time.

A vague scent of spice came to her as Julia entered the small dining room. But this was soon overwhelmed by the platter of veal and bowls of potatoes and vegetables that were placed on the table, which was bolted to the floor. There were no portholes, and the lamps were fixed to the wall. Julia assumed the crew ate elsewhere, for there were only three settings.

"I dine informally," the captain said to her. "I hope you don't mind. . . ."

"Not at all," Julia said quickly.

With a charming display of gallantry, Captain Huckabee held her chair. As she went to sit down, the boat suddenly rose, hovered for a precarious second, and then came down with stomach-lurching swiftness. Julia landed in the chair with a thump and grasped the arms for support.

"What was that?" she asked weakly. "Are we in the storm?"

"No, no," Captain Huckabee said with a hearty laugh as he seated himself across from Lane. "That was just an oversized wave."

"Believe me, Julia," Lane said with a chuckle, "if we were in a storm, you'd know it." He helped himself to a large serving of potatoes, then passed the bowl to her.

"The *Sovereign* is a most seaworthy vessel, Mrs. Manning," the captain interjected in a tone meant to be reassuring. He piled several slices of veal on his plate, then added, "She can handle anything she gets into."

Julia put one small potatoe on her plate and stared at it dubiously as it rolled to one side. "I know so little about boats," she murmured, carefully choosing the thinnest slice of meat on the platter.

"Well, the *Sovereign* is a clipper, Mrs. Manning," Captain Huckabee went on to explain. "Or more properly, a clipper schooner, and she's full rigged. That means we have square sails on each mast as well as the usual complement of spankers, jibs, and staysails. She's one of the fastest of her kind; better than fifteen knots, under normal conditions. When we have a following wind, she can easily do twenty. But though we carry a full complement of masts and sails, we are right now under steam power."

He spoke with such unabashed pride that his comments drew a smile from Lane.

"And because of the chickens and livestock in the hold," the captain added, "we can travel many weeks without any inconvenience."

Julia looked up at him. "Livestock?" she murmured faintly.

"Yes," he nodded with a smile. "It insures that we have fresh meat for the whole voyage." He tapped the plate of veal with his fork. "This fellow was slaughtered only hours ago."

Julia hesitated, then put down her fork. Was the room tilting or was it just her imagination?

Though Julia had doubted it would ever happen, the meal at last came to an end. Lane and Captain Huckabee shared a bottle of port, discussing the pros and cons of French wines versus those from Germany, and then Lane finally got up to escort Julia to their cabin.

They made their way down a narrow corridor lit by lanterns, and Lane opened the door, assisting her as she stepped over the raised threshold. The cabin was quite large, with plush carpeting and two portholes draped with silk that appeared to have been hand-embroidered with gold thread. The furniture was dark and heavy, and here, as in the dining room, the lamps were fixed to the wall.

"I hope you approve of your accommodations," Lane said with an expansive wave of his hand.

"Very much," Julia replied truthfully, turning to face him. She hoped she sounded more enthusiastic than she felt.

Lane's hand rested briefly on her shoulder. At least, he thought to himself, she didn't appear to be nervous tonight; that was a step in the right direction. He would be gentle, patient, and, with a little luck, they both might achieve a degree of satisfaction. With that in mind, his hand dropped to curve around her small waist. Pulling her closer, his mouth found hers in a kiss that was at first gentle, then became more insistent.

Of a sudden, the nausea she had been fighting for hours would no longer be denied. With a sharp cry, Julia bolted from him and ran into the bathroom, where she became violently sick.

Taken by surprise, Lane stood there a moment, mouth agape. Then heated anger flushed his face as he stared at the closed door. *What the hell have I gotten myself into?* he wondered. *The woman either faints or gets sick each time I get close to her.*

"Well, be damned," he muttered to no one in particular, storming from the cabin. If his presence was so disturbing to her, then let her spend her time alone!

Julia heard the cabin door slam, but felt too weak even to call out. When she finally caught her breath, she splashed cold water on her face, welcoming the icy sting on her skin.

Feeling altogether miserable, she headed for the bed and threw herself down on it. Even relieving her stomach of its unwanted burden hadn't helped any.

After some time had passed, Julia was able to rouse herself sufficiently to undress and return to bed. She wondered where Lane had gone and what he must think of her. On that gloomy note, Julia fell into a restless, intermittent sleep.

A warm sun, slanting through the portholes to touch her face, awoke Julia the following morning.

Listlessly, she opened her eyes, then turned away from the brightness. Beneath her, the bed felt as though it were moving of its own accord.

God, she thought, burying her face in the pillow. Does

nothing remain still on this wretched boat? There was no doubt in her mind that she would never survive this trip. By the time they arrived in Athens, there would be nothing left of her but skin and bones.

Awhile later Julia heard the door open, but she didn't have the energy to raise her head. When Lane came into her view, she saw that he still looked angry. Her lower lip trembled at the sight of his scowling face.

"Why didn't you come to breakfast?" Lane demanded as he came to stand beside the bed.

Lane was completely out of sorts and didn't care if the world at large knew it. The *Sovereign* was primarily a cargo ship. Aside from the captain's quarters, this was the only cabin available. He had spent the night in a hastily rigged hammock in the captain's quarters and had a stiff neck to prove it. Twice he'd almost fallen out of the damn thing, and Huckabee's ill-concealed amusement hadn't helped matters any.

When Julia made no answer, he peered closer, taking note of her ashen face and overbright eyes. "You're seasick!" He sounded affronted.

"I'm sorry," she whispered weakly. "I should have told you."

He hesitated a moment, then spoke cautiously. "Were you sick last night?"

"Yes. . . ."

A frown of exasperation was followed by a sigh. "You're right! You should have told me. I thought . . . Well, never mind; it's unimportant. But you must eat. You'll only feel worse if you don't."

She groaned at his words. "I couldn't. I don't even want to think about food!" She glared at his suddenly grinning face. "Go away! Leave me alone." Rolling on her side, she presented her back to him. She heard the door close but didn't turn around, wanting nothing more than to be left alone.

But a short time later, Lane was back, this time carrying a tray.

"Here. . . ." he said gently, placing the tray on the bedside table. "Try to get as much of this down as you can."

"What is it?" she asked in a small voice, not bothering to look.

"Dry toast and hot tea with a bit of brandy. Come on now." Ignoring her protests, he raised her to a sitting position and placed the pillows behind her back. "Just take one small bite and one small sip," he coaxed.

It took almost thirty minutes for her to consume the light repast, but to her relief, Julia found that she did feel much better.

Lane arranged the covers, tucking them close around her. "You sleep for a while, then I'll take you up on deck for some fresh air."

By the time Lane returned a couple of hours later, Julia was dressed and sitting on the edge of the bed. Her hair was neatly coiffed, her color had returned to normal, and she even managed a smile when he came in.

On deck, as she strolled beside Lane a few minutes later, Julia inhaled deeply of the cool sea air. The sky had cleared and the sun shone brightly. Julia noticed that the sea had calmed. The waves didn't appear to her to be as menacing as they had the day before.

"Are you all right?" Lane inquired, looking down at her. Fine tendrils of her hair had escaped the confinement of her chignon and wafted about her face.

"I'm feeling fine," Julia answered truthfully.

"I should have recognized the symptoms," Lane said,

sounding annoyed with himself. "My sister April has the same problem."

It took a second for his words to register. When they did, Julia paused to view him with astonishment. "I didn't know you had a sister. . . ."

"I have two: April and Hester. They're twins, physically identical right down to a mole on the right side of the cheek." He laughed as they resumed walking. "But there the resemblance ends."

"How so?" Somehow the thought of Lane having sisters was a comforting one to Julia. She had always disliked being an only child, never having anyone to confide in, to share secrets and dreams with.

He pursed his lips as he considered her question. "It has to do with personalities, I guess," he said, after giving it some thought. "April is of a quiet sort. Always was, ever since she was a child. Hester . . . well, she's like our mother. She can be quick to temper when provoked." He took Julia's hand and slipped it beneath his arm. "You'll meet them all soon enough." Momentarily diverted, Lane gave a sigh at the thought of his mother and sisters. Doubtless he would be subject to their annoyance when they discovered he had gotten married without all the fanfare that would have been expected had the event taken place at home. But it was just as well, he decided. It was enough that he and Julia had had so little time to get to know each other. It would have been unfair of him to foist his whole family on her all at once. He turned his head as Julia spoke.

"Do they know that you've married?"

He nodded. "Yes. I wrote to my mother before we left and told her the news. I'm sure she'll be very happy."

"Did you . . . did you tell her about me?"

He frowned. "What do you mean?"

Glancing at him, Julia saw that he really didn't know to what she was referring. "I meant . . . about my mother, and everything. . . ."

Lane came to a halt, put his hands on her shoulders, and spoke sternly. "Julia, all that doesn't matter! It's unimportant. I don't want you to think about it anymore. It all happened a long time ago. And, in answer to your question: no, I didn't mention it. It never even occurred to me."

She looked at him wilth curiosity. It really *didn't* matter to him, she realized. The idea was a new one for her to contemplate. As angry and as upset as she had been over the attitude of Mark and her friends, Julia had understood it. She had lived with this attitude all her life: People were only as good as their background. Money helped, but it wasn't necessarily the only criterion. Had her father merely gone bankrupt, her status would not have changed. Even the fact that he had taken his own life wouldn't have appreciably altered that status. It was the news of her own birth that had done that. Yet, here was this man telling her that it was unimportant, of no consequence. Nor was he mouthing platitudes; he really meant it.

Julia took a deep breath as they resumed walking. She felt lighter somehow, as if a great burden had been removed from her shoulders. A giddy warmth took hold of her, and for a moment she was in the grip of a crazy impulse to run and skip like a child on Christmas morning; instead, she linked her arm through Lane's and forced herself to walk sedately.

Looking down at her, Lane smiled, pleased with the small intimacy. "It's almost time for dinner, Mrs. Manning," he said, brushing a knuckle across her chin. "How do you feel about that?"

"I'm famished!" she replied with a happy little laugh, and meant it.

Julia's dark blue eyes were shining as she gazed up at her husband, unaware that the respect she felt for him had taken a hesitant step toward affection. The past was over, the future beckoned, and Julia now eagerly looked forward to it.

That night when Lane crawled into bed beside her, Julia felt his arms go around her as he settled himself in the softness. But he made no move to kiss her or caress her, just held her close.

For a few minutes, Julia held herself rigid, but when the sound of his breathing told her he was falling asleep, she relaxed, her head on his bare chest, feeling the soft hair beneath her cheek, hearing the steady beat of his heart. There was, of course, no source of heat in the cabin, and the warmth of Lane's body—which only last night she had found annoying—was now most welcome.

Julia snuggled a bit closer. No man had ever held her this way before. She decided she liked it; very much, in fact.

With a deep sigh, Julia let herself drift off to sleep, feeling more content than she had ever felt in her life.

chapter
seven

Willa Manning was anything but happy as she sat at the writing table in the sitting room that adjoined her bedroom. It was from here that she ran the household known locally as Manning House. She was a tall woman in her late forties. Her black hair was now tinged with an ample sprinkling of silver, a condition she made no attmept to conceal. Her features were at once strong and patrician.

Right now a deep frown etched her brow as her vivid blue eyes stared at the paper she was holding in her hand. It was not Lane's letter. She had received that more than a week ago. No, it was not her son's marriage that prompted her annoyance. It was the woman he had married. The information hadn't been difficult to come by—word to her lawyer, a few discreet inquiries, and she had known all she needed to know about Julia Trent.

How could Lane have acted so irresponsibly? she wondered in growing anger, flinging the paper aside. To have actually married such a one. What could he have been

100

thinking of? Did he really think he could keep it a secret that his wife was the illegitimate daugher of a prostitute?

Of course not. Knowing Lane as she did, Willa was certain that it didn't even matter to him. She had never been able to impress upon him the importance of social contacts, of associating with the right people, of keeping up appearances. He thought nothing at all of flaunting convention when it suited his purposes.

She was also certain that Lane didn't love the young woman he had taken to wife. How could he? He was still in love with Rosalind.

Rosalind would have been perfect, but that foolish girl hadn't been able to see past her nose. Not that she had done so badly, Willa had to grudgingly admit. Rosalind had married Otis Langley, a rich man more than twenty-five years her senior.

"Mama?"

Startled, Willa turned in her chair and scowled at her daughter. "What is it, April?"

The seventeen-year-old girl smiled tentatively. "Would it be all right if Andrew stayed for dinner?"

"Well, he does almost every Sunday," Willa replied irritably. "I see no reason why today should be any different." She waved an impatient hand. "Tell Mrs. Litton to have an extra place set."

As her daugher left the room, Willa made an effort to calm her nerves. No reason to be upset with the girl, she told herself. April and Andrew Hollinger were engaged to be married. It was only natural that the young man came to call each Sunday.

Leaning back in her chair, Willa let her gaze rest on the view framed in her window. Today being Sunday, the Schuylkill River was host to many small boats as people lazed away the hours of the afternoon, courting and socializing. And along the grassy banks, couples strolled, the ladies holding their open parasols at an angle that would protect their fair skin from the sun. Even at this distance their brightly colored hats and dresses were in cheery contrast to the tranquil blue water.

The pleasant scene did little to lighten Willa's mood. Turning away, she surveyed her lavishly appointed sitting room, noting the Chippendale furniture, the costly brocades and damasks, the expensive Persian rug, and she sighed.

Though not on a scale such as this, the Mannings had always lived comfortably, if not grandly. Willa's husband, Charles, had been a cabinetmaker and had made a respectable income. They'd had some money put away, but when Charles died, Lane had been only sixteen, disinclined to follow in his father's footsteps.

It was just about this time when the Bothwells moved next door to their house on Walnut Street. Rosalind was their only daughter, and Lane had been smitten when first he laid eyes upon her. Three years after that, Lane had proposed. But Rosalind, even at the tender age of eighteen, had known exactly what she wanted: a man with money, a man who could give her all the fine dresses and jewels and servants to which she thought she was entitled. She had rejected Lane in no uncertain terms.

For many months, Lane had moped about, depressed as only youth can be when the heart is broken. Lane had matured during those unhappy months, stepping from boyhood into manhood. And with a man's determination, he grimly set about accumulating a fortune.

Willa had had serious misgivings about turning her savings over to her son so that he could begin his first venture: bringing back a shipload of goods from the Orient and selling them in this country at a huge profit. But it had worked out just as he'd said it would. From that day until this, the money poured in, in a never-ending stream. Willa's initial investment had been paid back to her a hundredfold. She was now a wealthy woman in her own right. As for Lane, even Willa had no idea of his worth. More than ten million, she guessed, and that was probably a conservative estimate. And the irony of it all was that Lane was now far more wealthy than Otis had ever been.

Thoughtful now, Willa tapped a finger against her lips. A friend had told her that Otis Langley had recently died in Paris, where he and Rosalind had been living for the past five years. Not surprising, since he was more than twenty-five years older than Rosalind—who was twenty-seven if she was a day—and had already suffered one heart attack before they had married nine years ago. Willa wondered if the news of his demise was accurate, sorry now that she hadn't written to Lane while he was in Boston. But who could have forseen that he would marry a girl he'd met only once? Willa had never thought of Lane as being impulsive. Yet surely that was what had taken place: an act of impulse.

One he would live to regret, Willa predicted dourly.

After April had informed the housekeeper, Thelma Litton, that there would be a guest for dinner, she went into the library, where Andrew was waiting for her. Entering, she smiled as she saw her sister.

"Hester! How very nice of you to keep Andrew entertained in my absence."

Andrew Hollinger immediately sprang to his feet. Tall and lean, he had brown hair and dark eyes that now brightened when April came into the room. He adored her and was always a little uncomfortable when left alone with

Hester. If pressed, he really couldn't explain why this was so. There were those who thought the sisters identical, but Andrew wasn't one of them. April was sweet, demure, soft-spoken. Hester, while every bit as beautiful, had a certain intensity that put him off.

Hester did her best not to glare at April, whose constant affability set her teeth on edge. No, that was not true, she thought, watching as April seated herself beside Andrew on the sofa—at a proper distance, of course. April seldom acted otherwise. Hester admitted to herself that she dearly loved her sister. It was only... It was only that she loved Andrew more. And the fool was so besotted that he couldn't see that she, Hester, would make a better wife for him. She knew that, felt it in the most secret part of her heart.

"Andrew," April was saying in her somewhat breathless voice, "we have the most marvelous news! Lane has gotten married!"

"Has he?" Andrew smiled broadly. "Is it anyone we know?" His gaze shifted to Hester, but she wasn't looking at him. She had picked up a magazine from a side table and was absently flipping through it. He wished she wasn't in the room so that he could be alone with April.

April shook her head. "No. She comes from Boston, and her name is Julia. That's all any of us really knows. Hester and I are so looking forward to meeting her." Glancing at her sister, April's sweet smile broadened. She did not recognize the hating reproof that glinted in those blue eyes that were identical to her own, for she was gentle in her heart and saw only what she wanted to see: goodness.

"When are they coming home?" Andrew asked, and April returned her attention to him.

"Not for several weeks, I should imagine. They're honeymooning in the Greek isles."

April blushed as she said that, and Andrew thought he

had never seen anything as lovely as her flushed cheeks. He resented it when someone remarked on the likeness between April and her sister. April was like a day filled with sunshine, full of kindness and with a gentle consideration for everyone. To Andrew, she was more precious than any jewel could hope to be.

Standing by the marble fireplace, Hester clenched her hands tightly, unable to look at the young couple as they gazed into each other's eyes. Andrew should be looking at her like that, she thought, feeling an anguish that cut to the core of her. Would have been, if she'd met him first, or even at the same time.

A maid appeared in the doorway just then to announce that dinner was being served in the family dining room, a considerably smaller room than its formal counterpart. Andrew immediately got to his feet and offered April his arm. He seemed to have forgotten that Hester was in the room.

When they were all seated at the table, April turned to her mother. "Mama," she said. "Do you think it would be a nice idea to have a reception for Lane and his wife when they return?"

"I do not," came the brief reply.

"But why?" April persisted, looking perplexed. "It will be a wonderful way for her to meet everyone."

"I suggest we leave that decision to your brother," Willa replied, picking up her fork.

Undaunted, April continued her argument. Hester looked up at the ceiling, then at her sister. April was such a dolt! It was so obvious that their mother was in one of her moods, and had been since yesterday.

Briefly, Hester wondered if her mother's ill-temper had something to do with Lane's marriage. Then she dismissed the thought; only her own concerns occupied her mind for any length of time.

After dinner, they all went into the drawing room. Sitting in her favorite chair, Willa positioned her tapestry board so that it caught the light, then began to thread a needle.

"Melissa Stapleton is having a croquet party next Sunday afternoon," April said to Andrew as she settled herself on the sofa. "Hes is going with Philip Maynard. If you have nothing else planned," she went on as he sat down beside her, "I would very much like to go."

Andrew grinned at her. "If I have, I'll cancel it. Of course we can go."

Hester stared at them, mouth tight. Andrew was hanging on April's every word as though she were imparting the secret of the universe to him.

"She's been seeing rather a lot of Philip. Haven't you, Hes?" April teased.

Hester lowered her eyes. "On occasion," she replied noncommittally. Philip Maynard, she thought to herself in disgust. The only reason she allowed him to escort her anywhere was because he was the least obnoxious young man she knew. With superb effort she managed to keep her features composed, revealing none of her turbulent thoughts. She headed for a side table. "Andrew," she said brightly, "may I pour you a glass of port?"

He turned his head and viewed her in surprise, as if she had suddenly appeared out of nowhere. "Why, yes. Thank you, Hester."

Picking up the decanter, she poured wine into a crystal glass. Handing it to him, their fingers briefly touched. The contact made her hand tremble, sending the ruby liquid splashing onto April's gown. With a soft cry of surprise, April jumped to her feet.

"Hester!" Willa said irritably, looking up from her handwork. "Must you be so clumsy?"

Quickly, Hester drew forth a handkerchief from the sleeve of her dress and began to mop April's skirt.

"I'm so sorry," she exclaimed. "It just slipped from my hand. Oh, April, if I've ruined your dress, I'll never forgive myself."

April extended a hand and rested it on Hester's arm. "It was just an accident, Hes. Please don't be upset. I'm sure it will wash out."

"Perhaps you'd better change," Hester suggested. "If you soak it quickly enough, it might not leave a stain."

"Yes," Willa interjected, getting up. "Come along, April. I'll ask Mrs. Litton to take it to the washroom immediately."

April nodded, then viewed her sister. "Will you please keep Andrew company until I return?"

"Of course I will," Hester responded warmly. "It's the least I can do."

As her mother and sister left the room, Hester sighed and gave Andrew a crestfallen look. "It was clumsy of me...."

Andrew thought so, too; but he shook his head and murmured: "Not at all."

Pouring another glass of wine, Hester placed it on the table beside him. She smiled and touched the flower at her bosom, knowing his eyes would follow the gesture. "I stole one of the rosebuds from the bouquet you sent to April. I hope you don't mind."

"Of course not," he said quickly. He did look at the flower, then the rest of her. He didn't like her dress, a rather garish shade of pink that seemed to absorb her color, leaving her looking pale. Hester had a penchant for bright colors, he thought disapprovingly, not realizing that this was one of the main reasons he could see the difference in the sisters at a glance. That, and the quality of their voices.

Hester gave a soft laugh and sat down beside him, keeping her manner casual. It was an effort. She wanted to throw herself into his arms. "April takes forever to change her clothes," she said with a light laugh. "I'm usually dressed in half the time she requires."

Andrew gave a weak smile, but didn't respond to the observation for the simple reason that he didn't know what to say. The subject of a woman's toilette was one he had never encountered before. He cleared his throat. Then, though he had already asked the question, he asked it again. "When is Lane scheduled to return?"

Hester shrugged. "In a few weeks, I guess. He wasn't certain as to the exact day...." Unable to resist, she allowed her arm to brush against his sleeve, and the resulting tingle of pleasure that coursed through her was almost unbearable in its sweetness.

"Well, it will be good to have him back," Andrew said with a glance at the door. Quickly, he got to his feet as April swept into the room, now wearing a taffeta dress of pale lilac.

In resignation, Hester pushed herself up and excused herself for the evening.

That night, in the room they shared, April slept soundly, but Hester, sitting in the window seat, a light blanket over her, was wide awake. In the distance, the lights along Market Street twinkled brightly, though there was very little traffic, since it was after ten o'clock.

Such had not been the case earlier in the day. Most of the residents of Philadelphia had fallen into the habit of taking a Sunday drive to Fairmount Park, and, consequently, the streets were jammed with carriages as people went to and fro, inspecting the progress of the construction taking place there.

Hester opened the window a fraction to catch the breeze that swept off the river; but she was careful not to open it too wide, lest April take a chill from the night air.

The clock downstairs tolled eleven, but Hester continued to sit there, her thoughts on her sister's fiancé.

Andrew Hollinger worked for Lane as head bookkeeper, a prestigious position for a young man just barely turned twenty-two. Six months ago, Lane had invited Andrew to the house for supper. As it was, Hester had accompanied her mother to New York, where Willa was prone to do her shopping. By the time they returned two days later, the die had been cast. At first Hester had only listened in amusement to April's description of the handsome young man who worked for Lane. He had stayed for supper that first night, a Friday, and had requested permission to return the following day.

But Hester's amusement had quickly vanished the first time she was in the company of Andrew Hollinger.

On occasion since that first meeting with Andrew, Hester wondered if her attraction to this man was based on the close relationship between herself and April. They were twins after all. Perhaps it was inevitable that they would both fall in love with the same man. Although they'd both had their share of beaux, until now neither one of them had seriously considered any man.

There had been a time when Hester thought that April might choose Desmond Carlyle, a young man they'd both known for some years. The Carlyles were Lane's friends, and their son, Desmond, had courted April. But as soon as

Andrew had come on the scene, April had eyes for no one else.

It shamed her to admit it, but Hester had to confess to herself that for months now she had been deliberately going out of her way to catch Andrew alone, plotting to be with him when she knew April was otherwise occupied, even for a few minutes.

All to no avail. Andrew smiled politely, nodded in the right places, and kept an eager eye on the door for April's return.

But it wasn't fair! All she needed was a chance. Once Andrew was aware of her own true love for him, he would be able to see that April's feelings were only a pale imitation of the powerful emotion she felt.

Why couldn't Andrew see the difference between herself and April? she wondered in exasperation. Even their constitutions were completely different: April's, delicate; her own, robust. Once a month, April took to her bed when her flow made its presence known. She never passed a winter without at least one cold of sufficient severity to render her helpless for the better part of a week. Every childhood ailment known to man had been visited upon April. As for herself, Hester disdained infirmity. On those rare occasions when she had been ill, she stubbornly refused to stay in bed, ignored all the doctor's advice, and spat out any medicine given to her.

And April was the wife Andrew wanted! The injustice galled her.

But it was only because he didn't know! Well, the error of his ways would have to be shown to him, she decided. April would be upset for a while, but she would get over it. April lacked fire, the passion, the hot blood that poured through the veins of her sister. Hester was convinced of that. To April, love was romance, a beautiful sunset, a bouquet of flowers. What could any woman like that offer Andrew?

The clock tolled twelve, and Hester flung the blanket aside and got up.

All I need is a chance, Hester resolved, eyes burning with determination as she got into bed. And I will have it, one way or the other.

chapter
<u>eight</u>

Summer laid a heavy hand on the isle of Santorini, the most southerly of the Cycladic islands, holding it in a grip of heat and glare that Julia had seldom before experienced; but there was a stark and primitive beauty about it that called forth admiration and even awe.

Having arrived in Athens the day before, this morning they had boarded a packet that had, only an hour ago, deposited them on the southeast coast of the island, where Lane had rented a villa overlooking the Aegean Sea.

"Lane, it's beautiful!" Julia said breathlessly, looking down at the small coastal village of Périssa.

"It is," he agreed solemnly. He had been to this island twice before, the first time by accident when an unexpected storm had forced his ship to harbor here until the weather cleared. Each time he had left with a sense of regret, and each time he returned with a feeling of anticipation. Turning to Julia, he gave a short laugh. "Let's hope, however, that we're not treated to one of their famous volcanic eruptions while we're here.''

Frowning, she looked down at the village again. "Are there many such eruptions?" she inquired, suddenly conscious of the ground beneath her feet; it felt solid enough at this moment.

"Enough," Lane admitted. "But the Santorinians are a very persistent people," he went on. "For thousands of years they've battled earthquakes, high winds, heat, not to mention eruptions. But no matter how many times they've been forced to leave their island, they always return."

Shading her eyes with her hand from the glare of the sun, Julia turned and gazed up at the mountain behind them. "Are there people living up there?"

"Yes. Tomorrow I'll take you up there."

She looked a bit surprised. "It looks like a long walk," she ventured uncertainly.

"I imagine it is," he responded with a chuckle. "But we'll not be walking. A boat will take us to the other side of the island, then we'll go by mule." He put his hands on her shoulders. "Now . . . how would you like to go for a swim?"

Julia bit her lip. Until recently, she had always thought of herself as being sophisticated, but in the short time she had been married to this man, Julia was beginning to feel woefully inadequate. "I . . . don't know how to swim," she confessed at last. "I don't even own a bathing dress."

"Well, we'll have to do something about that right away." Lane went back into the house, and she heard him talking to Elena Doumas. The thirty-year-old woman had been retained to cook and take care of the villa while they were in residence. When Lane returned a few minutes later, he looked satisfied. "Elena assures me that she can supply you with an outfit by tomorrow afternoon."

A moment's apprehension took hold of Julia, but when she looked at the expanse of incredibly blue water, it suddenly seemed enticing.

That night Julia slept soundly, worn out by the long journey. She awoke the following morning to see Lane peering down at her. He was fully dressed and sitting on the edge of the bed.

"Are you going to sleep the day away?" he teased with a smile.

Turning her head, Julia viewed the clock, her eyes widening. "It isn't even six!" she protested. Slowly, she sat up, and in so doing she brought her face closer to his, feeling rather disappointed with the light kiss that landed in the vicinity of the corner of her mouth. She found it incredible that only a few short weeks ago she'd had reservations about his mouth on her bare flesh.

"Rise and shine, Mrs. Manning! We have a full day ahead of us," Lane informed her cheerfully as he stood up. "Elena has breakfast ready. She makes the most marvelous scrambled eggs," he went on as Julia swung her legs over the side of the bed. "Covered with mushrooms and black olives and tomatoes." He patted his stomach appreciatively, then made for the door. "While you dress and eat, I'll see to the boat. . . ."

Getting out of bed then, Julia went to the wardrobe, reached for her dark green riding habit, and sighed. Even though it was made of lawn, meant to be worn in summer, it seemed as though it would be warm in this type of heat. Throwing the jacket aside, she substituted a calico blouse in its place. It didn't match, but that couldn't be helped. Dressing quickly, she went into the dining room. There were windows on two sides, the shutters folded back, and sunlight flooded the room.

Elena was just putting the food on the table. She was short and plump, with eyes as black as the hair that she wore braided and wound around her head like a coronet. Her English was scanty at best, so she smiled and nodded a lot whenever Lane or Julia spoke to her.

Since Lane had already eaten, the table was set for only one. Julia sat down and began to eat what Elena placed in front of her.

Lane had been right. Breakfast was delicious, the coffee strong and sweet. By the time she went outside, a wide-brimmed hat on her head to protect her from the sun, Julia felt as if she could take on the world.

It was already warm, promising to turn hot before the sun reached its zenith.

The fishing boat took them around the southwest coast of the island and deposited them in the harbor just below Phera, the main village, where Lane secured the services of a guide and mules for them to ride. Unlike the serenity of Périssa, this side of the island was barren and rocky. Their guide was a strapping young man in his twenties named Pieter, who had an engaging smile that he saw fit to display every time he was addressed.

"This one's yours," Lane said to Julia, patting the head of the smaller mule. "Pieter assures me that he's a gentle beast. You'll have to ride astride, though. They seem to have only one type of saddle on the island."

Julia kept silent as she warily approached the mule. It couldn't be all that different from riding a horse. "They don't go fast, do they?" she asked hesitantly as Lane assisted her in mounting. She had never ridden astride before, and it took a few minutes to position herself correctly. It wasn't comfortable.

"No faster than a walk," Lane assured her, making

certain that both her feet were securely in the stirrups. He mounted with ease, and his mule began to go forward.

Julia sat there, staring at the twitching ears of the animal beneath her, wondering how to get it started. Having no riding crop, she reached behind her and gave him a gentle smack on the rump. That elicited no response whatsoever. Ahead, Lane turned in his saddle and grinned at her.

"Nudge him with your knees!"

Nothing happened the first time. With a bit more pressure, however, the mule finally moved reluctantly. Julia decided then that she preferred horses to these somewhat unattractive creatures. Soon she caught up to Lane and rode beside him. His white shirt was open at the neck, the sleeves rolled up to his elbows. He was also wearing tight-fitting tan breeches that encased his powerful thighs in a way she could not help but notice.

It took better than thirty minutes for the mules to pick their way daintily up the six hundred broad and shallow steps that separated Phera from the harbor; Julia was glad she didn't have to walk the distance, but the view once they reached the summit was breathtaking. A multitude of small chapels dotted the island from one end to the other, their icons being the works of local hagiographers, at least half of which, Pieter explained to them in surprisingly good English, were clerics.

Leaning forward to peer over the mule's head, Julia stared out across the blue waters. She could see the small isle of Thirasia, which was no more than three square miles in area, and Aspronisi, which was even smaller.

"Does anyone live there?" she asked Lane, pointing to the small islands.

He nudged his mule closer. "No. They're both uninhabited," he answered. "At one time they were a part of

Santorini, but during the last century there was a severe volcanic explosion. Thirasia and Aspronisi separated from Santorini at that time.''

They followed as Pieter led them through the cobbled streets of the village. There was very little activity. Here and there, chairs placed in the shade, groups of old men gathered to gossip and reminisce, the smoke from their pipes etching little gray columns into the stifling air. A young boy, riding bareback on a donkey, skin as brown as a nut, waved cheerfuly to Pieter as he passed by. And an occasional dog, roused from its lethargy, would come to lope at their side for a short distance, but its curiosity would be dampened by the pressing heat, and it soon returned to whatever shady haven it had momentarily deserted.

In an effort to offset the blinding glare of the Aegean and the burning heat of summer, all the houses were whitewashed, having small windows fitted with wooden shutters that were on the inside, a position that protected them from the piercing winds that occasionally swept the island. The houses themselves were arranged in a terraced fashion, the roof of one house supporting the courtyard of the house above it. They were small, consisting of one oblong room that was constructed of stone and one or two smaller rooms that were dug out of the dense layer of pozzolana, a substance that was readily available, it being the ash mantle that settled after a volcanic eruption.

A short distance from Phera was the small village of Merovighli, which Lane insisted Julia must see. Along the cobbled route they stopped to view the Orthodox convent of Aghios Nicholaos. Julia was glad for the respite; her thighs were beginning to ache from riding astride.

On their mules again, Pieter directed their attention to the pitch-black rock that projected below the road. It appeared to Julia that there had at one time been a city there, though now there was nothing but ruins to see.

"Skaros," Pieter informed them. "It used to be the Venetian capital of Théra, as our island was then known. Then came the Turks; it's no more than fifty years since they've gone." He grinned at them. "That's the reason we have so many churches. First the Venetians built them, then the Turks."

Wind gusted up at them in short, hot bursts of air as they continued on to Merovighli, the main attraction being the Church of the Virgin of Malta. The outside had been recently whitewashed and seemed dazzling beneath the sun. It owed its name to the icon of the Virgin, which had been brought all the way from Malta. Julia viewed the carved wooden altar screen with reverent silence. Complete scenes from the Bible were rendered on the lower panels, sculpted in the round. To Julia, the most impressive was the sacrifice of Abraham and the decapitation of Saint John the Baptist.

By the time they returned to the villa later that afternoon, it was so hot that Julia was more than ready for a lesson in swimming. But when Lane showed her the bathing dress that Elena had given him, she gasped.

"I can't possibly wear that!" she cried, staring at the garment. "It . . . it has no bottom! The overskirt stops at the knees, for goodness sakes."

He chuckled at her shocked outrage. "Elena is familiar only with the European style of bathing dress, which is what this is."

"Where on earth did she get it?" Julia found it impossible to believe that Lane actually expected her to wear the dress.

"I've no idea," he replied, still chuckling. "I didn't ask. Perhaps it was left by a previous tenant, or perhaps she borrowed it from someone on the island. For all I know, she made it herself. What difference does it make? You need a bathing dress, and this one looks perfectly serviceable to me.''

"It doesn't even come close," Julia protested, her mouth settling into a prim line of censure.

"It will do just fine," he insisted. "Besides . . ." He put an arm around her and led her to the window. "Look! There will be no one on the beach but you and me."

Julia frowned. "There are fishermen down there!" she protested indignantly, turning to glare at him.

"And they are all used to seeing this style of bathing dress," he explained in a patient way. He handed her the garment. "Now, get into it, and we'll have our first lesson. Elena will help you. I'll change in the sitting room."

Julia rolled her eyes upward, but she did as he said.

She refused to look at herself until she was dressed in the outlandish costume. When she did, she cringed at her reflection. Never in her life had her lower limbs been exposed to public view. She looked positively indecent!

"Isn't there a hat that goes with this?" she asked Elena, tugging at a puffed sleeve in an effort to lower it to her elbow.

Elena shrugged. "No more," she offered, shaking her head. Julia was again viewing her reflection. "Very nice," Elena added, nodding vigorously, a twinkle in her large dark eyes.

When she emerged from the bedroom a few minutes later, Julia's face was scarlet, but Lane gave her no time to change her mind, quickly ushering her outside.

Glancing at him, Julia swallowed a gasp of surprise. She guessed that Lane was also wearing a European-style bathing outfit. The pants barely reached his knees, and the shirt with its V-shaped neck did little to conceal the hair on his chest.

Oh, Lord! Julia thought to herself, as she dutifully trudged beside him. *What would my father think if he saw me now?* Bathing in anything other than a tub had always been on her list of forbidden activities.

Even low in the sky, the August sun felt hot on her arms and legs. Doubtless the sun would call forth all her freckles, she thought crossly, sorry now that she had agreed to this foolishness.

"Better leave your shoes on," Lane instructed as they reached the water's edge. "There may be loose stones in the sand, or even clam shells." He took her arm, leading her into the water until it reached her waist. It was pleasantly cool and so clear it could have been made of glass.

Julia trailed her fingertips along the surface, then lowered her head, delighted that she could see her feet as clearly as if she were on shore. "Are there fish down there?" she asked nervously, her nose no more than an inch above the water.

"If there are, they won't bother you," Lane said offhand-edly. "Now, bend forward. . . ." Lane placed a hand on her abdomen for support. "Raise your legs."

With a shrill cry of alarm, she clutched at him. "No, no!"

"Julia, put your arms in the water!" Lane laughed as she began to flail at the water. "Take it easy." He put his free arm around her waist, holding her securely. "Relax . . . you won't sink, and even if you do, you can hold your breath until you stand upright again."

"Easy for you to say," she muttered, annoyed by his calm logic. Gritting her teeth, Julia did as she was told. Lane kept walking through the water, always parallel with the beach, careful to keep the water at a level just above his waist.

"First one arm, then the other," Lane said. "That's it. . . ."

It was easier than she thought it would be, and Julia relaxed a bit.

For the next quarter hour, Julia practiced, becoming more confident and enjoying the refreshing feeling of the water as it engulfed her body. The sea was calm, its blue expanse broken only by an occasional fishing boat.

Finally Lane removed the support of his hands. "All right. Now try it on your own."

Julia did, and promptly sank.

She emerged gasping and sputtering, her hair drenched and clinging wetly to her neck. Lane's arms went around her to steady her balance.

"I must say, you're the prettiest fish I've ever caught. One of the biggest, too." Laughing heartily, Lane pulled her against him and gave her a small hug.

For a moment, also laughing, Julia rested her head on his chest, feeling the warmth and safety of his arms around her. It was a good feeling. She had decided that being held was the nicest thing about being married. She felt so very safe, so very secure within these muscular arms. It was as if nothing in the world could touch her unless it went through her husband first.

Then she went very still, staring up into those gray eyes, wondering at the pleasurable little darts of warmth shooting through her body. This curious tingling feeling had claimed her several times now, mostly during the last few days of their voyage. So far, it had happened only when Lane caressed her; but he was doing no such thing now. Why then, did she want so desperately for him to kiss her?

Lane's eyes searched hers for a long moment, the smile fading from his mouth, his expression holding a hint of bewilderment.

Abruptly, he released her, his voice again infused with that businesslike tone she was coming to know so well.

"All right, that's enough for today," he said curtly. Placing a hand on her back, he firmly propelled her toward shore. "We'd better go back inside before you get sunburned."

At first confused by his sudden abruptness, Julia's cheeks flushed with embarrassed realization. Obviously Lane had caught her unladylike thoughts and was displeased with her. She must not let that happen again!

That evening, after they had dined on moussaka and spinach pie, Julia and Lane strolled along the beach, enjoying the coolness of the early evening. The sun was gone from view, leaving in its wake a sky washed with color, the scanty clouds brushed with gold and crimson slashes that were reflected on the calm surface of the sea.

"Tell me about your home," Julia said as they walked.

"Our home," he corrected gently, looking down at her. She was wearing a brown muslin dress that was, as usual, buttoned to her throat. A fine dusting of freckles decorated her nose, which, despite her precaution of donning a wide-brimmed hat, was slightly sunburned. She had washed her hair but, for once, had not wound it into its usual chignon. It cascaded well beyond her shoulders, halfway down her back. He thought it a lovely color, cool and warm at the same time, reminding him of chilled champagne sipped beneath a warm spring sun. "It's big," he went on, resisting the urge to touch that pale softness. "You'll see it soon enough."

For a while they walked in silence, then headed back for the villa.

On the stone terrace, they paused beneath a gnarled mimosa tree that spread its branches every which way, proudly displaying lush and abundant blossoms that filled the air with their sweet scent. A sudden warm breeze lifted the pale hair from Julia's neck and splayed it out like a golden veil. Without thinking, she raised a hand to smooth it.

"No," Lane said, catching her hand in his own. "I like to see it flowing and free. You're quite lovely, you know." Still clutching her hand, he drew her closer. "Are you still afraid of me?" he whispered. Shyly, she shook her head.

Bending forward, Lane kissed her in a lingering, unhurried fashion, his hands solid and warmer than any sun on her back. A delicious lassitude swept through Julia as she clung to him.

Drawing back, Lane caressed her satin-smooth cheek. "Come inside," he said in a voice that was suddenly husky. He opened the French doors that led to their bedroom, but didn't bother to close them.

Reaching out, he began to undo the top buttons of her dress, and Julia's hand flew to her throat.

"What are you doing?" Her voice was a squeak of shock.

Lane sighed. "Julia . . . it's damned inconvenient to make love through the impediment of clothes."

His hand had fallen away, and she automatically buttoned her gown. "But I can't," she cried. "I've never . . ." Her voice fell to the merest whisper. "I've never been unclothed before anyone. . . ."

His lips curved, but he spoke gravely. "You've been unclothed before me."

Her eyes grew round. "I've never!" she protested, then

flushed a deep crimson when he reminded her of their wedding night.

A small frown creased her brow. "I don't suppose you . . . refrained from looking," she murmured, sounding hopeful with the prospect.

"I don't suppose," he retorted, shaking his head. He hesitated, then asked, "Julia, do you find the coupling of a man and a woman a shameful thing?"

She was quiet for a long moment before she answered him. "Let us say I consider it a necessary thing," she replied carefully.

He frowned, his patience at an end. "Take off your clothes, Julia!" He spoke in a voice that brooked no contradiction.

Clumsily, with fingers that suddenly felt like spaghetti, Julia fumbled with buttons and ribbons, noticing that Lane made no pretense of looking away while she disrobed.

At last she stood before him, naked as the day she had been born. He removed his own clothes and came to stand close to her, hands on her shoulders. Her eyes had been lowered, but when they encountered his throbbing manhood, she quickly raised them. As he bent his head to kiss her, she closed her eyes. Feeling his tongue probe gently at her lips, they flew open again, and she stiffened.

Lane ignored her reaction. His arms went around her, and he pulled her against him. The kiss, to Julia, seemed without end. Gradually, a feeling of lassitude enveloped her; in spite of herself, she relaxed, feeling as though her legs would no longer support her.

They were in bed, but Julia had no idea how they had gotten there. The lamp was lit, but she gave no thought to it, was aware of nothing but Lane's hands and mouth as he caressed her. She squirmed, wanting to move away, to ease the unbearable tension that seemed to be building up inside her with each passing second. But Lane only held her tighter.

At last he entered her. Julia gripped his shoulders so tightly her nails dug into his flesh. His pace began to quicken.

A small whimper emerged from her lips, and Julia wanted desperately to surrender to these thrilling sensations that were leaving her dizzy with a longing she was unable to express.

Another small cry escaped, and Lane drew back, his brow knitting into a frown, not recognizing the silent plea in those dark blue eyes.

"Am I hurting you?" he whispered, pausing a moment.

"No. . . ." Was that ragged sound her voice? she wondered in astonishment.

He regarded her a moment longer, then began to move again. Finally his body shuddered, something Julia now recognized as the end of the act. Rolling to the side, Lane lay there, looking at her with that little hint of bewilderment she had seen once or twice before.

She wet her lips. "Can I put my clothes back on now?" she asked in a small voice.

His gray eyes held hers a moment longer, then he sighed. "Yes, Julia. You can dress now."

Grabbing her nightclothes, Julia ran into the sitting room. She did not, however, immediately dress. She was trembling too badly to do that. The strange quivering sensations were still in her stomach, and her breasts ached in the oddest way. Weakly, she sat down in a chair for once unaware of her nakedness. What on earth had happened to her in there? For a time she had wanted—what? She really didn't know. Had she, for just a little while, been enjoying herself? Julia put a shaking hand to her cheek. Lane must never know! He would think her a harlot, no better than the mother she'd never known.

In the other room, Lane had donned a robe, then walked out onto the balcony, his expression at once thoughtful and saddened. He was experienced enough to know that some women liked sex, others did not. For the latter, there was little a man could do except perform as quickly as possible so as to cause them the least discomfort.

Perhaps if he could come to love Julia, he could break down that barrier, he thought to himself. That, however, was a useless conjecture; one did not will one's heart.

Slowly, he ambled to the railing and leaned on it. The gentle lap of the water as it snuggled closer to the beach before retreating again seemed to echo a name he had thought to banish from his heart and mind. But it was not to be. It returned when it was least expected, when he was least prepared to deal with it. This afternoon he had looked into the eyes of the lovely girl he had married, and thought of the woman he had loved for so long, a woman who was forever beyond his reach.

He lowered his head. Even the breeze seemed to whisper her name: Rosalind. . . .

With a deep sigh, Lane went back inside and crawled into bed. Julia was already there, and he moved quietly so as not to disturb her.

But Julia was wide awake, a part of her wanting him to take her in his arms, and a part of her fearful that he would do exactly that. He lay on his side with his back to her, however, and was soon asleep.

Raising herself up on an elbow, Julia studied the sleeping form of her husband. How could she ever have thought him to be anything less than the most handsome man in the world? Wanting to touch his broad shoulder, her hand reached out, then hovered an inch or so before coming to rest on his bare flesh.

Julia couldn't bring herself to do it. With as little movement as possible, she lay down again, trying to analyze her confused emotions. She didn't quite know what it was she was beginning to feel. Was this what people referred to as a physical attraction? Or was it something deeper?

No! she cautioned herself sternly, eyes staring into the darkness. *Don't let yourself care for this man. You'll only get hurt if you do. He doesn't love you, probably never will. He wants a wife who is a lady, and he wants children. Five,* she reminded herself ruefully. *In return, he will give you a fine home to live in and the protection of being a married woman.*

That was the agreement.

And in the dimness of the room, with only the mournful ticking of the clock to bear witness, Julia resolved to honor that agreement.

It was a resolution that, during the coming days, began to crumble like a sand castle before the incoming tide.

chapter
nine

Perched on a rock, Julia bent down, picked up a handful of sand, and let it trickle through her fingertips. In the rays of the setting sun it looked like countless grains of gold.

Beside her, Lane was munching on the last of the cold chicken Elena had supplied for their picnic. When he was through, he sailed the bone into the sea, then carefully placed the half-empty bottle of wine back into the wicker basket.

"You'll spoil your supper," Julia murmured to him, still toying with the sand. "I think Elena is preparing something special for us tonight."

"I'm sure she is," Lane agreed, grinning at her. "But supper is more than two hours away." He stood up, stretched, then extended a hand toward her. "Come on. We'll walk a bit farther down the beach, then head back. By then, we'll both have worked up an appetite."

For a time, hand in hand, they walked in silence, the

solitude broken only by their elongated shadows that trailed along like mute companions.

Finally Julia sighed, turned to look at Lane, and wondered where the past ten days had gone. She and Lane had been together every minute of the time, exploring the island from one end to the other, boating, fishing, and strolling along the beach at the end of the day, as they were now doing.

Aware of her look, Lane returned it. "Why so pensive?" he asked quietly.

"We'll be leaving tomorrow," she answered in a small voice.

He squeezed her hand. "Is that why you've been looking so sad all day?" he teased.

"I haven't been!" she protested, knowing it was all too true. Her slim shoulders moved in a helpless shrug. "It's just that this is so . . . perfect."

In these past days, Julia had discovered a freedom she hadn't known existed. She could now swim without the assistance of Lane's support. Riding astride no longer presented a problem. The heat had forced her to divest herself of half the clothing she was used to wearing, and going about without her shoes and stockings was a delight she was loath to relinquish.

Lane had even taught her how to go clamming. They had spent many enjoyable hours walking through shallow water in their bare feet, toes pressing into the satiny sand in search of the elusive hardness of a shell, scooping up their treasure, and placing it into a pail. Then they had sat on the steps of the terrace while Lane deftly opened the clams, after which they had eaten the delicacies with much appetite and appreciation.

Her only regret was that the relentless sun had tanned a

portion of her skin; she was appalled at the color of her face, arms, and, ludicrously, the lower part of her legs and feet. Her hair, so pale to begin with, had lightened so much that parts of it were actually white! Her nose had peeled, and she groaned unhappily whenever she looked at herself in the mirror, seeing a patchwork of light and dark she thought most unattractive. When she had lamented her appearance to Lane, he had laughed, and said: "It makes your eyes look as blue as the sea...."

Well, perhaps it did; but that didn't make up for what was most assuredly an unfashionably dark complexion.

She glanced at Lane again; he, too, was deeply tanned. On him, however, it was most attractive.

"You know, it must be nice to live here," she mused, following the observation with another sigh.

He chuckled. "I would imagine that even a steady diet of paradise would grow boring after a while. Besides," he added, in an effort to lighten her mood, "there's still Athens. I want you to see the Parthenon and the Acropolis. So we still have a few days left before it's time for us to return home."

Home... Pursing her lips, Julia pondered the word, a word that usually brought with it a measure of comfort and anticipation, a word that, right now, held no meaning for her.

"I've never been to Philadelphia," she murmured after a while. With a display of agility that drew a smile from Lane, she sidestepped a sand crab. They were both barefoot and walking at the water's edge. "What's it like?"

"It's a beautiful city," he said, displaying an enthusiasm that marked his sincerity. "Filled with history and growing every day. Fairmount Park is where the Centennial Exhibition will take place. A few years ago, it was no more than an open field. Now there are one hundred and eighty buildings being constructed on it.''

"The Centennial,'' Julia echoed, glancing at him with sharpened interest. ''I've read about that in the newspapers. Is it true that they will have exhibits from all over the world?''

"Well, thirty-eight foreign nations have so far contributed artwork crafts; I guess that's a fair sampling of the world. I understand they've also received exhibits from almost every state and territory. It's a huge undertaking, of course. The Exhibition is something that has never been tried before.'' He stopped a moment to light a cigar.

Julia looked to the horizon. A pale lemon-yellow sky blazed a final triumph to the day. Even as she watched, lilac fringed the high clouds, deepening to purple. By the dock, a few late-arriving fishing boats were being secured, their catch piled on the wooden slats of the pier that jutted a distance into the water.

A sense of peace and serenity made itself known to Julia; here, life was at its simplest, the basics of food and survival taking precedence, no room for tears or petty acts of grievance, only laughter and determination as man coped with nature in its most primitive form.

"I imagine there must be a lot of work involved to coordinate something that large,'' Julia speculated as they began to retrace their steps back to the house. Ahead of her, she could see the imprint of their footsteps, the only intrusion in the otherwise pristine expanse of sand.

"And time-consuming,'' Lane added. ''The idea was first presented to Congress in 1866, but few people even considered it then. It was just a dream, a fantasy. No one took it seriously until Daniel Morrell brought it up again five years ago.''

"And it was his intention to collect artwork, crafts, and inventions from all over the world and from every state in the Union and display them all in one place," Julia said, remembering the news article she had read.

"Exactly." Lane nodded. They had reached the spot where they had picnicked, and Lane detoured to retrieve the wicker basket. "And still another year went by before the President finally appointed a commissioner from each state and territory," he continued as they resumed walking. "The following year, Congress appointed a Board of Finance, and at last the money became available." He took a final puff on the cigar, dropped it into the sand, then took Julia's arm to assist her up the steps that led to the terrace.

"The government, then, is funding the Centennial?" Julia asked with a touch of surprise. It had been her understanding that the Centennial was, in a sense, a private undertaking on the part of the city of Philadelphia.

"Oh, no. The Board of Finance has been issuing stock at ten dollars a share," Lane explained to her. "People from all over the Union have been buying it, myself included."

The merest hint of a smile touched her lips, but the meaning of the gesture was lost on Lane. This was the first time a man had spoken to her of such things as stocks and shares and finances in a manner that suggested she might be intelligent enough to understand.

In the house, they both washed and dressed, and by eight o'clock, Julia had to admit that she was indeed hungry again.

Just before she left the bedroom, Julia paused and regarded the small table set in a corner. After a moment, she walked toward it and picked up a chessman. Holding it in her hand, she viewed it thoughtfully, storing away yet one more memory of this trip.

Two days ago, for the first time since they had arrived in Santorini, it had rained all day long, forcing them to remain indoors. From the bottom of his trunk, Lane had produced the chessmen. The set was truly a work of art, one army crafted from ivory, the other from ebony. Setting the pieces on a teakwood board, he announced his intention of teaching her how to play the game.

Julia, of course, had never played chess in her life. It was common knowledge, backed up by the most respected physicians of the day, that a woman's brain could be seriously imparied if she attempted to sort out the intricacies of such a complicated game. Lane had pronounced the theory "blatant quackery."

"There are countries ruled by queens," he further went on to point out. "And those women think nothing of pitting real armies against each other. I cannot see that playing chess with real soldiers is less harmful than moving inanimate ones around a board."

And Lane must have been right, she mused, returning the chessman to its rightful place. They'd played several games— none of which Julia came close to winning—and she could honestly say that her brain felt fine.

Turning away from the ebony and ivory soldiers, Julia headed for the door.

Elena had supper waiting for them. Only one look told Julia that the woman had made a special effort tonight. The dining room had been set with a lace cloth and candles gleamed, creating soft shadows that danced on the walls and flickered on the ceiling.

"Mmm . . ." Julia sniffed appreciatively as she sat down. "I don't know what that is, but it certainly smells good!"

Elena's head bobbed up and down. "Stifatho," she

supplied, but was unable to tell them that the dish was one of her specialties.

Julia and Lane exchanged a quick glance, their eyes sparkling with mirth. Neither one of them had the faintest idea what stifatho was.

It turned out to be a delicious concoction of beef and onions, cooked in red wine and brown sugar, and seasoned with cinnamon, cloves, and garlic. Complementing the spicy dish was a huge Greek salad and, for Lane, a glass of ouzo, the fiery national drink of Greece.

There was a bittersweet gaiety to this last meal that both of them felt. Tomorrow they would be returning to the real world again.

At the end of the meal, Lane drained his glass, and even he blinked at its strength. Then he viewed Elena, who had entered the room to see if they needed anything else.

"Elena," he said, putting his glass down next to his plate. "I compliment you and your countrymen. Not only is your food delicious, the ouzo is"—he paused—"stimulating," he concluded with what he was certain was an understatement.

The woman grinned at him, having understood only a few words of what he had said. She did sense, however, that he was pleased. Holding up the bottle, she asked: "You want more?"

"No!" Lane said quickly. Laughing, he raised a hand. "A little ouzo goes a long way!"

"Warms the belly," Elena declared seriously, giving him an exaggerated nod and rubbing her free hand on her well-rounded stomach.

"You'll get no argument from me," Lane retorted with another laugh.

Shaking her head, in what was clearly a sign of disapproval, Elena headed toward her kitchen, to return a short while later with a dessert of nuts and honey, encased in pastry.

"Pieter said this island was at one time called Thera," Julia said as she began to eat the confection. "How did it come to be called Santorini?"

"It was named by the Venetians, who ruled here for many years," Lane replied. "Pieter told me it was named after a chapel, Santa Irini. Then, of course, came the Turks. Finally, in 1829, Santorini came under the dominion of Greece. Strangely, the Turks never influenced the religion of the people. You've probably noticed that the churches are either Roman Catholic or Greek Orthodox."

"Yes," Julia murmured, for the first time thinking about it. "Perhaps the Turks weren't here for very long," she mused, scraping her plate clean. Sweet though the pastry was, it made a satisfying impression on her palate.

"Not really," Lane retorted, shaking his head. "Their suzerainty lasted better than two hundred years; however, it was benevolent, perhaps because the island had very little wealth. Probably the most important benefit was that the Turks protected the island from pirates, and, as a consequence, they gradually achieved a certain degree of economic independence."

Julia put down her fork. "You like this place," she noted softly.

"Yes," he agreed. "But it's . . . seductive. A man could easily forget there's another world out there. Then, too," he went on, getting up, "I don't believe I'd like to be here when the ground begins to shake."

Holding a hand out to Julia, he assisted her to her feet and led her out onto the terrace.

The sky was a carpet of soft purple, the stars tiny

diamonds to decorate the rich fabric. A pale moon glowed, appearing larger than it was, due to the ring of haze that encircled it.

Lane viewed it thoughtfully. "Might rain tomorrow," he speculated.

"Will that delay our departure?" Julia didn't sound too upset by the prospect.

"Only if it's severe," he answererd. Turning, he winked at her, rubbing his hands together in an anticipatory manner. "You know, I think we should celebrate our last night on Santorini in a very special way."

"And what did you have in mind?" She smiled because she thought she knew.

"A moonlight swim," came the quick retort.

Smile fading, Julia gaped at him in amazement. She had never heard of such a thing. What would the man think of next? "Lane, you can't be serious!" she protested.

He was.

A short while later, as they headed for the water, Julia reflected dourly that at least no one would see her in the ridiculous bathing dress.

They both entered the water at the same time, Julia pausing when the water reached her waist, Lane diving in and swimming with firm strokes. The evening was warm, and Julia had to admit that the coolness felt delightful.

Playfully, she splashed Lane as he swam by, and he dove underwater to grab her legs, causing her to emit a pretended squeal of alarm.

He surfaced, his hair even more curly from the water that clung to it. "Did you think I was a shark?" he inquired, grinning at her.

Laughter bubbled up. "Sharks don't have as much hair as you have!"

Picking her up, he fell onto his back, arms working at his sides, letting her rest on top of him as he paddled through the water.

"Lane . . ." she murmured, feeling embarrassed by their position. "Suppose someone is watching?"

Turning his head, Lane looked toward the villa. "You're right," he said in a low voice. "Elena is at the window, looking at us through a spyglass!"

Unable to help herself, Julia turned to look before she realized he was teasing. "Lane! There's no one there!"

"Well then, we have nothing to worry about," he concluded cheerfully.

Righting himself, he stood her on her feet. Then his hands went to the buttons of her bathing dress.

Julia bit back her question. No need to ask; she knew perfectly well what he was doing. She had a crazy mental image of the two of them trying to make love in the water . . . and sinking to the bottom.

Having opened the front of her dress, Lane now pushed it over her shoulders and down past her waist. Picking her up, he freed the garment from the lower part of her and flung it toward shore. In a moment, his own clothes had followed.

Then, as he was wont to do, Lane said something that took her tortally by surprise.

"Swim!"

"What?"

"Swim."

After a moment's hesitation, during which time she looked at him to be sure he wasn't joking, she leaned forward and pushed with her feet as he had taught her to do. To her utter astonishment, her body, freed from the impediment of clothes, cut through the water with the ease of a knife slicing through a ripe melon.

The sensation was so exhilarating that Julia spent the next ten minutes enjoying the freedom of moving back and forth, circling Lane, who stood there, hands on his hips, watching her with approval. When he saw the confidence in her movements, he plunged in beside her, matching her stroke for stroke.

Finally Julia stopped and stood upright again, stretching her arms to the velvety sky. "Oh! That was marvelous!"

Lane came to stand beside her, staring at the vision she presented. Bending forward he kissed the droplets of water from a breast highlighted by moonglow. "You look like Circe," he said softly.

Lowering her arms, she gave him an impish grin. "No one knows what she looked like!"

"I do. Now."

Julia's grin erupted into a delighted laugh. "Circe was a sorceress! She did terrible things to men; she put them under a spell. . . ."

"You're doing terrible things to me right now," Lane retorted huskily.

"Odysseus was immune to her enchantment," she pointed out, arching a brow.

Lane grabbed her, kissing her soundly. "But I am not Odysseus, and I find myself completely under your spell." He took her hand. "Come on, I'll race you back to the villa."

They were on the beach when Julia realized they were both still naked. Lane scooped up their clothes, but instead of giving her the bathing dress, he began to trot toward the villa, still holding her hand.

"Lane!" her free hand was uncertain as to which part of her to cover. Being unclothed in the water was one thing! But here, in plain view. . .

Giving her a quick glance, Lane laughed, and without a pause in his stride, said, "I'll bet if Elena is watching, it's not you she's looking at."

They were both breathless by the time they reached the seclusion of their bedroom.

Dropping their clothes carelessly to the floor, Lane reached for her and spoke with an affected leer. "I may be the only man in the world to discover what it's like to bed a sorceress. . . ."

As his mouth found hers, Julia shuddered, filled with the disquieting idea that her reaction was not at all due to the night air on her bare flesh.

chapter
ten

Julia was glad she had worn her lime-green pelisse over her yellow silk dress. Although sunshine blazed from a cloudless sky, a chilly breeze made the September day less than comfortable.

The station was crowded, and Lane put a protective hand on her elbow so that they would not become separated in the throng of people. As they went to board, the train whistle blared, uncaring of the assault it produced on human ears.

She and Lane were back in New York, on the final leg of their journey to Philadelphia. Julia had experienced no discomfort on the return voyage.

Well, perhaps that was not true. She had experienced discomfort, but the ocean had had nothing to do with it. She was getting to the point where, each time Lane touched her, she felt as if molten lava were coursing through her veins. The strain of keeping herself in check and not losing her self-control was beginning to tell. Her nerves were stretched to the breaking point.

For the most part, Lane was unfailingly kind and gentle, but on one or two occasions in this past week, Julia had detected a certain annoyance, an abruptness with her that she could not explain.

About thirty minutes after the train left the station, they went into the dining car. They had no sooner placed their order when Lane, hearing his name called, turned in his chair, then broke into a wide grin at the sight of the man and woman heading in his direction.

"William!" Lane immediately got to his feet and clasped the man's hand, then smiled warmly at the woman. "Leah! You're looking lovely as ever. Won't you both join us?"

The man hesitated, glancing at Julia, then back at Lane. "We wouldn't want to intrude. . . ."

Lane laughed. "I can't imagine a time when the presence of my two best friends could be called an intrusion!"

The woman seated herself beside Julia and held out a gloved hand. "I'm Leah Carlyle. This is my husband, William."

Julia murmured a gracious acknowledgment as the man sat down next to Lane. In his early forties, he was above average in height, though not as tall as Lane. His features were irregular, the mouth too wide, the nose too broad, but somehow the combination produced a pleasant, attractive face. The woman, however, was striking, with dark auburn hair and green eyes that sparkled with mirth even when she was not laughing. Although Julia guessed that Leah Carlyle was also in her early forties, she gave the appearance of being a decade younger than that.

Julia couldn't contain a smile when she saw the looks of astonishment as Lane presented her to his friends.

"Married?" William gave Lane an accusing look. "Why

didn't you tell us? I'll not forgive you for not inviting us."

Lane laughed easily, raising a hand to summon a passing waiter. After William and Leah had ordered, Lane regarded his friend.

"No one was invited to our wedding," he explained with a smile at Julia. "We were married two days after Julia honored me with her acceptance. We've just returned from Santorini."

"How romantic!" Leah exclaimed. Placing a hand on Julia's wrist, she gave it a small squeeze. "I may not be the first to offer congratulations, but you will receive none more sincere."

"Thank you," Julia responded, feeling warmed by the obvious acceptance of Lane's friends.

"And how is Desmond?" Lane asked of the Carlyles' twenty-year-old son.

William replied with a humorless laugh. "Still moping about, as he has been since he learned of April's engagement to Andrew."

Lane nodded solemnly. "It's too bad their courtship didn't work out . . . ."

The waiter placed their first course in front of them: broiled trout in anchovy sauce. The conversation was smooth and easy, and by the time their dessert arrived, Julia felt as though she had known the Carlyles all her life. William was an architect. He had, in fact, designed Manning House, and was now engaged in several projects for the Centennial Exhibition, scheduled to open the following year. Leah, too, was involved with that long-awaited event, being a member of the Women's Committee, a group planning the Women's Pavilion.

Even after the meal was completed, the four of them continued to sit there, sipping coffee and chatting easily.

Only once did Julia falter; that was when Leah asked her where she and Lane had met. "At my engagement party" didn't seem to be an appropriate answer. Julia contented herself with: "At a social function in Boston."

"It must have been a whirlwind courtship," Leah said with a gay little laugh.

Julia nodded. "More or less," she murmured, refusing to meet Lane's eye, well aware that he was watching her with amusement.

Only one other incident marred the enjoyable trip from New York to Philadelphia, and that was when William mentioned to Lane that a man named Otis Langley had died some weeks before. His statement was greeted by a silence that left Julia perplexed. Leah gave her husband a look that was clearly an admonishment of the sort only a wife could convey to her husband without speaking. William looked decidedly uncomfortable, his face turning beet red.

But it was Lane's reaction that caused Julia's heart to skip a beat. He paled noticeably and for several long minutes stared out the window in silence.

Then Lane's eyes turned slowly in her direction, and Julia was baffled by the enigmatic look in those gray depths. She longed to reach out to him, to offer as much comfort as she could. It was obvious that the death of this man had affected him profoundly.

And just who, Julia wondered uneasily, was Otis Langley?

Lane had wired ahead with the time of their arrival, and the Manning carriage was waiting for them at the station. They drove the Carlyles home first, Leah promising to call on Julia as soon as she was settled. Then they continued along the road that paralleled the Schuylkill River, until the carriage finally turned onto the drive that led to Manning House.

Julia had expected her new home to be large, but she was momentarily speechless when she first caught sight of it. Crowning a wooded slope, it was fronted by the river. Tall columns rising from the veranda to the second story were of white marble. The steps, too, were of that material, though Julia had noticed as they had driven through town that quite a few houses had marble steps. The mansard roof was flanked at either end with towers, the panes of oriel windows appearing gold in the rays of the setting sun.

The carriage pulled up to the front entrance, and a tall, thin Negro dressed in smart livery hurried down the steps to open the door of the vehicle. Julia assumed that he was the butler, but she was to learn later that the man was Lane's personal valet.

"Welcome home, Mr. Lane," he said, flashing a bright smile.

"Thank you, Joseph," Lane responded with a smile of his own. "It's good to be back again." He assisted Julia down. "This is my wife."

"Welcome, Mrs. Manning," Joseph said, offering a deferential nod, then addressed Lane again. "Your mother and sisters are waiting." He chuckled as they made their way up the steps. "Miss April hasn't moved from the window in the past thirty minutes."

Suffering a surge of doubt, grateful for the support of Lane's strong hand, Julia climbed the four marble steps that would take her into her new home to meet her new family.

As they entered, a servant stepped forward to relieve them of their outer clothing.

The entrance hall was a huge expanse of black and white tile crowned by the largest crystal chandelier Julia had ever seen. On either side were two matching Boulle cabinets containing priceless Dresden figurines.

Julia glanced at the three women standing in the foyer, and her smile was unsteady as Lane presented her to his mother and sisters. She so wanted them to like her.

The family resemblance was immediately apparent to her, the color of their eyes being the most notable distinction. Willa Manning's skin was like alabaster, polished and chiseled, her vivid blue eyes inherited by both her daughters, who had Lane's black and slightly wavy hair. At first glance, the girls were truly identical, but then Julia noticed a subtle difference in their expressions. April had a Madonna-like look about her, a serenity that appeared unshakable. Hester, on the other hand, had a look Julia could only describe as impatient.

Willa merely nodded to her, saying nothing; but April immediately stepped forward and embraced Julia. Standing back, Hester's eyes were coolly appraising at first, then they softened, as if the image that met her eye also met with her approval. Coming forward, she kissed Julia's cheek.

Without appearing to, Willa was studying Julia with great care. She took note of the yellow silk dress with its high collar, sleeves to the wrist, and the shining cap of hair without so much as a ringlet or curl to mar its severity.

In her cynical fashion, Willa decided that the dress was meant to offset Julia's immodest background, designed to fool the observer into thinking her demure and respectable. Her mouth tightened. A man could be fooled easily enough; no doubt about that.

The girls were clustered around Lane, both asking questions at the same time, Hester demanding to know whether Lane had brought her a present.

"Girls!" Willa's voice rang with stern authority. "Show

Julia to her rooms and see to it that she is properly settled. I'm sure she would like to rest before supper.''

April was the first to respond. With a warm smile, she shyly took hold of Julia's hand, leading her to one of the two staircases that flanked the foyer like an inverted horseshoe.

''Mother's right. You mst be exhausted from your trip. You and Lane are in the north wing.'' She gave a little laugh that was as breathless as her voice. ''The house is so large that I expect it will take awhile for you to get your bearings.''

Willa watched until they were gone from view, then turned toward her son. ''I would like to see you in the study, Lane.''

Without waiting for an answer, she headed down the hall to the rear of the house. Lane hesitated a moment, wondering why his mother couldn't wait to speak with him until after he had taken a bath. Then, with a sigh of resignation, he followed her.

''Why did you marry that girl?'' Willa demanded without preamble as she closed the door.

Lane's dark brows arched. The question took him by surprise. ''I thought you'd be pleased, Mother,'' he said lazily. ''You've been after me for a long time now to settle down, to begin a family.''

''Of course I have!'' she snapped, then jerked her head toward the door. ''But not with the likes of her!''

Lane's eyes narrowed. ''Explain yourself,'' he said quietly, watching her closely. Although, he thought ruefully, explanations really weren't necessary.

Willa gave a sound of disgust. ''I know all about her. The illegitimate daughter of a prostitute! Really, Lane. How could you have acted so irresponsibly? What will people think?''

"I don't give a damn what people think!" Lane retorted harshly. "Julia is my wife! That's all anyone needs to know." He came closer, his voice lowered to a dangerous level. "I would not take it kindly if you brought this subject up in her presence, or anyone else's for that matter." Willa made no response. Back stiff, she continued to regard him with angry eyes. "Let me put it this way, Mother," Lane went on quietly in an almost threatening tone. "If the story becomes general knowledge, I shall know at whose door to lay the blame."

Willa's mouth was a thin line as she viewed her son, but she knew better than to cross him when he was in a mood of this sort. "No one will hear it from me," she muttered at last.

Lane's manner eased. "I knew I could count on you."

chapter
eleven

Upstairs, Julia followed April and Hester into the bedroom. It was large and airy. A comfortable-looking four-poster was positioned against one wall, with a light blue velvet canopy and matching counterpane.

It took her a moment to realize that the room was far too feminine in its furnishings and materials to be inhabited by a man. Was she, then, to sleep alone?

April's next words confirmed it. "Lane's rooms are right next to yours, of course," she said, opening the adjoining door.

Beyond, Julia saw the bedroom and then the sitting room on the other side. She turned, hearing Hester's voice.

"I just know you're going to like this," the girl said, beckoning Julia into the sitting room.

Coming to stand beside Hester, Julia couldn't contain a gasp of pleasure. The room was octagonal, with windows on three sides, two of which offered a veiw of the river. Light poured in on plush carpeting and Queen Anne furniture.

Stepping to the window on the far wall, she looked outside. Set toward the rear of the grounds she could see the carriage house and stables. A charming gazebo decorated the formal gardens, which had stone walkways and curved benches. And, in the midst of it all, there was a small pond that glistened like a sapphire in an emerald setting. She turned toward the girls, both of whom were watching her with expectant eyes.

"Oh, it's lovely!" she said to them.

April beamed. "Hes and I chose the colors," she related proudly. "But of course you can change anything you wish," she added hastily.

"I wouldn't change a thing," Julia said sincerely, turning as a servant entered. The woman, who appeared to be in her late twenties, smiled shyly at Julia. Her dark hair was tucked neatly beneath a starched white hat that framed her fair complexion.

"This is Mary," April said by way of introduction. "She'll see to your needs." She motioned to her sister. "Come along, Hes. I'm sure Julia would like to freshen up before supper." She looked at Julia again. "We eat at eight o'clock."

The servants had brought up her trunks, and Mary now proceeded to open them. "I'll see to it that all these are washed and pressed tomorrow." She went to the wardrobe. "Your other things arrived a few weeks ago. They've all been cleaned." Her hazel eyes sought Julia, and she hesitated before she added, "If you want them arranged differently, I'll . . ."

"Oh, no," Julia said quickly, pleased with the woman's efficiency. "This will do just fine." She looked at the watch pinned to her bodice, thankful to see that there was time enough to take a bath.

Mary seemed to read her thoughts. "I've a hot tub waiting," she said, "unless you'd like to rest first."

"No," Julia answered with a short laugh. "Definitely a bath first. . . ."

At a quarter to eight, Julia, having changed into a peach chiffon gown, went downstairs and was directed by a servant to the drawing room.

Lane smiled as she entered. Stepping forward, he clasped her hand. "Did you find everything to your satisfaction?"

"Oh, Lane, that octagonal room is absolutely the most charming I've ever seen!"

"I'm glad you like it. It's one of the towers." He led her to one of the sofas, then picked up a half-finished drink from a table. "Hester and April share the other one."

Seated in a deep-cushioned chair, Willa, too, had changed her clothes for the evening meal and was now wearing a turquoise velvet gown that was obviously a Worth original. She had greeted the entrance of her daughter-in-law with silence, but now she spoke.

"Would you care for a drink, Julia?" she asked. "A glass of wine, perhaps?"

"Oh, no, thank you," Julia said as she sat down, for the first time taking note of her surroundings.

The room was high-ceilinged, the walls covered with Beauvais tapestries. The carpet was a very fine Savonnerie, patterned in muted crimson and gold.

But the clutter! Every table—and there were more than any one room needed—was covered with a fringed cloth, the surface jammed with porcelain statues, enameled music boxes, and fragile vases. Heavy drapes, fringed and tasseled, covered the tall, narrow windows, blocking any light that might be offered, for Willa well knew that sun faded and bleached materials.

"We are all so disappointed that we couldn't attend your wedding," April said to Julia, then pouted charmingly at her brother. "Why didn't you come home and have the ceremony here?"

Lane dropped a light kiss on the top of her black curls. "Because the *Sovereign* was scheduled to leave on the tenth," he explained patiently. "Had we returned here, we would have missed the boat."

"Oh, Lane!" Hester laughed and gave him a playful slap on the arm. "You own the *Sovereign*. You could have set any date you wanted!"

"She's right, Lane," April said, then looked at Julia. "I hope that members of your family, at least, were there."

Julia knew her face had flushed. "I . . . have no family," she said quietly. "My mother died some years ago, and my father . . . passed away earlier this year."

Both girls looked stricken at their faux pas. April hurried to Julia's side and put her arms around her. "How awful for you." Her arms tightened in a hug. "But you have a family now."

"Indeed you have," Hester exclaimed. She came to sit on the other side of Julia and took her hand. "April and I have always wanted another sister."

"Sorry I couldn't have accommodated you," Willa remarked dryly as she got to her feet, seeing a servant standing discreetly in the doorway. She nodded before the girl could speak. "Supper is ready," she announced, walking from the room.

Lane helped Julia to her feet. She was quite moved by the declarations from Hester and April and blinked her eyes several times as they headed for the family dining room.

This room was charming. There were two, probably large, windows; Julia couldn't tell for sure because the white satin drapes were drawn. The walls were painted a light green and potted plants in brass pots, showing a profusion of greenery, all combined to imbue the room with an informal intimacy.

To Julia's surprise, the food, while abundant, was quite unskillfully cooked. The pork roast had apparently sat too long before being brought to the table, and a fine film of fat had begun to congeal on top. Julia viewed it with distaste. The vegetables were overdone to the point where they were mushy and unpalatable, at least to her. No one else seemed to mind, though. Lane was eating with the enthusiasm she had come to expect of him. Good, bad, or indifferent, Lane ate heartily.

Both girls chatted incessantly, plying both Lane and Julia with questions, and again the subject of how they had met came up, affording Julia a moment of embarrassment. Willa was strangely silent during the meal, but Julia didn't know the woman well enough to ascertain whether this was normal behavior for her or not.

Distancing herself from the table conversation, Willa was eating fastidiously, picking at the small portions on her plate with almost mechanical movements. Julia received the impression that food wasn't especially important to Willa Manning. No doubt she was one of those people who ate to refuel their body, taking little satisfaction or enjoyment in the process.

And no wonder, thought Julia, swallowing the last of the mushy carrots. She stole a glance at Lane; he was on his second helping of everything.

After the meal was over, Willa, Hester, and April went upstairs.

In the hall, Lane gave Julia a light kiss on her forehead. "I have some papers to go through," he said quietly. "I know you must be tired. Can you find your way to your rooms, or shall I call a servant to show you the way?''

''I can find my way,'' she replied quickly, summoning a cheery smile. After all these weeks, sleeping alone seemed oddly unsatisfactory to her. She had become used to rolling over and being captured within those strong arms.

He gave her another kiss. ''I'll see you tomorrow, then. Sleep well. If you need anything, call Mary.''

I don't want to call Mary, she thought with a silly urge to cry. *I want to call you. . . .*

The next morning, April enthusiastically guided Julia through the twenty-two rooms that comprised Manning House.

The house was a colorful blend of French and Queen Anne. With the exception of the two dining rooms and the large ballroom, all other rooms were, in a sense, asymmetrical, replete with delightful alcoves in the most unexpected places, and featuring bay windows with cushioned seats. Though heated by warm-air furnaces, all rooms were equipped with fireplaces of Italian marble, and all had gas-illuminated chandeliers, the most elaborate being on the first floor, which, in addition to the ballroom and dining rooms, consisted of a drawing room, library, glassed solarium, and a truly huge kitchen with several long trestle tables at one end where the servants took their meals. The second floor was given over entirely to bedrooms, most of which were adjoined by sitting rooms. The servants' quarters were on the third floor.

The household staff, presided over by the housekeeper, Thelma Litton, numbered eleven, and included three personal maids, one valet, one cook, who had two assistants, an upstairs maid and a downstairs maid, and two girls who did the washing and ironing.

Later that morning, Julia caught sight of Thelma Litton emerging from the kitchen. Before the woman could go upstairs, Julia approached her.

"Mrs. Litton!" she called. "May I have a word with you?"

Hand on the balustrade, the woman paused for an instant longer than was necessary before she turned to face Julia. Widowed, and secure in her post as housekeeper of Manning House, Thelma Litton was a plain-faced woman who was fifty-two years old and looked every day of it. Her hair was iron gray and pulled so tightly into a bun on the back of her head that the corners of her eyes tilted upward slightly, giving her face the look of a weathered mask.

"I would like to see the day's menu," Julia said. "Would you please bring it to me in the library?"

The woman's black eyes studied Julia for a long moment. Not much happened in this house that she didn't know about. Though Willa had not disclosed her information on Julia, Mrs. Litton had found the lawyer's letter in the trash.

Julia was regarding the housekeeper in puzzlement. Was the woman hard of hearing? she wondered. She repeated her request in a sharper tone.

"We use a weekly menu here. Mrs. Manning takes care of that," came the cold reply.

Julia frowned. "I realize that," she said, containing her annoyance at the woman's tone. "Still, I would like to see them!"

"I can't do that unless Mrs. Manning gives her permission. You'll have to take it up with her."

Keys jangling at her waist, Mrs. Litton continued on her way, leaving Julia dumbfounded. All her life she had dealt with servants, and never had she encountered the likes of Thelma Litton. True, the woman had the exalted title of housekeeper; she was not to be considered a mere servant. Still, there was a very definite line she ought not to cross between confidence and disobedience.

As Mrs. Litton disappeared in the shadows of the upper landing, Julia stood there and chewed on her inner cheek. Her instinct was to follow the woman immediately and issue a severe reprimand. Yet this was her first day here; perhaps, she decided, it would be prudent to deal with Mrs. Litton at a later date.

She was about to go into the kitchen to have a few words with the cook when Hester came tripping down the stairs with a most unladylike display of haste.

"Julia!" she called out. "April and I were looking for you. We're going for a ride along the river. Would you like to come along?"

Julia hesitated, then smiled. "Yes. I'd like to join you. Just give me a minute to change...."

"Take your time. April isn't ready yet. I'll meet you both at the stables."

At that moment, Willa, garbed in a walking dress of indigo wool, a black felt hat perched atop her dark hair, emerged from her room.

"Hester!" she exclaimed, coming down the stairs. "How many times have I told you to walk, not run!"

"Yes, Mama," Hester said over her shoulder, without a break in her stride.

As Willa passed by Julia, she asked, "Did you sleep well last night?"

"Yes, I did—" Julia was about to speak of Mrs. Litton, but Willa sailed on out the front door without a pause.

Well! Julia thought to herself as she climbed the stairs, obviously she wasn't going to accomplish anything today.

The following afternoon, a Sunday, Lane took Julia for a

carriage ride to acquaint her with the city that would now be her home.

Cobblestoned streets were lined with houses constructed mostly of brick, though some were built of brown- or free-stone with pressed-brick fronts. White marble steps gleamed brightly in the sun.

First Lane took her to Market Street, where his warehouse was located. One hundred feet wide, the great thoroughfare extended from the Delaware to the Schuylkill rivers. Here were located the publishing offices of Lippincott & Company, as well as Hood, Bonbright & Company, and on the corner of Market and Sixth was the vast clothing warehouse of John Wanamaker & Company.

They drove by the Walnut Street Theatre and the American Academy of Music, the latter being somewhat unimpressive on the outside.

Between Walnut and Locust, Lane halted the carriage and they strolled through Rittenhouse Square with its shaded walks, benches, and fountains, all surrounded by elegant residences.

Although she was a Bostonian born and bred, it took very little time for Julia to fall in love with Philadelphia. Independence Hall, the Liberty Bell, Carpenters' Hall—home of the First Continental Congress—all breathed vitality and history; the city was steeped in it, and Julia could not help but respond to the powerful tug it exerted on her.

chapter
twelve

The October day was cold, holding a threat of rain or snow, depending on how much farther the temperature dropped. With biting intensity, the wind came rushing in off the river, howling like a troubled animal seeking shelter. The leaves that still remained on trees succumbed to the assault and fluttered through the air to cover the ground eventually with a carpet of crimson and gold.

Coming downstairs on this gloomy Thursday afternoon, Julia went into the library.

The room felt chilly to her, and she rubbed her hands on her arms, feeling the roughness of wool beneath her palms. The house was quiet. Hester and April had gone out to visit friends, and Julia had no idea as to Willa's whereabouts.

Without even being aware of it, Julia frowned as she thought of her mother-in-law. In the two weeks since she and Lane had come home, Julia had, on more than one occasion, tried to participate in the running of this household; her efforts were akin to wading through molasses. Mrs.

Litton never carried out an order unless it was prefaced with: "I'll speak to Mrs. Manning about it." Willa absolutely refused to listen to any complaints with regard to the housekeeper's attitude.

"Can I get you anything, Mrs. Manning?"

Startled, Julia turned to see the downstairs maid, a cheerful girl named Nancy, who possessed springy brown curls that seemed disinclined to stay tucked under her cap.

Julia smiled at her. "Well, I think a fire would be nice. . . ."

The girl bobbed her head. "It's a cold one today," she said, heading for the hearth. "There was even a thin coating of ice on the pond this morning."

While the girl saw to the fire, Julia sat down in a comfortable chair. The nap she had taken after dinner had left her feeling groggy. She was beginning to feel bored. Her days were settling into a routine that was anything but exciting. Twice she had accompanied April and Hester on shopping excursions, mainly for April's trousseau, and yesterday they had again gone horseback riding along the river. The girls were a delight to be with, and she enjoyed their company. Understandably, April talked of little but Andrew and their upcoming wedding. Hester, too, seemed to talk a great deal about Andrew, and Julia thought it was marvelous that the sisters were so close.

"There!" Nancy said with satisfaction as the blaze took hold. Straightening, she regarded Julia. "Is there anything else I can do for you, Mrs. Manning?"

Drawn out of her reverie, Julia started to say no, then realized that the chair she was sitting in was positioned so far from the fireplace that she could feel no trace of its warmth. Glancing around, she saw the other chairs, too, were at a distance.

"Yes," she said on an impulse, getting to her feet. "If you've a few minutes, I'd like you to help me rearrange some of the furniture in here."

"Yes, ma'am," Nancy agreed enthusiastically.

For the next ten minutes, Julia and Nancy moved furniture, placing two chairs before the fire and repositioning several tables Julia thought would complement the change. Then she stood there, tapping a finger on her lip as she studied the effect.

"Turn the chairs just a few inches more in the direction of the fireplace, Nancy," she instructed, nodding with satisfaction as the girl complied. "That's much—"

"What do you think you're doing!"

Both young women spun around, startled by the harsh voice. Willa stood in the doorway, glaring at them. Her yellow-and-brown-striped taffeta bodice moved up and down with her angry breaths.

"Why, I was just rearranging a few things," Julia replied, wondering at the older woman's reaction and transfixed by the coldness of those blue eyes.

"Please confine that to your own rooms!" Willa snapped quickly. "I dislike having things moved around in my house."

Clasping her hands at her waist, Julia raised her chin. "I was under the impression that this was Lane's house," she said carefully.

"And I am Lane's mother! For the past four years I've seen to the running of this household. It functions smoothly and will continue to do so under my guidance! I will thank you not to interfere."

"I . . . didn't mean to interfere," Julia retorted stiffly, upset with the accusation and even more upset that Willa would use such a tone when speaking to her. "Still, this is now my house as well, and I feel that I have a right to—"

"Any rights you have in this household will be accorded by me!" Willa's eyes narrowed to slits, and a pulse throbbed in her jaw as she clenched her teeth. "I suggest you do not try to circumvent my rules or give orders to any of my staff." Turning from Julia, she glared at Nancy, and the girl seemed to shrink beneath the hard look. "Be about your business! And in the future do not move any furniture without my permission or you will be seeking employment elsewhere!"

"Yes, ma'am. . . ." The girl looked about to cry as she scurried for the door.

When Nancy left, Julia returned her mother-in-law's angry look with one of her own. "There was no need to speak to the girl like that!" she exclaimed, appalled that anyone would be so unfair. "Nancy was only obeying my instructions."

"I know." Willa's smile was cold, her tone not much warmer. "And be assured that the next time she does, she will be discharged."

With that, Willa turned abruptly and left the room. Releasing a deep sigh, Julia sank down in the chair. The fire was burning brightly now, its cheerful crackle mocking her dark mood. It had been her intention to curl up with a book, but she didn't feel like reading now. Willa's hostility was thick enough to cut with a knife. But why? Was it herself, or would any woman Lane have married be treated in the same way?

With her elbow on the arm of the chair, Julia cupped her chin and stared moodily into the dancing flames. Lane had left the house right after breakfast, as he always did. She would not see him until supper. Should she speak of what had taken place here this afternoon? Should she mention the cold way in which Willa continually addressed her?

She sighed. No. This was not a man's concern. She had no right to burden her husband with household matters. That was one lesson her mother had firmly instilled within her: "Men have important problems on their minds," she always used to say. "There is no need to trouble them with ours when they come home."

Julia heard the front doorbell ring, but paid it no mind. She wasn't expecting any visitors. When Leah entered the library a short while later, however, Julia emitted a glad cry and sprang to her feet.

"Leah! How happy I am to see you."

Coming forward, Leah Carlyle gave her a quick embrace, a brushing of cheeks. "My, you do look well! I'm not intruding, am I?"

"Heavens, no! I was about to expire from a lack of anything to do."

"Ahh. . . ." Leah removed her gloves and sat down in the opposite chair. "If it's boredom that's afflicting you, I have the perfect solution!"

"Let me ring for refreshments," Julia said, heading for the bell cord. "What would you like?"

"On a day like this, a glass of sherry would be most welcome." Feeling the warmth of the fire, Leah unbuttoned her dark gray wool jacket to reveal the crisp white silk blouse she was wearing beneath it.

When Nancy appeared, Julia requested the sherry for Leah and a cup of hot chocolate for herself.

"Are you settled?" Leah inquired as Julia again sat down.

"Yes, I think so," Julia replied with a laugh that didn't sound sincere to Leah. She suddenly noticed that Julia looked tired, and mentioned it.

"Oh, no," Julia disclaimed with a wave of her hand. "Just the opposite. I've never napped in my life, but find myself doing so now."

Nancy entered and placed the tray on a table, then discreetly withdrew.

Extending a hand, Leah picked up her glass of sherry, took a sip, then asked, "Would you consider joining our committee? We're in desperate need of help."

"Of course!" Julia said quickly, reaching for the hot chocolate. "You are speaking of the Centennial Women's Committee?"

"Yes, I am."

"I will certainly do anything I can to help, although I must confess, I've never been a part of anything like this before. I wouldn't know where to begin." She viewed Leah with interest, her hands wrapped around the warm cup.

"That will make itself known to you when I give you some background. You see, when the plans were drawn up, there was one glaring omission: women were not represented in any way. Elizabeth Gillespie, who founded our committee, did her best to convince Dr. Loring, who heads the Board of Finance, that we should have our own pavilion." She gave a short laugh and a shake of her head. "There are one hundred and eighty buildings in the plans, but they would not give us one! Dr. Loring informed Mrs. Gillespie that if we wanted our own building, we would have to have our own plans drawn up, and see to the exhibits as well; in short, they would offer us no assistance at all."

Julia pursed her lips, took a sip of chocolate, then placed the cup back on its saucer. "Perhaps I can convince Lane to make a contribution."

"He already has," Leah said quickly. "He's been most generous. Actually, money is the least of our problems at this point. We have already raised the thirty thousand dollars we need to construct the building. What we need now is help in writing letters and making contacts; and above all, we are running out of space. We did rent a small warehouse, but I fear it's already jammed to the rafters—and still the exhibits arrive.''

Julia thought of the vast warehouse that belonged to Lane. Perhaps there was space available in the building for the committee's use. She said nothing to Leah at this point, however, thinking it best to speak to Lane first.

Leah finished her sherry and looked up as Willa entered the room.

"Oh, it's you, Leah," she said. "I thought I heard voices in here. . . .''

"Good afternoon, Willa," Leah said as she put the glass back on the table. "I've just persuaded Julia to join our committee.''

Willa regarded Julia with a tight smile. "Well, it will give her something to do. . . .''

Besides moving the furniture? Julia thought to herself, feeling a resentment she was careful not to display.

Leah stood up and faced Julia. "If you're free tomorrow morning, I'll take you to Fairmount Park. Have you been there yet?''

Julia got to her feet and walked beside Leah as they headed for the front door. "No, I haven't gone yet, and I'd very much like to go with you tomorrow.'' Anything, she thought, to get out of this house and away from Willa for a few hours.

Leah paused and allowed Nancy to assist her as she put on her fur cloak. "Fine. Will ten suit you?''

"Yes. I'll be ready.''

Nancy opened the door, and a frigid blast of air swirled

in. Leah gave a startled gasp and waved at Julia. "Ten, then—unless it snows!"

The following morning, however, dawned clear and sunny. Julia found herself excited at the prospect of an outing and was ready well before the appointed hour, pleased that Leah arrived promptly at ten o'clock.

"I'm glad it didn't snow after all," Leah said as Julia settled herself in the carriage. "Mrs. Gillespie would be furious if the construction had to be halted. We only started two weeks ago."

Julia regarded her friend with surprise. "I thought the Exhibition was scheduled to open in May! That's less than seven months away!"

"You're not the only one to be surprised," Leah retorted with a small laugh. "Everyone is telling us it cannot be completed by May tenth, but if Elizabeth Gillespie has anything to say about it, it will be done on time."

Instead of going directly to Fairmount Park, Leah had instructed her driver to take them to the small warehouse on Market Street where the exhibits were currently being stored.

As the vehicle slowed, Leah leaned forward to peer outside. "Ah . . . here we are."

The two women got out of the carriage. Producing keys from her reticule, Leah unlocked the door.

Julia's first impression as she entered the unheated building was one of haphazard clutter, but then she saw that the exhibits were arranged by country.

"Everything you see in here," Leah explained as they strolled along, "was done by women."

Julia paused before the most magnificent writing table she had ever seen. It was made of teak, its front and sides adorned with delicate ivory figures. Wonderingly, her fingertips traced the mother-of-pearl inlay. "This is the most beautiful thing I've ever seen!'' she exclaimed, turning to look at Leah. ''Did a woman really make this?''

Leah laughed with delight at Julia's skeptical tone. ''Every bit of it. It comes from Japan. Come over here. I want you to see this. It's my favorite.''

''Ohhh,'' Julia breathed as she viewed the six-paneled screen pointed out by Leah. The framework itself was of ebony, but Julia's eye was immediately drawn to the yellow silk inserts upon which were painted a variety of ladies' fans. Each fan had been embroidered in silk thread to represent the figures of mandarins and merchants.

Although she was certain she had seen the best, Julia spent the following hour in a state of awe. From Brazil there were embroidered table covers and delicate gold lacework, and pincushions of every size, some of which were made from shells.

Canada's women had sent antimacassar and cretonne work, as well as silk flowers and laces.

''Look at this,'' Leah said, holding up a richly embroidered velvet door cover from Egypt. ''This was sent to us by the wife of the Bey of Tunis. It was done by her own hand.''

Julia just shook her head. ''What you have here is . . . overwhelming!''

''And still they arrive. Wait until you see the featherwork from the Netherlands. . . .''

By the time they left the warehouse, Julia's enthusiasm was at a high level.

It was close to noon when they arrived at Fairmount Park. The threat of an early winter seemed to have fled in the face of the returning sunshine, and the day sparkled with a brilliance peculiar only to the season known as autumn.

At first glance, the scene was one of utter confusion.

Construction workers were everywhere. Carpenters, masons, bricklayers, and roofers milled about.

Everywhere she looked, Julia saw buildings in various stages of completion. Leah cautioned her to step carefully.

"The roads are rutted from the wagons," she explained. "It's really dreadful when it rains. Everything turns to mud."

Holding their skirts an inch or so off the ground, they made their way through a veritable forest of lumber, piled high in stacks that were taller than they were.

As they passed what would be the Japanese Pavilion, Julia couldn't resist stopping to watch the workers. They were all Japanese, and all of them were dressed in their native costume.

"They use ink instead of chalk to mark their walls," Leah informed her. "Isn't that strange?"

Julia regarded one of the carpenters with open curiosity. The man was wearing a bright crimson sash around his waist, but not for effect. It served a very utilitarian purpose. Little pockets in the material held tools, and suspended from one side was a small wicker basket that held the nails he was using.

When they reached the site of the Women's Pavilion, Leah beckoned to the lone female figure, who immediately headed in their direction.

Elizabeth Gillespie appeared to be in her late thirties. She was attractive rather than pretty, with a formidable look and a no-nonsense air that precluded familiarity.

She gave Julia a penetrating look when Leah introduced them, then said in clipped tones, "I'm glad to have you with us, Mrs. Manning. Ours is no easy task. We welcome all the assistance we can get."

"I'm delighted to be a part of it," Julia responded warmly, liking the woman despite her brisk manner.

During the next hour, Julia watched Elizabeth Gillespie with growing admiration and more than a touch of amazement. The woman was everywhere, cajoling masons, arguing with bricklayers, consulting with the architect. No detail seemed too small for her attention. Ignoring the roughness of the terrain, the hem of her gown trailing carelessly in the dust, she even at one point climbed up on the scaffolding to inspect the workmanship.

Julia turned to Leah and shook her head. "I confess I had my doubts when you told me this was to be completed by May tenth, but if today is any indication, I'd venture a guess that it will be done ahead of time, if Mrs. Gillespie has anything to say about it."

"She is indefatigable," Leah agreed solemnly, with a nod of her head. "For the past two years she has worked tirelessly, organizing subcommittees in all states, and she has traveled extensively in order to raise money for the construction of our building."

"Where does she get her energy?" Julia gave a small laugh as she followed Leah back to the carriage.

"Passed down to her from her famous ancestor, I would say." At Julia's puzzled look, Leah said, "Benjamin Franklin, my dear. Mrs. Gillespie is his great-granddaughter. I thought you knew."

"No, I didn't."

"Oh, blood will tell; it always does."

When she returned to Manning House later that afternoon, Julia was surprised to discover that Lane had come home early. Nancy told her that he was in the study, and Julia quickly headed in that direction, full of what she had seen, and anxious to learn whether he would donate some of the space in his warehouse for the committee's use.

Lane listened patiently, a bit amused by her enthusiasm; then, to her delight, he readily agreed.

"I must send word to Leah right away!" Julia said, but as she went to leave, Lane got up and came to stand at her side.

"That can wait," he said firmly. "Right now, I have something to show you."

"What is it?" Julia asked as the took her arm.

"You'll see," he replied enigmatically, grinning at her. He led her down the hall to the drawing room. Pausing before the closed doors, and still grinning, he flung them open in a dramatic gesture.

Puzzled, Julia stepped into the room, then caught her breath at the sight that greeted her. Tears gathered in her eyes as she viewed the piano. The wood was dark, almost black, and it was polished to such a degree that it reflected images like a mirror.

"Do you like it?" Lane asked, watching her closely. "It was delivered just an hour ago. I was afraid you would return before it got here."

Julia's heart melted at this touching display of consideration. "Oh, Lane," she breathed. Throwing caution to the wind, she flung her arms around him and pressed herself close to him.

Lane chuckled. Raising his hands, he gently disengaged her arms from around his neck, giving her wrists a gentle squeeze before he released them. Then he walked to the piano, resting a hand on its polished surface. "I'm glad you're pleased, Julia," he said with a smile. "I confess that I know little about these instruments, but I was assured it was the best of its kind. It's a Steinway."

There's also something else you know little about, Julia thought to herself, more hurt than she could have imagined by the small rejection she had just endured. With a fingertip, she brushed away a tear that had nothing at all to do with being pleased, then forced a bright smile as she came to stand beside her husband.

"Would you play something for me?" Lane asked.

"Of course," Julia responded quickly. "What would you like to hear?"

He shrugged. "Anything you'd care to play."

Leaning on the piano, Lane listened in polite attentiveness as the beautiful melody of Schubert's Impromptu in B-flat major filled the room. But before another minute had passed, his mouth dropped open in astonishment.

"My God," he exclaimed. Straightening, he gave her an incredulous look. "You play at concert level! I had no idea. . . ."

Julia paused, smiling at his obvious amazement. Before she could continue, April and Hester came into the room.

"Julia!" April came forward, a look of surprise on her lovely face. "Was that you playing just now?" At her nod, April grasped Hester's hand and pulled her toward the sofa. "Please go on—I'd love to hear more!"

chapter
thirteen

That night, Julia sat up in bed, pillows propped behind her, an unopened book on her lap. Usually her evening bath left her feeling pleasantly drowsy; tonight, however, she was wide awake.

Discontentment was a feeling she had rarely encountered before; now it seemed to tear at every nerve in her body. It troubled her because she could find no reason for it. Lane was generous, thoughtful, kind. And, for reasons she could not even begin to explain, these very commendable traits were, at times, leaving her with a heavy sadness. Her moods of late were swinging from high to low, tears threatening at the slightest provocation.

Inclining her head, Julia picked up the book, then with a sigh put it down again. Tension coursed through her, precluding any inclination she may have had to read or even to remain still.

With a sound of disgust, she threw aside the blankets and got up. Her annoyance with herself growing with each step she took, Julia walked aimlessly into her sitting room, then back into her bedroom.

What on earth did she want? she wondered irritably. She had never considered herself to be self-centered, but right now she could come up with no better explanation of her distressing attitude. Today Lane had given her a piano, a beautiful instrument, the best of its kind. She should be deliriously happy at this moment! Instead, she was acting like a child, hurt because Lane hadn't swept her into his arms.

Nor did logic help. Julia told herself that his mother and sisters—not to mention the servants—were close by; how could a man be expected to do something like that under those circumstances?

Getting back into bed, she plumped her pillow, then became still as she heard Lane enter his room. Usually he spent an hour or less in his study after supper before coming upstairs; tonight it had been closer to two hours. Glancing at the clock, she saw that it was after ten-thirty.

The breath she drew was involuntarily deep, reflecting a quickened heartbeat and a tension she was coming to know all too well. Lane visited her almost every night, but he never stayed in her bed. Julia was beginning to wonder whether men, too, should have a "marital duty" to perform.

She punched her pillow in a furious gesture, again wondering what the devil it was she wanted! Not too long ago, sleeping alone had been bliss; not too long ago, nude bodies were an abomination; not too long ago, a body pressed against hers in sleep was an annoyance.

What had happened to her?

Tilting her head, Julia strained to hear any sound from the adjoining room that might indicate that Lane would come to her. She heard nothing; probably the hour was too late, and he had decided to retire.

Reaching out, she extinguished the lamp and fell back on the pillow with a deep sigh.

She bit her lip, again thinking of what a child she was—an ingrate! Yes, that was it, an ingrate! Lane had fulfilled every promise he had made. "You will never want for anything," he had said. "You will live in the style to which you are accustomed."

Well, he had made good on every promise.

Then, why was she discontented?

The door opened, and Julia sat up straighter as Lane came into the room. The light was behind him, but she sensed his smile.

"I thought you might be asleep," he said softly.

"I'm not," she whispered, longing for those strong arms to hold her tight. His hair was tousled, slightly damp, and even at this distance she could smell the good, clean scent of him. Although he was wearing a robe, she was certain he wore nothing beneath it. A hot wave of emotion swept over her.

Coming closer, Lane took off his robe and sat on the eadge of the bed. Julia made no resistance as he began to remove her nightgown; indeed, it now seemed natural to her that they made love unclothed. She didn't think to question the fact that she no longer felt the painful embarrassment that had afflicted her initially when she had exposed her body before his unrelenting gaze. Nor did she find the sight of him anything but pleasing.

As she usually did, Julia remained passive as Lane began to caress her; but then, as always seemed to be happening to her of late, that unbearable tension began to make itself known, threatening her composure. Gritting her teeth, Julia told herself it would soon be over.

Tonight, however, Lane seemed to be in no hurry. He continued to stroke her for minutes on end, until Julia felt like screaming. Her breath quickened to the point where she had to part her lips in order to get enough air into her lungs.

Her eyes were closed, and when his mouth found her nipple, she shuddered. His mouth moved lower, trailing hot darts of flame wherever it came in contact with her quivering flesh, and now her body began to tremble like a leaf in a storm.

"Julia . . ." he whispered, lips now on her ear as he eased himself on top of her. "Don't fight me. Make love with me. . . ."

His mouth was upon hers, his tongue seeking her honeyed sweetness.

All resistance fled, and when he entered her moist warmth, Julia began to move beneath him like a wild thing, all control gone as she sought to follow wherever these sensations would lead her.

They spiraled upward as if reaching for the heavens, and Julia let herself ascend to the top, where a starburst of ecstasy awaited, enfolding her in its rapturous embrace.

Then she lay there, panting, spent, a fine film of perspiration setting her body aglow.

Lane was next to her now, but Julia couldn't remember when he had removed himself from her warmth. Leaning on an elbow, he was staring down at her, brushing the damp tendrils of her hair from her forehead with a gentle hand.

After a few minutes went by, Julia's breath calmed, and the enormity of what she had done made itself known to her.

"Ohhh . . ." she moaned, covering her face with hands that

were shaking. Had she been able to crawl into a hole and pull it in after her, she would have done so.

"Julia . . . ?"

She heard his voice, but could not bring herself to look at him, could not bear to see the revulsion she was certain his face was reflecting.

"Julia . . . look at me," Lane said quietly, caressing her shoulder.

"Nooo. . . ." A wrenching sob of despair erupted from her throat.

His arm went around her. Rolling onto his back, Lane pulled her up and held her against him, cradling her head on his chest. She still had her hands pressed to her face, and he made no effort to remove them.

"Why did you try to hide it from me?" he whispered, lips pressed in the fragrance of her hair. "I've suspected for weeks now that you could be a warm and sensual woman, if only you would allow yourself to be."

"I'm nothing of the sort!" she cried out, words muffled behind her hands. "Don't talk to me like that! I'm not a harlot. . . ."

Frowning, Lane sat up and now firmly pulled her hands away from her face. "What on earth are you talking about?" he demanded, clearly displaying his puzzlement. "What the hell does sensuality have to do with being a harlot?"

Tears sparkled and hung in droplets on her golden lashes. She kept her eyes lowered, refusing to look at him. No means of explanation came to her, so she remained silent.

"Answer me, Julia!"

Her lips trembled, and the words came between gulping sobs. "No lady would ever have acted as I have just done. I don't doubt you think me a harlot. Oh, God, I'm so ashamed. . . ." Her hands again covered her face.

A moment went by before Julia became aware that, beneath her, the bed was shaking. In confusion then, she raised her eyes to look at Lane.

He was laughing! At first he made no sound, but he apparently could no longer control himself, and now the sound emerged, hearty and robust . . . and infuriating! Julia's tear-filled eyes blazed with indignation. She had bared her heart, her innermost thoughts, and he thought it was funny!

Sitting up, Julia folded her arms across her breasts, averted her face, and stared angrily across the room.

"I'm . . . I'm sorry," he gasped, wiping tears of laughter from the corners of his eyes.

Her angry gaze swung toward him again. Shoulders heaving, Lane seemed to be in imminent danger of being unable to regain his breath anytime in the near future.

And it would serve him right, she thought, grinding her teeth. As far as she could see, there was absolutely no cause for such high amusement.

Reaching out, he took hold of a strand of her hair, rubbing the softness between his thumb and forefinger. "I don't know who put those foolish notions into that lovely head of yours," he said softly. "But I do know one thing: they're wrong! What happened between us tonight is right and normal and wonderful." His hand moved to cup her chin, and he stared deeply into her eyes. "Do you understand me, Julia?"

Hesitating, she studied him for a long moment. "Do you really mean that?" she whispered, still a bit doubtful.

He pulled her close to him, his warm hands caressing the satiny smoothness of her back, causing a shivering delight to fire her banked passion. "My lovely Circe . . . I'm going to show you exactly what I mean. . . ."

And he did.

It was close to midnight by the time Lane fell asleep, for once in her bed instead of his own. But Julia was feeling too happy to sleep, her body still tingling with remembered pleasure. Never in her life had she felt so alive!

Outside, a full moon shone with icy brightness, throwing pale ribbons of light into the room.

Turning her head, Julia gazed at her sleeping husband. He was on his back, one arm flung over his head, the blanket wrapped around his ankles. As usual, he was not wearing a nightshirt, or anything else; for that matter, neither was Julia. She hadn't bothered to put on her nightgown again.

In her mind, Julia relived their lovemaking. It was right, she decided; just as Lane had said. Nothing so beautiful could possibly be wrong. "Sensual," Lane had called her. Her lips curved in a soft smile. He had been right about that, too. Mavis was the one who had been wrong.

Sitting up, Julia clasped her arms around her legs and put her chin on her knees, her eyes viewing the length of the man beside her. She couldn't help but marvel at his male beauty. When her gaze reached his manhood, she hastily turned away, but then, with renewed confidence, she returned to study it in more detail. And why not? She had given in to temptation and touched it. A hand went to her lips to smother a small laugh. Mavis hadn't been entirely wrong after all; it certainly did change shape!

With a happy sigh, she rested back on her pillow and looked out the window. The draperies were parted, and she could see the night sky. The moon was so bright, the stars seemed to have disappeared, as if overwhelmed by a superior force they could not hope to compete against.

Sleep just would not come.

Finally Julia got out of bed, slipped into her nightgown, and donned a robe.

A glass of warm milk was just what she needed, she decided, careful to close the door as quietly as she could so as not to disturb Lane.

Downstairs in the kitchen, she lit the gaslight, found a bottle of milk in the icebox, and poured some of it into a pot.

While it heated on the stove, the coals still warm from the evening meal, she walked over to one of the cupboards. Perhaps there was still some chocolate cake left over from supper.

One thing was certain, Julia thought to herself, repressing a giggle: being happy gave her a ravenous appetite! Come to think of it, for the past few weeks she had been eating more than she normally did, mostly sweets. And it was beginning to tell. She suspected she had put on a few pounds. Her corset was beginning to feel uncomfortably tight.

Taking hold of a porcelain fitting, Julia gave it a tug, then another. It took her a second to realize that the cupboard was locked. All of them were!

Puzzled, she chewed her lower lip, staring about the kitchen. After a moment, she walked toward the pantry. The door was locked, the key nowhere in sight.

"I don't believe this," she murmured to the empty room. She knew of only one woman, a neighbor named Hortense Willoughby, who did this sort of thing. Parsimonious in the extreme, Hortense locked her pantry and cupboards at night, a practice that prevented servants from stealing food. To find it being done here, at Manning House, was a shock.

A hissing sound from the other side of the kitchen startled her. Julia spun around with a sharply drawn breath, making a face when she saw that the milk had boiled over. Hurrying to the stove, she lifted the pot from the heat. The handle was hot, and the pot landed back on the stove with a clatter, spilling some of the liquid. Julia licked her fingers and reached for a towel to wipe up the mess.

The door to the kitchen flew open just then with a force that slammed it against the wall.

"What is going on in here!" Thelma Litton, a flannel robe over her nightgown, her hair falling down her back in one long, thick braid, spoke crossly. She occupied the only two-room apartment allotted to the staff, and it was off the kitchen with its own door to the outside. When Julia turned to face the woman, Mrs. Litton's eyes widened in surprise. "Oh, it's you, Mrs. Manning. Sorry. I thought it was one of the servants."

Ignoring that, Julia pointed. "Why are these cupboards locked?" she demanded.

"Why do you suppose?" came the insolent retort. "If they were not locked, the servants would help themselves to whatever they pleased. . . ."

And what of it? Julia thought to herself, but said: "Is Mr. Manning aware of this?"

The woman looked incredulous. "Mr. Manning has better things to do than concern himself with trivial household matters." She spoke as if Julia were an absolute dolt not to know that.

"Mrs. Manning, then?" Julia persisted, more than a little irritated by the woman's continuing insubordination. With the exception of Mary and Nancy who were everything servants ought to be, the other servants treated her correctly, if with reservation. But Mrs. Litton went too far. "Does she know?'' Julia asked again when she received no immediate answer.

Thelma Litton folded her hands at her waist and, though the same height as Julia, managed to look down her nose at her. ''Well, of course, she does. Nothing happens in this house without her say-so.''

''I want these cupboards left open at all times!'' Julia said sternly. ''Day and night!''

Mrs. Litton's shoulders moved in a careless shrug. ''I'll speak to Mrs. Manning about it, if you insist.''

Julia's eyes narrowed, but she refused to lose her temper. ''You are speaking to Mrs. Manning,'' she reminded her, keeping her voice even.

For once, Mrs. Litton seemed to be at a loss for words. When she recovered, she spoke stiffly. ''I was, of course, referring to the elder Mrs. Manning. . . .''

With that, the housekeeper turned and stomped from the kitchen. A few low mutters told Julia that she was more than a bit annoyed at having her rest disturbed.

Julia had no appetite for milk or anything else now. She washed the pot and left it on the drainboard, determined to have a talk with Willa first thing in the morning. Mother-in-law or no, she wasn't about to allow such goings-on in her own home!

Returning to her room, Julia removed her clothes and got back into bed. Lane rolled over, and his arms went around her.

''Where did you go?'' he mumbled, sounding as if he was still half asleep.

''Nowhere,'' she whispered softly. Snuggling close to him, she felt the protective warmth of his body envelope her, and she sighed with contentment. The cloying seduction of sleep tugged at her, and Julia finally closed her eyes.

The following day, however, was Sunday, and despite her resolve of the night before, no opportunity for a private talk with Willa presented itself.

After church, not only did Andrew Hollinger arrive, as he always did, for Sunday dinner, but afterward friends of Hester and April came to call. The young people whiled away the afternoon playing charades, creating a happy, high-spirited atmosphere that everyone seemed to enjoy.

The next morning, Julia kept her own counsel until Lane left the house. Hester and April, on their way to the stables, asked if Julia would like to accompany them for a ride. She declined. Then she went upstairs, knowing that Willa would be in her sitting room.

The confrontation would not be pleasant, but neither could it be avoided.

On the landing, Julia paused a moment, wondering how she should address her mother-in-law. So far, she had avoided calling her anything. In view of their less than cordial relationship, "Mother" seemed inappropriate, not to mention unwanted.

Approaching the sitting room, Julia saw that the door was open. She knocked anyway.

"Come in," Willa murmured without looking up.

Slowly, Julia made her way toward the writing table, behind which Willa was seated.

The room was larger than her own sitting room and of a rectangular shape. Though the fabrics and furnishings were costly and elegant, Willa's penchant for clutter was noticeable everywhere Julia looked. Her eye lit on a table crammed with priceless Chinese porcelain arranged in no particular order, and she frowned in distaste.

A long minute passed. Willa, garbed in a morning dress

of brown linen with a white lace collar, continued to pen numbers in a ledger book.

With growing impatience, Julia stared down at the top of Willa's head. Well, sooner or later she'd have to address this woman in some way, she thought, and took a deep breath.

"Willa, I think we should talk."

"Very well, Julia." Reaching up, she removed her steel-rimmed spectacles. She didn't seem surprised; in fact, she wasn't. Mrs. Litton had told her of her midnight encounter with Julia in the kitchen. With a slow movement, she put down her pen and closed the ledger.

"I think I should have a hand in certain matters in this household—"

"There's no need," Willa interrupted, displaying a calmness that reflected her unperturbed state of mind. Absently, her fingers drummed on the ledger. "This household was running smoothly before you came, and it will continue to do so. Besides"—she offered a frosty smile—"your committee work will be taking up a great deal of your time. Certainly I wouldn't want you to be overworked."

Julia's frown deepened. The woman was being deliberately obtuse. "That's not the point, and you know it! Not only is Mrs. Litton insolent, but she also refuses to carry out a single order I give her without first consulting with you."

Willa gave a short, humorless laugh. "I don't find that in the least bit unusual," she murmured. "I was the one who hired her, you know. It's only natural that she displays a certain loyalty to me."

"I don't question her loyalty to you; it is her insubordination toward me that I take exception to." Julia made a sound of exasperation. "I cannot believe that you would condone such a petty and unnecessary practice as locking the cupboards each night!''

Willa's mouth tightened. "Petty it might be," she conceded, "but unnecessary it is not. If the servants confined their pilfering to themselves, the cost would be inconsequential. Unfortunately, they have a distressing tendency to take food home to their families. All the servants in this house are well fed—I see no need to supply meals for their families as well!'' She raised her chin. "Quite frankly, Julia, it would be wise of you to rid yourself of your unfortunate habit of interfering and apply yourself to something for which you may be better suited.''

"And what might that be?" Julia inquired, trying to conceal her sarcasm.

"Having children, of course." Willa made a gesture of vague irritation. "Why do you suppose my son married you?''

Julia's mouth tightened. "Why don't you tell me?" she muttered, now making no effort to contain her sarcasm. "It appears that you have all the answers.''

"Indeed I have," Willa acknowledged with a short nod of her head. "And probably to questions you haven't even thought to ask.''

Julia tried another tack. "I realize you are not very fond of me," she began. That was an understatement, if there ever was one. "Still, Lane and I are married, and that situation is unlikely to change. . . .''

Gazing up at the slim woman in front of her, Willa's eyes glinted with animosity. She had given Lane her word never to mention Julia's background, but she had not given her word that she would not speak of other things.

"How can you be so certain?" she asked at last, her

voice deceptively soft. She leaned back in her chair and viewed Julia with interest.

Confusion shaded Julia's dark blue eyes. "I . . . don't know what you mean. . . ."

"Of course you don't," Willa murmured in a soothing tone, then fixed her daughter-in-law with a hard look. "Has Lane ever expressed love for you?"

Julia was so shocked by the question that she could only stare at the woman.

Willa's smile was thin. "I thought not," she mused softly. "But then, how could he? He's in love with another woman; always has been." Ignoring the suddenly pale face of her daughter-in-law, Willa got up and walked slowly to the window, staring for a long moment at the tranquil blue waters of the river, over which a brown cloud now seemed to hover.

Since this was a weekday, construction was in furious progress at Fairmount Park. Willa wrinkled her nose. "All that dust!" she muttered, sounding annoyed. The observation was not commented upon. Turning, she viewed the dark blue eyes that were staring at her. The young woman seemed incapable of speech. Willa cleared her throat and spoke briskly. "Lane, as you know, is twenty-eight. To be honest, until recently, I had despaired of his ever marrying. I'm sure I don't have to tell you that there are people in this world for whom love comes only once in a lifetime."

Weakly, Julia sat down in the nearest chair, her eyes never leaving Willa Manning's face. All strength seemed to have deserted her. She could not refute the words, could not refute the small suspicions that had been taunting her of late. She remembered the impression she had received when she had asked Lane if he'd ever been in love. "No," he'd said; but he had not spoken the truth.

"Her name is Rosalind Langley," Willa went on, then proceeded to tell Julia the whole story. There was one thing she omitted: the death of Otis Langley. She needn't have bothered, however, for with her first mention of the name, Julia recalled William Carlyle telling Lane about the death of that man. Feeling ill, she now realized the meaning of Lane's expression upon learning the news.

A chill coursed down Julia's spine, and she shivered. As clearly as if he were standing in front of her, she could see that enigmatic look he had leveled at her soon after learning that Otis Langley had died.

It was no longer a mystery. Now Julia was certain she knew what was behind that look: Lane was sorry he had married her!

"Why. . ." Julia's mouth seemed suddenly parched, and she swallowed. "Why have you told me this?"

Willa sighed and waved a hand in a gesture that clearly indicated impatience. "Wouldn't you agree that a person is better served by knowledge than ignorance?"

There was a moment of silence before an answer was forthcoming.

"You . . . were doing me a favor?" Julia retorted cuttingly. The back of her throat stung with tears she refused to shed.

"That was my intention," Willa replied blithely. Arching a brow, she paused, gave Julia a meaningful look, then added: "Although I would imagine that a woman . . . like yourself probably wouldn't think so."

Julia caught her breath at the insinuating tone of Willa's voice. Staring into those cold blue eyes, she suddenly understood. The message was so clear, it could have been carved into stone. Somehow Willa had found out about her; not from Lane, of that she was certain. She also felt certain that in the best interest of her own family, Willa would never reveal her knowledge to an outsider. It would, in a sense, remain a wall between the two of them. Everything now fell into place. Feeling incredibly weary, Julia's shoulders slumped. She had neither the heart nor the energy to spar any further with her mother-in-law.

Slowly, she got to her feet, her initial reasons for being here forgotten.

Julia spent the remainder of that day in her rooms, feeling dazed. Pleading a headache, she did not go down to supper.

It was well past nine o'clock when Lane tapped on her door. Opening it, he regarded her with a show of surprise. Although a fire burned in the hearth, not a single light was lit.

"Julia? Why are you sitting in the dark?" he exclaimed, coming closer.

Raising her head, she looked at him and felt a pain of anguish that seemed to sear her soul. "Why didn't you tell me?"

Puzzlement creased his brow. "Tell you what?" Hunching down beside her chair, he placed a warm hand over her cold one.

"Rosalind. . . ."

He drew a sharp breath, and a moment went by before he spoke. "Oh. I'm sorry, I . . ."

". . . never meant for me to find out?" she finished, viewing him with a level look.

His mouth compressed. "How did you find out about Rosalind?"

She turned away. "Does it matter?"

He gave a deep sigh. "No . . . I guess it really doesn't. . . ." He squeezed her hand, but it remained limp beneath the pressure. "Julia," he said softly, "you are my wife. . . ."

"Do you still love her?" As soon as the words were out, Julia wished she'd never asked the question.

Lane, however, didn't answer it. Her words had caused a heaviness in his heart. He had known that, sooner or later, this time would come, and he had dreaded it. He had no wish to speak of Rosalind, for she was his past, and he was not a man to look backward. A stirring of resentment coursed through him as he regarded Julia. Even though she had learned about Rosalind, she should not have spoken of it. Wounds he had thought to be healed now burst open to cause fresh pain.

"Do you?" Julia cried out into the void of silence. In a quick movement, she wrenched her hand from his.

Lane got up, and Julia could sense his sudden anger. "Be quiet! I don't want to discuss this now." Going to the window, he plunged his hands into his pockets and stared outside.

"Not discuss it now?" she echoed in a faint voice, turning in her chair to stare at his back. "Would tomorrow be a better time? When can we talk about it?"

In a movement that took her by surprise, he spun around and glared at her, a tide of angry color staining his cheeks. "Never! This is no concern of yours! It happened long before I met you." When Julia opened her mouth to speak, his voice thundered at her. "I forbid you to bring up this subject again!"

Shrinking back in her chair, Julia put her fingertips to her trembling lips. In all the months they had been married, this was the first time Lane had raised his voice to her.

Turning from her, Lane stormed from the room before she could speak.

The fire burned scarlet behind the brass screen, but it did little to ease the chill in her heart as she watched him go.

Oh, God, she thought, wrapping her arms around her stomach. Is this what it was all about? This longing, this burning desire that threatened to consume? Two nights ago, she had found ecstasy in Lane's arms, and in so doing had lost her heart forever. If this was love, she hated it! Didn't want any part of it!

Her head dropped lower, and her hair fell forward in a shimmering cascade too pale to be called golden. She could no longer deny it. No matter how much she protested, her heart refused to listen.

She was in love with Lane Manning.

Circe, he had called her; well, perhaps that was true in one sense. When Circe discovered that Odysseus was able to resist her wiles—the only man in her experience to have done so—she fell in love with him.

Pity poor Circe, Julia thought in profound despair; Odysseus stayed with her for one year. All her spells, all her seductive charms had not been enough to hold him longer than that. . . .

chapter
fourteen

Emerging from the carriage, Julia paused before the two-story brick house. Except for the gleaming marble steps that shone whitely beneath a weak November sun, it was a rather plain structure. Several huge elms decorated the small front lawn, now looking as brown and as bare as the branches on the trees.

To the side of the brick walkway, a neatly lettered sign advised the onlooker that the residence was inhabited by Dr. Morris Blodgett. Julia had managed to elicit the name of the Manning family physician from April, who had casually mentioned during the course of a conversation that she had suffered a severe earache the previous winter.

Taking a deep breath, Julia now moved determinedly up the stairs and rang the bell. She had missed one period, but she had no other symptoms of pregnancy, a situation that both confused and alarmed her. After giving it much thought, she had decided to come here to the doctor's office, which was actually the front room of his house, and find out for certain before she said anything to anyone.

The door opened, and a kindly faced woman dressed in black bombazine and a floor-length white apron ushered her into the front room.

Some thirty minutes later, Julia sank into the straight-backed chair before the doctor's desk and stared at the man in disbelief.

"That's impossible," she breathed. "I've missed only one period. . . ."

Dr. Blodgett nodded. He was a tall man, with stoop shoulders that made him appear older than his sixty-two years, aided by a mane of white hair that was leonine in its disorder. "Nevertheless, Mrs. Manning, you are more than four months pregnant. It's not all that unusual to have a showing for the first three months."

"But I haven't had any nausea!" she insisted. "I feel fine."

His smile was benevolent. "Not every woman has morning sickness," he explained patiently. "Consider yourself fortunate that you are among the minority who experience no discomfort." His smile broadened as he saw that she was still having trouble accepting what he knew to be a fact. A teasing note crept into his voice. "Surely you have noticed that your clothes are becoming a bit tight around your waist?"

"Yes," Julia conceded with a slow nod. "But only for the past week or so. I thought that I was beginning to show early. . . ."

His laughter boomed as he slapped the arm of his chair. "Right on schedule, I'd say." He stood up, assisting her to her feet. "I suggest you return home and tell your husband the good news. You can expect to deliver around the second week of March. I'll come to see you in about six weeks. If you have any problems, however, send word to me, and I will come sooner.''

On the street a few minutes later, Julia headed for the waiting carriage, still feeling dazed.

It must have happened on her wedding night, she mused. Now that she thought back, she realized that the first three periods after her marriage were abnormally light, lasting only about two days. She had thought nothing of it, reasoning the change had to do with being married.

The prospect of having a baby was beginning to excite her, and for a time, as the carriage wended its way back to Manning House, Julia found herself thinking of names.

Before she reached home, however, her euphoria began to dim. Lane would be pleased, she had no doubt about that, but what of their personal relationship? Julia was sorry now that she had ever brought up the subject of Rosalind. The atmosphere had been strained between her and Lane since that night; in the past two weeks, he hadn't come to her bed once.

And now, when he learned of the child, she had no doubt that he would refrain from doing so until it was born.

That night, when she knew Lane was in his room and she was certain that Joseph had gone upstairs, Julia walked to the closed door, put her hand on the knob, then let it fall to her side again. For the moment, she stood there, uncertain as to whether she should just walk in or call out.

At last she knocked. Receiving permission to enter, she did so. Lane was seated in a chair, reading the newspaper. He had removed his jacket and cravat but was otherwise dressed.

As she came farther into the room, he put the newspaper

aside and got up, his face a curious mixture of surprise and concern.

"I . . . saw the doctor today," Julia said before he could speak.

Now there was only concern as he asked: "Is anything wrong? Are you ill?"

She shook her head. "I'm going to have a baby. . . ."

It took him several seconds to react, then his face brightened with anticipation. "This is marvelous news!" he exclaimed. Coming forward, he put an arm around her. "When is it to be?"

"In March. . . ." She saw his confusion and quickly explained.

"Well," he said with a delighted chuckle when she was through, "we have less than five months to prepare for the happy event." With an arm still around her, Lane headed toward her room, enthusiastically outlining plans for a nursery.

As solicitous as if she had suddenly become an invalid, Lane helped her into bed. When he straightened, smiling down at her, Julia could see how his face glowed with love. With a pang of sadness that momentarily dimmed her own happiness, she knew very well that the emotion was not for herself; it was for his unborn child.

The next morning when Lane broke the news of Julia's pregnancy to the rest of the family, April and Hester reacted with squeals of delight. Willa's reaction was a nod of cold approval.

Finally a show of approval! Julia thought to herself, feeling a resentment she took care to conceal. Willa's look said that at last Julia was doing what she was "best suited for." Then she became aware that Lane was beaming at her, a broad grin crinkling the corners of his eyes. He looked so happy, Julia couldn't help but offer a smile of her own.

The strain between them dissipated as if it had never existed. It was as though they had both reached an unspoken agreement to pretend that their discussion about Rosalind had never taken place. Lane became so attentive and considerate that Julia was almost able to make herself believe they hadn't had a disagreement, and it was only at night, in the darkness of her room, that doubt assailed her.

Now hardly a day passed that Lane didn't return home with a gift for her; nor did he by any means confine himself to jewelry. There were lace fans, a gold enamel needle case, a clock decorated with Meissen birds, a tortoiseshell music box, and a mother-of-pearl bonbonnière filled with her favorite chocolates.

The following weeks passed swiftly. Julia assisted Leah and some of the other members of the committee in the momentous task of compiling a complete inventory of the exhibits, some of which were now being stored in Lane's warehouse. Almost every day more were arriving via ships or trains. Julia, still feeling no discomfort, participated gladly, knowing that very soon she would have to curtail her activities.

One Saturday afternoon, as she and Leah drove into Fairmount Park, Julia leaned forward to peer outside, a look of bewilderment of her face.

It was far too quiet!

"Isn't anyone working today?" she asked, turning to look at Leah, who also appeared to be surprised by the lack of activity.

"Construction must have been stopped," she speculated, "although I can't imagine why." She regarded Julia with a furrowed brow. "Perhaps Elizabeth will know." She again looked outside and heaved a sigh of relief. "The workers are still at our pavilion. . . ."

Elizabeth Gillespie did indeed know why construction had been abruptly halted.

"The Centennial Committee has exhausted its funds," she told them.

After a moment of stunned silence, Leah asked: "Can more be raised?"

"Not in the usual way," the woman answered. "There is not enough time. They need better than a million dollars, and they need it right away."

"But what are they going to do?" Julia cried out. "Surely they don't mean to abandon the Exhibition?"

Elizabeth Gillespie sighed and shook her head. "I certainly hope it doesn't come to that," she replied slowly, sounding concerned in spite of her words. "Dr. Loring has known for some time now that the money is running out. A few weeks ago, he sent a letter to President Grant in hopes that he might be able to persuade Congress to come up with the necessary funds."

"More than a million dollars?" Leah exclaimed, her green eyes going wide. "They will never agree to that!"

"We can only hope. . . ." Elizabeth murmured. "The President has agreed to come to Philadelphia to review the situation. That, at least, is a step in the right direction."

"Even if the President agrees, that doesn't mean Congress will vote to fund a private undertaking!" Julia protested. As the full meaning of the situation made itself known to her, she was filled with a feeling of helplessness. The work, the preparation, the concerted effort of thousands of people, all of it now in danger of coming to naught!

"And what of our committee?" Leah put in with an

anxious look at Elizabeth. "Will it be necessary for us to halt construction as well?"

For the first time, the woman smiled. "Not at all. We have all the money we need. If you recall, we are entirely independent of the Centennial Committee."

Leah chewed her lip. "Even if they get the money, they will never finish in time if the delay continues," she lamented.

"It will be close," Elizabeth agreed dourly. "We will all know the answer to that in a few days, however. President Grant is coming here this Wednesday evening, and he is bringing several senators with him. Dr. Loring is planning a dinner for them to be held in the Horticultural Building. Except for some interior painting, it is now completed." At Leah's look of surprise, she added, "He feels the President might be more impressed if he could see what had already been accomplished. Mr. Grant has, thankfully, offered one note of encouragement. He knows that the country is still reeling from the depression of 'seventy-three and he has told Dr. Loring that the Exhibition might be the very thing needed to bolster morale. I sincerely believe that he is on our side and will do everything he can to assist us."

As it was to turn out, the senators in no way shared the optimism of Elizabeth Gillespie. They predicted dire repercussions should Congress set a precedent of this sort. Dr. Loring's carefully staged dinner turned into a battleground of opposing forces.

In the end, however, they did agree to at least put it to a vote.

The Centennial Committee, at this point, could do nothing but wait for the outcome. A pall of enforced quiet blanketed Fairmount Park, the stillness broken only by the continued construction of the Women's Pavilion, prodded onward by the dauntless will of Elizabeth Gillespie.

By the middle of December, even Julia couldn't doubt Dr. Blodgett's estimate as to the length of her pregnancy. All she had to do was look at herself in the mirror. With a small sigh of regret, she knew that the time had come for her to remain in seclusion.

On a particularly frosty afternoon just two days before Christmas, Lane entered her sitting room, carrying a large box, his rosy cheeks attesting to the fact that he had entered the house only minutes ago.

Surprised, Julia glanced at the clock; it was not yet four o'clock. "What are you doing home so early?" she asked him.

"Do I need a reason?" he retorted with a laugh. Placing the box on a table, he removed the cover and threw it carelessly to the floor.

"Ohh. . . ." Julia put her hands to her cheeks and stared in amazement as Lane removed not one, but two fur cloaks from the box, then held them up for her inspection. Both were full-length and hooded, one sable, the other chinchilla.

Julia was at a loss for words. Dropping the chinchilla onto the sofa, Lane came forward and draped the sable around her shoulders.

Turning to him, Julia's eyes sparkled with tears. "Lane, you shouldn't have," she protested. "You're far too generous. How can I possibly choose. . . ?"

"Choose?" He chuckled. Putting his hands on each side of the collar, he pulled her close and planted a light kiss on her nose. "Did you really think I brought them home for you to decide which one you want? They're both bought and paid for. I'll not have you and my child shivering through the winter!"

Biting her lip, Julia turned away, longing to tell him that there was only one thing she wanted from him: his love. But she knew very well that one could not ask for love; if it was not freely given, it was worthless.

Lane gave her a look filled with concern. "You are feeling all right, aren't you? Shall I send for the doctor?"

With the back of her hand, Julia brushed the droplets from her cheek and summoned a bright smile. "There's nothing wrong. It's just that . . . I'm so happy." Despite her effort, her voice cracked with a sob. *I love you, you foolish man!* she wanted to scream, but could not bring herself to say the words. It would only embarrass him; even, God forbid, make him feel as though he would have to profess love, whether he meant it or not. Then she would never know.

Lane put his arms around her, resting his chin in the softness of her hair. "I'll never understand why happiness brings tears to a woman's eyes." Inclining his head, he grinned at her. "Do you?"

"No," she responded in a small voice.

Drawing back, he rubbed her cheek with his fingertips. "Why don't you rest awhile before supper? I'll send Mary in to straighten up." He gave her another kiss. "I'll see you downstairs."

Nodding, she watched him go. Then her tears came in earnest. How could a man be as sensitive and as astute as Lane was and not be able to recognize the love she felt for him?

Or . . . perhaps he did know. Perhaps he knew and was able to respond only with kindness. The thought was chilling in its implications. Maybe that was why he continually showered her with expensive gifts.

It was all he could offer. . . .

chapter
fifteen

Well before midnight on this New Year's Eve, the last day of 1875, every building in the city, regardless of whether it was residential or commercial, turned on its gaslights, and flares were lighted. The resulting brightness gave one the impression that daylight had returned.

Along Chestnut Street, the crowd was so thick there was barely room enough for people to move. As there was no hope of taking the carriage into the throng of revelers, Andrew halted it on a side street.

Willa, however, refused to get out, sorry now that she had let the girls talk her into this madness. The weather was bad enough. It was so cold and damp that she felt chilled to the bone; but she wasn't about to set foot on that overcrowded street. A person could be trampled to death!

"Oh, Mama! Please come with us," April begged, trying not to shiver, fearful that if her mother noticed, she would be forced to stay behind and miss all the fun.

"I have no intention of getting into that mob of rabble-rousers!'' Willa declared emphatically, pulling the fur carriage robe closer about her. She waved a gloved hand at her daughter. ''You go along. I'll wait here!''

''Are you sure, Mrs. Manning?'' Andrew asked, looking up at her with a frown. He had already helped April out of the carriage and now, as an afterthought, did the same for Hester. ''I don't feel right about leaving you here alone. . . .''

''I'll be fine!'' Willa snapped, grimacing as another cannon was set off.

''Perhaps I ought to take you back home,'' Andrew shouted over the din.

April tugged on his arm. ''It's almost midnight, Andrew! We cannot possibly go home and be back in time.''

He smiled down at her. The hood of her fur cloak hid her hair and framed her lovely face. Her cheeks were rosy with excitement as well as pinked by the cold air.

''All right,'' he said with an indulgent laugh. ''But I want you to hold on to me! If we do get separated, I want you to come directly back here!''

''I will, Andrew. I promise.''

April linked her arm around his elbow. On his other side, Hester did the same, achingly aware of how hard and muscled his arm felt, even beneath the fabric of a jacket and coat.

Andrew took a deep breath. ''All right. Hold tight; here we go. . . .''

Amid much shoving and pushing, they were able to make their way a distance along Chestnut Street. Parades were in progress, and men dressed as clowns or Indians cavorted and mimed for the cheering crowd. People who were not even in the parades were banging on drums, blowing on horns, or rasping on fiddles, creating a sound that bore no relation whatsoever to music.

On the stroke of twelve, every bell rang and every cannon in the city was fired again and again. Boats and trains joined the melee, their steam whistles blaring. At Independence Hall, the bell was rung exactly one hundred times, once for each year of the nation's existence. Fireworks were set off, and there was a sudden surge of people as everyone pushed for an advantageous viewpoint.

The crowd, boisterous and rowdy to begin with, went wild.

Try as he might, Andrew found himself unable to maintain his grip when a burly man plowed into him, almost knocking him from his feet. When he regained his balance, he peered around him in rising panic, shouting April's name.

After a minute that seemed an eternity, he spied both girls about five feet away. They were clinging to each other, both of them laughing, and didn't appear to be in any imminent danger.

With much difficulty, Andrew began to elbow his way toward them, shouting at them to stay in place, although he was certain they couldn't hear him.

Finally, he battled his way to their side. Extending his arms, Andrew experienced a moment of complete disorientation. The fur cloaks that April and Hester were wearing were almost identical. Their voices were lost in the deafening crescendo of noise that seemed to have no end.

Andrew couldn't tell which one of them was April!

The anxious moment lasted only a second, until April threw herself into his arms, the familiar scent of her perfume making itself known to him.

With one arm tightly around April, Andrew grabbed Hester with his free hand, and said shakily, "That's enough! We're getting out of here!"

* * *

At Manning House, as elsewhere, light blazed from every window.

From her sitting room, Julia peered outside, seeing a spray of fireworks shoot up into the sky. The effect, however, was lost in the glow from all the other lights.

With a deep sigh, she turned to Lane, watching as he vigorously applied the poker to the logs in the hearth. The flames leapt higher, and Lane put the poker down, brushing his hands together.

"Oh, Lane," Julia said, coming toward him. "Can't we go out? Just for a little while?"

"Absolutely not!" Lane retorted with a sharp shake of his head. "You have no idea what the crowds are like out there," he went on when she pouted. "No carriage can get through the streets, and I will not even consider having you jostled."

Julia emitted another sigh, knowing he was right. It would be unwise to take chances in her condition. "Very well. But I would feel better if you were to join your mother and the girls. There's no need for you to miss the festivities."

"I've given the servants the night off, and I have no intention of leaving you alone," he declared with a firmness she knew could not be questioned. "Andrew is escorting April, so they'll all be well looked after." He glanced out the window and frowned. "Well, with all the hootin' and hollerin' going on out there, I guess it would be pointless to try to sleep right now." Facing her again, he smiled at her continued disappointment. "Tell you what I'll do," he said, making his voice cheerful. "I'll go downstairs and make us both some hot chocolate, then we'll play a game of chess. We'll have our own celebration. You do remember how to play, don't you?" he asked teasingly.

"I remember," she answered bleakly, still upset to have missed the excitement. There would be other New Year's Eves, of course; but there wouldn't be another one like this for another hundred years!

By one o'clock, the noise had abated, though by no means had it come to an end. Willa, Hester, and April arrived home shortly after, and as they passed by the door, Lane got up and walked toward the hall.

"There you are! Did you all have a good time?" he called out.

Willa, looking frazzled, her hat askew, mumbled something inaudible and kept on going in the direction of her bedroom. But April and Hester came in, each of them talking at once.

"So many people . . ."

"So much noise . . ."

"We were almost crushed to death!"

Lane laughed and raised a hand, and both girls took a breath as they calmed down.

"Oh, Julia!" April exclaimed, as she took off her hat. "I wish you could have seen it. The lights . . ."

"Every building in town has them turned on," Hester finished. "It looked like noon instead of midnight."

"I was most impressed with Carpenters' Hall," April went on. "They had their gas jets arranged to spell out 'The Nation's Birthplace.'"

Julia got up from her chair. "Oh, how I wish I had been there to see it! Still, having you tell me about it is the next best thing. . . ."

"But not tonight," Lane declared, putting an arm around her. "It's late, and it's about time we all went to bed. New Year's Eve is over for another year."

The revelery that would mark the country's one hundredth birthday did not end with the New Year's celebration, however; it had only begun.

The following Saturday, Andrew was to take April to the Academy of Music. That morning, April woke up with a light-headedness that left her feeling queasy. Rather than dissipating, the feeling increased during the afternoon. By evening, she knew she would be unable to go out.

She lay on her bed, curled up into a ball, and viewed Hester. "I don't feel well at all; even my head aches." Contrary to her words, April put a hand to her throat, aware of a certain soreness when she swallowed. "I think I must be getting another cold. Hes, you'd better tell Andrew that I can't make it tonight."

"I will, dear," Hester replied, then gave her sister a worried frown. She did look pale. "Let me get you a glass of blackberry brandy." Before April could protest, Hester hurried from the room and returned a short time later, holding a crystal wineglass. "Here, drink this. Perhaps it will ease your stomach."

April smiled wanly. "Oh, Hes. You know brandy puts me to sleep. . . ."

"And that's just what you need," Hester retorted with a short nod of her head. "A good night's sleep."

Dutifully, April drank, then rested a hand on Hester's arm. "You will tell Andrew. . . ?"

"I will, dear." Hester took the glass from April's hand and put it on a table. "Please get some rest." Seating herself on the edge of the bed, she brushed April's dark curls from her forehead, relieved to find the skin cool beneath her touch. Among other things, April was prone to raging fevers. "I'll sit right here until you fall asleep."

"You used to do that when we were children," April

reminisced. "Do you remember, Hes? When I had a bad dream and was afraid of the dark?"

"I remember. . . ."

April leaned back against the pillow and closed her eyes. In only minutes she was fast asleep.

Hester got up, intending to send word to Andrew. Then she paused, glancing at April's wardrobe.

Dare I? she wondered.

Determination came to her with the stealth of a cat. In her heart she knew she would dare this and more to be alone with Andrew.

Quickly, Hester crossed the room and opened the door to April's wardrobe. Every dress was meticulously arranged according to morning, evening, or formal wear. After a moment's consideration, she selected a blue-and-white silk dress. It was, she knew, Andrew's favorite. She'd often heard him tell April so.

Removing her own dress, she donned April's. Going to the mirror, she critically scrutinized her image; even she thought she was viewing April. When they were children, she and April would occasionally try to change places, mischievously trying to fool the other members of the family. It rarely worked, though, because April always gave herself away. While it was incredibly easy for Hester to adopt April's breathless tone of voice and her demure, almost effacing manner, April was unable to imitate her sister's somewhat authoritative tone and brisk way of walking.

Well, April wouldn't be around tonight to give her away, Hester thought, glancing at the bed to make certain April was still asleep. She had no real concern, however. Even when she was feeling well, brandy made April as sleepy as a cat dozing beneath a warm summer sun.

A few steps took her to April's dressing table, where she

put on a few dabs of the lilac perfume her sister favored. She wrinkled her nose, much preferring her own jasmine scent. Opening April's enameled jewel box, her hand hovered over the contents for a long moment; then she smiled, selecting the opal pendant that Andrew had given to April on her birthday. Finally, she took April's fur cloak and draped it over her arm.

No twinge of conscience presented itself as Hester left the room. It was only for a few hours, she told herself. And only this one time. If she could not have Andrew, she would at least have this one night to remember.

Coming down the stairs, Hester hesitated as she saw her mother emerging from the drawing room.

First test, she thought uneasily, steeling herself, thankful to see that her mother wasn't wearing her spectacles. She descended slowly, one hand on the banister. April always did this. She herself was inclined to trip down the stairs in a hurried fashion that always drew a rebuke from her mother.

Pausing, Willa looked up. "Oh, there you are, April. I was about to send Nancy after you. Andrew's been waiting for ten minutes. . . ."

"I'm sorry, Mama. . . ." The voice sounded perfect even to her own ears. "I just couldn't decide what to wear."

"Well, don't dawdle! You'll be late for the opera." She motioned toward the drawing room. "Andrew's in there. Where is Hester?"

"She's asleep, Mama. She was feeling . . . indisposed, and decided to retire early."

"Hummph!" Willa dismissed the complaint. "Most likely it was that second piece of pie she indulged herself with at the supper table. Your sister has a most unladylike appetite."

"Yes, Mama."

Hester held her breath as her mother came up the stairs, releasing it only when Willa passed by without so much as a glance in her direction.

Entering the drawing room a few moments later, Hester experienced a moment of panic. She had thought that Andrew would be alone. Instead, she saw that Leah Carlyle and Julia were in the room. Where her brother was, she had no idea; probably he was in the study having a brandy and cigar with William. Wherever he was, he would certainly be joining the rest of them at any minute. The more people she met, the greater was her chance of being exposed. The Carlyles didn't concern her in the least; even Julia, she felt certain, would not see through her impersonation. But Lane . . .

Nervously, Hester cast a quick glance at Andrew. She had a dismaying mental vision of Andrew denouncing her in a loud voice that would summon the household to witness her disgrace.

Andrew, however, jumped to his feet at her entrance, his face brightening as it always did at the sight of April, and Hester expelled a sigh of relief.

"I'm sorry I'm late. . . ." she said, thinking how handsome he was in the dark green frock coat, beneath which his shoulders seemed so broad.

Coming forward, Andrew pressed her hands. "You're worth waiting for," he whispered, then grinned as his eyes swept over her from head to toe. "I'm glad you wore that dress. You look so lovely in it."

She smiled and lowered her eyes, afraid that he might see the longing in their depths. "Thank you, Andrew."

"Andrew is right!" Leah called out from where she was sitting on the sofa beside Julia. "You do look lovely, April.

I understand that you are going to see the presentation of *Tristan and Isolde* this evening. . . ."

Slowly, Hester nodded.

"I'm sure you're going to enjoy it," Leah went on in an enthusiastic way that was maddening to Hester. "William and I attended last night's performance. It was splendid!"

"I am looking forward to it," Hester murmured, grateful when Andrew moved forward to take the fur cloak from her grasp.

"Well, we'd best get going." He assisted her with the cloak, then put on his coat and hat.

Outside, the temperature was close to freezing. Each expelled breath turned into a steamy little puff that hovered on the frigid air for an instant before dissipating. Earlier in the day, clouds that had dropped an icy rain on the city had now fled, leaving behind a black sky decorated with a multitude of diamond-bright stars that dazzled the eye.

As Nancy closed the front door behind them, Hester allowed herself to relax. She hadn't realized how tightly she had been holding herself until she felt her muscles protest against the enforced restriction she had inflicted on them.

Andrew had hired a carriage to take them to the American Academy of Music on Broad Street, as there was no convenient place to park it once they arrived at their destination.

After they had settled themselves, the vehicle moved forward. Gloved hands in her lap, fingers toying with the strings of her reticule, Hester listened to Andrew as he extolled the merits of the opera they were about to see. She was paying only enough attention to nod in the right places.

She was actually here, alone with Andrew, and couldn't believe that she had actually done this thing! Not that she was sorry; far from it. She knew that if she had taken the time to think it through, she would never have mustered the courage to act this way.

But then, what harm was there in it? Tomorrow she would, of course, have to explain to April. Her sister would not be angry; in fact, they would laugh about this little deception. She had no doubt that April would tease Andrew about it for a long time to come.

As for herself, Hester thought, turning to look at the man beside her, she would have a cherished memory to savor for the rest of her life.

chapter
sixteen

The carriage came to a halt. Broad Street was crowded with people: ladies bundled in fur cloaks, gentlemen in winter coats and beaver hats and boots that reflected a high polish beneath the glow of streetlights. There was still a trace of holiday gaiety in the air, the breeze carrying with it the silver sounds of jangling trappings and merry laughter.

"Come back for us at eleven-thirty," Andrew instructed the driver as they got out. Hester loved the forceful tone of his voice. He was so much in command! She glowed beneath his smile as they began to walk. "Hold on to me," he said, "There may be patches of ice on the ground. . . ."

A moment later they entered the front door of the rather plain brick building. Inside, plainness gave way to grandeur.

Built in 1857, the Academy of Music was a study in opulence, a delight to all those privileged to be within its confines. No expense had been spared in its decor or its furnishings; and it showed.

In the large, plushly carpeted lobby, Andrew's hand cupped

Hester's elbow as they ascended the broad, curving staircase that led to the balcony as well as to the private boxes, one of which Andrew had reserved for their use this evening.

Upstairs, a uniformed attendant opened the door for them, and they entered the cubicle.

Seating herself in one of the cushioned chairs that had been richly upholstered in crimson and gold, Hester sighed in contentment as Andrew slipped the fur cloak from her shoulders and draped it over the back of the chair. This was where she belonged, an arm's length away from the man she loved.

Settling herself comfortably, Hester viewed her surroundings. Across from her were the counterparts of the private box in which they were seated, each separated by a towering Corinthian pillar.

The theater was crowded on this Saturday night. A subdued rustle of satin and taffeta blended with hushed voices of expectation as the members of the orchestra took their places.

Raising her head slightly, Hester looked upward. The first time she had been here, about three years ago, she had been fascinated by the domed ceiling. It was painted to resemble a night sky, complete with stars. Only the magnificent chandelier in the center gave lie to the illusion.

Now, as she glanced up at the ceiling, Hester smiled, admitting to herself that it still held a certain fascination for her.

They were no sooner settled when the lights dimmed and the audience stilled with anticipation.

Andrew leaned forward as the orchestra began the prelude, and, from the corner of her eye, Hester watched him, her heart filled with the love she felt for him.

So quietly that one would have thought it was accomplished without mechanical aid, the heavy velvet curtain rose to reveal the huge stage that was ninety feet wide, fifty feet high, and fully one hundred feet deep. Long moments passed, however, before the opera gained Hester's attention.

Finally, she directed her eyes to the stage, seeing the replica of a ship. Isolde had commanded her servant to bring her a death potion and was now receiving, instead, the substituted love potion. Hester knew that shortly Tristan and Isolde would toast each other, but instead of drinking death, they would be filled with passion and love for each other forever.

Unaware that she did so, Hester released a deep sigh. It was the part she liked best. She really wasn't an enthusiastic operagoer, though April was; but she liked this one, liked the romance, the pageantry, the bittersweet culmination of a love that was never meant to be.

The music filled the theater. Andrew was engrossed. That was all right with Hester. She was content just to be with him, the dimness of the theater providing a soft intimacy that allowed her to glance at his handsome profile from time to time. If only this night would never end.

By the time Hester again directed her attention to the performance, Isolde was cradling Tristan in her arms, her voice raised in testimony to their undying love.

Fumbling in the depths of her reticule, Hester located a lace handkerchief and proceeded to mop the corners of her eyes. So sad. How she wished the lovers could have lived happily ever after. She was about to replace her handkerchief when Andrew's voice gave her a start.

"You always cry at this part. . . ."

Bending close to her, his whisper was in itself a caress, infused with a tenderness that made her catch her breath.

Hester swallowed. Did April cry at the end? She really

didn't know. "I'm not the only one," she responded shakily as Andrew squeezed her hand.

The curtain descended, and the audience gave the performers an enthusiastic accolade that continued for more than ten minutes.

"That was one of the best performances I've ever seen!" Andrew exclaimed as the lights brightened. Hester nodded her agreement as he helped her don her cloak.

When they were once again seated in the hired carriage, Hester remained silent until it had wended its way several blocks from the theater. The evening was over, the idyllic interlude at an end. Hester couldn't accept it.

Impulsively, she blurted, "Andrew . . . I've had such a lovely evening, and I'm not in the least bit tired. Could we stop by your house?"

He frowned and gave her a quick glance. "It's getting late, April."

Slipping her hand beneath his arm, Hester rested her head on his broad shoulder. "Just for a little while," she whispered, making her tone as imploring as she could. "I've never seen where you live." She knew this because April had mused on the subject once or twice.

Turning his head, Andrew kissed her brow, and Hester went weak. "I guess it will be all right." Leaning forward, he tapped on the window and instructed the driver to take them to Arch Street, where his house was located. He lived alone, though a maid came in during the day to clean and to make his evening meal.

"Here we are," Andrew said a few minutes later. Getting out, he went around the carriage to open the door for her, instructing the driver to wait.

The night was calm and clear and cold. A pale crescent moon shed only a faint light over the land. The hour was late enough that they were alone with only the night sounds to break the stillness.

Inside, Andrew escorted her through the rooms on the first floor. By comparison to Manning House, it was small but cozy and well furnished.

Finally, they came into the front parlor. Going to the hearth, Andrew stoked the banked fire and added a few more logs. Crimson color flared to tint the white walls with a rosy hue.

Moving slowly, Hester came to stand beside him. A sudden heat flooded through her. The fire? His nearness? She didn't know what had caused it, but she did know that her cheeks had flushed.

"It seems like such a long time until we can be married," she noted with a tremulous sigh.

Andrew's arm went around her, his brown eyes searching the depths of hers. "I count every hour," he said huskily, overcome as he always was when she was close to him. His hands trembled as he placed them on her cheeks. "I love you, April. I can never tell you how much. Each day that I don't see you is a wasted day. . . ."

"As it is for me," Hester replied quickly. Unable to resist the moment, she put her arms around his neck. "I love you more than anything in the world. . . ."

Andrew's lips brushed hers in what was to be the gentle kiss he always gave her; instead, to his surprise, she clung to him fiercely, pressing her body close against him, her mouth demanding more.

For a moment, Andrew was startled, but the scent of her perfume combined with the softness of her sweet body made his senses reel.

"April . . ." he moaned as she nuzzled his ear. "I think I should take you home now. . . ."

"My home is with you, my darling."

Hester had no trouble in maintaining the charade of a breathless voice. The breath seemed to have been forced from her lungs. Her body was filled with such longing she felt certain she would die if Andrew did not make love to her. For this one night, Andrew belonged to her. Pressing her mouth to his, Hester slowly sank to the sofa, pulling him down with her.

For endless minutes they kissed, until at last Andrew drew back, roused to the point where he was shaking with his need.

"April ... I don't think ..." He fell silent when she put her fingertips to his lips.

"We'll be married in only a few weeks," she reminded him. "I don't want to wait, Andrew. I want you now." She paused, then asked, "Don't you want me?"

"Oh, my God!" Andrew crushed her to him. "I want you more than life itself. ..."

"Then this night will be ours, my darling."

Without further ado, Hester began to remove her clothes, her body tingling with an anticipation that left her feeling giddy. She stretched out on the sofa, her body glowing in the firelight.

Andrew stared in mute wonder at the splendor that was his darling April. He took off his clothes and lay beside her, for the moment content to hold her close to him, flesh against flesh.

In a dreamy state that bordered upon intoxication, Hester listened to his loving endearments, and the fact that he was using her sister's name didn't faze her in the least. It was her body he was caressing, her body that had set him aflame with passion.

"Oh, April," Andrew whispered. "I never realized just how beautiful you are."

Gently, Andrew's hand caressed a small, perfect breast, slid down to her tapering waist, and paused on the swell of her hip. Bending forward, he kissed the hollow of her throat, aware of how her pulse fluttered like a captured bird beneath his lips. Then his eager mouth sought the cleft between her breasts and trailed a hot flame as it came to rest on a taut, rose-tipped nipple.

"Andrew . . ." Hester moaned, running her hands along his well-muscled back.

The urgent tone of her voice set his loins afire, and Andrew could think of nothing except possessing her. He eased himself on top of her fragrant softness. Even the light, sharp pain that she felt when Andrew thrust into her could not dampen her ardor as Hester arched her body to meet and meld with his passion.

They were aware of nothing but each other. Release came to them both with shattering impact, and for a time, Andrew collapsed against her, feeling as though he were incapable of movement.

They clung to each other for long minutes until their heartbeat slowed and their breath calmed. Andrew toyed with a glossy black curl.

"Your hair is as dark as a night sky. . . ." He kissed the silky strand, inhaling the elusive scent of lilac she emanated.

"Is this the first time you've noticed that?" Raising herself up on an elbow, she stared at him. "Look at me, Andrew!" Hester said in her normal voice. "Tell me what you see. . . ." Whatever the consequences, whatever the price to be paid, she knew she could never let him go.

At first, only the words registered, and he answered softly, "I see the most beautiful woman in the world." Then he paused as he realized what he had just heard. So quickly did he draw away from her, he almost tumbled them both from the couch. Sitting up, he continued to stare at her, his face paling with the shock of recognition. "Oh, my God!" he exclaimed in a choked voice. "Hester!"

She gave him a lazy smile and a slow nod. "Yes. April doesn't know," she went on quickly, anticipating his question. "She wasn't feelilng well and is safe in bed, sound asleep." She sat up, bent toward him. "It was the only way, Andrew," she said earnestly. "The only way to make you see what a terrible mistake you are making. . . ."

Getting up, Andrew hastily reached for his clothes, his hands shaking with a feeling too great to be called anger, causing his motions to be clumsy and awkward.

"Get dressed! And, by God, if you ever mention this to anyone, I'll . . ." He clamped his teeth together against his rage, fearing he would strike her.

"Andrew, I meant everything I've said to you tonight! I love you. . . ."

"And I love your sister!" came the sharp retort. "I meant every word I said, too. But it wasn't you that I was talking to!"

Hester was silent for a long moment, studying him with an intense look. "Are you sure, Andrew?" she asked quietly. "In your own heart, are you really very sure of that?"

His eyes brightened with renewed anger. "What are you saying?" he hissed, bringing his face closer to hers.

She was sitting there, weight on one buttock and the palm of her left hand, her small breasts thrust forward to catch the fire glow. Her black hair, tousled and loosened from its confines during their lovemaking, threaded its way in a dark cloud about her face and shoulders.

Viewing her, Andrew's hands clenched into fists. That she was beautiful he could not deny. As beautiful as a deadly serpent. . . .

Hester didn't flinch at his threatening attitude. "April would never have done this, and you know it! You know it, Andrew!"

He straightened, anger turning cold. "You're right about that, at least. April doesn't hold herself cheap!" Picking up her clothes, he flung them at her. "Get dressed!"

Tears welled in her eyes. Had what they just shared meant so little to him? Hester reached out an imploring hand. "Andrew—"

Roughly, he slapped her hand. "Damn you!"

Andrew presented his back to her, and after a moment Hester rose to put on her clothes, noticing that he never once turned to look at her.

The trip back to Manning House was made in silence. Even when Hester got out of the carriage, Andrew refused to speak to her. She knew, though, that he would never speak of what had taken place between them any more than she would.

But he would remember this night; of that, Hester was certain. And when his anger cooled, perhaps his ardor would rekindle, and he would finally realize that he was in love with the wrong woman.

The lights were lit in the drawing room, and Hester could hear voices. She had hoped that everyone would be asleep by now, but obviously the Carlyles had stayed longer than they normally did when they came to visit. Hester tiptoed upstairs to her room, afraid that everyone would be able to tell what had happened just by looking at her tearstained face.

She entered quietly. April was just a mound beneath the covers.

After undressing, Hester crept into bed, but knew she would find no sleep.

Hearing footsteps in the hall a few minutes later, Hester held herself very still. When her mother opened the door to peer inside, Hester closed her eyes until she left.

Hester was uncertain as to how much time had passed, or how long she had been hearing the sound of April's irregular breathing, but it burst into her awareness with a suddenness that made her eyes go wide. With a gasp, she sat bolt upright in bed.

"April?" Her voice was a jagged whisper that sliced through the darkness, to be greeted by a silence broken only by the eerie noise that had first captured her attention. Fear swept through her in an icy wave, setting her heart to hammer painfully in her breast. "April!" Jumping out of bed, Hester ran across the room, lit the light, and stared down at the slim form.

April's skin was an unhealthy blue, and she appeared to be unconscious. In rising panic, Hester noticed that her sister's chest was rising and falling in an exaggerated manner, as though she was straining for air.

"*Mama!*"

Her scream rent the stillness with a piercing, devastating urgency, causing everyone who heard it to come running at top speed.

Lane, who had been on his way up to his room, reached Hester first.

"My God, Hester! What is it?" Almost stumbling in his haste to reach her side, he grabbed her by the shoulders, thoroughly alarmed at the sight of her white face.

Hester couldn't speak and only pointed a trembling finger at April.

"What's wrong?" Willa burst into the room just then. She had her nightgown on but hadn't taken the time to don a wrapper. Brushing past Hester, who was rigid in her terror, she went to April's side. Bending over, she placed a hand on her daughter's forehead. It was cool and damp. The absence of fever, however, did little to calm her.

Kneeling by the bed, Lane turned to his mother, his own face ashen. "Send for Dr. Blodgett immediately. Tell him to get here as fast as he can."

Willa wasted no time asking futile questions.

When Julia entered the room a moment later, Lane hastily ushered her out to the hall again with firm instructions for her to wait downstairs. Then he sent his mother and sister out of the room as well.

The next twenty minutes seemed an eternity to them all.

Only when the doctor arrived did Lane leave April's side. With a worried look at the girl, he went downstairs to join the others.

Hester, still in her nightgown and barefooted, hands clenched at her waist, paced about the room like a caged cat, her mind filled with only one tormenting thought: if she had been in her room where she belonged, April would have received help earlier. What if April died because of the delay?

Pausing, she buried her face in her hands and began to weep uncontrollably, a harsh and grating sound that tore at Willa's nerves.

"For heaven's sake, Hester!" she exclaimed, gripping the arms of her chair and glowering at her daughter. "Do not lose control of yourself. This is difficult enough without you making it worse!"

Pushing herself up from the chair in which she had been sitting, Julia went to the distraught girl and put an arm around her shaking shoulders. "Come, Hester," she said quietly. "Please sit down." Firmly, she propelled Hester to the nearest chair and gently pushed her down into it.

Still upset, Willa turned to look at Lane. He was standing by the doorway, eyes riveted to the stairs. "Did the doctor give you any indication of what it might be?" she asked him.

"No," he sighed, not moving from his vigil.

"Well, you'd think he was smart enough to know just by looking at her," she muttered crossly.

When the doctor entered the parlor awhile later, his grave bearing caused them all a feeling of dread.

"Diphtheria. . . ." he murmured quietly, sitting down heavily.

"How serious?" Lane asked from a throat that was suddenly tight with apprehension.

Dr. Blodgett shook his head. "There are no cases to be viewed otherwise. She must be kept in complete isolation. No one"—he paused to give them all a stern look—"no one is to be allowed in her room. I will send a nurse to see to her needs."

"But she has no fever. . . ." Willa protested, composure slipping.

Dr. Blodgett nodded at the observation. "Fever is not an indication of diphtheria. As a matter of fact, the temperature usually is below normal at the beginning. That's what makes this disease so insidious. In its early stages, it is difficult to diagnose. . . ."

"Then how can you be certain?" Hester demanded in a loud voice. Her eyes were bright with unshed tears and with a fear that left her feeling faint.

"I am certain," Dr. Blodgett stated flatly, sounding a

trifle annoyed at being questioned. "Had I examined your sister yesterday, or even this morning, I might not have been. But when the false membrane, as it is called, makes its appearance in the throat, diagnosis is clear-cut." He got up and stood facing them all, hands clasped behind him. "Her youth and general state of health are in her favor. I must warn you, however, that convalescence is very prolonged in these cases. She must be considered to be in danger of cardiac failure for the next four weeks. She must stay in bed for at least this length of time. And I mean complete bed rest!"

Slowly, Willa shook her head from side to side. "I don't understand it! April was all right two hours ago. She went out this evening, and I looked in on her before I went to my room. There was nothing wrong then. . . ."

"As I've told you, the onset of this illness is a gradual thing."

"Dr. Blodgett . . ." Hester spoke in a shaky voice as she got to her feet. "She's going to be all right, isn't she? I mean, she's not going to . . ." she broke off, unable to speak the word.

The doctor averted his gaze and passed a weary hand across his mouth. Questions like that always left him feeling uneasy. "I can't answer that, Hester," he replied at last in a low voice. "For now, it's in the hands of God."

Putting her face in her hands, Hester began to weep again, this time softly, a mournful sound of despair. Moving quickly to her side, Lane gathered his sister to him, holding her close. Despite the unspoken reassurance, there was no comfort for Hester, who was ridden with a guilt that formed in the pit of her stomach like a heavy stone.

That very night, Hester moved into a guest room directly across the hall from the room she shared with April, refusing to go farther than that. When Willa insisted she take a room at the end of the hall, Hester screamed at her in such a frenzied fashion that Willa threw up her hands and retreated. There was, she knew, no reasoning with Hester when she went into one of her tantrums.

For the next five days, except for meals, Hester refused to leave the guest room. During the day, she left the door open and sat on the chaise, positioning it so she could keep an eye on the door across the hall. The only time it opened was when the day nurse was relieved by the night nurse. Their answers, when Hester eagerly sought news of her sister, were maddeningly alike. "She's doing fine," they would each report with a solemn nod of a white-capped head.

On the sixth day, Willa's patience was at an end.

"For heaven's sake, Hester!" she exclaimed. "Do stop moping about. The world has not yet come to an end!"

"How can you talk like that?" Hester retorted hotly. "April could be dying!"

"She's not dying! She's doing fine. . . ."

Hester gave her mother a withering look. "You got that from the nurses," she observed scathingly. "You don't really know!"

Pausing, Willa regarded her daughter in puzzlement. That the girls were close she didn't have to be told; yet April had been sick in the past, too many times to count, actually, and Hester had never acted in this manner before. Willa put her thoughts into words.

"But not like this!" Hester shouted. "You saw what she looked like. . . ." For herself, Hester couldn't seem to erase from her mind that last image of April's face as she struggled for air. Wringing her hands, she let out a soft moan.

Skirts swirling with her exasperated movements, Willa

crossed the hall and knocked on the door. It was opened a moment later by the day nurse, a strongly built woman named Rose Fullerton.

Frowning, she peered at Willa. "You can't come in here. . . ."

"I know," Willa said quickly, beckoning to Hester. "Just open the door so that we can see April."

The woman hesitated, seemed about to refuse, but at the sight of Hester's pleading eyes, reluctantly swung the door wider.

Hand on the door frame, Hester looked inside, almost fearful of what she might see. "April?"

April's dark head turned on the pillow, and she managed a smile.

"How are you feeling?" Hester was unaware that she had whispered the words, but the room was so quiet she felt compelled to speak softly.

"Much better, Hes. . . ."

The voice was weak, the face far too pale; nevertheless Hester took heart.

"That's enough now!" the nurse said sternly. Putting a hand on Hester's shoulder, she gently but firmly pushed her back from the threshold. "You know what the doctor's orders are: complete bed rest!"

The door closed with a sound of finality that was not to be questioned.

"Are you satisfied?" Willa demanded, showing more annoyance than she actually felt. It was enough that she had April to worry about without adding Hester to her list of concerns.

Without bothering to answer her mother, Hester returned to the chaise and sank into it. For the moment, she was satisfied; but in the back of her mind, Dr. Blodgett's words seared a tormenting path through her awareness: "In danger of cardiac failure," he had said. It was a condition that would prevail for four weeks, one of which, thankfully, was almost at an end.

On Sunday morning, Hester dragged herself out of bed. There was no chance of excusing herself from church. Whether she wanted to or not, there was no question of her missing services.

Resigning herself to the inevitable, Hester put on one of the linen dresses that she usually wore for this weekly occasion. She had several, all of them fashioned in dark gray or brown. Bright colors were not to be considered for church, but Hester had never discovered why this was so. "Unacceptable!" her mother had declared when, one day, she had innocently donned a yellow dress embroidered with pert green flowers.

Hester had never thought to question; she did not now.

In the victoria awhile later, with Lane, Julia, and her mother, Hester couldn't resist a backward glance at April's window as the carriage rolled down the drive. She saw nothing, of course; there was nothing to be seen, except the blank reflection of glass.

When they entered the church, Hester felt the cold wrap itself around her. Hot in the summer, cold in the winter, she thought disgruntledly.

As her eyes adjusted from the bright glare of sunshine, Hester caught her lower lip between her teeth, seeing that Andrew was already seated in the Manning pew. He had been joining them there ever since his engagement to April.

Deliberately, Hester slowed her steps as she walked down the aisle so that her mother would enter first. Sitting next to Andrew for more than an hour was something Hester was certain she could not accomplish without mishap.

The sermon, for Hester, dragged on interminably. She could in no way concentrate on the words of the minister, an energetic man who banged on the lectern with his fist each time he wanted to make a point. His oratory was usually peppered with threats of hellfire and damnation; today was no exception.

Restless beyond endurance, Hester fidgeted, earning more than one warning look from her mother.

At last it was over.

Outside, each of them exchanged a few words of greeting with the minister, who stood by the door to greet his parishioners, after which they paused on the front walkway before going to their respective carriages.

"How is April?" Andrew inquired of Lane, appearing vastly reassured when told she was apparently on the road to recovery. In a weary gesture, he rubbed the bridge of his nose with his fingertips. "God, I've been so worried. How I long to see her."

Hester averted her eyes, feeling as if a heavy hand had suddenly clutched her heart and was now squeezing it tightly.

Lane put a hand on Andrew's shoulder. "None of us is allowed to see her, Andrew. The doctor will not permit it; and of course he's right. Rest assured, she is being well cared for. Dr. Blodgett told me that both of her nurses have had a great deal of experience with this illness. April is not alone at any time." His hand fell away. "Will you be coming to the house for dinner? You are more than welcome, you know."

Andrew hesitated, then slowly shook his head. "Please excuse me. I would not be good company just now."

Lane nodded. "I understand." Taking Willa's arm, he

began to walk toward the carriage. "I'll see you tomorrow, then," he called over his shoulder.

Hester did not immediately move, unable to tear her gaze from Andrew's face, trembling as he stood before her, even now overcome with longing. She hated herself for this feeling she could not control, but there was no ignoring it.

A brief glance was all she received from Andrew, one that was chilling in its accusation. Turning from her, he strode away. Not a word had passed between them since they had left his house more than a week ago.

Hester only barely got back home without expressing her unhappiness in a wail of despair.

chapter
seventeen

At Fairmount Park, construction was resumed at a frantic pace. Workmen were now toiling day and night, six days a week, in an effort to meet the May 10 deadline. Though the vote had been too close for comfort, Congress had finally agreed to provide the Centennial Committee with the money they needed.

Elsewhere, too, were signs that the opening was not too far distant. The Pennsylvania Railroad was busily constructing a spur that would convey passengers right to the gates of Fairmount Park, and eighty-eight miles of new track were being laid between New York and Philadelphia. Existing tracks were being replaced where needed, and the railroad was adding new cars to its line as fast as they could be built. Their goal, in conjunction with the Wilmington and Baltimore railroads, was to transport an expected 145,000 visitors each day from every accessible part of the country to the city of Philadelphia.

The numbers astounded everyone; no one could imagine

what sort of a crowd that many people would produce. No one had ever seen that many people in one place at one time. 145,000 visitors in one day! Multiplied by an average of thirty days in a month, it became inconceivable.

While she could no longer appear in public due to the advanced state of her pregnancy, Julia was able to continue with her committee work from the privacy of her sitting room.

Leah visited at least once a week, sometimes alone and sometimes with other members of the committee, keeping Julia informed of their progress.

A very real problem had developed on this February day: they needed to locate a woman capable of operating the vast network of machinery in their pavilion.

At first this did not really seem to be much of an obstacle, but in the past weeks, Julia had written more letters than she could count, to every subcommittee in every state and territory in the nation. All responses had been negative. It appeared there wasn't a woman in the country who could do what they required.

"Well, I can't say it wasn't expected," Leah mused, throwing aside one of the responses they had received from Rhode Island. She sounded dejected in spite of her assessment.

They were in Julia's sitting room. A fire burned brightly in the hearth, and the room was warm and cheery. Outside, it was cold and crisp, the countryside whitened by the snow that had fallen during the night.

"I've tried to tell this to Elizabeth," Leah went on after taking a sip of tea. "But you know how she is. She's determined that only women will run the pavilion."

Getting up from her chair, Leah went to one of the oriel windows and stared at the snow. Julia repressed a sigh of envy at the sight of the other woman's trim waist and flat abdomen. Now going into her ninth month, Julia was beginning to feel as though she had been pregnant all her life.

"It wouldn't surprise me in the least if she barred male visitors altogether," Leah speculated. Turning from the window, she regarded Julia with some amusement. "She has barred them from the opening ceremony. Did you know that?"

Absently, Julia nodded, her thoughts returning to the problem at hand. With effort, she pushed herself up to her feet. Sitting for any length of time was now very uncomfortable for her.

"Leah," she said finally, "exhibits are coming in from other countries. Why can't we contact some of them? Does our operator have to be from our country?"

Leah regarded her in surprise. "Why, no. I guess not. . . ." She thought about it for a moment, then nodded excitedly. "Yes, of course! That's exactly what we must do! What do you suggest?"

"Well, there's no harm in trying them all, is there?" Julia replied with a laugh. "I'll begin on the letters tomorrow."

Going back to her chair, Leah drained the last of the tea from her cup, then picked up her fur muff. "Now, I don't want you to overtax youself. . . ."

"I won't." Julia walked with Leah to the door. "Hester has offered to help me in any way she can. I know that she won't mind writing a few letters."

As they crossed the threshold, Leah glanced at the room directly across the hall. "Is the nursery completed?" she asked.

"Yes. Would you like to see it?" At her enthusiastic nod, Julia opened the door. Lane had given instructions that the room be completely renovated. It had been freshly painted in soft blue, and all the furnishings were new.

"Oh!" Leah exclaimed with delight, walking toward the cradle in the center of the room. "It's lovely. Wherever did you find something this ornate?"

"Lane had it specially made."

Motioning to the trundle bed in a corner, Leah laughed. "Is that for when he outgrows the cradle?"

"No," Julia said, also laughing. "That's for the nurse, whom I haven't met yet. She'll be arriving next week."

"I must say Lane believes in being prepared," Leah commented as they left the room. Pausing in the hall, she gave Julia a light kiss on the cheek. "Remember, don't tire yourself! I'll see you next week." She started to walk away, then turned back again. "How is April?"

"Doing very well," Julia assured her with a nod of her head. "It's been more than a month since she became ill, and there have been no problems. Of course, she's very weak, but at least she's allowed to sit up now. The doctor feels she can get out of bed in a few days."

"Marvelous! Desmond will be relieved to hear she's almost recovered. He asks about her every day. I'll stop in to see her for a few minutes before I go."

Leaving Julia's side, Leah continued down the hall, taking a moment to wave to Hester, who was in her bedroom, sitting at her writing table.

Hester offered only a vague nod, too preoccupied to return the greeting. She stared at the calendar in front of her and again counted the days, certain she was wrong. They totaled twenty-one, the same total she had come up with four times in a row. She had never been this late.

But it couldn't be! she thought, feeling a chill of apprehension that left her weak. No one gets pregnant the first time; everyone knew that.

She glanced at the calendar again and resisted counting the days yet one more time. In a hurried movement, she flung it into a drawer. If only there was someone she could talk to, but who? Not her mother. Not Julia. Lane would never forgive her if she upset Julia at this time.

April? Oh, God, no; not April, though under any other circumstance, her sister would be the first one in whom she could confide.

Wait. That was all she could do at this point.

"Hester?"

She almost jumped a foot at the sound of Julia's voice.

"Oh, I'm sorry!" Julia's brow furrowed in concern. "I didn't mean to startle you."

Hester licked her dry lips. This would never do. She must remain calm! "It's not your fault, Julia. I was . . . daydreaming and didn't hear you come in." Stretching her mouth into a smile, she asked, "Is there anything I can do for you?" Hoping her legs would support her, she got shakily to her feet.

"Well, as a matter of fact, there is." Quickly, Julia explained what she required. "Would you mind helping me write the letters? I wouldn't impose, but"—she gave a rueful laugh—"there are a lot of them to be sent out, and time is running short. . . ."

Hester came closer, the smile still in place, her mind working on two levels. Julia looked so . . . big! Since most women of her acquaintance went into seclusion after their sixth or seventh month of pregnancy, Hester couldn't recall ever seeing a woman this far along. Right now, she found it terrifying!

"Of course if you are busy, I don't want to impose. . . ."

Julia viewed her sister-in-law doubtfully, not certain how to react in the face of her obvious hesitancy.

With effort, Hester shook herself free from her troublesome thoughts. "I'd be happy to help you, Julia. We'll begin in the morning if you like. . . ."

During the days that followed, Hester kept herself as busy as possible. She spent several hours each morning helping Julia write letters, visited April in the afternoon, reading to her so that she would not overtax herself by talking; then she tried, without much success, to sleep at night.

Never did a week crawl by with such excruciating slowness; each day seemed to be a week in length.

But pass it did.

On a frosty early March morning, there was no longer any doubt in Hester's mind: she was carrying Andrew's child.

Somehow she would have to get to Andrew, see him alone, and tell him what had happened. But how? He came here every Sunday to see April, though he hadn't actually been allowed to visit with her until this past week when the doctor finally declared April well enough to leave her bed. Hester, however, still hadn't returned to her former room because April napped in the afternoon, and she feared disturbing her rest.

Hester chewed her lower lip in thought as she paced the floor. Andrew didn't arrive home much before seven o'clock in the evening—too late for her even to consider leaving the house unescorted, even if she could think of a reason for doing so.

Sunday? She shook her head. Andrew was here on Sunday, but there was no chance of their being alone. Besides, that was five days away; almost another week!

It had to be during the week. Today, if possible. They would have to make plans to be married right away.

Abruptly, she halted her aimless prowling. What would she do if Andrew refused to marry her? Hester's hands worked nervously against each other, her palms damp with sudden dread. No, she would not even think about that. He would! He must!

Then, taking a sharp breath, Hester suddenly realized how it could be done. More often than not, Andrew returned home for his midday meal. Was the maid there? Hester didn't know. No matter. It was the only way.

Going to the wardrobe, Hester grabbed hold of a heavy woolen cape, then set out for the carriage house, where she instructed one of the grooms to ready the buggy. It would be prudent, she decided, to drive herself.

While she waited, she glanced back at the house. No one except Nancy had seen her leave. The girl would have no reason to mention it unless she was questioned. With any luck, her mother wouldn't realize she wasn't in her room; if she did, there was a good chance that Willa would think she was in Julia's room, helping to write those infernal letters.

When he came up the front walk shortly after noon, Andrew halted in surprise at the sight of Hester waiting on his doorstep. She was the last person he expected, or wanted, to see.

"What the devil are you doing here?" he demanded harshly.

These were the first words he had spoken to her since the night of the opera. Not exactly a warm greeting, Hester thought morosely. She spoke firmly.

"Andrew, I must talk to you. . . ."

Concern flashed in his eyes. "Is it about April? Has she had a relapse?"

Impatiently, Hester shook her head. "No. April is fine." She looked nervously up and down the street. "Please, Andrew. Let's go inside. What I have to say to you would be best said in private."

"I have nothing to say to you, in private or otherwise!" Fumbling in his pocket, he brought forth his latchkey and angrily jammed it into the lock.

Viewing him, Hester's eyes blazed like blue fire. She felt like shouting it out to the world, and wondered what he would do if she screamed: *I am to have your baby!*

Of course she didn't; she spoke the words quietly.

Tilting his head, Andrew viewed her with disbelief. "You really expect me to believe that?"

"We must get married!" Hester insisted, touching his arm.

With a rough motion, he brushed her hand away. "I have no intention of marrying you," he gritted through clenched teeth. "If you are pregnant—and I have my doubts about it—then it's your own fault! As far as I'm concerned, you can do what every other female does when she finds herself in such a condition: go abroad for a year. Come home a widow with a child." His smile was not pleasant. "I suggest you invent a struggling artist for your husband. Impoverished noblemen are grossly overdone."

Anger was building deep inside her; Hester always knew the signs. Who did he think he was? Regardless of how it had come about, she had certainly not gotten pregnant by herself.

Hester's chin lifted, and she looked him in the eye. He was still pretending he hadn't known who was on that couch with him. Until the moment they entered his house, Hester was willing to concede that he thought he was with April. Nevertheless, no matter how well she could impersonate her sister, there was no way she could possibly know what sort of a kiss April would bestow on a man. Surely she, Hester, could not have duplicated that! If Andrew had been fooled, it was only because he had allowed himself to be. . . .

"There is to be a child," she repeated slowly, evenly. "We must get married. And soon!"

Andrew's features hardened, and his eyes reflected the same anger she was feeling. "Get that out of your mind! I'll marry no one but April!"

Before she could speak again, Andrew pushed the front door open, entered, then slammed it in her face.

Fury bubbled up in Hester, flushing her face and making her tremble.

We'll see about that, she thought, turning back to the street. *We'll see.* . . .

As she drove the buggy home, Hester's anger melted into despair. She could think of no solution; yet one must be found.

When she arrived back at the carriage house, the sun was still high, its cheery brilliance holding a promise of warmth that was not realized; the day remained cold.

The groom helped her from the buggy, and Hester stood there a moment, feeling as though events beyond her control were crowding in on her, snatching the decision from her grasp. Visions flooded her mind, none of them pleasant.

Raising her head, Hester viewed the cloudless sky, and for the first time she thought of her child. If it was a boy, it might be able to overcome the stigma of bastardy. If it was a girl . . .

Hester blinked against threatening tears and bit her lip so hard it hurt. Circumstances suddenly took on a new perspective, and the realization gave her a determination that stiffened her spine. No longer could she consider the feelings of those around her. The child must now be her only concern.

Just before she opened the rear door, Hester bent down, scooped up a handful of dirt, and smeared it on her cape.

Entering then, she removed the cape and took it directly into the washroom.

"I've discovered a spot on this. Please see to it that it is cleaned," she instructed, handing it to one of the girls.

She felt better about going upstairs without wearing anything that would indicate she had been out. She was in no mood for any questions.

Hester needn't have worried; except for servants, she encountered no one on the way to her room. Glancing at the clock, she was surprised to see that she had been gone less than an hour.

But then, how long did it take for one's life to collapse in ruins? A few minutes of pleasure . . . and all was lost.

Turning sideways, Hester viewed herself in the mirror. Tightly corseted as she was, her abdomen looked as flat as it always did. Time, however, was running out at an alarming rate.

She would have to tell someone. And soon. Hester expelled a deep breath as she turned from the mirror. There was only one person she knew of who could convince Andrew to marry her. Andrew may have been right as to its being her own fault, but he was wrong not to acknowledge his own child.

Hester remained in her room until it was time for supper. She got through the meal as best she could. Unless they had guests, Lane always spent an hour or so in his study after the evening meal. Julia, for the past two weeks now, had been having her meals in her room, for the doctor had cautioned her against walking up and down the stairs unless it was absolutely necessary.

When Lane excused himself, Hester waited a few minutes until she was certain her mother was otherwise occupied, then she walked down the hall, pausing before the open door to the study. Lane was seated behind his desk, riffling through a pile of papers in front of him.

"Lane? Are you very busy?"

He looked up and smiled. "Never too busy to see you, Hester." Although he said that, and meant it, he reluctantly put aside the geology report on the one-thousand-acre parcel of land he had recently purchased in Titusville, and on which he hoped to find petroleum. "What is it? Did you see an especially fetching Worth gown that you cannot live without?" He smiled indulgently. Hester was always badgering him for a new dress. He had no idea how she managed to cram them all into her wardrobe.

Hester strove for an answering smile, then gave it up. She and April had always been close to Lane, and Hester now said a silent prayer, infinitely relieved that this news would be imparted to her brother and not to her father.

She swallowed, then closed the door. "No . . . Lane, promise me you won't be angry with me. . . ."

He frowned, then saw she was serious. "I promise," he said slowly, wondering at her attitude. He was used to April being serious. Hester, however, was like a fast-moving stream, changing direction with a swiftness that took everyone by surprise.

"Lane . . ." She began to cry softly.

Alarm fluttered in his stomach, leaving him with a distinct feeling of unease. Getting up, Lane went to her and put his arm around her. "Hester? What is it? You know you can tell me."

She pressed a tearstained cheek against his shirt. "Lane . . . I'm going to have a baby. . . ."

He stiffened, and she quickly looked up at him. "You promised!"

Grabbing her by the shoulders, Lane forced himself to speak calmly. "Who . . . who did this thing?"

She made no response, and he shook her.

"Tell me! Who is the father?"

"Andrew. . . ." Her voice was so inaudible, Lane wasn't sure he had heard her correctly.

"Andrew? Andrew Hollinger?" His voice ended on a rising note of incredulity.

At her nod, Lane scowled at her. He couldn't imagine why she was doing this, but he did know he didn't find it amusing. Sighing, he ran a hand through his hair. "Hester, if this is a joke, I don't find it funny at all!" Turning from her, he headed back to his desk. "You should be ashamed of yourself."

"I am," she replied in a small voice. "But not for the reason you mean, Lane. It's true. I'm to have Andrew's child."

Shock, confusion, and anger battled for supremacy within Lane. "Perhaps you'd better tell me all about it," he suggested.

She wet her lips. "It happened the night April got sick. I thought . . . I thought it would be a lark to pretend that I was her and go to the opera with Andrew. I . . . didn't mean any harm. I had no idea that April was really ill." She waved a hand in a helpless gesture. "You know how she gets every month. . . ."

Confusion won out, and Lane shook his head. He was

well aware that Hester could fool most people into thinking she was April when the mood overtook her, but he couldn't believe that Andrew wouldn't see through the ruse.

"Are you telling me that Andrew thought he was with April?"

"Yes. . . ."

"Continue."

"Well, after the opera, Andrew took me to his house. . . ." She paused at the look on her brother's face.

Lane scowled at her as he thought of the implications. "You mean April goes to his house?" He spoke slowly, face flushed.

"Oh, no!" Hester said quickly. "She's never been there. It's just that . . . Andrew thought it would be a treat for her to see where they would live." Her hands reached out for the back of a chair, and she gripped it tightly, as if it offered support. "And after we got there . . ." She averted her eyes, looking everywhere but at her brother.

Lane slammed a hand on the desk, causing Hester to start with the sudden noise. "Why the hell didn't you get out of there?" he demanded.

"I tried." Tears coursed down her cheeks. "Really, I did. But before I knew what was happening . . . it was all over. I must have fainted; I'm sure I did. He's much stronger than I am. . . ."

Lane turned away, his hands clenched at his sides. "I'll kill him!"

Relinquishing the security of the chair, Hester ran toward him, clutching at his arm.

"Lane, you gave me your word that you wouldn't get angry!" she cried. Looking at her brother's face, she felt icy cold, not at all certain that he wasn't about to do exactly as he said.

Inclining his head, Lane gave her a penetrating look. "Have you told Andrew about this?"

She lowered her eyes and brushed the tears from her cheeks. "Yes. But he sent me away." She flung herself into his arms. "Oh, Lane, you must make Andrew marry me! I couldn't face the scandal. I'd die! Really, I would. I'd die!" She began to sob again.

"You'll not have to face anything," Lane said gruffly. "Andrew will marry you, I promise you that!" Awkwardly, he patted her shoulder. "Go upstairs now. But for God's sake, don't say anything to Mother—or to April. Especially to April. . . ." he muttered, feeling ill.

When Hester left, Lane cornered a servant and instructed him to send the carriage for Andrew Hollinger and fetch him back to Manning House, posthaste.

What a night this was turning out to be, Lane thought morosely. Pouring himself a brandy, he sat down to wait, his thoughts now not on Hester or Andrew but on April. The girl would, of course, have to be told; but not of the child. People would guess, certainly. They must never know for sure, however. He would arrange it so that it would appear that Andrew and Hester had eloped. He would tell everyone that they were now, this minute, married, and had kept it a secret until April was recovered.

Lane was still sitting behind the desk when Andrew arrived some thirty minutes later.

"Close the door," Lane instructed quietly. "And sit down." Getting up, he poured another brandy, placing the glass on the desk before Andrew.

Andrew looked uneasy and gave some thought to asking if this unexpected summons had to do with business; but deep inside him, he knew it did not.

"Hester is to have your child," Lane stated bluntly and to

the point. If he had any doubts, Andrew's lack of surprise now convinced him that Hester had told the truth.

Clearing his throat, Andrew stared down at the floor. "I'm not entirely convinced of that," he murmured.

"Are you calling my sister a liar?" Lane's face darkened, and he fixed the younger man with a hard look.

"No, no!" Andrew ran a hand through his hair. He stared at the glass of brandy, then took a quick swallow of the fiery liquid. "For God's sake, Lane! I thought I was with April. . . ."

Lane's eyes grew flinty as he studied Andrew. "And you expect me to excuse you for that?" he asked softly. "If a man is so stupid that he doesn't know the identity of the woman he has lain with—"

"It was Hester's fault!" Andrew interrupted, grimly determined to make his point.

"Hester is young and impressionable!" Lane cut him off. "It was your place to show restraint!"

Hester was never young, Andrew thought resentfully. Women like that were gifted with guile before they left their cradle.

Lane gave a long, drawn-out sigh. "I cannot believe you didn't know you were with Hester," he said slowly, shaking his head. Then he gave Andrew a sharp look. "Not that I would condone all this if that were the case! It would just . . . make it easier to understand."

Andrew moved restlessly in the chair under Lane's relentless stare. On more than one occasion since the night of the opera, he had searched his mind in an effort to discover whether he, in fact, knew he wasn't with April, or at least suspected that he wasn't. He had had no suspicion at all . . . until they'd kissed. Never before had such fire claimed him. Any suspicions—if indeed he had any—were consumed in the heat of the moment. No man could be expected to think clearly in a situation like that. In the end, however, it remained a question he could not answer honestly, even in the privacy of his own mind.

"You will be married tomorrow," Lane continued. "In Lancaster. Then you will tell everyone that you and Hester eloped several weeks ago."

"No!" Andrew jumped to his feet. "I'll marry no one but April. I love her!"

Lane's eyes narrowed dangerously as he got up. "You'll do as I say, or I'll have you brought before the authorities. The resulting scandal will benefit no one—certainly not April!"

Authorities! Andrew was thinking as he sank back into his chair. He didn't give a damn about authorities. All he'd have to do would be to leave town, and they'd never find him. His job, now. That was different. Lane was generous to his employees; he paid well, and there was always a little extra at the end of the year. There was no doubt in Andrew's mind that he would lose his job if he didn't marry Hester. And if that happened, where would he go? New York and Boston were out; Lane spent too much time in both those cities.

Clasping his hands between his knees, Andrew morosely contemplated the tip of his boots. Was Hester really going to have his child? Or was this another one of her tricks?

Even though Lane was waiting, Andrew's thoughts turned inward. He had been only eighteen when he first joined Manning Enterprises as an assistant to the bookkeeper. Ordinarily it would have taken him years to work himself up to the top. But he had been there just short of two years when he discovered that his supervisor, Harry Dillman, was embezzling funds and falsifying the books. Andrew prided

himself on his honesty and had been genuinely appalled at
the deception he had uncovered. After three weeks of
serious soul-searching, he had at last placed the books
before Lane and pointed out the falsifications. Dillman had
been discharged, and Lane, in a move that surprised everyone, installed Andrew as head bookkeeper.

From that day until this, Lane Manning had received
Andrew's loyalty and devotion.

But, Andrew wondered now, was loyalty and devotion
enough for him to marry a woman he didn't love?

Seeing Andrew's hesitation, Lane came forward and now
spoke earnestly. "Regardless of how this unfortunate incident came about, you should now have only one concern:
your child. The responsibility is yours, Andrew. No matter
how you try to shun it, you are responsible for bringing a
child into this world."

Andrew looked up at him. "Can I . . . can I talk to April
first?" he implored.

"No!"

"Just for a few minutes. . . ."

"No! I'll not have her upset any more than is necessary."

Wearily, Andrew stood up. "She'll have to know sooner
or later."

"It will come about in the proper time. In view of the
fact that Hester is underage, I will accompany you to
Lancaster. After the ceremony, Hester and I will return here.
You will join us for supper, after which you will announce
the news."

Andrew paled. He had thought, hoped, that Lane would
take care of that. "How . . . how will I do that?"

Lane's smile held no trace of mirth. "You're a bright
young man, Andrew; that's why I hired you. I'm sure you'll

think of a way—a convincing way," he added grimly, escorting the young man to the foyer.

After the front door had closed, Lane went upstairs to tell Hester that she would be married tomorrow.

When her brother left her room, Hester sagged in relief.

Then she glanced at the door. Should she tell April? Clasping her hands tightly, Hester brought them to her trembling lips.

She was halfway across the room when her courage deserted her.

"Oh, April!" she whispered as tears welled in her eyes. "You are my only regret. . . ."

chapter
eighteen

The next morning, before Lane even opened his eyes, he was aware of a feeling of depression.

Sitting up, he yanked on the bell cord that would summon Joseph, then frowned at the bright sunlight that flowed from a cloudless sky. It did nothing to lighten his mood.

All he could think of was that he wished this day was over.

"Good morning, sir," Joseph said in his usual cheerful voice as he entered the room a few minutes later.

Lane didn't answer.

Going to the wardrobe, Joseph brought forth a suit, holding it up for Lane's inspection.

"I thought perhaps the black broadcloth," he suggested.

That would be appropriate, Lane thought to himself with a sigh, running a hand through his hair. Getting to his feet, he said, "No. I'll wear the light brown today."

After he had washed, dressed, and shaved, Lane went into Julia's room. She was awake, but still in bed.

"How are you feeling this morning?" he asked, bending forward to give her a tender kiss.

"Fat and bored!" She giggled. "And not necessarily in that order."

He squeezed her hand. "It won't be long. I'm sorry about the piano."

Julia made a face, and sighed. Lane had wanted to have the Steinway moved up here so that she could while away a few hours playing. Dr. Blodgett had insisted it would be a strain on her back, however, and had firmly vetoed the idea. "Well, I suppose the good doctor knows what he's talking about. . . ." She didn't sound convinced.

"Indeed he does!"

They both fell silent as the nurse, Alma Gwenn, came into the room at just that moment. She had arrived two days ago, one of four nurses who had been highly recommended by Dr. Blodgett. Lane had personally interviewed each applicant and, impressed with her credentials, had finally decided on the thirty-four-year-old woman from Shropshire, England. She had been trained at the Nightingale School and Home for Nurses at Saint Thomas's Hospital in London.

"The doctor was quite right in his judgment, Mrs. Manning," the nurse went on, viewing Julia as though she were a naughty child. "The muscles in your back are under a strain as it is. Sitting on a bench without support would only add to that strain."

Meekly, Julia nodded. She was a bit intimidated by Alma Gwenn. One did not question a Nightingale nurse.

Just then, Mary entered with Julia's breakfast tray. Attention diverted, Miss Gwenn quickly went to inspect the morning fare that would be served to her patient, nodding in satisfaction at the coddled egg and tall glass of warm milk. That last had caused a heated discussion between Julia and

Miss Gwenn. Until the nurse's arrival, Julia had been drinking coffee, a practice Miss Gwenn immediately discontinued. Julia's protests—for she greatly enjoyed her morning coffee—were ignored.

"Your child is eating what you are eating!" Miss Gwenn had declared, and the subject was closed.

"I could sit in a regular chair and use a pillow," Julia suggested to Lane, still thinking about the piano. She said this in a barely audible voice, hoping that Nurse Gwenn would not overhear this medical blasphemy.

Lane patted her abdomen, for a moment letting his hand rest there as he felt the child move. For the first time since he had opened his eyes this morning, he felt a measure of comfort.

"I don't think you can get close enough to play anyway," Lane answered with a laugh. "Your arms aren't long enough."

Julia glanced down at the mound beneath the covers. "I guess you're right." Then she brightened. "Besides, it won't be long now. I can start counting days, instead of weeks and months!"

"Indeed you can," he agreed, giving her another kiss. Straightening, he saw that Mary had removed the plates from the tray and had set them neatly on a table. "I'll see you later today," he said to Julia, making for the door.

Getting out of bed, Julia headed for the table that held her breakfast.

"Will you be having supper with me?" she asked Lane. He had been doing that several times a week since she had been eating in her room.

He hesitated, seemed to consider it, then said slowly, "Not tonight." He looked at her and smiled. "Tomorrow, for sure."

When he entered the dining room a few minutes later, Lane saw that Willa, Hester, and April were already at the table.

"Do you think you should be up this early?" Lane asked April as he sat down.

"The doctor said I could resume my normal routine," April reminded him, after she took a sip of her orange juice.

"Still, it wouldn't be wise to overdo just yet. . . ."

"April is fine, Lane," Willa interjected, signaling the serving girl to fill her coffee cup. "Don't coddle her."

Lane was silent as the servant piled scrambled eggs onto his plate. "That's enough," he said, after she had doled out two spoonfuls. Picking up his napkin, he unfolded it, put it on his lap, then said, "Hester, I've got to go to Boston today. How would you like to come along for the ride? You've been cooped up here for weeks now. . . ."

"I would like that," Hester replied quickly, giving her mother a tentative look. What, she wondered uneasily, would they do if she suddenly decided to join them? They were not, of course, going to Boston. After fetching Andrew, they were going to Lancaster.

But Willa merely said, "Lane is right, Hester. It will do you good to get out of the house for a while."

Hester released a breath she hadn't known she was holding, then caught it again as she heard April speak.

"Can I go, too?" she asked, giving Lane an eager look.

"You may not!" Willa said hastily before Lane could speak.

Leaning back in her chair, April pouted, but knew better than to question her mother when she used that tone.

Viewing his sisters, Lane repressed a sigh. He loved them both, and never could it be said, even now, that he loved one more than the other. He knew that his mother, though she would be the last to admit it, favored Hester; probably, he thought, because they were so much alike. For himself, he could honestly say the girls shared an equal measure in his affections.

But damn! He wished this business were over. He glanced at April. Her shining black hair was pulled back and secured with a large white calico bow patterned with embroidered red flowers, the same material and design as her morning gown. He hadn't seen her wear her hair like that since she was a child. She looked so very young to him, so vulnerable, that his heart ached.

A moment's doubt assailed him. Was he doing the right thing? Perhaps he should have a talk with April before he and Hester left for Lancaster.

And what would he say? Your sister is pregnant by your betrothed? But don't feel bad, April; Andrew thought he was with you?

Lane released the sigh he'd been holding back and saw Hester give him an anxious glance. He responded with what he hoped was a reassuring smile.

It was all a can of worms, he thought, draining his coffee cup and feeling resigned. There was no easy way.

With breakfast concluded, Lane stood up. Both Hester and April left the room, then Lane turned to look at his mother.

"By the way," he said as casually as he could, "Andrew will be here for supper tonight."

A frown of irritation creased Willa's brow. "On Wednesday!"

"Does it matter?" He forced a small laugh that sounded hollow, even to himself. "After all, he will be a member of the family soon." Very soon, he thought to himself, feeling depression once again crowd in on him.

"Not too soon," Willa countered sharply, getting to her feet. The wedding had been scheduled to take place two weeks ago. When April had taken ill, Willa had canceled all preparations. "You know, Lane, I really think we ought to postpone the wedding for another three or four weeks. . . ."

Pausing, Lane gave his mother a thoughtful look. "You don't like Andrew, do you?"

Willa looked startled by the question, and her face took on a faint flush. No, she didn't like Andrew Hollinger. There was a weakness there, one she could not define and would be hard-pressed to explain. She pursed her lips, aware that her son was waiting for an answer.

"Let us say that, in my opinion, Desmond Carlyle would have been more suitable for April."

"Well, we cannot always choose for others," Lane murmured as he left.

The trip to Lancaster was made within the constraint of a silence that plunged the three travelers into their own thoughts. Among them, only Hester dared hope.

Time, she thought to herself, staring out of the train window. Time would be her ally. She had so much love to give!

More than once during the course of their journey, Hester stole a look at Andrew, noticing how he seemed lost in his own thoughts. And were they of April? she wondered uneasily, twisting her gloved hands in her lap.

April can never love you as I do! she wanted to cry out to him.

Andrew was indeed thinking of April. He was also aware of Hester's looks in his direction, but he certainly wasn't about to acknowledge them. Marriage was something he was ready for and had, in fact, been anticipating, though he had never anticipated being miserable on this day of days! Here he was, about to wed a woman he didn't love, one who, incongruously, possessed the face and form of the woman he did love.

How had it happened?

Unable to bear his thoughts, Andrew studied the other passengers. There weren't many: a well-dressed man who looked preoccupied and who sat alone; a group of men who were laughing in a rowdy manner, their clothes indicating they were probably laborers or farmers; and a woman with three children, one of whom was crying fretfully.

Children.

He was about to become a father.

If Hester wasn't lying . . .

The train slowed as it approached the station.

Lane, as Hester had known he would, handled everything. There was nothing for her and Andrew to do except stand before the minister and recite their vows.

Hester had already replied when the minister asked the question of Andrew: "Do you take this woman to be your lawful wife . . . ?"

The ensuing silence caused the clergyman to pause and raise his brows as he studied the groom.

Hester felt as if she couldn't breathe.

The silence lasted a moment longer, then she heard Andrew's unemotional response. Fortunately, it was the correct one.

Only when Andrew turned to her at the end of the ceremony did his eyes finally meet hers. She could not read their depths. Their kiss was a mere brushing of lips.

They were married.

The return trip was no more cheerful than the one going, for they all knew what lay ahead of them.

"Eight o'clock," Lane reminded Andrew as they parted company at the station.

That, and no more, was said.

Hester would later wonder what she had been served at

supper that night, but she never would be able to remember. Her plate could have been filled with sawdust, for all she had tasted. Her nerves seemed to jangle in protest. Each time she brought the fork to her mouth, her hand had trembled to a degree that made her certain her food would land in her lap.

Lane and Andrew chatted easily enough, mostly about business, and at one point April had wanted an accounting of Hester's day in Boston. Thankfully, Lane had answered. Hester had never been to Boston and would have been at a loss even to prevaricate a credible story.

The end of the meal, however, did not lessen Hester's nervousness, for the time was now at hand.

While she waited for someone to make a move to leave the table, Hester absently plucked at the skirt of her taffeta gown. It was the color of amethysts, one of the prettiest dresses she owned. She had not, of course, worn it to her wedding; it was far too formal for daytime wear. Suspended from a silk ribbon around her neck, hidden beneath her bodice, was the gold wedding band Andrew had placed on her finger during the ceremony. The ring felt heavy and cold between her breasts.

Andrew, when he did speak, took her by surprise.

Getting to his feet, he said, "Lane, may I speak to you in private?"

"Of course, Andrew," Lane answered with a false joviality that only Hester caught. He clapped the young man's shoulder. "Let's have a brandy in the study; then we'll join the ladies in the drawing room." He held April's chair, assisted her to her feet, and kissed her brow. "How are you feeling? If you're tired, I want you to tell me immediately."

"Oh, Lane!" April laughed and gave him a light kiss on

the cheek. "Stop fussing. Even the doctor admits I'm recovered."

Lane continued to regard her a moment longer, as if to assure himself. Then he motioned for Andrew to follow him.

When he closed the study door a few minutes later, Lane gave Andrew a sharp look.

In the face of it, Andrew gestured helplessly. "I thought it would be more . . . convincing if they thought I told you first."

Lane relaxed, then nodded. "Yes. You did the right thing. We'll wait ten minutes or so, then join them."

The clock ticked the minutes away as both men sat in silence.

At last Lane got up. "Are you ready?"

Andrew nodded and tried to steel himself against April's reaction. If only he could have talked to her in private. Not that it would have made all that much difference, he realized unhappily. The end result would be the same.

As they walked from the study, Andrew had the disconcerting feeling that he was wide awake in the midst of a nightmare. He would have given half his remaining years if only he could turn back the clock.

From the first moment he had seen April, Andrew had wanted no other woman. And the agonizing thing to him was that he would be looking at April's face every day for the rest of his life.

A fire had been laid in the hearth and now blazed with cheery determination, reaching out to embrace the occupants of the room with invisible arms of warmth.

Nevertheless, Lane felt chilled as they entered the drawing room. "Andrew has something to say to us all," he said in a tone more curt than he had intended.

Crossing the carpeted floor, Lane came to stand behind

April's chair. Even though the doctor had assured him that she was completely recovered, Lane felt the need to protect her and would have gladly taken on himself the ordeal she was about to face in the next few minutes had it been at all possible for him to do so.

Willa, needle poised above the tapestry she was working on, gave Lane a questioning look, alerted by the tone of his voice. A sudden apprehension beset her, and her hand trembled, causing the needle to waver with uncertainty. Carefully, she set the tapestry board to the side of her chair and waited.

Several times Andrew opened his mouth, only to close it again. "I've . . . told Lane . . ." He broke off and cast a beseeching look at Lane, but received only a cold stare in return. He then looked at April, and was certain his heart would break at the sight of her trusting smile.

"We're waiting to hear your news, Andrew!" Lane said, sounding impatient.

Andrew's eyes swung to Hester. Her beautiful face was composed, but her breast rose and fell at a pace that gave lie to the calmness she was displaying.

"For heaven's sake!" Willa exclaimed irritably. "If you've something to say, Andrew, get on with it!" Her hands moved against each other as an uneasiness spread cold tentacles of dread throughout her whole body. She was certain she wasn't going to like this, whatever it was.

"Hester and I . . ." Andrew coughed and tried again. "Hester and I . . . were married several weeks ago. In Lancaster. We . . . didn't want to say anything about it until . . . until April was feeling better. I take full responsibility. . . ." He swallowed against the gorge in his throat.

While Andrew was speaking, Hester had removed the

gold ring from its place of concealment, and it now rested on her bosom, in plain view for everyone to see.

"Married . . . ?"

The word hung in the air, no more than a whisper as it emerged from April's parted lips. She was staring at Andrew as if he had spoken in a language she could not understand. Lane's hands were on her shoulders, feeling warm, gripping her tightly. That, more than Andrew's words, made it real for her. Her brother was always there when she needed him. With great effort, April resisted the urge to turn and fling herself into the safety of his arms.

As if all his energy had been expended in the short speech, Andrew now sank into a chair, hearing a thundering echo in his ears that he knew to be his own heartbeat.

Watching him, a crushing sense of desolation came over April, and she squared her shoulders as she fought to keep her emotions concealed. Her eyes went to her sister. Even though her heart felt as though it would shatter into a thousand pieces, April could not find it within herself to censure either one of them. Andrew could not help but love Hester, she thought, for there was much to love. Yet, how could he have done this to her?

An uncomfortable silence settled over them all.

Both Willa and April were stunned, unable to speak.

Willa, however, quickly recovered. She turned to glare at Hester, but her daughter wouldn't meet her eye. She was standing by the fireplace, eyes downcast, arms close to her sides, palms pressed against her abdomen. Willa took note of the unconscious stance, and her eyes narrowed as it all became clear to her in a flash of instant comprehension.

So, she mused, not at all fooled by the little charade being enacted here tonight. Even as she thought that, she knew that they would all play the game. Any chance remark overheard by the servants—and Willa had no doubt that some of them would be—could be bandied about only to corroborate the story of Hester and Andrew eloping.

With that in mind, Willa refrained from asking the one question that could have tumbled the story down like a house of cards: How did Hester manage to get married when, except for church, she hadn't left the house in this past month? Not until this morning, that is. Andrew, she realized, had been purposely vague. "Several weeks ago," he'd said, and everyone had left it at that.

The only person who might have asked was April. But she didn't. This was not surprising, since she had been unaware of her sister's activities during her illness.

The silence, unbroken till now, was suddenly shattered by Hester as she raced to kneel at her sister's side.

"Oh, April . . . please tell me you understand!" she implored.

"I . . . I wish you both every happiness." Her voice surprised her. It sounded . . . normal. Nothing else about her felt that way at just this moment. She had the oddest sensation of being trapped inside her body, looking out.

"April . . ." Weeping softly now, Hester put her head in her sister's lap.

"Hester!" Willa came forward, hands clasped at her waist. "That is enough. Your sister is still weak. She should not be troubled anymore this evening." Her attention turned to April and her tone softened. "Come along, April. You need your rest."

April got slowly to her feet. As she did, Andrew immediately stood up, but she cast not so much as a glance in his direction. Whatever they had been to each other in the past, he was now her sister's husband. Her proud, small head was held high. As she swept past Andrew, she gathered the folds of her skirt in one hand, drawing it close to her so that not even a ribbon or a piece of lace would come in contact with him.

Viewing her, Lane's heart swelled with pride at her display of dignity and composure. He knew very well that, had the situation been reversed, Hester would now be screaming and ranting uncontrollably.

Willa put her arm around April as they went to leave the room, and for the briefest of moments, her eyes and Lane's locked.

She knows! Lane thought to himself, feeling a rush of dismay, wondering how that was possible. Then, as his mother and sister headed for the stairs, he relaxed. Like himself, Willa would choose the lesser of two evils. For all their sakes, this was the way it had to be. As far as April was concerned, there could be no softening of the shock and hurt she bore in finding out that her sister and her betrothed had married each other. Whether she knew the truth or not, the facts could not be altered.

April managed to control herself until her mother closed the bedroom door. Then she threw herself on the bed to weep the tears that had been building up within her.

Sitting on the edge of the bed, Willa put a hand on April's shoulder; it was all the comfort she could offer. Hester was pregnant; she knew that with as much certainty as if she had been told.

What she couldn't quite figure out was when and under what circumstances such an intimate meeting between Hester and Andrew had come about in the first place! A little mental arithmetic brought her back to the night Andrew had taken April to the opera . . . the very night April had fallen ill . . . the very night Hester had supposedly taken to her bed, feeling indisposed.

Willa's mouth compressed into a tight line. It wasn't necessary for her to pursue her thoughts to their logical conclusion; it wasn't even necessary for her to ask April if she had, in fact, gone to the opera. Willa knew now that she had not.

April's sobs intensified, and Willa looked down at the girl on the bed. Compassion should have been there; it wasn't. To her chagrin, Willa had to admit that that feeling was for April's twin. . . .

Downstairs, another awkward silence had fallen. Lane broke it.

"Hester, in view of the fact that you are now a married woman, I suggest you pack a few things to see you through tonight. I'll have the rest of your belongings sent to you tomorrow."

With her hand, Hester brushed the clinging dampness from her cheeks and without a word, left the room.

Turning to Andrew, who was looking anything but a happy bridegroom, Lane put out his hand. "Welcome to the family," he said dryly.

Andrew refused the outstretched hand. Walking toward the fireplace, he plunged his hands into his pockets and stood there, staring at nothing.

Lane watched him a moment, then said, "Andrew, I realize that this marriage was not exactly of your choosing. . . ." The young man didn't turn, but a slight tensing of his shoulders told Lane that his words were being heard. "I urge you to make it as happy and as fulfilling as you can, however." Andrew made no response. Although Lane strove to keep his voice at an even level, a hard note crept into it. "It would displease me greatly if I were to discover that my sister was in any way being mistreated. . . ."

Turning then, Andrew stared at him for a long moment, then nodded.

When Hester and Andrew finally left the house, Lane made his way upstairs, his step heavy. He paused at April's closed door, hearing the low murmur of his mother's voice and the clear sound of April weeping. He put his hand on the doorknob but didn't turn it.

Feeling as if he had aged ten years in the past hour, Lane went into Julia's room. She was in bed, reading. As soon as she saw his face, she hastily put the book aside, alarmed by the look of him.

"Lane? What is it?"

He went to sit on the bed. Elbows on his knees, he put his face in his hands and told her that Hester and Andrew had eloped.

"Oh, Lane. . . ." Julia put her arms around him and drew his head to her breast. "How did April take it?"

"Better than I thought she would," he said tiredly, then shook his head. "But with April, it's hard to tell. She conceals so much. . . ."

"How could they have done such a thing?" Julia muttered, and her heart ached for April. She felt every bit as stunned as Willa and April had been. After thinking about it for a few moments, she moistened her lips, again viewing Lane. "Was there . . . a reason for their elopement?" she asked carefully.

Lane gave her long look, a brief nod, then turned away without speaking.

Many questions formed in Julia's mind, but she saw that Lane had no wish to discuss it further, so she remained silent.

Finally, Lane turned toward her. "Would you mind if I stayed here tonight?" he asked. "I don't want to trouble your rest, but . . ."

Reaching out a hand, Julia threw the covers back. "I'd like the company," she said softly. It took him only a moment to undress. Then his warm body was beside her own, and Julia settled herself comfortably within the circle of his embrace.

When Andrew unlocked his front door, he seemed about to enter, then he paused to allow Hester to precede him. He did not assist her, nor had he done so when she had alighted from the carriage.

In the dim hallway, Hester halted uncertainly. The only light came from the weak glow of embers in the fireplace in the parlor. She stood there, clutching the small valise with a hand that trembled. A nervous dread swept through her as she cast a look at the man who was now her husband, realizing that he had not spoken a word to her all day.

Nor did he now.

Chewing her lip, Hester watched as Andrew walked slowly into the parlor. With motions that were mechanical, as if his thoughts were elsewhere than on the task at hand, he stoked the bright red embers until a blaze took hold.

Putting her valise on the floor, Hester took the few steps necessary to enter the parlor.

Straightening, Andrew went very still, staring down into the little flames as if hypnotized, the poker held loosely in his hand.

Watching him, Hester knew that he was thinking of the last time they had been in this room together. That night, too, he had stoked the fire, and in its warming glow they had made love. And—Hester's mouth firmed imperceptibly—it had been right for them both!

She stared at Andrew's back through narrowed eyes. Men were such romantics. They would have us think otherwise, she thought with a trace of disdain, have us think that women were the silly romantics. Such was not the case. Men always thought they wanted a dutiful, sweet-tempered, and, above all, obedient wife. When they got one, they resented her, and didn't know why.

Fool! Hester thought to herself, even now overcome with love for him. *Had you married my sister, you would have been miserable.*

Finally Andrew turned toward her, staring at her face for a long moment before he spoke. The fire snapped, sounding loud in the stillness.

"Are you really going to have a baby?" he asked quietly.

"I am," she stated flatly. "And it's yours." Her eyes glittered like hard sapphires as she raised her chin and fixed him with an unwavering stare. "Do you doubt that, too?"

"No. . . ." He raised a hand and, with a knuckle, rubbed his nose in a weary gesture.

"Andrew!" Hester's voice was crisp, entirely out of context with the words she now spoke. "I love you. I shall never say that again until you can speak those words to me and mean them!" She drew herself up straighter and, hands clasped at her waist, added: "I would appreciate it if you would show me to our room. I'm tired, and it has been a long day."

Hester's eyes were as heated as the flames in the hearth. In spite of himself, Andrew felt a tightening in his loins.

Moving with a firm step, Hester then headed for the hall, where she halted, waiting, not looking at him. After a moment, Andrew followed.

"Please bring my valise with you," Hester said in that same tone as she began to climb the stairs.

chapter
nineteen

Winter was indulging in one last fling, turning the March night bitterly cold, tracing windows with delicate frost patterns and tipping trees with a brittle coating of ice that threatened to shatter thin branches with each gust of wind.

Opening her eyes, Julia moved restlessly on the bed. For a moment, she listened to the sound of the wind as it slammed into the house, then decided that this was what had awakened her.

Regardless of what had, she was no longer sleepy. Turning her head, she viewed the clock on her bedside table, its face illuminated by a shaft of moonlight. It was after three o'clock. The fire had burned down, gray ash covering what embers still remained. Though the room was chilly, Julia felt snug and warm beneath the heavy quilts.

Still, a cup of hot chocolate would be nice. Julia sighed. She couldn't bring herself to wake Mary for something so trivial. Nor could she light the lamp and read a book. Lane's door was open, and had been for the past week. He seemed to be awaiting the arrival of the baby with as much impatience as she was.

Of course, if she took care to move quietly, she could get up and close the door.

She sat up, went to throw the covers aside, and let out a startled scream as pain cut through her lower back with vicious force. As quickly as it came, it subsided.

"Julia!"

Hastily tying the belt of his robe, Lane burst into her room and lit the lamp with hands that were shaking so badly he almost tipped it over.

Pulling the covers up under her chin, Julia offered him a weak smile. "I think it's time. . . ."

Reaching to the side of the bed, Lane tugged on the bell cord that would summon Mary.

The door opened just then, and Alma Gwenn stepped into the room.

In some surprise, Lane saw that the woman was fully dressed, her light brown hair neatly combed and fashioned into its usual prim knot. For a moment, Lane wondered whether she slept in her clothes, then had to dismiss the idea. There wasn't so much as a wrinkle to mar the smooth expanse of her starched white apron.

In fact, except for the white apron, Miss Gwenn had not undressed. She had been sitting in a chair, occasionally dozing off, while she waited for Julia to go into labor. Though the child wasn't due for several days yet, Miss Gwenn's practiced eyes had noted subtle changes in Julia during the past forty-eight hours. She had a sixth sense about this sort of thing and was seldom wrong. At Julia's first outcry, Alma Gwenn had promptly gotten up, donned her apron, and come in here.

Now she took one look at Julia and said to Lane: "I'll send for the doctor, sir."

"Yes, please do that," Lane murmured, still viewing the woman as if he didn't believe what he was seeing. Hearing a gasp from Julia, he promptly forgot Miss Gwenn. "Are you all right?" he asked softly.

"Yes," she whispered breathlessly. "Oh, Lane . . . I'm so glad it's time. . . ."

When the doctor arrived, Lane, who had taken the time to dress, was sitting on the bed, holding Julia's hand.

"Well, well," Dr. Blodgett said cheerfully as he came into the room. "And how are we doing?" He took off his coat and jacket and rolled up his sleeves.

Lane looked up, annoyed by his jovial manner. Didn't the man realize how serious this was?

Approaching the bed, the doctor removed the blanket and flung it on the nearest chair, but left the sheet draped over Julia. Rubbing his hands together, he nodded to Mary. "Young woman, get that fire going and keep it high!" He turned to the nurse. "I'll need hot water and extra sheets."

"I've already seen to that," Alma Gwenn murmured with a short nod.

The doctor came to stand by the bed. Julia, in the grip of another contraction, was biting her lip and clinging to Lane's hands. He waited until the contraction passed, then dropped a hand on Lane's shoulder. "You'd better wait in the other room, Lane. It'll be awhile. First ones always take the longest."

"I'm not going anywhere," Lane growled. "I'm staying right here. I want to see my child born."

The doctor's hand fell away, and he viewed Lane in gaping astonishment. "Stay here? You can't possibly do that!"

Lane turned his head to stare at the man. "And why

not?'' He had made this decision weeks ago, refusing to leave town even for a day, lest he miss being here when Julia went into labor. He had not, of course, mentioned what he was going to do to anyone, certain he would meet with resistance. But, dammit, it was his child! He had every right to be here.

Thrown off guard, the doctor sputtered, ''A woman in labor is nothing for a man to see! I'll have no time to tend to you if you fall to the floor in a faint!''

''I doubt that will happen.''

''You can't stay here!'' Dr. Blodgett was outraged. For more than forty years he had been delivering babies, and not once had the father been present. In fact, most men fell over their own feet in an effort to get out of the room as fast as possible. Lane wasn't moving. The doctor tried reason. ''What of your wife's modesty?'' he demanded.

Lane wouldn't permit himself to laugh. Instead, he said, ''Why don't we ask her?'' He gave Julia a tender smile. ''Do you want me to leave?''

Julia, too, had been taken by surprise. She was still gripping Lane's hands, convinced that his strength was flowing into her like a warm stream. In truth, she really didn't want him to stay and witness her travail, but she couldn't bear to let go of him.

''Stay. . . .'' she managed before the next pain struck.

Slowly, the doctor shook his head. ''You're making a grave mistake,'' he warned dourly and said a silent prayer that there would be no complications.

Lane gave him a lopsided grin. ''Kings do it all the time, you know. I've never heard of one of them fainting. . . .''

''I wasn't aware that this was a royal birth,'' the doctor muttered under his breath. Reaching under the sheet, he grasped Julia's ankles, then pushed them toward her buttocks, raising her knees. Then he placed a hand on her abdomen. Satisfied, he drew up a chair and sat down. When Lane gave him a surprised look, he shrugged. "There's nothing to do now except wait."

Mary kept adding coals to the fire until Lane thought he couldn't bear the heat. Perspiration trickled down his back, and he finally removed his jacket. Bustling about, Mary hung a kettle of water on the trivet, put the sheets within easy reach of the doctor, who appeared to be dozing, then settled herself down to wait.

Alma Gwenn, hands clasped at her waist, stood to the side, prepared to assist the doctor should it become necessary. She cast a disapproving look at Lane, in complete agreement with the doctor. Husbands in a lying-in room! It was unheard of!

At one point, Willa peered around the door, saw Lane, and quickly backed out, shooing April back to her room.

After a time, the first rays of the sun crept in through the window, and Mary got up to extinguish the lamps.

Julia's face was bathed in perspiration, and Lane kept using his handkerchief to mop her brow.

At eight o'clock, Mary brought in a tray with coffee and slices of seed cake. After helping himself to several pieces of the cake, Dr. Blodgett went to the table where the clean linens had been stacked. He plucked one from the pile, wiped his hands, and threw it carelessly aside, never seeing the compressed lips of Nurse Gwenn. Cleanliness! It had been drilled into her. Easy to say, not so easy to enforce. Almost a decade had passed since Lister had given substance to his germ theory; it always astounded her how slow doctors were in accepting it. Perhaps the Centennial would help, she thought, turning away as the doctor now rubbed his hands on his shirt. Lister was scheduled to speak at the Medical Exhibit. Maybe then they would listen.

Going to the foot of the bed, the doctor again put his hands beneath the sheet, felt Julia's abdomen, then straightened. "Won't be long," he pronounced, sucking his teeth.

All through the endless hours, Julia had managed to contain her cries. Now the pain intensified as the child struggled to come into the world, and she was unable to remain silent.

Dr. Blodgett pulled the chair close to the foot of the bed and reached under the sheet. In growing amazement, Lane watched as the man fumbled beneath the linen, his face set in lines of concentration, as if he were searching his memory for the proper procedure.

"How the hell can you see what you're doing?" Lane demanded harshly. In a quick and violent motion, he flung the sheet to the floor.

With an audible gasp, Dr. Blodgett leapt from the chair, his face turning an alarming shade of crimson. "My God, Lane! What are you doing? You cannot expose your wife's body to me like this! Have you no shame? Any modest woman would—"

Julia, well aware of what her husband had done, didn't care. All she wanted was for this to be over. Right now, embarrassment and modesty were words that held no meaning for her.

"Why are you prattling about modesty at a time like this?" Lane bellowed. In spite of the tight hold he had on himself, Julia's distress was beginning to unnerve him. And this fool doctor was standing there preaching instead of administering!

Dr. Blodgett raised his hand. "Control yourself, Lane!" He straightened and assumed a dignified look. "I understand your concern, but you must understand—"

"Are you planning to deliver my child blindfolded?" Lane was incredulous and made no attempt to conceal it. For all his bravado, he was finding this business a lot more upsetting than he had thought it would be.

"I warned you!" the doctor retorted tersely, now feeling defensive. "I told you this was no place for you to be. . . ."

"Get on with it! This has gone on long enough."

Drawing in his chin, the doctor looked affronted. "These things cannot be hurried. . . ."

"She's in pain!"

"Of course she is. She's supposed to be."

Both men came to an abrupt halt as Julia gave a piercing shriek.

Forgetting Lane, the doctor addressed Julia. "Push hard now. It's almost over."

Irresistibly drawn, and feeling that he was about to witness an incredible event, Lane moved closer, standing just behind the doctor.

His annoyance evident, Dr. Blodgett turned and glared at him. "Dammit, Lane! If you must watch, stand back!"

Alma Gwenn came forward and gave Lane a stern look. "Sir? May I suggest that if you feel faint you try to fall backward?"

Lane's answering look was grave. "I'll do my best, Miss Gwenn," he retorted solemnly.

With a snort of exasperation, the doctor again applied himself to the matter at hand; in only seconds, he had forgotten Lane's presence.

And, with a feeling of fascination overshadowed by reverence, Lane watched as his child was born.

Quickly and efficiently, the doctor severed and tied the cord. With a murmur of satisfaction, he held the child up for view.

"A boy!" he announced triumphantly, sounding very

pleased with himself. Then he smiled broadly as the infant began to wail without any encouragement from him.

Miss Gwenn, swaddling linen in hand, was prepared to take the child.

"No!" Lane said quickly, reaching out. "I want to hold him. . . ."

Dr. Blodgett hesitated, frowned, sighed, then carefully handed the child to Lane with instructions to keep the tiny head supported, after which he returned his attention to Julia.

Lane stood very still, afraid to move, staring down at his son.

"He's not very pretty," he exclaimed with a catch in his throat, and thought to himself that he was viewing the most beautiful baby in the world.

The doctor gave a short laugh. "At this point, none of them are. But don't worry. As soon as the redness subsides, he'll look just like every other baby."

"Never. . . ." Lane murmured, with awe in his voice. His son. His son! "Julia? Look!" He held up the infant, who was now crying in earnest, his small hands clenched into fists. "Have you ever seen a child like this!"

Turning her head and viewing the infant with as much wonder as her husband was displaying, Julia smiled softly. He was perfect, his lusty cry giving testimony to his father's strength.

"First of five," she whispered, but Lane was too enthralled; he heard nothing but the squalls of his son.

Alma Gwenn was still frowning at Lane. "Give the child to me now, sir. We don't want him to take a chill." She spoke briskly. In her opinion, this unorthodox behavior had gone on quite long enough.

Lane made no immediate move, hard-pressed to tear his gaze from his son. Finally, with a show of reluctance, he handed the infant to the nurse. He turned as the doctor clapped him on the shoulder.

"My congratulations, Lane," he said, then lowered his voice. "I do think it would be wise for you leave now. I'm sure your wife would welcome a bit of privacy at this time." His hand moved in a vague gesture, and he spoke almost apologetically. "The bedding and her clothing should be changed. . . ."

Lane hesitated, then nodded. "I'll get some breakfast. . . ."

After reporting the news to Willa and April, both of whom hurried into the nursery to view the child, Lane went downstairs to get something to eat. A half hour later, he was back in Julia's room. The sheets had been changed, and she was wearing a fresh nightgown. Mary had brushed her hair, and it now fell softly, cresting into a silken wave at her shoulders. She looked pale and tired but was otherwise composed.

Coming forward, Lane sat on the edge of the bed and took hold of her hand. Raising it to his lips, he said, "Thank you. Every gift I've ever given you pales beside the one you've just given to me."

Julia gazed up at him, too weary to shed the tears that left an ache in her heart, an ache that was more hurtful than any labor pain.

"You have given me much happiness, Julia. . . ." he murmured.

And love? Do you never speak of that? Her lips pressed together so that the words would not come out of their own accord. Closing her eyes, Julia let her weary body relax. She felt Lane's hand on her cheek and resisted the impulse to press into it. *I love you so much*, she thought, feeling his warmth and, yes, his gentleness. *But I will never beg you for your love. Give it to me of your own free will, and I will cherish it forever. . . .*

Lane withdrew his hand and smiled down at her sleeping form. Then he got up and quietly left the room, his mind now filled with thoughts of his son. Charles, he decided happily. It was only fitting that he name his firstborn after his father.

The following afternoon, Leah came to visit, bringing with her an exquisite blanket she had made. It was just the right size to fit the cradle. Filled with down, it was covered with white satin onto which she had meticulously embroidered figures of small animals with silk thread.

"Oh, Leah! I've never seen anything so beautiful," Julia exclaimed as she lifted the covering from the box.

Leah beamed. "I sewed every stitch of it myself," she reported proudly.

"Have you seen the baby?" Julia asked, placing the blanket carefully back in the box.

"Of course!" Leah paused, then made a face. "Although I must say it isn't easy getting past that nurse! I had to speak sharply before she would let me into the room."

Julia laughed. "She is efficient. . . ."

Although they were alone in the room, Leah peered cautiously about, then lowered her voice. "Lane told William that he was present when the child was born. Is that really true?"

Julia giggled. "As a matter of fact, it is. I'm afraid the doctor was most upset." Her smile faltered at the sound of Leah's horrified gasp.

"Good heavens! How awful for you!" Leah's indignation darkened her green eyes. "Men can be so . . . insensitive at times. Thank goodness William isn't that way. Why, in all the years we've been married, he has never seen me unclothed. He wouldn't even enter our room at night without knocking first." Still viewing Julia, she shook her head.

"You must have been terribly embarrassed." The color in her fine-featured face deepened in consternation.

"Well," Julia responded slowly, "actually . . ." She considered telling Leah that Lane's presence had, in fact, been a source of comfort for her, but the other woman looked so shocked that she decided not to pursue the subject.

Leah touched Julia's arm. "And now that it's all over, how are you feeling?"

"Thin!" Julia responded promptly.

"That you are!" Leah was about to get up, then she said, "Oh, I almost forgot. . . ." Opening her reticule, she withdrew a letter, handing it to Julia.

Reading it, Julia smiled broadly. It was from a Canadian woman named Emma Allison, written in response to the committee's request for a female who was capable of operating machinery. Handing the letter back to Leah, Julia asked, "Do you suppose she really can do it?"

Leah raised her brows as she stuffed the paper back into her reticule. "I certainly hope so! It's the only affirmative response we've received." She stood up, then pressed her cheek to Julia's. "I'll let you get your rest now. . . ."

Julia sighed as Leah left the room. Rest! Two weeks, the doctor had said. Julia didn't think she could tolerate being in bed that long.

On the evening of the fifth day after the birth of her son, Julia irritably kicked off the covers and got out of bed. Mary gave her a disapproving look that ended in a sigh of resignation when Julia instructed her to fetch a dress from the wardrobe.

"Ahh. . . ." Julia smiled in delight a while later as she viewed herself in the mirror. Soft green linen hugged a waist once again small enough for a man's hands to span—

Lane's hands! God, how she longed to feel them caress her again.

Seeing that it was a quarter to eight, Julia went downstairs.

"You must stay in bed for at least another week!" Willa admonished, when she saw Julia enter the dining room. "The doctor told you that."

Julia waved a hand, dismissing this. "I see no reason to stay in bed when I feel as well as I do."

Getting up, Lane came quickly to her side, holding her chair, his brow creased in concern. "Perhaps Mother is right," he murmured as she settled herself. "It is a bit soon. . . ."

She grinned up at him. "I'm a mother now," she reminded him.

Despite the fact that she was up and around, it was late April before Julia left the house. Leah picked her up on a balmy Saturday afternoon and took her to Fairmount Park so that she could see what progress had been made in the past four months.

The local newspapers, in addition to printing a daily list of the exhibits that were arriving by train or boat, had been reporting the progress of the construction on a day-to-day basis, so Julia had an idea of what to expect. Even so, she was astonished at all that had been accomplished in a relatively short time.

Leah led her up State Avenue, where each state in the Union had its own building and exhibits. Viewing the buildings situated along the crescent-shaped street, Julia smiled and felt a sense of pride to see that Massachusetts had the grandest of them all.

Just before entering the Women's Pavilion, Julia stopped to view the now-completed structure, which had been painted gray.

The building, which sprawled across an acre of ground, was in the shape of a cross. The center portion, a full twenty-five feet higher than the rest of the edifice, was crowned by an impressive cupola.

"It's amazing," Julia murmured, impressed. "It looks so different from the last time I saw it."

Leah laughed. "Wait till you see the rest of it."

Inside, the walls had been painted a light blue. Julia caught her breath at the sight of the fountain that had been constructed in the center; it was made of rock and surrounded by ferns. High above, suspended from the ceiling and positioned directly over the fountain, was a gigantic prismed chandelier.

The northeastern section of the building was devoted exclusively to American contributions, while the southwestern part of the building contained all the foreign exhibits. In a place of prominence, so that it was not to be missed, was a glass case that held etchings done by Queen Victoria, who had graciously donated them to the Women's Pavilion.

"How beautiful. . . ." Julia murmured, trying to take it all in at once.

"We are all very proud of it, Mrs. Manning," said Elizabeth Gillespie, coming toward her. "I'm glad to see you up and around again. I understand that you have a fine son."

Julia nodded. "Charles. And I do hope you and your husband can attend the christening."

"I wouldn't miss it. Few celebrations in this life are as rewarding as the christening of a child." To Julia's surprise, she felt her hand being pressed by Elizabeth Gillespie as the woman added, "I would like to personally thank you for all your assistance." Her blue eyes twinkled. "Quite frankly, I was beginning to think that I myself would have to make an attempt to set the machinery in motion. I don't mind telling you that I was not looking forward to the experience—'' She came to an abrupt halt as she saw two men entering the pavilion at just that moment.

Julia recognized the taller of the two men, for she had seen pictures of Governor Hartranft. Leah, inclining her head, supplied the name of the other man. "Dr. Loring," she whispered. "In charge of the Board of Finance."

Julia's lips twitched with a repressed smile. So this was their nemesis, she thought to herself; he looked anything but. He was short, with receding brown hair, and a very noticeable potbelly.

Catching sight of them, Dr. Loring came forward, Governor Hartranft at his side.

"Well, Mrs. Gillespie," he said, offering a spurious smile that fooled no one. "I must admit I didn't think you could do it."

"I did not do it alone, Dr. Loring," retorted Elizabeth Gillespie. "Women from every state in the Union had a hand in this."

"Indeed, indeed." He gave the governor a small nudge with his elbow, as if sharing a joke. "Too bad you'll have to hire a man to run it all for you. You've a great deal of machinery in here. All those looms, and even a printing press, I see."

Mrs. Gillespie arched a brow. "That won't be necessary, Dr. Loring. The Women's Pavilion will function solely at the hands of women—and that includes the machinery."

Taken aback, Dr. Loring stared at her. "And where, pray tell, have you found this mechanic in skirts?" He began to laugh.

"Her name is Emma Allison, and she's from Canada. We

expect her to arrive next week. She will stay with me until November when the Exhibition closes.''

Both men were now laughing openly. Brushing the tears from his eyes, Dr. Loring addressed the governor. ''I cannot wait to see what she looks like,'' he said between guffaws. ''A stevedore in a dress, I should imagine. Doubtless she will be the main attraction of the Women's Pavilion.''

Still laughing, the men walked away.

Julia exchanged an uneasy glance with Leah. They both feared that the observation was probably not too far exaggerated. No one knew what Emma Allison looked like; but then, no one had ever heard of a woman who operated machinery before. It was difficult to imagine what such a woman would look like.

Arriving home later that day, Julia immediately went to the nursery. To her surprise, Willa was seated on a chair by the window, holding Charles in her arms, her face reflecting a softness Julia had never seen her express before.

For a moment, Julia stood motionless in the doorway. When Willa did become aware of her presence, she gave a startled gasp, and her face flushed.

''I . . . hope you don't mind. . . .'' she said stiffly, getting to her feet.

''Mind?'' With a smile, Julia came forward but made no move to take Charles from the arms of her mother-in-law. ''Of course I don't mind. It's every child's right to be held in the arms of a loving grandmother.''

Willa gave her a sharp look. Seeing no sign of sarcasm, she relaxed, looking down at the child again. ''He looks just like Lane. . . .''

''Was Lane a beautiful baby?'' Julia asked softly. Reaching out, she touched a tiny, petal-soft hand, pleased when the baby grasped her finger in a tight grip.

"Oh, yes," Willa answered quickly, then added in a low voice: "He was not my firstborn, you know. . . ." Julia did not know, and regarded her mother-in-law in surprise. Willa nodded. "My first boy died in infancy."

"I had no idea," Julia murmured, still feeling surprise.

"Well," Willa went on, sounding like her old self, "it's not something to dwell upon."

They both viewed the baby again. He was wide awake and seemed very pleased with the attention he was receiving. Julia gave a soft laugh.

"It won't be long before you have two grandchildren vying for your attention." On the previous Sunday, Andrew had finally made the announcement of the child he and Hester were expecting.

"Yes," Willa murmured, sounding strangely subdued. "It would appear that our family is growing. . . ." She went to place the child in Julia's arms.

Julia, however, took a step back and raised a hand. "I . . . have some letters to write." That, of course, was not true but could be easily remedied. "I wonder if you would mind staying with Charles until I am through. I would appreciate it. . . ."

Willa sniffed, then went back to sit in the chair. "Of course. It's no trouble at all," she replied, her expression melting into the timeless look of a woman gazing upon a beloved child.

Julia watched them a moment, then quietly closed the door.

The following week, Mrs. Gillespie, involved with the final positioning of some late-arriving exhibits, requested that Julia and Leah go to the station to greet Emma Allison and transport her back to Mrs. Gillespie's house.

They both stood on the platform, scanning the faces of all

females getting off the train. After twenty minutes went by, the train began to move forward again, and Julia and Leah gave each other a helpless look.

"Are you certain this was the train she was to be on?" Julia asked.

Leah removed a letter from her reticule and quickly scanned it. "Yes. That's what the letter says. Do you suppose she missed it? Perhaps we should wait until the next train comes in—"

She broke off as someone behind them spoke.

"Excuse me . . . are you ladies here to meet Emma Allison?"

"Yes." Both Julia and Leah spoke at once.

The woman smiled. "I am Emma Allison."

Julia and Leah stared in silent astonishment. If there was one word that would describe the appearance of Emma Allison, it would have to be "teacher." She had the prim, no-nonsense appearance of a schoolmistress. She wasn't more than five feet tall, slim to the point of appearing delicate, with skin as clear as porcelain and large brown eyes that sparkled with intelligence and wit. She was wearing a dark blue wool dress over which she wore a matching cape. Her hat was also blue, with a pert yellow feather set at a jaunty angle.

The young woman gave a merry laugh at the sight of the gaping mouths she was seeing, having encountered this reaction before.

"I have five brothers," she explained in a well-modulated voice. "They all work in my father's shop—he builds and repairs machinery. . . ."

chapter
<u>twenty</u>

Arriving home from church the following Sunday, Julia went upstairs to change her clothes.

Thank heavens the Carlyles were joining them for dinner today, she thought to herself, hurriedly removing her dark blue linen dress.

Sunday dinners were turning into an event that Julia was beginning to dread, and she was certain that she was not the only one to think so. Willa insisted that Hester and Andrew return with them to Manning House after church for this family ritual. They were downstairs now, awaiting the arrival of the Carlyles.

As she donned the cool chiffon she had selected, Julia was hoping that today's break in the routine would ease some of the tension that had been settling over the dinner table during these past weeks like some miasmic cloud that had drifted in through an open window. Andrew did little but stare at April; April did little but stare at her plate; and Hester did little but stare at her husband and sister.

Regardless, Willa remained adamant: her family would be together for dinner on the Sabbath.

By the time Julia went back downstairs, William and Leah had arrived with their son, Desmond. Julia liked the young man, who was just short of his twenty-first birthday. He was shy and soft-spoken, but very serious and intense about his work. Leah had told her that Desmond had finished his architectural studies a full year ahead of schedule, due to the fact that he applied himself so diligently and seemed to have a natural flair for his chosen field.

"He started to copy his father's drawings when he was only six years old," Leah told her one day. "By the time he was twelve, he began to incorporate his own ideas."

Because of the presence of the Carlyles, dinner was served in the formal dining room. Set on the north side of the house, it was nowhere near as cheery or as bright as the smaller one, and the heavy, dark furniture didn't help the situation. Even the walls were painted an unattractive brown that seemed to reject light in any form.

Its only saving grace, from Julia's viewpoint, was that it was one of the few places in the house that remained uncluttered. The table was set in the center of the rectangular room, positioned beneath a crystal chandelier. At either end were matching sideboards. In the middle of the longer wall was a white marble fireplace. Aside from that, the only other furnishings were a few straight-backed chairs and a tall cherrywood clock.

For once, Julia noted with relief, the cook had managed to conjure up a palatable meal. There was chicken soup, followed by ham that had been baked in cider, sweet potatoes, string beans, and blueberry pie.

"Desmond," Lane said after the soup bowls had been

cleared away, "I understand that you've joined your father's firm."

"Yes, sir." Desmond sat up straighter as he regarded Lane. He had Leah's auburn hair and green eyes and his father's irregular features.

"And he has some grand ideas, haven't you, son?" William put in with a chuckle, then winked at Lane. "Desmond likes to design buildings that reach up for the clouds. . . ."

"It's the young people who have the new ideas," Lane pointed out. "I, for one, would like to see some of his designs."

"Easy enough," William said, still chuckling. "He's brought one of them with him."

"I . . . thought perhaps that April might like to see it," Desmond murmured. A flush grew and deepened on his cheeks. He darted a quick glance at April, pleased to see her smiling at him. Had they been alone, he would have told her how beautiful she looked in her pink grosgrain silk dress. But then, in his opinion, April looked beautiful no matter what she wore.

"Of course, designing such buildings," William went on, after taking a sip of his wine, "is one thing. Getting them to stay up is another."

"They said the same thing to James Eads," Desmond pointed out quickly, turning in his chair to view his father, who was seated beside him.

Leah, dressed in dark green taffeta, smiled, and exchanged a knowing look with Julia.

"That is the engineer who designed the St. Louis Bridge?" Lane asked the young man.

"Yes, sir. Everyone said the Mississippi couldn't be bridged at that point. You see, until recently, we were limited to iron and masonry. The weight alone made such a thing impractical. Mr. Eads used steel and designed the structure using three cantilevered arches. It's been in service now for two years without mishap.''

"Well, we can't argue with success," Lane commented, amused by the young man's enthusiasm.

"Indeed," Desmond nodded seriously. "Mr. Eads is a visionary."

When the meal was concluded, Hester and Leah insisted on a visit to the nursery, where they tiptoed in to view a sleeping Charles, after which Andrew and Hester departed for home.

The rest of them settled down in the drawing room. With a graceful movement, April seated herself on the sofa, and after a moment's hesitation, Desmond headed in her direction.

"Would you like to see my design?" he asked as he sat down beside her.

"Of course, Desmond. I'd love to see it."

Reaching into a pocket, he brought forth a piece of drafting paper, then unrolled it for her inspection, watching her expectantly. April hadn't the faintest idea of how to read a blueprint, but she could count stories.

"Desmond!" she said with a laugh. "It's eleven stories high!"

She turned to look at him, eyes lit with amusement. Desmond felt his cheeks burn, but not from her words; Desmond wasn't entirely sure just what it was she had said. He was too busy noticing how her lashes fanned her cheeks, creating little shadows that came and went as she raised or lowered her eyes. And her mouth—it was so . . . soft. He had never kissed her, one of the great regrets of his life; but he longed to do so, longed to. . . .

"There are eleven stories," April repeated when he didn't immediately respond.

Desmond opened his mouth and had to clear his throat before he could translate his thoughts into words. "Yes, yes. I know," he said eagerly. "The steel framing . . ."

"Oh, Desmond," April interrupted, putting a hand to her lips. "People can't walk that far! All those steps. . . ."

"Elevators!" he said quickly. "Even though they go only five or six stories now, they can go higher! There's no telling how high they can go. With the elevator and the steel framing, there's no limit to the height of a building."

April smiled indulgently. She'd never been on an elevator and was certain the newspapers were correct when they portrayed the contraptions as death traps.

"Let me take a look at that," Lane said, coming to stand before Desmond, who got to his feet. Taking the paper, he studied it carefully. "I don't see why this wouldn't work," he murmured.

"I don't, either," Julia said, peering at the drawing with interest. "Our new city hall looks higher than that."

"That's because of the statue, Julia," William interjected. "The building itself is only seven stories; the statue of William Penn is more than twenty feet high; the height of the building is an illusion."

"If a steam elevator can go up seven stories, it can go eleven," Desmond insisted. "Even more!"

Lane handed the drawing back to him, then clapped the young man on the shoulder. "I think you're right." Then he viewed William's beaming face; there was no mistaking the man's pride. "Somehow I think your father does, too. A brandy, William?" he asked, heading for the decanter as the other man nodded his assent.

Desmond sat down beside April again. "Have you re-

ceived an invitation to Melissa's birthday party?'' he asked.
April nodded, and he went on. ''Umm . . . I was wondering
if you would allow me to escort you. . . .''

April turned away, feeling uncomfortable. She knew that
Desmond still cared for her, but her own heart felt empty. ''I
don't think . . .''

''Oh, please don't make up your mind right now,''
Desmond urged hastily. ''The party is two weeks away. I
thought . . . well, I thought you might at least consider
it. . . .''

April summoned a smile. ''I'll think about it, Desmond.
But I can't say for certain. . . .''

''I understand,'' he said, feeling relieved that she had not
refused him outright.

It was inconceivable to Desmond that Andrew Hollinger
would have turned away from April to marry Hester, but it
had been the happiest day of his life when he learned that
April was no longer engaged to be married. There had been
a time when Desmond thought that he and April were
heading toward marriage. The only reason he hadn't proposed was because he had been waiting to finish his school-
ing and become financially settled before taking on the
responsibility of a wife and family. And then, when Andrew
had come on the scene, it appeared that he had lost April
forever.

Now, as he viewed her beautiful profile, Desmond vowed
that he would not let her get away a second time. He wet his
lips.

''Perhaps I could call on you one night next week?'' he
pressed, leaning toward her.

''No,'' April said quickly, smoothing the folds of her
skirt. ''That would be inconvenient. I . . . I think I'm busy

almost every evening.'' She averted her gaze from the expression of disappointment on his face.

Desmond leaned back against the cushions, then his mouth firmed. April couldn't refuse to see him forever; he would present himself every day until she did receive him.

It was after ten o'clock by the time the Carlyles finally took their leave. Willa and April had already gone upstairs when Nancy closed the front door behind their departing guests.

''That'll be all, Nancy. You may retire now,'' Julia said to the young woman, well aware that she had to get up each morning at six.

She and Lane were halfway up the stairs when Julia realized that a lamp was still lit in the drawing room.

''I'll see to it,'' she said to Lane.

A few minutes later, having extinguished the forgotten lamp, Julia was once again about to go upstairs when she paused in the darkened foyer. Then, on an impulse, she went into the kitchen.

Lighting one of the gaslights, she thoughtfully viewed the cupboards, then approached one of them. It was locked.

Locked!

Angry now, she went to Mrs. Litton's room and knocked loudly on the door. Though she was certain that the housekeeper was asleep, Julia didn't care the least bit about disturbing the woman's slumber.

She had to knock a few more times before the door at last opened. Mrs. Litton didn't look too pleased to see her.

''I told you I wanted the cupboards and pantry to remain unlocked at all times! Can you give me an explanation as to why my instructions haven't been carried out?'' To her annoyance, Julia found herself trembling with anger.

The woman gave her a sullen look as she pulled her flannel robe closer. "Mrs. Manning said otherwise."

Julia put out her hand, palm up. "Give me the keys."

Mrs. Litton folded her arms across her chest. "I don't have them. I give them to Mrs. Manning at the end of the day." She paused, smiled unpleasantly, then added, "If you want the keys, you'll have to wake *her* up."

Julia hesitated, uncertain as to whether the woman was lying or not.

"Is there anything else you want?" Mrs. Litton asked, arms still folded on her bosom.

Julia sighed deeply. "No." Turning away, she left the kitchen. A few more words with that woman and Julia knew her anger would get the better of her. Then everyone in the house would be up.

Anger and annoyance vanished in an instant when Julia entered her room a few minutes later to see Lane waiting for her. This was the first time he had come to her bed since Charles had been born.

"Hello," she said softly, walking toward him.

And then she was in his arms and nothing mattered except the joy she felt at once again being in his embrace.

On the following Friday afternoon, Julia came out of the drawing room, having spent the last hour playing the piano. Pausing, she saw Desmond Carlyle in the foyer. The young man was standing there, hat in one hand, a bouquet of flowers in the other. Julia shook her head as she viewed the blossoms. She didn't think there was an empty vase left in the house. Even on those days when Desmond himself didn't show up at their door, the flowers did.

"Desmond! How nice to see you," she said, walking

toward him. "Would you care to come inside and sit down?"

"No, thank you, Mrs. Manning," he replied. "I'm just waiting. . . ." His voice trailed off as he saw Nancy coming downstairs. The expectant look on his pleasant face turned crestfallen as the girl shook her head. Again April had declined to see him.

With a sigh, Desmond handed the bouquet to Julia. "Would you please give them to April?"

"Certainly I will." Julia felt saddened for the young man. He was so obviously wearing his heart on his sleeve.

"And would you . . . would you please ask her if she has made up her mind about allowing me to escort her to the Stapletons' house next Saturday night? The party . . ."

"I know," Julia said, smiling. "It's Melissa's eighteenth birthday. I will speak to April."

"I would appreciate it," Desmond murmured, casting a wistful look in the direction of the top of the stairs. He turned then and left the house.

"Shall I put them in water, Mrs. Manning?" Nancy started to reach for the flowers.

"No," Julia replied. "I'll take them up to April."

The girl, however, was not in her room. Going to the window, Julia saw her heading toward the gazebo, a light shawl covering her brown muslin dress. She had obviously used the backstairs in order to avoid seeing Desmond.

Frowning, Julia left the bedroom. A few minutes later, she emerged on the back porch and began to walk toward April, who was sitting on the wooden bench, staring across the expanse of lawn that was only now beginning to show the vibrant green of spring.

"Am I disturbing you?" Julia asked softly as she sat down on the opposite bench.

April drew her shawl closer about her. "Of course not." She glanced at the flowers only once, displaying no interest whatsoever.

"Desmond was just here," Julia said, placing the bouquet next to April.

"I know."

"Don't you like Desmond?"

April shrugged. "He's nice enough. . . ."

"I think he cares a great deal for you," Julia ventured.

"I don't want him to care for me," April countered with a wave of her hand.

"Is that it?" Julia asked quietly after a moment, "or could it be that you are afraid to care for him?"

"That's not true!" April exclaimed too quickly, turning to look at Julia with angry eyes. In a swift motion, she picked up the bouquet and flung it out of the gazebo, where it tumbled across the lawn, coming to rest forlornly at the trunk of a tree.

Julia opened her mouth, then closed it again. Right now, April appeared in no mood for a discussion of this sort. She could do only harm, Julia thought to herself, if she pressed the issue at this point. With a weary sigh, she stepped down the wooden steps, retrieved the bouquet, and went back into the house.

That night, still feeling unsettled, Julia mentioned the incident to Lane.

"I do feel you ought to talk to her," she concluded.

"I have," Lane replied. He gave a short laugh. "There was a time when I thought Hester to be the stronger of my sisters. Over the years, however, I've come to know differently. Hester can be very determined and single-minded when it comes to getting what she wants. April's strength is of a more durable kind, not easily visible except to those who know her well. She is not as fragile as she appears to be." At Julia's doubtful look, Lane drew her into his arms. "You will see that I am right," he murmured, bending to nuzzle the softness of her neck.

Julia's inclination was to pursue the subject, but his warm breath was causing little shivers of delight to blot all thoughts from her mind. With a soft moan, she turned her head to kiss him, the palms of her hands caressing his broad shoulders. As they sank onto the bed, April's problems fled her mind.

But not for long. The following afternoon, Desmond appeared with yet another bouquet. The scenario of the day before was repeated. This time, when Julia headed for April's room, she was determined to have a talk with the girl. If it were only Desmond's invitations April was turning down, there would, Julia thought, be no cause for worry. April, however, was refusing each and every invitation that came her way. She was turning into a veritable recluse! The only time she left the house was to go to church. And Willa, for reasons of her own, seemed disinclined to interfere with her daughter's self-induced seclusion.

She found April seated at her writing table, making entries in her diary. The room appeared larger now that Hester's bed and wardrobe had been removed.

Coming closer, Julia placed the flowers on the writing table. "I don't have to tell you who these are from, do I?" Noting the high color that flooded the girl's cheeks, Julia pursed her lips. "I understand that there was a time when you liked Desmond a lot. . . ."

A short nod greeted that.

"Has Desmond changed?" Julia persisted.

"Oh, no," came the quick response. "I've known Desmond since we were children. He's always been sweet and kind."

Her voice lowered and took on a bitter note that Julia had never heard from her before. "But then, so was Andrew. If Andrew could betray me, then Desmond can do the same. I . . . just don't want to go through that again." Her chin rose. "I shall never marry. It would be unfair of me to take up Desmond's time." Appearing agitated, she got up and walked to the window.

Privately, Julia had her doubts as to whether it had been Andrew who had betrayed April. She said nothing of her suspicions, however.

"Please listen to me, April!" Julia was beginning to feel a bit desperate. There seemed to be no way of breaking through the barrier April had erected around herself. "You must not allow what happened with Andrew to destroy your life. No one wants to think of people—especially those we love—as being cruel or deceitful."

"Hester is neither!" April's defense of her sister was emphatic. Her expression dared Julia to take exception.

"Of course she isn't," Julia assured her in the face of that look. "I'm convinced of it."

Julia felt a tremor of alarm. The serenity April displayed was not so unshakable after all. The pain was there to see, in the large blue eyes, more touching because it was mute. How many times had she cried when no one was around to hear?

"I'm sorry," April breathed, genuinely contrite at the way her voice had risen.

Turning, April went to the window and stared outside, past the gazebo, past the flowering daffodils that bobbed in the warmth of the sun, her gaze coming to rest on the tranquil water of the pond, its surface reflecting the intense blue of the sky. She knew that Julia was trying to help, was sincerely concerned. But Julia didn't seem to realize just how much she was asking. Going out with Desmond was one thing—he really did care, she knew that—but the thought of facing her friends, each of them knowing that she had been jilted, was enough to set her heart pounding. Outwardly there would be a show of compassion. "Poor April. How dreadful for you. . . ." And behind fans, there would be titters of glee. Oh, she couldn't face that!

Julia sighed. "April, you must understand that . . . circumstances sometimes make people act in a way that they would not normally."

"I just can't believe that Andrew . . . " April's voice ended on a sob.

Viewing April's tears, Julia made a decision. "You mustn't feel as though you're the only one who has had to face this situation. I . . . I was engaged to a man before I met Lane."

Distracted, April's eyes went wide. "You? What happened?"

"He . . . he decided he didn't want to marry me, and so he broke our engagement."

"He fell in love with someone else?"

Julia smiled sadly and shook her head. "No. In some ways it would have been easier if he had. It wasn't that he loved someone else more, it was just that he didn't love me enough." She paused, then added, "I've not spoken of this to anyone else, and I hope you'll keep my confidence."

"Of course I will," April agreed with a nod of her head. Coming back to the writing table, she viewed Julia with open curiosity. "What . . . did your friends do? I mean, how did they take the news?"

Julia stared at the lovely, clear-complexioned face before her. Then she gave a short laugh. "I discovered that I didn't have any," she replied bluntly.

April blinked in surprise. "Oh, Julia! I can't believe that. . . ."

"Believe it!" Julia retorted wryly.

"Were you terribly unhappy?" April asked hesitantly, as if feeling her question was improper.

Julia tilted her head to one side as she thought about that. "For a while, I guess. But there comes a day when you must be brave enough to pick up the pieces and continue with your life. Sometimes, when we look back, we can see that misfortune can be a blessing in disguise. As it was for me," she added quietly.

April bit her lip. "Do you think Andrew's marrying Hester is a blessing in disguise for me?"

Reaching out, Julia clasped the girl's slim hands in her own. "Only time will tell," she said softly. "Wouldn't it be wise to give it a chance and discover the answer to that for yourself?"

April was silent for a time, and Julia did nothing to break her thoughts. Julia's revelations had really taken April by surprise. She had to confess to herself that she was indeed thinking of her situation as being unique.

Julia was right, April thought, now feeling ashamed. It was time she stopped feeling sorry for herself.

As for her friends . . . well, she couldn't hide from them forever, could she? At last, April sat down at the writing table and reached for a piece of notepaper.

"I'll write to Desmond," she said in a voice brisk with determination, "and accept his invitation." She flashed a smile at Julia. "Would you please tell one of the servants to put those in water?" She nodded at the bouquet, then picked up a pen.

Julia's lips twitched in amusement as she picked up the flowers. "I'll do it myself," she offered, wondering where she would find an empty vase.

Despite her newfound resolve, the following Saturday

seemed to arrive with undue swiftness for April. There was, however, no hope of backing down. The invitation had been accepted; it must be honored. Being just as adept at wielding a needle as her mother was, April had hurriedly embroidered Melissa's initials on several linen handkerchiefs and wrapped them attractively in paper and ribbon.

That night, April took great pains with her appearance. This was not so much to impress Desmond as it was to bolster her own morale. She chose a dress of bright yellow, with a pert little bustle and puffed sleeves. Her hair, as usual, was drawn back from her face and arranged in long, soft curls.

Willa was going with them. "To assist Germaine Stapleton," she told April and Desmond, neither one of whom believed her.

Desmond was unhappy with the maternal chaperoning, but he took it in stride. It was enough to be in the company of April for an entire evening.

By the time they walked up the marble steps that led to Melissa's house, April's knees were shaking.

Desmond seemed to sense her unease. Ignoring Willa's look of disapproval, he took April's arm as he rang the doorbell.

And then they were inside.

Her plump body encased in yards of pink satin, Melissa came rushing forward to greet them. She was a pretty girl, with wide-set brown eyes and deep dimples. Everyone said that Melissa would, one day, look just like her mother. Melissa always blushed in annoyance when she heard that; Germaine Stapleton weighed in excess of two hundred pounds.

"Oh, April! I'm so glad you could come." Melissa gave April—whom she considered to be her very best friend—a hug, receiving the proffered gift with a display of enthusiasm. She tugged on April's hand. "Come inside. I'm just about to cut the cake."

Melissa had invited about twenty of her friends to help her celebrate her birthday. Even though the number was modest, the small front parlor appeared to be crowded with young people, all of whom seemed to be laughing and talking at the same time when April and Desmond entered the room.

Was there a brief lull? April thought there was. Perhaps, though, it was just her imagination. People waved and said hello, their looks a bit more lingering than necessary. That, April decided, was not her imagination.

The topic had to come up. And soon it did.

Violet Partridge, a tall, thin girl whose full lower lip gave her an expression of a perpetual pout, sat down beside April, who was finishing the last of her cake. Her companion, a young man named Richard Nevins, came to stand beside Desmond, offering a brief nod as he did so.

"We were all so shocked to hear about Hester and Andrew," Violet said, assuming an expression of great concern. She patted April's arm. "I daresay it must have been a terrible shock for you, too." She sighed. "Poor April. Your own sister!"

"One would have thought that Hollinger would have been decent enough to wait until you were out of your sickbed before he jilted you," Richard put in with a laugh.

Carefully, April placed her plate on the table beside the couch. She had been right, she thought glumly; she should never have come here tonight. Desmond would have to take her home. Before she could express her wish, however, she heard Desmond speak.

"Did I hear you use the term 'jilted,' Richard?" Desmond turned to the young man and fixed him with a cold stare.

"Well, the term does seem apropos," Richard replied with another laugh, one that now contained a thread of nervousness. He didn't like the way Desmond was looking at him.

"I wonder how such rumors get started," Desmond mused softly, rubbing his chin.

Violet leaned forward. "Rumors? You mean they didn't elope?"

Desmond smiled at her. "Of course they did." Extending his hand, he raised April to her feet. "But after April broke her engagement, I would say that Andrew was free to marry anyone he chose. . . ." He paused to look at Richard through narrowed eyes. "Now, if I ever hear that word again in conjunction with April, I will know who started such an unkind rumor. . . ."

Gently, he led April to the other side of the room.

"They'll never believe that," she murmured, eyes downcast.

"People will believe anything, if it's repeated often enough," Desmond replied with a grin. Glancing across the room, he added, "Come on. Let's sit on the floor with the others. Melissa is getting ready to open her gifts."

chapter
twenty-one

It was late morning when Julia opened the door to the nursery. The room was, as always, spotless. More than one servant had run to the housekeeper in tears, overwhelmed by the impossible demands of Nurse Gwenn. But even Willa, when she heard the complaints, had backed down in the face of the formidable Miss Gwenn, who demanded a ceiling-to-floor cleaning each and every day of the week, during which time, weather permitting, she took her charge to the rear gardens.

After a brief nod to the nurse, Julia went directly to the cradle. "He's awake," she said, whispering as though he weren't.

Miss Gwenn nodded. She rarely saw the need to reply to the obvious.

Picking him up, Julia cuddled Charles in her arms, relishing the feel of the tiny hand pressed against her chin.

"It's almost time for his nap," the woman reminded her

in clipped tones, stalking Julia's footsteps as she, began to walk around the nursery.

"I know," Julia responded with a sigh, amused by the hawk-eyed vigilance with which the nurse was observing her. Julia felt like reassuring her that she wouldn't accidentally drop the child. She paused by the window, not wanting to relinquish the little warm body just yet.

Below, a carriage had just pulled up to the front entrance, and Julia was surprised to see Hester emerge. Since she and Andrew had been married, Hester had been coming here only on Sundays. Looking up at that moment, Hester waved, then disappeared from view.

Julia's attention immediately returned to her son. He was waving a small hand, the gesture accompanied by an interesting noise.

Julia's eyes widened in delight as she turned to Alma Gwenn. "Did you hear that?" she exclaimed. "I'm sure he said 'Mama'!"

The nurse folded her arms and frowned. "Gas, Mrs. Manning. Put his head on your shoulder and gently pat his back. . . ."

Downstairs, Hester was informed by Nancy that her mother was out. Hester already knew this. Today was Monday, the day her mother always made social calls. It was April she wanted to see.

For days now she had been trying to work up enough courage to talk to April. Oh, they spoke to each other every Sunday, but it wasn't the same thing. Hester had had no idea she would miss April as much as she did, and as the days flowed into weeks and then months, she was growing more and more upset by their estrangement.

This morning, after Andrew left for work, she had made

up her mind to tell April the truth, and she prayed to God that her sister would find it in her heart to forgive her.

April, however, was also out. Hester sighed as Nancy told her that April had gone for a ride on her favorite mount.

Thanking the servant, Hester returned to her carriage. She was about to instruct the driver to take her back home; then, on an impulse, she directed him to drive along the river. April always rode along the narrow path to the side of the road, usually as far as the Chestnut Street Bridge before returning home.

They had gone less than a mile when Hester caught sight of April, wearing her dark gray riding habit and perched sidesaddle on the bay mare that Lane had purchased for her two years ago.

As the carriage came alongside, April turned, her eyes widening as she saw Hester peering at her through the carriage window. Leaning forward, Hester told the driver to stop.

"Hes! What on earth are you doing out here?" April led the horse closer and smiled with pleasure.

"I went to the house to see you, but Nancy told me you'd gone riding." Extending a gloved hand through the window, she patted the mare's neck.

"I'll head on home. . . ." April started to say, then paused when Hester shook her head.

"No, no." She opened the door and got out. "I'd welcome some fresh air." Turning, she motioned for the driver to wait, then glanced up at April. "Could we walk?"

"Of course." April quickly dismounted. Holding the reins loosely in one hand, she fell in step beside Hester, the mare trailing behind her. "Do be careful of your footing, Hes," she cautioned with a frown of concern, noticing that Hester was wearing soft kid shoes that were entirely unsuitable for walking. She pointed ahead to a grassy rise. "Why don't we sit over there?"

"Good idea," Hester agreed with a small laugh, already feeling the strain of her brief exertion.

While Hester settled herself as comfortably as she was able, resting her back against the broad trunk of a tree, April tied the mare to a low branch so that the animal could graze. Then she sank down beside Hester.

"Is anything wrong, Hes?" she asked.

Hester wasn't aware that she had turned away until April's voice jarred her. "No, nothing's wrong," she answered quietly, plucking at a blade of grass. "I just wanted to talk to you." She offered a sad smile. "We . . . don't seem to do that much anymore."

April took a deep breath and expelled it slowly. "I know. . . ." She viewed her hands in her lap, then spoke plaintively. "I miss you, Hes. I've always known that one day we'd both get married and have to live apart, but I never thought it would be quite this way. . . ."

"You cannot miss me more than I miss you. That's why I came to see you today, hoping we could be alone . . . and talk." Hester fell silent and stared at the blue water. Only a few boats disturbed its pristine expanse. It was a perfect spring day: warm, but with a pleasantly cool breeze that eased the heat of the sun. Inclining her head, Hester caught her lower lip between her teeth. How was she to explain her treachery and deceit?

Begin at the beginning? Perhaps that was, after all, the best way.

"Do you remember the day Mama and I came home from New York," she began, "and you told me about the young man you had met?"

"I remember."

The sadness in the whispered voice was like a vise on Hester's heart.

"I thought it was amusing," she forced herself to continue. "And then . . . then I met him." Her eyes implored April's understanding. "From that first moment I saw him, I knew that I had fallen in love for the first and only time in my life. I couldn't help myself. Oh, April!" She pressed a hand to her lips, yet knew the words had to be spoken. "What happened was all my fault, every bit of it! You must never blame Andrew."

"I don't blame anyone," April protested hastily, giving a start of surprise. "Certainly I could never fault Andrew for loving you. It just happened."

"No!" Hester cried out. "Oh, God, you don't understand. It didn't just happen. I caused it. Andrew doesn't love me. The night we made love, he . . . thought I was you." Her voice fell to a ragged whisper. "I led him to think so."

As the meaning of what she was hearing sank in, April paled. "But when . . . ?"

"The night you were sick and couldn't go to the opera. . . ."

April got up and walked to the water's edge. "You . . . never told Andrew that I couldn't go?"

"No."

Slowly, April turned and regarded Hester for a long moment. "You went in my place, didn't you?"

"Yes." Turning her head, Hester absently watched as a squirrel cautiously left the safety of a clump of bushes and took a few tentative steps toward the water. Becoming aware of their presence, the little animal froze, then scurried back to his haven. For a moment, Hester wished that she could do the same. But there was no haven that could erase her guilt.

With a sigh, April returned to the grassy rise. "You always could imitate me better than I could imitate you," she noted as she sat down again.

Hester shifted her weight so that she could view her sister directly. "April, there's one thing I want you to know. I didn't know you were ill that night. I would never have left you alone if I'd had even the slightest suspicion."

"That is one thing you don't have to tell me, Hes," April said quietly.

"It was only after you fell asleep that I decided to . . ." She raised a hand, then let it fall to her lap again. "It was to be only one night. . . ."

One night that will go on for a lifetime, April thought, suddenly saddened. She shook her head. "But Andrew must have known!"

Hester wet her lips. "Only . . . only after we . . ." She took a deep breath. "He was very angry when he found out. That would have been the end of it, except for the fact that I got pregnant." She saw April's shock but pressed on. "Even after I told him about the baby, he didn't want to marry me. It was Lane who made him do that."

Frowning, April hesitated, then asked, "Does Mother know about all this?"

Hester raised her head to look at her twin, uncertain as to how to answer. No word had passed between her and Willa to indicate that she was aware of all that had taken place, not even when she had been told of the child; yet, Hester had the distinct feeling that her mother did know.

"I think she does, but I'm not sure," she answered finally.

A look of perplexity creased April's smooth brow. "When did you really get married?"

"The day Lane supposedly took me to Boston, we in fact

went to Lancaster. Andrew and I were married there, on the very day we told you about it."

April was silent while she tried to absorb it all. One thing, though, stood out sharp and clear in her mind: Andrew had not betrayed her. He had had to marry Hester because of their child; and that was only right.

The following thought, however, was one April could not accept. She could not find it in her heart to credit Hester with an act of betrayal against her. April knew very well that Hester had never had it in mind to hurt her, or anyone else for that matter. When all was said and done, Hester was guilty of falling in love.

And as if to confirm that in her own mind, she said, "You must love him very much." Her own unhappiness seemed unimportant to April in the face of her sister's real distress. And was she, in fact, unhappy? April wondered, feeling a jolt of surprise.

"I love him more than I can say," Hester admitted. A catch in her voice gave way to a sob.

There was silence for a time, only Hester's soft weeping breaking the stillness.

"I don't think I could love a man that much," April mused after a while, wistfulness in her voice; and she suddenly realized that was true. April wrinkled her brow. If the truth were told, she hadn't thought about Andrew in days. Maybe even weeks. She couldn't deny, even to herself, that it was Desmond who kept invading her thoughts of late. It was as though the two of them had picked up where they had left off before Andrew came into her life.

She thought about Melissa's party and smiled. Desmond had been like a rock! Buffering her from anyone rude enough to stare, never leaving her side for an instant. And, the most amazing thing of all, parrying questions with a sharp and cutting wit that more often than not left the inquisitor's face beet red! Several more incidents, in addition to the one with Violet and Richard, had occurred during the course of that evening. Until that night, April had never realized how . . . assertive Desmond was.

"Can you ever forgive me?" Hester implored.

Roused from her musings, April gazed into those vivid blue eyes, so like her own. "I would have no man, not even Andrew, destroy the bond between us," she said sincerely. "Andrew I will willingly let go; but I could not bear it if we were separated."

"We never shall be," Hester vowed, embracing her sister. Relief coursed through her with such force that it left her feeling light-headed.

"And now?" April asked, after a few minutes had passed. "How is everything between you and Andrew?"

Hester shrugged. "We don't argue, if that's what you mean; in fact, we are . . . most polite to each other." Like two tenants sharing the same lodging, she thought sadly. They did share the same bed, though, and on more than one occasion the heat of their bodies had flared into passion. But Hester could not say that those occasions were bringing them any closer. The next day, Andrew always seemed to be a bit embarrassed. "I think . . . I hope the child will make a difference."

"I'm sure it will," April said quickly. She stood up and helped Hester to her feet. Putting a hand on Hester's cheek, her thumb gently brushed away a clinging tear. "I do wish you every happiness, Hes. I'm sure things will work out for you and Andrew."

"I hope you're right," Hester sighed.

"He cannot help but love you and his child. . . ." Reaching out, April untied the reins and patted the mare's ears.

"How I wish I could believe that," Hester murmured as they began to retrace their steps. "Perhaps someday . . ." She hesitated, then spoke of her resolve, her voice filled with a determination that April knew all too well. "April, I will be such a good wife to Andrew, he will never have cause for complaint. This I swear before God. If I can earn his forgiveness, perhaps one day I can earn his love as well."

"You have mine," April said softly. Then, glancing down at Hester's thickening waist, she brightened. "Can you believe that I am to be an aunt again? Twice in one year!"

"Oh, April!" Hester clasped her sister in a tight embrace. "The good Lord made only one of you. . . ."

April gave a small laugh as she hugged her sister. "Not in this case, Hes," she said softly. Drawing back, she looked deeply into Hester's blue eyes. "There's not one of me; there's two of us. . . ."

chapter
twenty-two

On the morning of May 10, Julia opened her eyes, instantly awake, jumping out of bed with an enthusiasm she hadn't displayed since she had been a child. Going to the window, she flung the drapes aside.

"Ohh . . . ." she cried in dismay as she saw the rain.

It was not a light drizzle; it was a downpour! Thick, fat drops beat the ground with a vengeance, pocking the earth with countless little holes that immediately filled with water.

"Julia?"

She turned as Lane came into the room. Despite the early hour, he was already dressed, though he had not yet donned his jacket.

"Lane! It's raining!"

Coming to stand beside her, he draped an arm around her shoulder. "If I could do something about it, I would," he said with mock gravity, then grinned at her. "How would you like to huddle under an umbrella with me?"

"Lane, it isn't funny!" She was close to tears.

"I know." His tone turned gentle, and he gathered her to him. "But it's only six-thirty, Julia. The opening won't begin until nine o'clock. Perhaps the rain will let up by then . . . ."

And by eight-thirty, it did. Not only did the rain stop, but also the sun broke triumphantly through the clouds, evoking a collective sigh of relief from everyone.

And what a day it was! The air smelled clean and pure. Budding leaves and flowers, having been kissed by the morning rain, now glistened like tiny jewels.

Desmond, dressed in his best bottle-green frock coat over tan trousers, arrived to escort April; and in some amusement, Julia wondered whether he would be able to take his eyes off the girl long enough to view the exhibits.

Along Market Street, flags from every participating country flapped from lampposts. Long before nine o'clock people began to flock to Fairmount Park, leaving the city virtually deserted. Never before had anyone seen so many people all in one place. From all walks of life, they paid the fifty-cent note that was required for admission and came to gape in wonder. Ladies in silk dresses and gentlemen in top hats mingled with modestly dressed laborers and farmers clad in work clothes. Carriages, wagons, even ladies' hat trimmings were festooned in red, white, and blue.

It was fortunate that the stream of vehicles was, for the most part, going in the one direction, for there was little room in which to turn around.

As they drove up to the front entrance, Willa peered outside at what had been dubbed "Shantyville." The noise was ear-shattering as vendors tried to outshout each other in selling their wares. The odors of sausages and hot roasted potatoes mingled, sometimes unpleasantly, with pies and caramels, peanuts and oysters, and red, white, and blue popcorn balls.

Willa wrinkled her nose as they passed the Can Can Palace. "Have you heard about the dance they're going to do at that place?" she demanded of Lane, who tried not to smile.

"I have, Mother," he replied with a nod of his head. "But I've not seen it. . . ."

"From what I've heard, it's disgraceful!" Willa huffed. "It wouldn't surprise me in the least if the authorities close it down."

April leaned forward to stare at the building in question. "Is that the dance Mr. Twain wrote about? The one where the dancers lift their skirts up?"

"April!" Willa admonished with a glare. "That is not a fit observation for a lady!"

Properly chastised, April settled back again, a small smile tugging at the corners of her mouth when Lane winked at her.

Finally the carriage halted and they all got out.

A sense of excitement traveled on the breeze, touching everyone in its path. They all knew that today, on this plateau situated one hundred and twenty feet above the Schuylkill River, history was being made. Never before had such an event been attempted, much less brought to fruition. In all, thirty-eight countries and thirty-nine states and territories were represented here on this tenth day of May in the year 1876.

In the area set aside for the opening ceremonies, a 150-piece orchestra was playing "Hail to Columbia."

The crowd, however, was so noisy with anticipation that only those in the front rows were able to hear the speeches that followed. When President Grant concluded his oratory, the Emperor of Brazil stepped forward to say a few words. The monarch was greeted with such lusty cheers that many minutes passed before he could speak. In the few weeks since his arrival in this country, Dom Pedro II and his wife had gained the affection of the people. A man of much charm and grace, he dressed in a most ordinary manner, disdained pomp, and had a ready smile and a courteous word for everyone.

After the opening ceremony, they all made their way into Machinery Hall to see the Corliss engine put in operation. Nothing would operate until this one metal behemoth was set in motion, for it powered some eight thousand other pieces of machinery at various locations on the grounds. This single engine was supplying power for wool combers, cotten spinners, printing presses, lithographers, and even water pumps.

Everyone then rushed into the main building, a truly immense structure. In honor of the occasion, it was exactly 1,876 feet long and better than 460 feet wide. Although most of it was one story, it soared to 70 feet in height, making it appear even larger than it was.

At this point, Julia had to leave Lane and, with April and Willa, she went to the Women's Pavilion. True to her word, Elizabeth Gillespie refused to allow men to attend the opening ceremony—and that included the President and Dom Pedro! The Empress, however, had been selected as their guest of honor.

Leah Carlyle was already inside. Julia came to her side. "Oh, I do hope everything goes as planned," she whispered to her friend.

Leah only laughed. "Even fate wouldn't dare contradict Elizabeth. Look, there's the Empress. Isn't she pretty?" She fell silent as the woman began to speak.

Like her husband, Empress Theresa was on the stout side, but she was indeed pretty. Beneath her white satin hat, her luxurious dark hair was wound into an elaborate chignon. Over her lavender silk dress, she wore a white lace shawl so delicately made it could have been woven from cobwebs.

The speeches went off smoothly, and when it came time for Emma Allison to set the machinery in operation, even Willa was impressed.

"She doesn't look strong enough," was her bemused comment.

Julia smiled but refrained from telling her mother-in-law that strength had nothing to do with setting the machinery in motion.

Through it all, Elizabeth Gillespie wore an expression of satisfaction that Julia thought she was more than entitled to express.

As the ceremony concluded, the doors were thrown open to admit men, many of whom entered with an indulgent smile, only to leave in a state of wonder that in no small part was generated by Emma Allison. Dr. Loring had, in a sense, been correct. The young lady from Canada did indeed turn out to be the main attraction of the Women's Pavilion; but no one left laughing—not even Dr. Loring.

By noon, Willa declared she could no longer take another step, and April was complaining about a blister on her foot. Lane hastily rented rolling chairs for them all. No one, not even Julia, had realized that there were close to eighty miles of walkways in the grounds!

At an outrageous cost of sixty cents an hour, they spent the next few hours viewing exhibits in the comfort of a cushioned chair mounted on wheels and pushed by a uniformed attendant.

By three o'clock, they were all sufficiently rested to resume walking.

They took the circular elevator to the top of Sawyer's Observatory, where, at a dizzying height, it paused for a dramatic moment to allow passengers to view the grounds in their entirety.

Forgetting propriety, April emitted a gasp and clutched Desmond's arm. "Oh, I can't look down!" she cried, closing her eyes.

In an almost paternal gesture, Desmond patted her hand. Her fingers were digging into his arm, but he didn't care. "April, it's entirely safe," he soothed. "Look how far you can see!"

Tentatively, April opened her eyes, quickly closed them, then took another peek at the breathtaking panorama spread below.

A sea of flags, pennants, and streamers was creating a kaleidoscope of color. The huge expanse of iron and glass that was the Horticultural Building reflected sunlight in rays that dazzled the eye. The crowd of people appeared dwarfed by the immensity of the structures they filed in and out of like a fast-moving stream of humanity.

Lane regarded Desmond and chuckled. "Well, I'll never have any doubts about your theory, Desmond." He glanced outside. "How high are we, anyway?"

"One hundred and eighty-five feet, sir," Desmond replied with a promptness that suggested he knew exactly what he was talking about.

"Ohhh...." April shivered and closed her eyes again, tightening her hold on Desmond as the elevator began to descend with a swiftness that momentarily unsettled her stomach.

"Well," Julia remarked to Lane with a shaky laugh as

they stepped outside again, "I enjoyed that, but I don't think I want to do it again!"

"Nor I!" April exclaimed, then looked at her brother. "Let's go into Hudnut's and have one of those iced sodas everyone's talking about."

"Good idea," Lane agreed.

Just as they were about to move forward, April turned, hearing her name called.

"Hes!" Her eyes lit up as she saw her sister and Andrew coming toward them. Hester was wearing a brown linen duster over her clothing. Though they were not particularly attractive, many women of a practical frame of mind were wearing them. April suspected Hester's reasons were not of a practical nature; the garments were loose and concealing. Regarding Andrew, she nodded and said, "Hello, Andrew."

"April."

After the short acknowledgment, Andrew directed his gaze elsewhere. The sight of April was beginning to make him uncomfortable, though for the life of him he couldn't explain why that was so. He glanced sideways at his wife. Oddly, he no longer saw April in her face; he couldn't explain that, either. April's voice interrupted his musings, and he gave her another brief glance.

"I'm so glad you could make it," she was saying to her sister.

"We almost didn't," Hester retorted with a small laugh. "With all the rain this morning, Andrew was of a mind to wait until tomorrow. We did miss the opening ceremonies, though."

"Oh," April exclaimed with a deprecating wave of her hand. "You didn't miss anything. We could hardly hear a word anyone said. We're going to Hudnut's. Would you like to come along?"

Hester cast a timid glance at Andrew, relieved to see his short nod.

Happily, April linked her arm through Hester's as they began to walk.

"Oh, April . . . look!" Hester, wide-eyed, pointed to a huge display of spun white sugar fashioned into the shape of a cathedral; not far from it was a two-hundred-pound block of solid chocolate that had been carved into a rather ornate-looking vase.

Julia giggled as she viewed the huge display of confection, then turned to Lane. "A few months ago I would have attacked that mound of chocolate and made short work of it. I'm glad that craving has subsided."

Lane laughed. "I am, too." He patted the hand she slipped beneath his arm. "I wouldn't care for it if you looked like Germaine Stapleton."

"Oh, Lane!" Julia shook her head. She was well aware of how obese Mrs. Stapleton was.

Hudnut's soda fountain was crowded; everyone seemed to have developed a thirst at the same time. Inside, a huge steam calliope was offering a lilting rendition of "Listen to the Mocking Bird."

Lane peered inside the soda fountain and frowned at all the people. Then he glanced at April. "Are you sure you won't settle for a glass of lemonade?" At his sister's crestfallen look, he shrugged, then grinned at Desmond. "Well, let's make the best of it. . . ."

Lane, by the sheer size of him, managed to clear a way to the fountain. Chocolate, vanilla, and strawberry were their choices; they all agreed on strawberry.

"Mama?" Hester said in between sips. "Did you see the new floor covering in the main bulding?"

"You mean the lineoleum? Yes, I saw it."

"They claim it's waterproof!" Hester exclaimed. "It seems as though it would last forever."

Willa contained her smile at this wifely observation. Until recently, Hester's interest had rarely gone beyond the contents of her wardrobe.

Awhile later, having sampled the much-touted iced sodas, and having declared them delicious, they emerged once more into the crowd.

They had not gone far when a man bumped into Julia, mumbling a hasty "I'm sorry" as he did so. Julia turned and gave a startled gasp as she found herself face to face with Mark Eastwood. Feeling the reassuring pressure of Lane's hand on her elbow, Julia quickly recovered her composure.

"Julia!"

Only then did Julia notice Mark's companion, none other than Bunny Ramsey. She heard herself murmur an acknowledgment.

"Good afternoon, Mark," Lane said easily. He tipped his hat. "Miss Ramsey. . . ."

The girl blushed furiously and clung tightly to Mark's arm.

"It's no longer Miss Ramsey," Mark said quickly, his face red. "Bunny and I were married last month."

"My congratulations," Lane said dryly.

"Well, we all wondered what happened to you," Bunny said, looking at Julia with avid eyes that glittered with malice. "I had no idea you were in Philadelphia," she added in a trilling voice.

"Where else would my wife be?" Lane asked with a chuckle.

Mark blinked. "Your . . . your wife?"

A dark brow arched upward as Lane again regarded Mark. "My wife," he repeated evenly.

Mark and Bunny exchanged incredulous looks. "I didn't know," Mark said lamely, then gave a quick, embarrassed nod. "Well, it's nice to see you again, Mr. Manning. And you, too, Julia." Hastily, he ushered Bunny forward and they were soon lost in the crowd.

Lane and Julia turned to look at each other. Then, simultaneously, they dissolved into hearty laughter that drew bewildered looks from their companions.

When they gathered at the dinner table that evening, they were all footsore and weary. A cold meal graced the table because, together with everyone else in the city, the cook had also gone to Fairmount Park.

Although she usually viewed the food in this house with silent criticism, tonight Julia was too filled with excitement to notice what she was eating.

"Hmmph!" Willa offered Lane when he mentioned Alexander Graham Bell's invention. "A silly toy, if you ask me. It's easier to write a letter. Besides, the only calls one could make would be to people who also owned one of the contraptions."

"But the Emperor spoke into it, Mama!" April put in. "And it talked back to him!" She and Desmond had been impressed by the demonstration, even though both of them realized it was little more than a clever feat of magic. "Dom Pedro was so surprised, he dropped the instrument to the floor!"

"Well, of course he did," Willa retorted with a lift of her brow. "If a machine talked to me, I'd do the same thing. It's no wonder that Mr. Bell hasn't given it a name, though; it won't be around long enough to need one."

Realizing she could not win an argument with her mother,

April changed the subject. "I liked the Horticultural Building the best," she declared. "All those exotic flowers! I've never seen the likes of them before." She looked at her brother. "We are going back tomorrow, aren't we? There's so much we haven't seen."

"I would imagine it's going to take more than one more day to see everything," retorted Lane with a nod.

The following morning, and every day for the next two weeks, they all returned to Fairmount Park to see such wonders as a typewriter, an altogether ingenious contrivance that printed letters, thereby saving one the necessity of writing them with a pen; there was a new machine exhibited by Singer Sewing Machines, one that Willa insisted upon having when she learned that it made buttonholes and was capable of actually producing thirty thousand different types of stitches; and there was a truly amazing lamp that needed no gas or oil to produce its light. It used, instead, something called electricity.

One evening, after they had again returned home with throbbing feet and aching backs, Julia said to Lane: "What do you think of having a Centennial Ball right here in Manning House?"

He smiled. "I think that's a splendid idea, Julia. When would you like to have it?"

She thought. "July Fourth would be ideal," she mused, then sighed. "But it falls on a Tuesday this year."

"It seems to me that there will be so many celebrations on the Fourth, you might be wise to distance yours by a few weeks," he suggested.

"You're right," Julia agreed with a nod. "Perhaps the first week in August would be better. I'd like to decorate the ballroom in red, white, and blue," she went on, her enthusiasm growing, "and hire an orchestra, and have a fireworks display, and . . ."

Leaning back in his chair, Lane laughed. "You do anything you like, Julia. And don't worry about the cost."

Willa made a disparaging sound. "Have you ever handled an affair of this type before?" she asked Julia.

"Well, perhaps not on such a large scale, but . . ."

"I'm sure Julia will be able to take care of everything," Lane put in with a warning look at his mother.

Willa's expression clearly stated that she had her doubts, but, wisely, she said nothing more.

chapter
twenty-three

By July, Philadelphia was bursting at the seams. From the industrial cities of the East, from the farmlands of the Midwest, and from the far reaches of territories as yet unincorporated, people of all ages came to view the event of the century. Restaurants were running out of food long before closing time, and hotels were turning people away to fend for themselves as best they could.

The Fourth saw just as many activities and parades as had occurred on New Year's Eve, and this time Lane and Julia joined the throng of revelers.

As Lane had predicted, so many parties and celebrations had been scheduled that they were hard-pressed to decide which of the events to attend. One invitation, however, was accepted immediately: the twenty-second anniversary party of William and Leah Carlyle.

That evening, Desmond arrived early to escort April back to his house, delighted to discover that, for at least the length of the drive they would be alone. Willa, nursing a summer cold she declared she was certain would last until winter, had decided to forgo the party.

The Carlyles' house on Walnut Street was a two-story pressed-brick structure with a gable roof. It was beautifully landscaped, for Leah, when she had the time, liked to work in the garden. On this warm summer evening, her efforts were evident in the profusion of flowers that decorated both the front and rear gardens.

It wasn't a particularly large gathering, Julia saw as she and Lane entered the modest ballroom. No more than thirty people were in attendance to celebrate the Carlyles' anniversary. But Leah had hired a small orchestra, and on the table against one wall was a truly magnificent four-tiered cake.

Catching sight of them, Leah immediately left the group she was with and came forward, hands outstretched, palms down, in greeting.

"Leah! What a lovely gown," Julia exclaimed sincerely, her own hands reaching out to be squeezed affectionately by Leah Carlyle. She cast an admiring glance at the dress Leah was wearing. Of salmon-colored silk, it had an overskirt of fine white lace into which a floral pattern had been sewn with gold thread.

"Thank you. I know Lane has met everyone," Leah said as she took Julia's arm, "but I'm sure there are a few people you've not met. Everyone's here except the Stewarts. But they're always late," she added with a small laugh. "Come, I'll introduce you."

All twelve members of the Women's Committee, including Elizabeth Gillespie, were present with their husbands. Emma Allison, too, was there, looking crisp and lovely in ice-blue taffeta. Julia, of course, knew all the women but had met only one or two of the men.

When the introductions were over, Julia smiled at the sight of April and Desmond, who were dancing.

Leah, too, smiled. "They do make a lovely couple don't you think?"

"I think Desmond is just what April needs," Julia declared with an emphatic nod.

Turning her head, Leah regarded her curiously. "Did she take it very hard? About Andrew and Hester, I mean."

Slowly, Julia nodded. "More than she revealed, I think. She was devastated when Andrew told her. . . ."

"Well, it came as a shock to everyone," Leah murmured. "But these things happen, I guess. . . ."

The two women regarded each other for a moment, and they both knew they were thinking the same thing; but then, tacitly, as if they had reached a mutual agreement, they dropped the sensitive subject.

At that moment, Lane approached them. He gave Julia a fair imitation of a gallant bow.

"Pardon me," he drawled, straightening. "Would it be presumptuous of me to request a dance?"

Julia viewed him thoughtfully. "Have we met?"

"Only in my dreams. . . ." With a wink and a nod to Leah, he led Julia onto the dance floor. "Why are you smiling?" he asked her before they had completed one turn around the room.

"I was remembering the first time I danced with you," Julia replied, her smile dimpling her cheeks. "I thought you were holding me far too tight. . . ."

Throwing his head back, Lane gave a hearty laugh. "I probably was," he admitted. "But that was only because you kept stumbling about in your new shoes, stepping on my toes—"

"I never stepped on your toes!" she retorted, feigning indignation.

Lane chuckled, appeared about to reply, then came to an abrupt halt right in the middle of the dance floor! Julia glanced up at his face to see that his gaze was directed over her head, his expression one she could not fathom.

"Lane . . ." she murmured hesitantly, feeling a sudden unease she couldn't explain.

He seemed not to have heard her. Slowly, Julia turned to see a couple now entering the ballroom. The Stewarts, probably, she thought, remembering that Leah had told her they were always late. It was not, however, the Stewarts who had caught Lane's attention; of that she was certain. It was the woman who was with them.

Feeling suddenly ill, Julia knew, even before Lane murmured the name, the identity of the woman she was viewing.

"Rosalind. . . ." For Lane, time began to recede in an almost eerie way, almost ten years evaporating in the blink of an eye. It could have been yesterday that he had last seen her. The years had touched her gently, if at all.

Absently, Lane's hands dropped to his sides, and he headed slowly toward the newcomers, not bothering to escort Julia from the floor.

For a moment she stood there uncertainly, feeling a flush that burned her ears, vastly relieved when the music ended at just that moment.

With as much dignity as she could muster under the circumstances, Julia moved to the far side of the room. Unable to help herself, she stared at Rosalind Langley, who had moved forward to admire the cake. Where the Stewarts were, she didn't know or care; but Lane was there, right next to Rosalind.

Julia saw a woman whose beauty was marred only by the

lines of hard humor about the red lips. She was dressed in a velvet gown with an exaggerated bustle. Her dress was black, the color of mourning. Her dark eyes, however, reflected no sorrorw, nor did the pale ivory shoulders even hint at the slump of dejection. Her ebony hair was dressed fashionably, falling down the back of her slender neck in long, lush curls. If her dress was subdued, her accessories were not. Brilliant diamonds encircled the smooth, unlined throat, glimmered from a slim wrist, and flashed from tapered fingers that now reached out to rest briefly on Lane's cheek.

Someone touched her arm, and Julia gave a start. Turning, she saw Leah at her side, her pretty face a mask of concern. They stared at each other in silence for a moment, then Leah increased the pressure of her grip.

"Come upstairs with me, Julia," she instructed quietly.

Julia made no protest as Leah led her from the room. Upstairs, Leah closed the door to her bedroom and regarded Julia with a concern that creased her otherwise smooth brow.

"You know about Lane and Rosalind, don't you."

It was a statement rather than a question; nevertheless, Julia nodded.

"From the look on your face, I thought so." Leah sighed, then took Julia's hand in her own. Despite the warm night, it felt cold to her touch. "I want you to know that I didn't invite Rosalind here tonight; in fact, I didn't even know she was back in Philadelphia. Last I heard, she was living in Paris. Apparently she and her two daughters are staying with the Stewarts until she moves into her own house. She came with them."

"It doesn't matter," Julia replied dully, withdrawing her hand. She walked to the nearest chair and sank down into it as though her legs would no longer support her. Indeed, she was flooded with a weakness that left her light-headed.

Leah viewed her in alarm for a moment. Then, her steps hurried, she went into her sitting room, returning a short while later with a small snifter of brandy. "Here, drink this. You look as pale as a ghost."

Without any protest, and unaware of what was in the glass, Julia took a sip, sputtered, and waved it away. With a sigh, Leah put the glass on a nearby table, then stood there, looking down at Julia.

"How did you find out?" she asked finally. "Surely Lane didn't tell you. . . ."

"No. Willa did."

"Oh. . . ." Her mouth grew tight. "I've always known Willa to be a hard woman, but I never thought she was vindictive. But listen, Julia. All that happened a long time ago. More than nine years! People change. . . ."

Julia turned away. For some, she thought, an eternity could pass and their love for someone would remain unchanged. *And so it is with me*, she thought silently. "I saw the look on his face when she came into the room. . . ." Julia's voice broke, and she brushed the errant tears from her cheeks.

Unable to dispute Julia's words, Leah averted her eyes. She, too, had seen.

Moistening her lips, Julia asked, "Do you . . . do you know her very well?"

"Rosalind?" Clasping her hands, Leah considered the question. "Actually, I knew her parents better. They're both dead now. We all lived here on Walnut Street—the Bothwells, the Mannings, and the Carlyles. Rosalind . . ." She hesitated, then spoke the truth. "She's headstrong, knows exactly what she wants. . . . In all honesty, however, I must confess that I've always rather liked her. I know that, right now, you can't believe this, but under different circumstances I think you would, too.''

Julia felt something shrivel inside her. If Leah thought there was something worth liking in Rosalind, there was more to the woman than met the eye. ''She's . . . very beautiful.''

Leah sighed. ''Yes. Yes, I suppose she is. . . .''

Julia looked up at her. ''You mean Lane did not fall in love with her because of her beauty. . . .'' She spoke the words unemotionally and noticed that Leah made no response; her very silence was an affirmation.

Leah put a hand on Julia's shoulder. ''We must go back downstairs. . . .''

Reaching up, Julia covered Leah's hand with her own. ''I know.'' She stood up. ''It was unforgivable of me to keep you from your guests this long.''

Julia didn't know how she got through the rest of that evening. With a smile plastered on her lips as she and Leah came downstairs again, she forced herself to remain calm even when she saw Lane dancing with Rosalind. They were gazing into each other's eyes as though they were alone in the room.

William approached them and, after giving Leah a worried look, asked Julia to dance with him.

She did so, mechanically, the smile fixed in place with a determination she would have said was beyond her. Several times she became aware that Rosalind was observing her with a speculative look, but Julia could not bring herself to meet those dark eyes with any directness, afraid of what she might see.

With the exception of Elizabeth Gillespie, whose energies

and thoughts were so single-minded that she had no time for anyone else's problems, and Emma Allison, who was unaware of the situation, everyone else at the party was well aware of the small drama being enacted here this evening. Although Rosalind was, for the most part, well liked, sympathies were with Julia, and more than one compassionate glance was bestowed upon her.

April was plainly worried, and told Desmond of her concern.

Taking her hand, he murmured, "Let's go out on the terrace. It's getting warm in here."

April allowed him to lead her outside. "I wish she hadn't come back," she said, more to herself than to Desmond.

"That is not your problem," Desmond said, pausing at the far side of the terrace. A soft breeze brought with it the scent of Leah's prize tea roses.

"I can't help it!" April exclaimed. "I like Julia...."

"So do I," he responded quickly. "But I cannot bear to see your thoughts put a frown on that beautiful face of yours."

"Oh, Desmond." April smiled shyly, momentarily distracted. "You know I'm not beautiful. In fact, you once called me a tadpole."

He blinked. "You were only nine years old when I said that!" His face softened, and his voice dropped to a whisper touched with wonder. "You remembered that...."

Her sweetly curved mouth worked its way into a moue that strove unsuccessfully for primness. "I should think that any girl would remember a ... compliment like that."

With a will of its own, his thumb reached out to trace the pure curve of her jawline. "It was, you know. A compliment, I mean. When I was twelve, I thought tadpoles were awfully cute. In fact, I once tried to talk my mother into letting me keep a few of them in my room.'' He grinned. ''She declined.''

As he spoke, Desmond reached over the wrought-iron railing and plucked a single perfect rose from a bush so thick with blooms it was a solid mass of color. Handing it to April, he watched as she inclined her head to catch its fragrance.

''And now . . .'' He took a step closer. ''Now you are beautiful. I'd wager that any man who looked at you would say the same thing.'' He took hold of her slender wrists, and the rose tumbled from her grasp to land at her feet. Raising her hands to his lips, he kissed first one, then the other. ''April, I know I don't say things the way they should be said. I'm not very good at that. I just love you so much. . . .''

She pulled her hands from his grasp, suddenly afraid of the intimate moment. ''Please, Desmond . . .''

''No! I must speak of my feelings, put them into words. I should have done so long ago.''

''Sometimes a man's feelings change. . . . ''

''I could not live that long.''

Desmond spoke in such a serious tone that April's eyes were drawn to his. She was about to speak but broke off as Desmond, with hands that displayed a firmness she would have said he could not possess, took hold of her upper arms and drew her to him, his green eyes shining with the depth of his feelings.

In some surprise, April raised her head to look at him. For a long moment those eyes held hers, and she found herself unable to look away. They stood close to each other, not hearing the music or night sounds, oblivious to everyone but themselves.

Bending his head, Desmond's mouth claimed hers, his arms going around her in a tight embrace. It was not the gentle kiss April had experienced with Andrew. Instead, it was as if a hot flame had seared her lips.

Deep within April, something awakened. A mere flutter at first, it grew and expanded into an aching need to which April could give no name, one that left her with a curious weakness she had never felt before. . . .

chapter
twenty-four

Julia resisted using her fan as she settled herself in the carriage beside Lane. She felt faint with relief that this ghastly night had finally come to an end. She had danced, mingled, talked—and remembered nothing of what she had said. The strain of smiling when she had felt like weeping had left her jaws aching. Strange how no one thinks about smiling when it comes naturally.

Without turning her head, her eyes moved sideways, and she viewed Lane. They were so close their shoulders were touching. So close, and so far apart. He was staring out the window. The silence was louder than any cacophony could be. He was thinking about *her*. She knew that. About the woman he had loved and lost and who had now come back, free.

And was she to ignore the fact that that woman had come back into his life? Beneath her light shawl, Julia's shoulders slumped. She would not, dare not, speak. With painful clarity she remembered the scene that had taken place between herself and Lane the last time she had mentioned Rosalind.

Her hands clenched in her lap as they at last turned into the drive. April had left earlier, escorted by Desmond, and by the time Julia and Lane entered the house, everyone had already gone to bed.

Lane's silence remained unbroken until they went upstairs, where he murmured only a preoccupied "good night" to Julia before closing his door.

In her own room, Julia sighed deeply. Then, wearily, she undressed. Getting into bed, she wrapped her arms around her pillow, staring into the darkness, wondering why her eyes were dry. There should be tears to ease the ache she was feeling, but tears would not come. She couldn't shake the feeling of numbness that engulfed her, couldn't think, couldn't reason.

She wanted only to sleep, to blot out the memories of this night.

Determinedly, she closed her eyes. Things always looked worse at night. In the morning, the sunshine would throw its friendly light on everything, even the shadows of troubled unease that lurked in the corridors of her mind and which, right now, she could not bear to examine.

The following morning, having overslept, Julia discovered that Lane had already left the house by the time she came down to breakfast.

Having no appetite, Julia settled for coffee and a half of a muffin. She had barely finished when April came into the room. Her lawn morning dress was the color of cranberries and sported tiny white buttons down the front of the bodice.

"Julia," she said in her breathless way, "have you anything planned for today?"

Julia shook her head. "No."

Unless, she thought ruefully, moping about and feeling sorry for myself could be considered something to do.

"Oh, please come with me, then," April said, pausing to munch on the remaining half of Julia's muffin. "I want to buy some material for the baby's layette. I do think it's about time I got started. . . ."

Julia raised her brows and gave the girl a baleful look. "You are, I hope, referring to Hester's baby?"

Licking her fingers, April giggled. "Well, of course I am!"

"I don't know. . . ." Julia sighed, pushing herself to her feet. Somehow she didn't think she'd be very good company today.

"Oh, please, Julia," April implored. "I'm not at all certain what kind of material would be best. . . ."

Viewing the girl's eager face, Julia had to smile. "All right. You send for the carriage. It'll take me only a minute to get my shawl. . . ."

Two hours later, after having been in and out of almost every dry goods store in town, Julia and April strolled along Chestnut Street, the driver trailing behind them, his arms filled with their purchases.

The street was crowded as it had been since May. The whole city was crowded. Not too long ago, the newspaper had reported—with a trace of awe—that a record two hundred thousand people had disembarked from trains and boats in one day!

"I do think we have more than enough," Julia protested with a laugh as April headed for yet one more store.

April paused, peering in through the window. "I think we should buy some light wool. The baby will be needing blankets. . . ."

Julia was never to know what made her turn around at

just that moment. But when she did, the blood drained from her face. There, across the street from where she and April were standing, she saw Lane and Rosalind heading into a coffee shop.

"I think yellow would probably be the best color," April was saying, still peering into the window. She turned to Julia, waiting for a comment.

"I . . ." Julia swayed, and April's hands immediately reached out to steady her.

"Julia! What's wrong!" the girl cried out in alarm. "Are you ill?"

Fighting a sudden dizziness, Julia forced a smile. "No. It's just that I have . . . a headache. I'm sorry, April. Would you mind if we returned home now?"

"Of course not!" the girl exclaimed, her hands still on Julia's arms. She then turned to the driver. "John, please fetch the carriage and bring it here. Mrs. Manning is not feeling well enough to walk back."

When they arrived home some twenty minutes later, Julia went to her room to rest. By now, she did indeed have a headache, a splitting one! By evening, though, she had managed to compose herself enough to go downstairs for supper.

Willa, nose red and sniffing audibly, came downstairs for the first time in more than a week. Julia thought she knew why. Most likely, April had told her mother that Rosalind had returned.

They had not yet finished their first course when Julia's suspicions were confirmed.

"I understand that Rosalind has come home," Willa remarked to Lane.

Julia poked her fork into her salad and tried to maintain her equilibrium.

"Yes," Lane murmured. "Her appearance was a surprise to everyone, including the Carlyles." He did not look at Julia as he spoke.

Willa coughed delicately. "I'm sorry now that I didn't go to the party. It would have been nice to see her again. I must call on her soon." A slight smile hovered on her lips as she buttered a piece of bread and took a bite out of it.

"She . . . hasn't moved into her house yet," Lane said. "She's staying with the Stewarts."

Julia looked up. Now would be the time for Lane to mention that he had seen Rosalind today.

He said nothing.

As soon as the meal ended, Julia hurried to her room. With hands that trembled, she lit the lamp, then sat down at her dressing table, absently removing the pins from her hair.

Raising her head after a few minutes, Julia regarded her reflection in the mirror, shocked by what she saw. Her eyes looked large, dark, pain-filled, her mouth a hard white line.

Damn! she thought.

Getting up, she clenched her hands and stared angrily about her room. Lane was her husband, and she loved him with all her heart. Was she ready to give up without a fight? Without even trying?

She glanced back at her image, scowling with determination. No! By God, it was time she put her house in order. Win or lose, it wouldn't be because she didn't make the effort!

The following morning at breakfast, Lane announced his intention of going to New York.

"I may be home late this evening," he added. "Don't wait supper for me."

And are you going alone? Julia wondered; but of course

she did not ask it aloud. Her pride would not permit her to question him.

When Lane left the house, April wiped her mouth with the linen napkin and smiled at Julia. "Melissa Stapleton and I are going to Fairmount Park today. Would you like to join us?"

"No, thank you. I . . . have some things to do today." As the girl got to her feet, Julia asked: "April, who is the best dressmaker in town?"

Pausing, April pursed her lips as she considered the question. "Lisa Arquette. Her shop is on Market."

When April left the dining room, Julia went into the hall. Nancy was dusting the Dresden figurines housed in the Boulle cabinets. Julia motioned to her.

"Please find Mrs. Litton and tell her to meet me in the study. Right away," Julia added.

Going into the study, Julia seated herself behind the desk. She felt certain that Nancy had delivered her message immediately; nevertheless, a full fifteen minutes went by before Thelma Litton condescended to respond to the summons.

"You wanted to see me?" she asked, coming into the room. Her frown clearly conveyed her annoyance at being interrupted in her duties.

"I did," Julia replied curtly. She viewed the woman a long moment before she spoke. "Mrs. Litton, how long have you been here?"

"Four years," the woman reported proudly, with a trace a hauteur. "Ever since the family moved into Manning House."

Julia nodded thoughtfully. "Your services are no longer required, Mrs. Litton. You are discharged."

Anger spread a vibrant color across the woman's cheeks. She drew back, then gave a short laugh of disbelief. "You can't discharge me!"

Julia smiled. "I already have," she noted softly. "Today
is your last day. You will have your belongings packed and
be gone from this house by noon tomorrow. However, you
may do one last thing before you leave, Mrs. Litton," Julia
went on coolly. "And if it is done properly, without any
fuss, I will see to it that you receive a favorable letter of
reference." The woman turned hating eyes on her, but Julia
ignored this display of futile defiance. "You will notify the
cook that her services are no longer needed."

Unable to contain her outrage, Mrs. Litton gave a strangled cry and almost ran upstairs in her haste to get to Willa
Manning's sitting room.

Calmly, Julia leaned back in the chair and waited for the
inevitable confrontation she knew would have to take place
between herself and her mother-in-law.

It was not long in coming.

"How dare you take it upon yourself to discharge members of my staff without my permission!" Willa sputtered as
she sailed into the room.

"I do not need your permission, or anyone else's for that
matter," Julia retorted, her voice as cool as Willa's was
heated. "I am through tolerating insubordination, insolence,
and inefficiency in my house."

"Your house?" the woman choked.

Julia stood up and looked directly at her mother-in-law.
"Exactly. Nor are the dismissals of Mrs. Litton and the
cook to be the only changes that will be made. From now
on, I am mistress of this house!"

"You!" Willa looked positively choleric. "You're nothing but a . . ."

"A what?" Julia asked softly, with a deceptively sweet
smile.

Willa straightened, nostrils flaring with her quickened

breathing. "I don't have to tell you what you are! You already know!"

"I do indeed," Julia replied, still smiling. Then her brows dipped, and the smile vanished. "But in the event that you have forgotten, I will refresh your memory: I am Lane Manning's wife, and I am mistress of Manning House."

With that, Julia swept past Willa and, head high, left the room.

Upstairs, Julia put on her hat, picked up her reticule, and went downstairs again.

Just before she left the house, Nancy approached her.

"Excuse me, Mrs. Manning..." she began, with new respect in her voice. "Is it true you'll be needing a new cook?"

"Yes," Julia nodded, drawing on her gloves.

"I happen to know of someone who's looking for just such a post. She's very good," Nancy continued before Julia could comment. "It's my aunt. She's newly widowed and has been looking for employment."

"Has she any experience?"

Nancy looked crestfallen. "Not of the type you mean. But she's cooked all her life. She makes the best seed cake I've ever tasted," she added with a shy laugh.

Julia hesitated. Her first inclination was to say no. Then she remembered her own brief fling at trying to secure employment. How she had resented it when everyone insisted on experience backed up by references.

"Very well, Nancy," she said, making up her mind. "Tell your aunt to come by to see me in the morning. I'll give her a one-week trial; if all goes well, I'll hire her."

"Oh, thank you, ma'am."

In the carriage, Julia instructed the driver to take her to the newspaper office. There she placed a notice for a new housekeeper. In the carriage again, Julia gave orders to be taken to the shop of Lisa Arquette.

The shop appeared small from the outside, but when she entered, Julia was pleasantly surprised by the roomy, uncluttered look of the front part. The walls were painted a soft green, trimmed with white molding. Several well-positioned mirrors gave the illusion of vastness. The Queen Anne chairs were upholstered in dark green damask, and the matching tables, highly polished, supported glass vases filled with flowers.

The shop was empty of customers at this moment. Upon Julia's entrance, a woman came in from the back room. She was tall, statuesque in bearing, with white hair piled high on her head. A measuring tape slung carelessly over one shoulder suggested she had been interrupted while at work.

"Yes? May I help you?" she asked, coming forward.

"I am Mrs. Manning," Julia stated without preamble.

Deference immediately crept into the pale blue eyes. The woman clucked like a mother hen as she quickly ushered Julia to a comfortable chair, sent for refreshments, and snapped her fingers for her assistants to come forward.

Julia ignored it all. When she was certain she had the woman's undivided attention, she stated crisply and to the point: "I shall require a whole new wardrobe."

The woman seemed taken aback. "Everything?"

"Everything." She removed her gloves. "I would like to view some of your better materials. . . ."

Fingers snapped again. "Miss Erwin!" she called to one of her assistants. "Fetch the new bolts, the ones from Paris. . . ."

One after another, bolts of material were presented for Julia's inspection. After viewing a score or so, Julia frowned.

"Please, Mrs. Arquette, do not show me colors of such

dreary shades. If you must show me blue, make certain it is vivid! I have no objection to pastels, but the colors must be vibrant, with depth.''

''Exactly!'' Mrs. Arquette beamed, throwing the bolt carelessly out of the way. ''Now this . . .'' She held it up for inspection and was rewarded with a smile. The material was of iridescent satin, changing from a gleaming turquoise to an emerald green as the woman moved the bolt from side to side.

''Beautiful!'' Julia said with a nod of her head. ''Set that one aside. . . .''

That evening, from her bedroom window, Julia watched as Lane arrived home. She had no doubt at all that he was about to receive a few words from his mother.

No matter, Julia thought, leaving her room. She had no intention of backing down.

She was only halfway down the stairs when she could hear Willa's raised voice coming from behind the closed door to the study. She could hear nothing at all from Lane.

A moment later, the door opened and Willa appeared. From the look on her mother-in-law's face, Julia knew that Lane had upheld the dismissals.

Supper was, if anything, even more unpalatable than was normally the case; everything was either underdone or overcooked.

Julia sighed. Obviously the cook was determined to have the last word, even if it was a silent one.

Even April wrinkled her nose. ''Mama . . . I don't think these potatoes have been cooked long enough.''

''They do seem to be crunchy,'' Lane commented, putting down his fork.

''Shall I send it back?'' Willa asked Lane in a voice of

contained anger. She wasn't at all certain that she would ever forgive him for siding with his wife. "It's her prerogative," Lane had said. Prerogative, indeed! Willa sniffed her displeasure while she waited for her son's answer.

"No," Lane sighed, getting up. "I'm really not very hungry. . . ."

Four days later, the first of Julia's newly ordered gowns arrived: an emerald-green dress of chiffon that seemed to float like a cloud with each step she took. The dress was a bit formal for ordinary evening wear, but for once she and Lane would be dining alone, so she decided she would wear it. Willa had gone to New York and had taken April with her. Her excuse had been that she wanted to go shopping; Julia suspected otherwise, for Willa was making no attempt to conceal her displeasure at being thwarted by her daughter-in-law.

Julia twirled before the mirror a few times, pleased with the effect and with the workmanship of the gown. It was low on her shoulders, with a more pronounced décolleté than she normally wore.

Expensive. And worth every penny, she decided.

"Ohh . . . it's so pretty," Mary exclaimed, stepping back to view the overall effect. "The pearls, I think. . . ." she suggested, heading for the dressing table.

"Yes," Julia agreed. She sat down at the table while Mary fastened the clasp around her neck. Chewing her lip, Julia regarded her image, then turned to Mary. "Do you know how to fashion a pompadour?"

Mary's smile was broad. "I certainly do."

Entering the dining room awhile later, Julia nodded in silent approval as she took her seat and saw the food being placed on the table. Nancy's aunt, Elsa Quayle, had been doing the cooking for three days now, and Julia could honestly say that she had not one complaint as to the outcome.

Tonight the meal began with a clear beef broth that was as delicious as any she had ever tasted.

Lane leaned back in his seat as the serving girl removed his soup bowl. He had a bemused expression on his face as he viewed his wife across the table.

"You've a new hairdo," he commented, sounding surprised at his own observation.

"I thought it was time for a change," Julia replied with a smile. She watched as the girl now placed the main course on the table. The roast beef was beautifully carved and arranged on a silver platter surrounded by potatoes that had been first boiled then sautéed in butter and parsley. Sprigs of mint had been added for decoration.

Lane was on his second helping before he spoke again. "That's a lovely gown. . . ." he said, then paused as if he were about to say more but thought better of it.

Julia tilted her head. "Except what?"

"Well, it's a bit . . . "

Leaning forward, she regarded him with interest. "A bit what?"

"Oh, nothing. . . ." Bending his head, he concentrated on his food.

Afterward, Julia followed Lane into his study. "How are things going in Titusville?" she asked, seating herself on one of the leather sofas.

Lane poured himself a small brandy, then sat down behind his desk. "Fine. I'm convinced there's petroleum down there. Unfortunately, I have conflicting reports as to how deep it is."

"A third opinion?" Julia suggested.

He rubbed the back of his neck and sighed. "Yes, I suppose; but it's risky at best."

"Is this the first time you've tried this sort of thing?"

"Yes, but there's a first time for everything. . . ."

They were communicating on two different levels, Julia thought to herself; making polite conversation when so much remained unsaid between them.

"Dinner was very good tonight," Lane murmured, taking a sip from his glass. "I'm . . . I'm glad you dismissed both Mrs. Litton and the cook. I think you did the right thing."

"Thank you. Although I'm afraid my decision . . . upset your mother."

"Oh . . . well. Mother can be a bit opinionated at times. Still, it was about time you showed an interest."

She regarded him in surprise. About time? Well, perhaps it was, she thought. Perhaps it was.

"You don't mind, then?"

"Of course not." He grinned, and her heart turned over. "To be truthful, I've never thought the food in this house was the best it could be."

"You never complained," she pointed out.

"No. . . ." He got up and replaced his glass next to the decanter, then stood there, staring at it.

What is it you're not saying! Julia demanded silently, wanting to scream the words at him. But she dared not ask.

She stood up. "I think I'll retire now." She waited a moment. There was no response.

In her room, she undressed and then dismissed Mary. And waited.

More than an hour passed before she finally heard Lane enter his room. His footsteps came as far as their adjoining door. She could sense that he was standing there, motionless.

A few minutes later, she heard him speaking softly to Joseph.

Then the light, visible as a ribbon beneath her door, went out.

Resting back against the pillow, Julia tried to will herself to sleep. Dawn thrust tentative fingers of pink and yellow through her window before she succeeded.

chapter
twenty-five

Late afternoon sunlight drifted in through the library window. Julia had been sitting in the same chair for more than an hour, her thoughts going round and round in a whirlpool of dark despair that seemed to have no bottom.

It was a week after the Carlyles' anniversary party. A week that had gone by with a sameness that made Julia want to scream. Not a word—not a word!—had been spoken between her and Lane with regard to Rosalind.

Lane had not come to her bed once, and Julia agonized over the reasons. Was it because he was thinking of her? Was it because he was trying to make a decision? Was it because, God forbid, he was in *her* bed?

Glancing down at the unopened book on her lap, Julia made a sound of disgust, mostly directed at herself for her inability to concentrate. Getting up, she returned the volume to its rightful place on the shelf, turning then as she saw Nancy come into the room, holding a cardboard box.

"This was just delivered for you, Mrs. Manning," she

said. "It's from the dressmaker's shop. Shall I put it in your room?"

Julia reached for it. "No. Thank you, Nancy. I'll take it."

Hurrying upstairs, Julia opened the box and removed the nightgown it contained.

"Beautiful," she murmured, making a mental note to congratulate Lisa Arquette on her skill with a needle. The silk was so delicate that she could see her hand through the material. She wondered what Lane would think of it.

That night after supper, Lane, as usual, spent an hour or so in his study. When he did go upstairs, he went directly into his own room. In some surprise, he saw that the adjoining door to Julia's room was open and, inside, he could see her seated at her dressing table, brushing her hair.

His attention captured, Lane walked slowly into her room. The lamp was lit, and as she raised her arms, the light seemed to flow through the silken material of her nightgown, outlining the perfection of her body.

For a few minutes, he stood there, observing her with a half smile on his face. At times, her beauty caught him unaware. Coming closer, he put his hands on her shoulder and, bending forward, kissed her neck.

Getting to her feet, Julia turned to him, allowing him to draw her into his arms.

Lane was just about to kiss her when he paused, hearing the doorbell ring. He glanced at the clock. Seeing it was almost nine-thirty, he frowned.

"Now who the devil could that be?" he muttered in annoyance, then smiled at Julia. "You wait right here. I'll get rid of whoever it is."

Lane left the room, and Julia waited.

Fifteen minutes later, she made a sound of exasperation as she slipped on her peignoir.

In the hall, Julia placed both hands on the banister and, leaning over, peered down to the entrance hall below.

She couldn't see anyone, but she could hear voices coming from the drawing room. They were mostly male, with one exception. As the silvery, wind-chime laughter of Rosalind Langley wafted up to her, Julia tensed, her hands tightening on the banister.

The laughter finaly subsided, and Julia straightened, scowling down at the foyer as if it had personally affronted her.

Well, she thought after a moment, she'd have to dress and join them, she supposed. It would be rude to ignore guests, however inconsiderate they had been in calling at such an ungodly hour.

In her room again, Julia went to her wardrobe and yanked the door open in an angry gesture that made its hinges squeal in protest. She grabbed the first thing her hand made contact with: a dark blue muslin dress. It was not one of her favorites. But then, she thought grimly, pulling the nightgown over her head, she wasn't especially fond of her guests, either.

Swiftly, Julia put on her underclothes and struggled into the dress, wishing now that she had called Mary to help her.

She put her shoes on, and headed for the door.

"Oh, no!" Julia's hands flew to her unbound hair.

Muttering now, she raced back to the dressing table and twisted her hair into a knot that wasn't particularly attractive, but at least she was presentable enough to appear in public.

Again she headed for the door.

Julia had one foot on the top step when they all emerged into the hall. Rosalind, Lane, and two men she didn't know.

The men, including Lane, were laughing in delight at some witticism offered by Rosalind, who then addressed her two companions.

"Lane has kindly consented to escort me home. Now, now," she said with a gay little laugh as they both began to protest. "Lane has yet to see my new house. Besides"—she slipped an arm through his and gave him a languid look from beneath her dark lashes, and her voice took on a hushed note— "we are old friends who have not seen each other in a long time, and we have much to discuss."

Straightening, Julia glared down at them, her back rigid with the sudden flare of anger that swept through her. Old friends? Much to discuss?

Turning on her heel, she ran back to her room, her breath tight in her throat. Going into her sitting room, she went to the one window that offered a clear view of the carriage drive.

The two men were entering the victoria waiting at the front entrance, presumably the vehicle in which they had arrived. Only moments later she saw the Manning carriage pull up, and Lane was there, opening the door for Rosalind.

Mouth compressed, Julia moved away from the window. Lane had told her to wait. And she had. Well, she was through waiting!

Anger began slowly building to a pinnacle that Julia feared would cause her to lose her self-control.

Passing by the chaise, the silk nightgown caught her eye. Picking it up, she vented her fury on the flimsy material, ripping it to shreds. With hurried steps, she then went to the door that led to the hall and firmly turned the key in the lock. Moving to the door that separated her room from Lane's, her movements quick and decisive, she locked that one, too.

Then she sat down and stared at the clock.

* * *

Rosalind had purchased a house on Locust Street, one that offered a fine view of Rittenhouse Square. While not as large as Manning House, it was every bit as elegantly furnished.

They had talked steadily on the brief ride, mostly engaging in the age-old game of "do you remember?" It was as if, by tacit agreement, they had both decided to skirt anything of a personal nature. Since Rosalind's return, the two of them had been together only once before, on the day that Lane had taken her to the coffee shop. Their meeting had been quite by accident, their conversation casual, stilted, alive with words that could not be spoken.

Rosalind led him into the rear parlor. It was small but tastefully appointed. Two oil paintings flanked the marble fireplace, both of them early works of Canaletto. A pianoforte and a harp were positioned in a corner. The Hepplewhite furniture was upholstered in cream-colored satin sporting finely crafted needlepoint.

"Would you care for a drink?" Rosalind asked, turning to look at him. Her black taffeta gown rustled and whispered each time she moved.

"I can't stay long," Lane murmured. He was beginning to feel guilty about having left Julia, but she would understand. "Where are your daughters? I've not met them yet."

"Oh"—Rosalind waved a hand in a careless gesture—"long since in bed, I would imagine. Margaret is five, and Catherine is a year younger." She came close to him, so close he could smell the elusive French perfume she was wearing. "I had forgotten how handsome you are...." Her fingertip brushed his cheek with feathery lightness.

"Your beauty is as I remember. . . ." Lane said, striving for a bantering tone.

Her creamy shoulders moved in a delicate shrug. "Nine years is long enough for a woman to lose her youth. . . ."

"Not in your case!" he objected quickly, and thought it was true. She was still as slim as the girl he had first seen so many years ago; her hair was still as black and glossy as ever, her waist trim.

"Lane . . ."

Her voice turned husky. It had always had an effect on him. So soft, so sensual. As a young man, it had reduced him to a quivering mass of desire.

"It's been so long. . . ." Putting her arms around his neck, Rosalind raised her lips to meet his.

Lane placed his mouth on hers, fully expecting the remembered flame of desire to ignite in his loins.

Nothing happened.

The kiss went on for a moment longer. Lane's heartbeat remained calm and steady. He could have been kissing his mother on the cheek for all the passion he was experiencing. Suddenly, behind the lids of his closed eyes, he saw the image of Julia's face. With a quick movement, he drew away from Rosalind, taking a step back, a look of incredulity widening his gray eyes.

"I . . ." Lane choked on the word and clamped his mouth shut, quite at a loss for words.

With her head tilted upward, Rosalind was viewing him with open surprise. This was not the same young man who had been devoted to her. Where was the eager suitor who had pleaded so fervently for her hand in marriage? "I will love you forever," he had declared. And when had forever come to an end? Arching an expressive brow, she offered a rueful smile.

"Well . . . it would appear that the quaint tales of eternal love are no more than myths. . . ."

"Rosalind, I . . ." Lane still hadn't recovered. Until this very moment, he would have sworn undying love for this woman. "My God," he groaned, turning away from her. "How could I have been such a fool!"

"You love her, don't you. . . ." Rosalind said in wonder, not even posing her observation as a question.

But Lane, who still appeared overcome by some inner revelation, made no answer; indeed, he seemed not to have heard her.

Rosalind's smile broadened, and she touched Lane's arm with affection. "My dear Lane, there was a time for us," she whispered softly, and with a sigh. "But that time has passed and can never be recaptured." Her hand fell away, and her dark eyes held a gleam of sadness. "Much as we would like, I guess we can never return to the passions of our youth."

On the drive home, Lane sat in the carriage, feeling dazed. Rosalind was like a stranger to him, a woman he had never met before! The dream he had carried in his heart all these years had nothing whatsoever to do with reality.

Impatient now, he tapped on the window and instructed the driver to hurry.

Home again, Lane took the stairs two at a time. The hall door that led to Julia's room was locked, but he thought nothing of it. Quickly, he went into his own room. The adjoining door was also locked. He knocked, softly at first, then more insistently. There was no response.

"Julia! Open this door," he commanded, growing angry. He conceded the fact that she was probably miffed by his long absence; however, that didn't warrant barring her door to him! He rattled the knob. "Open it, I say!"

He waited, ear to the door, but there was no sound of movement from the other side. A few minutes went by, during which time he tried to cajole his wife; but his words were like puffs of smoke that dissipated into the air without a trace.

Standing back, he glared at the door. "Open it or I'll break it down!" he bellowed, patience gone.

Another long minute went by. A growl built up in his throat, and Lane put his shoulder to the wood panel.

On the third thrust, the lock broke, cracking the jamb, and the door swung inward. Catching his balance, he scowled at Julia. She was no longer wearing the silk nightgown. Beneath the satin of her peignoir, he saw the familiar flannel.

Across the hall, awakened by the unaccustomed loud noises, Charles began to cry. Only a few seconds passed before his sobs sank to a fretful whimper, and Julia knew that he had been picked up by Alma Gwenn.

"How dare you lock your door to me!" Lane's voice ended on a rising note that stopped just short of a shout.

Standing very still, Julia gave her husband a cold look. "My door was locked because I did not want you in my bedroom," she retorted cuttingly. Lane took a step forward, and Julia raised her chin. "Don't touch me." Her voice had a deadly calm that stopped him in his tracks.

If Lane hadn't been looking at her, he wouldn't have recognized this woman to be his wife. He'd never heard her use this tone.

Julia wrinkled her nose. "Since when have you taken to wearing expensive French perfume?"

Lane's face flushed darkly. "You don't understand. . . ." he choked.

"Nor do I want to!" she spat out swiftly, angrier than she had ever been in her life. Her eyes flashed blue fire. "Please leave my room! You reek with a smell I find offensive."

His jaw worked, muscles throbbing in protest at the enforced restriction.

"Julia!"

She turned from him, feeling an anguish she never thought possible. "Get out!" she gritted, not certain she could control herself.

Slowly, his steps sounding heavy, Lane made for the door, where he paused.

"We must talk, Julia," he said, without facing her. "I'll be leaving for New York tomorrow. When I return, and when you're calmer, we will talk. . . ."

The door closed, the gaping hole in the jamb mocking her with its ray of light.

Sinking into a chair, arm across her forehead, Julia stared at the ceiling. The tears came then, crushing in their intensity, making her feel as though she had turned herself inside out.

At last she got up and washed her face.

All right, Mrs. Langley, she thought grimly, throwing the towel aside. *If it's a fight you want, it's a fight you'll get.*

Images of Rosalind swam before her eyes: bare shoulders, tempting curve of bosom, lips tinted with rouge. . . .

The image of the woman Lane Manning loved.

Going into her sitting room, Julia opened a drawer in her writing table and removed a piece of paper on which she had drawn a sketch of a ball gown that she planned to give Mrs. Arquette tomorrow.

Sitting down, she reached for a pencil and thoughtfully

nibbled on one end of it while she considered the sketch. Then she nodded once. With deft strokes, she altered the front and back of the gown.

Satisfied, she went to bed.

The following morning, Julia stayed in her room until she was certain that Lane had left the house.

When Mary came in to help her dress, her eyes widened at the sight of the door, but she made no comment.

Julia motioned toward it in a casual gesture. "Please see to it that the door is repaired," she instructed, offering no explanation.

Coming downstairs a while later, Julia firmly pushed aside any thoughts of her husband. The ball was scheduled to be held this coming Saturday. Only four days in which to complete all preparations. No time to think of anything else.

Mentally, she listed those things to be done today: First, make arrangements for the ballroom to be painted. The decorations needn't go up until Friday. Next, see to the hiring of an orchestra and procuring special uniforms for them. Perhaps she'd better do that first. Food. Extra servants. Fireworks display—that she could do tomorrow. And finally, visit Lisa Arquette.

Just before she entered the dressmaker's shop later that day, Julia halted and stared at the man coming in her direction. Jacques Offenbach! Although she had not seen the famed composer for more than two years, there was no mistaking the pince-nez, side whiskers, and the bright colors he favored in his attire. The composer of numerous operettas considered by most critics to be masterpieces of satire, Jacques Offenbach had, at fifty-seven, a slight build and blond hair that held only a touch of gray. He carried himself with a grace and a certain savoir faire that was reflected in his music. Julia had met him at a party held in the Eastwood house. Mark had insisted that she play for the guests after supper. Although somewhat intimidated by the presence of this famous man, she had done so.

"Monsieur Offenbach!" Julia called out as he came abreast of her.

Pausing, the man touched the brim of his hat, then peered at her through his pince-nez. "Mozart's Sonata in A major!" he exclaimed, then wagged a finger. "I may forget a face but never a rendition." Julia flushed, hoping he meant that as a compliment. "Miss Trent, is it not?"

"It's Mrs. Manning now," she murmured, then asked, "Are you in town for long?"

"Awhile," he answered. "I've several concerts scheduled for the Exhibition. You've been there, of course?"

"Oh, yes. Every day for the better part of two weeks."

"A remarkable achievement."

"It is. . . ." She hesitated as a thought struck. "Monsieur Offenbach, if you are free this Saturday night, my husband and I are planning a Centennial Ball to be held at Manning House. I would be so pleased if you could attend."

"I would be delighted," he exclaimed enthusiastically.

"Where are you staying? I'll be glad to send a carriage for you."

"No need," he responded with a laugh. "I daresay anyone in Philadelphia knows where Manning House is, and I have my own carriage."

"Marvelous!" Julia held out her hand, and the composer gallantly bent forward to brush his lips over it. "Nine o'clock?"

"I shall be there!" Jacques Offenbach promised, moving away.

As she opened the door to the shop, Julia decided she would say nothing about her encounter with the composer.

Jacques Offenbach's appearance at Manning House would be her little secret.

Catching sight of her, Lisa Arquette hurried forward.

Before the woman could speak, Julia handed her the sketch. "Can you have this done by Friday?"

"Of course, Mrs. Manning." The professional smile faltered as the woman regarded the sketch. "Are you . . . are you certain you want . . . ?"

"I'm certain!" Julia said shortly. "The material will remain as we previously decided upon. You still have my measurements?"

"Of course." The woman spoke absently, still staring at the paper in her hand. Then she shook herself free of her feeling of amazement and viewed Julia. "I'll bring it to you on Friday afternoon. Any last-minute alterations can be done at that time."

"That will be just fine."

Outside again, Julia inhaled deeply and passed a hand across her brow. The air was humid and heavy. Although the sky was hazy, the sun beat down with a summer intensity that quite took her breath away.

Gathering her skirt, Julia headed for the waiting carriage, anxious to return home.

"Mrs. Manning!"

Julia paused and turned, her smile disappearing as she saw Rosalind Langley heading in her direction. The woman was, as always, dressed in the height of fashion. Her walking dress was made of light cashmere, the hem a bare inch from the ground. Her stiff-brimmed velvet hat was decorated with artificial flowers and small velvet bows. As she approached, she lowered her parasol and closed it.

"What a pleasant surprise," she said, sounding as if she meant it.

Julia nodded curtly. "Mrs. Langley. . . ."

"Oh, please call me Rosalind." She placed a hand lightly on Julia's arm. "I do hope you have a few minutes." She gestured toward the Bingham House across the street. "Please join me for a cup of tea."

"I'm sorry, I can't. I'm in a hurry." The woman had her nerve!

"Nonsense!" Rosalind protested quickly, refusing to release her hold. "This won't take long."

Rather than make a scene, Julia reluctantly allowed herself to be led forward. And what, she wondered uneasily, wouldn't take long?

The Bingham House, one of the finest hotels in the city, took up the whole corner of Market and Eleventh. The dining room, set to the side of the lobby, was almost empty at this time of day. All the tables were covered with dark blue linen cloths and fine white china.

After they had been seated at a table by the window and ordered tea, Rosalind removed her gloves and placed them to the side of her reticule.

"I've always wondered what kind of woman Lane would marry," she said, observing Julia with an amused expression.

"And his selection surprised you?" Julia inquired stiffly, wondering how she could gracefully take her leave.

Rosalind's dark eyes sparkled with mirth. "As a matter of fact, it does. You are so . . . young, so . . . genteel, so . . ." She waved a hand.

Uninteresting? Julia wondered, irritation growing as she viewed her companion. How did the woman manage to look so crisp and cool and unruffled? Julia was positive that she herself looked wilted; certainly she was beginning to feel that way.

They both fell silent as the waiter placed their tea on the

table. Julia stared at it desultorily and wished she were elsewhere.

Rosalind put her elbows on the table, hands folded beneath her chin, as she regarded Julia. "You know that Lane took me home last night, don't you?"

"I do, but I do not feel the need to discuss it!" She was about to get up, but Rosalind's hand on her wrist detained her.

"Please, let us talk." When Julia reluctantly seated herself again, Rosalind went on. "When Lane and I first met, we were so very young. He was only a lad of sixteen, and I was a year younger. Ahh..." She raised a hand. "The dreams of youth! We all have them. Nothing seems impossible when you are young."

"I don't think I want to hear this," Julia murmured through a throat tight with emotion.

"I think you'll change your mind," Rosalind noted softly. "Sugar?"

"No."

Rosalind put a generous helping of the sweet stuff into her cup before she spoke again. "Nothing happened last night," she stated flatly, stirring the tea. Then she gave Julia a level look. "I confess I would have had it otherwise. But Lane..."

"Why are you telling me this?" Julia cried out.

"Because it's true," Rosalind replied, looking surprised by the outburst. "But that is not the question you should be asking me."

"I... don't understand."

"When Lane asked me to marry him nine years ago, he was very much in love with me." She lowered her head and stared into her cup. "I wanted him. But I wanted money more, and Lane didn't have any; nor any prospects that I could see. Otis had been courting me for more than six months when Lane proposed. I . . . well, I considered it; but when Otis proposed, I accepted him immediately. Otis was a good man," she added quickly before Julia could comment. "I have not been unhappy, and I dearly love my two daughters." She paused a long moment. "But even though I accepted Otis, I was in love with Lane."

"Lane is now my husband!" Julia clasped her hands in her lap so that Rosalind couldn't see how they trembled.

"Indeed he is," Rosalind remarked dryly. She stared out the window, a pensive look shading her beautiful features.

"What do you mean?" Julia was growing annoyed with the enigmatic statements being thrown at her.

Turning toward her again, Rosalind smiled as if she alone knew a secret. Reaching over, she patted Julia's hand. "Lane loved me once; he no longer does, though I suspect he didn't learn that until last night." She laughed lightly. "My dear Julia, your husband is in love with you! The only thing that remains to be done is for you to bring it to his attention."

Julia was dumbfounded and couldn't quite believe what Rosalind was saying. If Lane loved her, he would have told her so!

Rosalind's smile softened in the face of the incredulous expression she was seeing. "You didn't marry Lane for his money, did you?"

"No," Julia said shortly, then chewed her lip. And yet, didn't she do just that? she wondered, feeling uncomfortable again.

For just an instant, Julia's curiosity was piqued. It was inconceivable to her that a woman would marry a man for no other reason than that he had money.

Though Julia said nothing of her thoughts, Rosalind seemed to sense them.

"Do you really think that the only ingredient for a happy marriage is love?" she asked quietly.

"I think it helps," Julia murmured.

Rosalind leveled a shrewd look at her. "I know I don't have to tell you that once a woman marries she is entirely dependent upon her husband, at his beck and call, ready to cater to any whim he may have, however distasteful she might find it to be. How much better, then, to be the wife of a man of wealth, one who adores her and is prepared to indulge her whims instead of his own."

Julia was silent a moment, then couldn't resist asking, "Was . . . was your husband in love with you?"

"Yes, he was. And every day of our life together, he let me know how much." Rosalind paused to take a sip of her tea. Placing the cup back on its saucer, her dark eyes danced with merriment. "Oh, we did have a time," she sighed with a slight smile, running a fingertip around the rim of her cup. "Otis was in his forties when we married," she went on after a moment. "Yet he had the energy and stamina of a man half his age." Her eyes raised to view Julia. "He wasn't handsome, you understand, but he had charm—" She broke off, drew a sharp breath, and put the knuckle of her forefinger to her lips.

Julia's head tilted to one side, and she blinked as she regarded the older woman in wonder. "Are you very sure you didn't love your husband?" she asked quietly.

The dark eyes widened, then lowered. "Perhaps I did," she murmured after a moment. "Perhaps I did. . . ."

There was a silence as both women contemplated their thoughts.

Finally, Rosalind regarded Julia with open curiosity. "How did you and Lane meet?"

That question again. Julia made no immediate reply, but

something in Rosalind's attitude prompted an honest answer. Julia began to talk, at first hesitantly, then with greater confidence.

The tea cooled and was replaced, and still they talked. By the time they were through, there was little they didn't know about each other. In a flash of insight, Julia realized why Rosalind Langley was so well liked. There was absolutely no artifice about the woman; she was candid, honest. She possessed a presence that was commanding but not threatening.

The sun was low by the time they finally left the restaurant. On the sidewalk, both women paused to view each other, knowing that, despite all odds, each had found a friend.

"You've lifted a great burden from my heart," Julia said softly with a smile at Rosalind. Then she placed a hand on the older woman's arm. "Will you come to Manning House Saturday night for the ball?"

Rosalind raised an amused brow. "Do you really want me to?"

"Yes. Yes, I do."

Rosalind gave one of her light laughs. "Then I will be there."

chapter
twenty-six

Lane arrived home from New York on Friday afternoon, feeling weary and disgruntled. His meeting with several bankers whom he had hoped would partially finance the drilling operations on his thousand-acre parcel had not gone as well as he'd hoped.

He could fault no one but himself. Morning, noon, and night, he had done nothing but think about Julia. That last image of her cold and angry face had robbed him of sleep. He had taken his business associates to the finest restaurant in New York, only to find that he himself had no appetite. All his geology reports had been in meticulous order; yet when he had been questioned, he found himself stammering and groping for words like a dullard!

Entering the house, he handed his hat to Nancy and gave a curt nod to the new housekeeper. Theresa something-or-other; he couldn't remember. An improvement, he thought, over the stone-faced Thelma Litton.

"Where is my wife?" he asked Nancy, frowning at her

357

frazzled appearance. She always looked as neat as a pin. Today her apron was so smudged that Lane wondered whether she had been using it to dust the furniture.

"I'm not really sure, Mr. Manning." A hand went to her springy hair to reposition a wayward curl that immediately bounced back as soon as she released her hold. "Things are pretty hectic around here. . . ."

"Lane!" April offered a bright smile as she came down the stairs. "If you're looking for Julia, she's in her room. Mother's visiting with Mrs. Stapleton. I expect she'll return shortly."

All that was delivered while April was in motion. Reaching the bottom of the stairs, her skirts aswirl with her haste, she headed for the rear of the house.

Unusual sounds coming from the ballroom drew Lane closer. Workmen were on ladders, fastening papier-mâché decorations to the wall. Bemused, he noticed that the whole room had been painted white, which was all right with him; he never had liked the dark green Willa had chosen.

Turning, he watched as servants, most of whom he had never seen before, scurried back and forth, intent on errands that appeared to be of the utmost importance.

"Excuse me, sir. . . ."

"Oh! Sorry." Quickly, Lane stepped aside, realizing that he was in the way of two men straining beneath the weight of a heavy trestle table they were moving into the ballroom.

Noises coming from the direction of the kitchen told him that absolute turmoil was in progress in that part of the house.

Climbing the stairs, he opened Julia's door, but hastily backed out again when confronted by a bevy of chattering seamstresses clustered around Julia, who offered him nothing more than an absent smile of greeting.

Crossing the hall, he went into the nursery, emitting a

sigh of relief at the peaceful quiet that greeted him. Here was an island of serenity in the midst of chaos. Today, as on every other day, Miss Gwenn had insisted that the servants perform their usual chores. "From floor to ceiling!" she insisted, unmoved by the extra work being generated by the ball. And so it would be tomorrow when the great day arrived.

Lane tiptoed to the cradle. Charles was fast asleep as he usually was when Lane came home at the end of the day. But Lane always visited in the morning before he went downstairs for breakfast. Then Charles was awake. It was the most treasured time of day for him.

He looked at Miss Gwenn and spoke in a whisper. "Do you think he'd wake if I picked him up?"

"Probably," Miss Gwenn replied dryly, not at all pleased by this unexpected visit.

Lane grinned as he reached for his son.

Supper that night was simple: soup, salad, and freshly baked bread.

Unobtrusively, Lane kept darting looks at his wife, wishing they were alone. Was she still angry? He couldn't tell. Whenever they made direct eye contact across the table, Julia offered a vague smile that told him nothing. His mother did most of the talking. After a while, Lane gathered that Melissa Stapleton was to be married. In the way of women, the conversation dwelt endlessly on wedding preparations. It appeared that April was to be maid of honor.

The news finally sank in. Lane looked at his mother. "Who did you say she was marrying?"

Willa's face creased in exasperation. "I told you! The Logan boy. Stanley."

Lane blinked, receiving an impression of a portly young man with a red face.

Willa continued as if there had been no interruption. Colors. Patterns. Flowers.

Lane tuned it out. He had just time enough to get through the meal when Andrew appeared with a pile of papers he claimed needed Lane's immediate attention. He also brought with him the disquieting news that one of Lane's ships was more than two weeks overdue. There was a good chance that the vessel, together with its cargo, had either sunk or been pirated. With that in mind, they both settled down to compile a list of probable losses should the assumption prove to be accurate.

Finally, more than three hours after he had arrived, Andrew stacked his papers neatly and got to his feet.

"How is Hester?" Lane asked as he walked Andrew to the door.

"She's doing well. Terribly upset, of course, that she will be unable to attend the ball tomorrow night. Better prepare youself for a barrage of questions when we come to dinner on Sunday." Shaking his head, Andrew gave a rueful laugh. "From the size of her, I wouldn't be surprised if she gives birth to twins!" He said that with an odd mixture of embarrassment and pride.

Lane laughed. "It wouldn't surprise me, either; it does run in the family, you know." He sobered, knew it was none of his business, but couldn't resist asking: "Is . . . everything all right between you and Hester?"

Andrew shrugged as he put on his hat. "I suppose we're both getting used to each other," was the noncommittal reply.

Andrew didn't meet Lane's eye as he said that. His feelings for Hester were now so ambivalent that they left him feeling helpless at times. One minute he hated her, and the next he desperately wanted to possess her; even more, he wanted to conquer her, conquer that rebellious spirit he knew was at the very core of her being. Outwardly, she was everything a wife should be: acquiescent, always deferring to his wishes or needs. His home was comfortable, the servants—all of whom Hester had engaged—were capable and efficient. But beneath it all, he knew there was in his wife a strength of will that far exceeded his own. Hester was acquiescent only because she chose to be.

Andrew's answer had been less than satisfactory to Lane, but he let it go. On the surface, everything appeared to be running smoothly, and he took comfort from that. For one thing, Lane was grateful that the bond between Hester and April had remained strong, undamaged by what had taken place. April visited Hester several times a week, and on Sunday, it pleased him to see the girls chatting with the happy animation he had come to expect of them.

When Andrew left, Lane climbed wearily up the stairs. There was no light showing under Julia's door, which was not surprising in view of the fact that it was past eleven o'clock.

For a moment, Lane was tempted to try the door, just to see if it was locked; then he turned away. She was, no doubt, exhausted. He felt certain that his mother had not lifted a finger to assist her with the preparations for the ball. Probably it would be best to wait until this business was over and done with; certainly he and Julia could not talk surrounded by all this pandemonium.

As he undressed, Lane reflected that he was glad he had to go to work in the morning. If tomorrow was anything like today, he had no desire to be around the house.

Saturday dawned clear and stayed that way, much to Julia's relief. The ball was to begin at nine o'clock, the fireworks display scheduled to go off at midnight.

Julia spent the morning in the kitchen, overseeing the

preparation of the food to be served. She was well pleased with Nancy's aunt; not only was the woman an excellent cook, but also nothing could diminish her calm and cheerful manner. She was handling the extra work incurred by the ball as if it were merely a few extra people for dinner.

During the afternoon, Julia checked to see that all the decorations were displayed as she had specified, then watched as the gigantic fireworks display was set up in the rear gardens. Colorful Chinese lanterns were hung in the gazebo but were, as yet, unlit.

Coming upstairs awhile later, Julia peered into the nursery, amused to see Willa in the chair by the window and holding Charles. Much to her surprise Willa had been completely won over by the child, spending several hours each day in the nursery, incurring the annoyance of Alma Gwenn, who had strong ideas about schedules and sticking to them.

Insofar as Willa's attitude toward her daughter-in-law was concerned, that, too, had changed recently, ever so slightly. Whether this was because of her grandchild or because Julia had asserted herself, no one would ever know except Willa herself.

By four o'clock, Julia retired to her room, took a long, hot bath, then rested until it was time for her to dress.

After Mary had fashioned Julia's pale hair into a sweeping pompadour, Julia dismissed the servant, wanting to be alone while she dressed. When the door closed behind Mary, Julia gazed thoughtfully at the ball gown draped carefully over a chair. Made of the sheerest silk, it was a startling shade of red that seemed to glow like a brightly burning flame, deepening into the hot crimson of burning embers in the softly flowing folds of the skirt.

It was also the most daringly cut gown she had ever seen. At first glance it was deceptively simple: no lace, no ribbons, no flowers, no flounces. From top to bottom it was a glorious sweep of shimmering fabric and unbroken color.

Julia loved it. And when she put it on and viewed herself in the mirror, she knew she had made the right choice.

At a quarter to nine, the door opened, and Lane, dressed formally in black broadcloth, came into the room.

"The orchestra has arrived. They're setting up—" He came to an abrupt halt as he stared at her, mouth agape. "What the hell are you wearing!"

Julia's lips twitched at the sight of his open shock. "Do you like it? I had it made especially for tonight." She did a little pirouette before him.

Lane drew a strangled breath. The front was bad enough, but he'd never seen a dress cut that low in the back. "Take that off!" His voice climbed to a dangerous level. "I'll not have you appearing in public like that!"

"Like what?" she asked innocently.

"Half undressed!" he shot back.

She tossed her head. "Don't be silly, Lane. I have no intention of changing my gown."

"You'll do as I say!" He was about to say more, but the sound of carriages coming up the drive alerted him to the fact that their guests were beginning to arrive. "Change your dress," he growled. "Put on that"—he waved a hand—"that yellow thing with all those flowers on it. The one with the ruffles at the neck."

Hand on the doorknob, Lane gave her one last look, making it as stern as he could. He had no real concern, however; despite her defiance, Julia would never dare disobey him.

Straightening his cravat, Lane stepped confidently into the hall. When Julia made her appearance, it would be in her usual ladylike fashion. Anything else would be unthinkable.

In keeping with the motif of this centennial year, Julia had instructed that the ballroom be decorated in red, white, and blue. A huge ice carving of the Liberty Bell dominated the center table, one of five that held an assortment of food and pastries. The orchestra, abandoning their usual black formal wear, were clad in replicas of the uniforms worn by the soldiers of the Revolution. The waiters all wore red or blue jackets over spotlessly white trousers.

Lane noted it all with approval. Julia had done a good job. He smiled at his mother, who, together with April, was standing just outside the ballroom, greeting guests as they arrived. Willa was dressed in a gray satin gown sewn with silver thread. Emeralds glinted from her neck and ears. April looked fetching in blue chiffon, the color enriching the blue of her eyes.

"You both look lovely," he exclaimed sincerely, coming toward them.

Willa scowled at him. "I should think that your wife would be here to greet the guests she has invited," she grumbled.

"She'll be down shortly," Lane answered easily, nodding to the Carlyles, who, together with Desmond, had just arrived. "She hasn't finished dressing. . . ."

Desmond paused, gazing at April with such open admiration that the girl blushed. Lane touched his sister's arm. "Why don't you go inside with Desmond," he suggested. "I'll stay with Mother." He smiled, watching them go. "Julia's done a fine job," he said after the Carlyles moved into the ballroom.

"It cost enough." Willa wasn't about to concede. The front door opened again, and her eyes went wide. She didn't need to be told the identity of the man who now entered. Every hostess of any note knew who Jacques Offenbach was. His picture appeared in the newspaper each time he was in town, and never a night passed that he was without an invitation. Sadly for the hostess who hoped to enliven an otherwise dull evening, Offenbach turned down more invitations than he accepted. Raising her fan, Willa caught her breath and exclaimed: "That's Jacques Offenbach! I didn't know he was to be here tonight. I didn't know Julia even knew him!" She rushed forward. "Monsieur Offenbach! What a pleasure to have you join us this evening."

"The pleasure is mine, madame." He nodded to her, then shook Lane's outstretched hand.

"I didn't know you were in town," Willa gushed, still overcome with the presence of such a well-known personage in her house.

"Even in Paris the Exhibition is a topic for conversation," Offenbach offered with a laugh. "Like everyone else, I felt I must see it."

With a happy smile, Willa slipped her arm through his, then led the composer into the ballroom, abandoning an amused Lane in the hall.

For the next twenty minutes a steady stream of people entered, and Lane kept glancing at the stairs, wondering why it was taking Julia so long to change her dress. He had a moment's surprise when Rosalind Langley appeared, and was even more surprised when he learned that she was here at Julia's invitation.

Finally, around nine-fifteen, the traffic began to thin and Lane finally ambled into the ballroom. If Julia didn't get here soon, she's miss her own party, he thought with annoyance.

chapter
twenty-seven

In her room, Julia pushed herself up out of the chair she had been sitting in for the past thirty minutes, smoothing the skirt of the red silk dress as she did so.

Going to her dressing table, she selected a necklace of red rubies, fastened it around her throat, then put on the earrings that matched it. Checking her appearance once more in the mirror, she picked up an ostrich-plumed fan, gathered her skirt, and calmly left her room, certain that everyone had arrived by now.

Downstairs, Julia hesitated for a dramatic moment in the arched entryway. With her appearance, the orchestra began to play.

As sound ripples across a room with a sudden spurt of excited conversation, so it now seemed to retreat into a heavy silence as one by one the guests turned to view their hostess.

Every eye was upon her. Julia had never seen men look at her with such admiration. She decided she liked it. Only one man was viewing her with something other than admiration, and that was her own husband.

Julia ignored him.

Jacques Offenbach was the first to reach her side. As usual, the man's attire was anything but subdued. Tonight he was wearing a maroon jacket of heavy satin with a bright pink velvet collar and cuffs over a hand-embroidered silk vest that was an eye-catching canary yellow in color.

"I do hope this first dance isn't taken," he murmured with a charming smile. "I suspect your company will be much in demand this evening."

With a graceful movement, Julia held out her hand. "The ball will not begin until I dance with its most honored guest," she replied softly.

As Julia swept past Lane, she flashed him a bright smile that set his teeth on edge.

Julia and Monsieur Offenbach circled the ballroom once, then other couples joined them.

Standing to the side, Rosalind gave a delighted laugh as she viewed Julia. Even in Paris that gown would occasion a second glance. Her companion gave her a questioning look, and, as Rosalind allowed him to lead her onto the dance floor, she murmured, "The swan has turned into a stunning peacock, my dear Frederick!" and her laughter trilled higher at his confused expression.

As the evening progressed, Julia glowed under the steady stream of compliments being whispered into her ear, and all the while she was aware of her husband's burning gaze as those gray eyes followed her around the room in relentless pursuit.

Lane saw nothing of the glittering whirl that surrounded him: the ladies in gowns of every color in the rainbow, the flash of satin, the rustle of taffeta, the dazzle of jewels—all went unnoticed. He could see only the color of red, the softness of silk that so lovingly molded the lissome body of the most beautiful woman in the room, in the world! A beauty that constricted his chest with fury. That vision should be for his eyes only!

Rosalind had been doing little but watching both Lane and Julia, more than a bit amused at Lane's scowling countenance. He certainly didn't look like he was enjoying himself. Finally, she approached him.

"I do think that this will be considered the event of the year, Lane," she said, noticing that he did not turn toward her as she spoke. "How fortunate you were in having Monsieur Offenbach attend. Every hostess from New York to Philadelphia would give her eyeteeth to have such an important guest."

Lane made no response; indeed, he seemed not to have heard her.

"I must say, Julia looks lovely this evening," Rosalind ventured after a moment's silence. "Quite the belle of the ball, wouldn't you say?"

"What . . . ?"

"My goodness, Lane!" Her red lips curved into a wide smile. "I always thought you were more articulate."

"Hmm? Oh, I'm sorry, Rosalind. What did you say?"

"It's not important, Lane. I suspect you'll find out in your own good time."

Lane gave her a look mixed with puzzlement and annoyance as she walked away. What the devil was the woman prattling about? he wondered irritably. But before the thought was fully formed in his mind, his eyes had again sought Julia. Damn her! She was dancing with that blasted composer again; was this the second or third time?

As she glided by, the prismed chandelier highlighted the

creamy swell of her breasts, fuller now since the birth of Charles. Caught unaware, Lane gasped at the sight and clenched his hands, his scowl as black as night. If he could see it, so could every man in the room!

His angry eyes scanned the assemblage. Yes, every man was looking at her! He was certain of it! A knot of rage formed in his throat. He had an almost irresistible urge to remove his jacket and drape it around her shoulders—after which he would take great pleasure in throttling her to within an inch of her life!

A waiter passed by, and Lane plucked a glass of bourbon from the tray, downing half of it in one long swallow. He had to forcibly restrain himself from putting his fist into the face of every man who was looking at Julia.

In spite of Lane's assumption, however, there was one man in the room who never once looked at Julia. For Desmond, there was only one woman worth looking at, and that was April.

Having concluded a particularly strenuous polonaise, they were standing by the tall French doors, now open to receive the cooling breeze that swept up from the river. April waved her fan and tried to catch her breath. Her cheeks were delightfully pink, and her eyes shone with excitement.

Desmond reached for her hand. "Come outside, so we can talk. . . ."

April hung back, casting a wary look across the room. "I can't," she whispered. "My mother is watching us. . . ."

Following her glance, Desmond sighed at the sight of Willa's forbidding scowl as she viewed them. His eyes again swung to April. "We could stand just outside the door where she can see us," he suggested.

"Well . . ." April closed her fan. "I suppose that would be all right."

They took a few steps over the threshold, where they paused.

"When I look at you, so many feelings fill my heart," Desmond said quietly, "but I cannot find the words to do them justice."

"And what sort of feelings are they?" April darted a quick look at him.

"I would need a lifetime to tell you." Unmindful that Willa was still watching them, Desmond put his arms around April's slender form. "If you would marry me, I would have all the time I need. Providing, of course, you didn't get bored with hearing how much I love you. . . ."

April tilted her head, and a light of mischief danced in her eyes. "I don't think you could ever bore me, Desmond." Then her voice lowered to a whisper as she added, "I think you're quite the most exciting man I've ever known. . . ."

Inside, having finished his drink, Lane put the glass on a table. He knew he should be circulating, dancing, but he couldn't bring himself to act the part of congenial host. Right now he felt anything but congenial.

His gray eyes scanned the ballroom. Where was she now? He saw her deep in conversation with Jacques Offenbach. A lot of nodding and hand waving ensued; then, when the orchestra concluded the current song, the composer stepped up on the dais.

"Ladies and gentlemen!" he said, pausing until he had everyone's attention. "A few years ago, I was privileged to hear a rendition of Mozart's Sonata in A major. Tonight, it will be your privilege to hear this piece played as Mozart intended." He turned to Julia, kissed her hand, then gave it a gentle squeeze as he whispered: "Only play it half as well as you did before, and it will be a delight to these old ears."

Gathering her skirt, Julia seated herself at the piano, aware of the surprised hush that surrounded her, more devastating than any uproar could hope to be. She knew why: women played a pianoforte, a harpsichord, and they offered the popular tunes of the day. They did not dare tread into a male pianist's domain.

Her hands hovered a moment over the keyboard, and before she began, the melody flowed into her being. The first movement was less than half completed when Julia knew she held everyone's rapt attention. Then her awareness of the external world fled, and there was only the music of a master to claim her interest.

Even Lane, whose ear was not in the least attuned to music, was enraptured by Julia's talent, and for this short while, his anger was buried beneath the sheer beauty of the melody.

When it was over, there was a moment of stunned silence. Then the applause began, led by Monsieur Offenbach, whose eyes gleamed behind his pince-nez. Getting to his feet, he shouted: "Bravo!" And the exclamation was soon echoed by everyone, including Lane, from whose throat the word emerged in choked fashion.

Leah Carlyle, laughing and crying at the same time, rushed forward to embrace Julia.

Then the dancing began again, and Julia was so surrounded by people that Lane made no attempt to get to her. Instead, he danced with his mother.

"I must say, Julia plays the piano rather well," Willa commented, sounding thoroughly flabbergasted. Although she had heard Julia practice on the Steinway at various times, Willa had paid little attention, because, like Lane, she had little appreciation for music, classical or otherwise. And to think that even Monsieur Offenbach had applauded!

"Yes, she does." Lane sounded as though his thoughts were far away.

Willa glanced up at him, saw he was preoccupied, and fell silent.

Before the dance ended, Lane's anger had returned in full force. Julia would have played just as well in a sensible dress! It hadn't been necessary for her to sit up there on that dais, in plain view of every man in the room, looking so damned . . . beautiful! All right, he'd admit that she looked spectacular, but he couldn't believe that she had disobeyed him. He had been most explicit, had left no room for argument. Her delayed appearance had been meant to throw him off guard, to lull him into thinking that she was changing her clothes. . . .

"Lane!"

Startled, he glanced down at his mother's frowning face.

"You're squeezing my hand so hard it hurts! What on earth is the matter with you?"

Realizing that his hands had clenched, Lane immediately released his hold. "I'm sorry, Mother. I was thinking of something. . . ."

The music ended, and, still frowning at Lane, Willa stalked away.

When the clock struck midnight, Julia led everyone out to the rear gardens. The night was clear and calm and moonless. At her signal, the fireworks were set off, blazing into the black sky with a spray of color and design that drew exclamations of delight from everyone.

Supper followed, and by two o'clock, people at last began to take their leave. Lane and Julia stood side by side in the entrance hall, bidding their guests farewell, never speaking a word to each other.

Lane held his temper in check until they were upstairs, where he all but slammed the door to her bedroom.

If Julia was in any way upset with his attitude, she gave no indication of it. Her movements calm and deliberate, she removed her jewelry and placed it carefully into her jewelry box. She seemed to be unaware that he was even in the room.

He came closer, brows drawn together. "How dare you appear in public as you did tonight?" His voice was low and menacing, but it drew only a small smile from Julia.

"I'm sorry you didn't like my dress," she murmured, removing the pins from her hair. The paleness cascaded like a silvery waterfall as it fell about her shoulders.

His temper exploded. Grabbing her, his fingers digging painfully into her upper arms, he shook her. "You are never to wear that dress again! Do you hear me?"

Her head tilted up, and her blue eyes viewed him levelly, and with an innocence that only fueled his rage. "Why?"

Beneath his hands, the soft, satin smoothness of her flesh seemed to burn his skin. He released his hold so suddenly, Julia stumbled back a step.

"I don't want any other man looking at you!" he shouted.

She raised a brow. "And why not?"

"Because . . . because, dammit, I love you! You belong to me!" Reaching for her, Lane crushed her against him, burying his face in her hair. "Oh, God, I love you more than life itself. . . ."

If it was possible for a heart to sing with joy, hers did at that moment, a precious interlude that, for her, would never be surpassed. Drawing back slightly, Julia gazed up at her husband. When her eyes met his, delight dawned on her face.

"Oh, I love you so much," she breathed.

Lane kissed her with such intensity that even thoughts of love fled her mind, to be replaced by the passion she had for so long kept repressed. She needed no inducement now to remove the red dress.

Still holding her, Lane sank onto the bed. Their arms entwined, bodies pressed so close they were as one.

"Make love with me. . . ." Lane whispered, as he had once before.

But this time, Julia needed no encouragement. Completely and without reservation she gave herself to the ecstasy she had come to expect in his embrace, and to it was added the sweetness of a love shared, a glorious crescendo Julia was certain not even the most accomplished composer could capture on paper.

Afterward, Lane held her tightly, reluctant to release her even for a moment, and when they finally fell asleep, it was within each other's arms.

When Julia opened her eyes the following morning, it was to see Lane looking at her, his chin cupped in his hand, an elbow propped on his pillow.

"How long have you been staring at me?" she asked, feeling a trifle embarrassed.

"Hours."

She raised her chin slightly, certain she was about to receive a kiss.

But Lane, ever unpredictable, said, "I'm going to have that wall torn down."

She blinked. "What wall?"

He pointed to the wall that separated his room from hers.

"That one. We'll have one big room. . . ." He grinned. "The better for me to chase you around in. But only one bed!"

"I think I'd like that." Julia slipped her arms around his waist. Her dark blue eyes studied him. "Then you did mean what you said to me last night?" she whispered. "That you love me?"

"I don't believe there was ever a time when I didn't love you," he murmured. "From that first moment I saw you standing there in that ridiculous dress. . . ."

Julia's eyes widened, and she pulled away from him. "Ridiculous?" she echoed indignantly.

He grinned at her. "You looked like a schoolgirl who'd wandered into the Eastwood house by mistake," he replied, smothering a laugh.

She sighed, twining her fingers through his dark curls. "You're right. I used to hate the way I had to dress." She jumped up, hands on her hips, feet planted wide, her glorious unbound hair tumbling about her shoulders, spilling down her back. "But I'll have you know I'm a changed woman, Mr. Manning!"

She strutted before him, naked, proud of her body. Then, bending over, she picked up the red dress and held it in front of her. She hated to give it up. It was far and away the most beautiful creation she had even seen.

Lane scowled, catching her thoughts. "I meant what I said," he growled. "You are never to wear that dress in public again!"

Julia wasn't paying attention. A bit of lace, she was thinking, a slight alteration . . . She let out a startled gasp as Lane sprang out of bed and grabbed her from behind, nuzzling the back of her neck, his hands roaming her body as if he were trying to memorize every inch of her.

"Lane!" she protested with a laugh. "It's broad daylight!"

She cast a quick glance at the door, hoping Mary wouldn't pick this moment to come into the room.

"I hadn't noticed. . . ." As he hugged her with playful roughness, the dress slipped unnoticed to the floor.

Julia turned so that she was facing him. "Oh, my dear heart . . ." She put the palms of her hands against his cheeks—his marvelous, clean-shaven cheeks, warm and smooth and sensuous beneath her touch. He pulled her closer, and she shivered, having no doubt as to his urgent need. She glanced at the door again. "What if Mary comes in?" she whispered, her voice turning breathless as his hands slid down her back to firmly cup her buttocks.

Lane picked her up in his arms and grinned at her as he headed toward the bed. "If she does, I have an idea she'll be in for the shock of her life. . . ."

Because of the late hour at which they had all retired the night before, no one came down to breakfast until after ten o'clock in the morning. When Lane and Julia entered the family dining room, April had just finished eating; a moment later, Willa entered, heaving a deep sigh as she sat down.

"Thank goodness that's all over," she declared as she picked up her fork, then gave Julia a look of grudging admiration. "Although I must admit that it went off rather well."

Julia just smiled at her mother-in-law, then turned her attention to April as the girl addressed Lane.

"I have something to tell you, Lane. All of you, in fact," she qualified with a shy smile. "Desmond asked me to marry him last night. I think . . . I think he plans to speak to you later today. . . ." Her cheeks warmed to a rosy color as she regarded her brother.

Lane leaned forward over the table to view her closely. "And what would you like me to say to Desmond?" he inquired with a smile. "Or shall I simply show him the heel of my boot . . . ?"

April's eyes went round. "Oh, no!" Then she giggled as she saw he was teasing her. "I . . . want you to give your permission."

"Oh, April!" Julia got up to give the girl a hug. "I'm so glad. Congratulations. . . ."

"Mine, too," Lane said quickly. "When would you like to be married?"

"We both thought around Christmas. I want Hester to be my matron of honor."

Willa cast her daughter a quick glance and breathed a sigh of relief. Putting her napkin aside, she got to her feet. "Come along. Let's see how much of your trousseau can be salvaged. It's for certain all the monograms will have to be changed," she grumbled.

When his mother and sister left, Lane got up and gathered Julia into his arms. "Now that that's settled, I have a suggestion to make. How would you like to return to the isle of Santorini for a few weeks?"

She hesitated. "I don't think it would be wise for me to travel that far right now," she answered slowly. "I'm going to have another child. . . ."

He drew a sharp breath. "Oh, Julia," he whispered, and felt no shame as his eyes misted.

She went on to say, "There is something I would like to do, however. . . ."

"Anything!" He held her close and thought he had never been as happy or as fulfilled in his life as he was right now. To think that at one time he'd thought money was all-important!

"I want to return to New York, to the Fifth Avenue

Hotel.'' Burying her face in his shirt, she giggled, thinking of her wedding night. How long ago it seemed! Beneath her cheek, she could feel his chest rumble with the beginnings of a laugh.

"Perhaps I could get the same suite," he suggested, now chuckling openly as his memories turned vivid. He couldn't believe that the woman he now held in his arms was the girl he had married. Love suddenly seemed an inadequate word for what he was feeling.

"And would you order pheasant?" she asked, toying with his lapel.

"That would be my only choice," he replied with mock seriousness.

Raising her head, Julia looked up at him, eyes dancing. "Lane . . . what did you really think of that night?"

Ruefully, he shook his head. "It was the most unexciting experience of my life," he answered truthfully.

"Mine, too," she quickly agreed. "Somehow, I think a wedding night should be more memorable. . . ."

He pursed his lips. "Would you like to repeat it?" he asked huskily.

Julia nodded as she put her arms around his neck, gazing deeply into those gray eyes she loved. "I plan to repeat it until we get it right," she declared solemnly.

Then she gave him a kiss that took his breath away.